THE RAPHA CHRONICLES

the fall

a novel

by

Chana Keefer

the fall

Published by:
Intermedia Publishing Group, Inc.
P.O. Box 2825
Peoria, Arizona 85380
www.intermediapub.com

ISBN 978-1-935906-55-1

Printed in the United States of America

What people are saying about *The Fall*:

"Earth-shattering yet subtle. I found God revealing Himself to me personally as Chana described the indescribable as if she was actually there!"

Victoria Jackson
Former SNL cast member, Author

"After reading this book, I guarantee you'll never think about God or the fall of Lucifer the same way again. Rapha's story is a massive, visual spectacle, yet it's also one angel's intimate, personal perspective on the battle for all creation. 'Epic' doesn't begin to cover it."

Cory Edwards
Writer / Director of *HOODWINKED*

"*The Fall* has the potential to be the *Screwtape Letters* of this generation. Chana Keefer manages to sidestep all the pitfalls of debate to provide a layered, complex, and character-driven look at the birth of mankind that places its focus not on the how of creation but on the why: redemption and resurrection. I wish I was that talented."

Adam Palmer
Author of *TAMING A LIGER—UNEXPECTED SPIRITUAL LESSONS FROM NAPOLEON DYNAMITE*

"As a Pastor I often hear the questions: What was going on before creation? What was happening in Heaven? How did the battle between good and evil begin? *The Fall* paints a picture that can give image to the answers."

Rusty George
Lead Pastor, Real Life Church, Valencia, California

To Mark.

Love of my life and best friend.

You never once said I couldn't.

10-12-2011

Acknowledgements

A heartfelt thanks to my family; Mark, McKenna, Sky, Madeline and Micah—my first guinea pig. Thanks for thinking Mom's obsession was cool. Undying gratitude to my parents, Lynn and Glenda Vowell, for loving and encouraging me from day one. Thank you to Tawni and Mark, for putting up with your crazy baby sis; to Mrs. Barrett, my literary buddy, for all the time, tea, cake and excellent taste; to the Keefers, Vowells, Gilstraps, Dillahuntys, McClungs and Pannells of my family tree who raised up your kids to live for God.

Thank you to the many writers who inspired me through the years; J.R.R. Tolkien, C.S. Lewis, Gene Stratton Porter, Jane Austen, Catherine Marshall—the list would be unending. You inspired a little girl to dream and a woman to delve deeper.

A special thank you to our family at Real Life Church and our amazing Life Group. Thank you Brenda, Melanie, Tara, Jeanne, Emily, Dennis, Shannon, Lucy, Vicky, Jennifer, Amy, Terri, Gina and so many others who let me run-on about this story. Your encouragement is priceless.

As always, Robert and Andrea; yours is a world without limits. Adam and Michelle, you started down this path ahead of me and encouraged every step of the way. Cory and Vicki, you live outside the box and make it fun. Much appreciation to you, Jeff, for gushing about this idea when it was embryonic. Blessings on you, Janis, editor extraordinaire, for the word "Tolkienesque." To the crew at Intermedia—Terry, Larry, Yvonne and Johanna—thank you for your expertise and professionalism.

Thanks also to the crew at Starbucks for the green tea, Chai, and office space! You really should be charging me rent.

Delirious, U2, Sting, Cold Play, S.C.C, Foo Fighters, Fleming and John, Mutemath, Switchfoot, John Michael Talbot, Dan and Leland, and so many others, thanks for providing uncomplaining accompaniment and inspiration no matter how early or late.

Special thanks to Pete Greig for his excellent book, ***Red Moon Rising***, that helped me fall in love with prayer. This is just one of the results of that addiction.

Finally, thank you God for making the impossible reality. You were and are the best part of this journey, providing the adrenalin, perseverance, kick in the pants, pat on the head and anything else needed to see this through. You truly are the author and finisher!

C.L.K.

Table of Contents

Chapter One

End of an Age

There was a time they were best friends...
a distant memory almost forgotten. Almost.
It would be so much easier if he could forget.

Peace, peace, but there is no peace... Rapha clutches his head in his hands oblivious to the rare trace of fresh air and woodland noises around him, too lost in fractured, tortured memories.

> *A child's eyes, wide with fear; a woman's ripe belly, torn; screams and cries of anguish splitting the darkness of night; innocence lost; purity destroyed; life swallowed in death. And weaving through every image, the sound of cruel laughter—feasting on mankind's pain.*

That face. Rapha squeezes his head but the image burns clearer—a face bathed in shadows as fumes of death cast waves of beauty and horror, eyes of leeching evil. Those eyes suck him into darkness, willing him to join the nightmare.

With all the force of his formidable will Rapha wrenches his thoughts from that realm, forcing his eyes open to light and life. A flower—tiny, bright, thriving no more than a few brave hours—faces the sun's feeble light. With a need for comfort, Rapha stretches face down, breathing in soil and weakly pulsing life. Although fires burn, smokes of destruction rise and death reigns, here is a patch of green. His fingers grip deep into soft earth as fresh pain rips through him.

> *Flashing, intelligent eyes; a carefree smile; beautiful hands gesturing with enthusiasm; boyish laughter filtering through a forest glade—ancient memories that bring unbearable torture.*

Sobs rumble from the depths of the earth itself, erupting through Rapha's muscular frame.

"I cannot," he gasps, wrestling in his mind with an unseen companion. "It's impossible. He's gone too far for too long. There's nothing, nothing pure—he's made it so…." Rapha's body writhes like a tortured serpent, with agony greater than he's ever experienced, threatening to rip his immortal soul from his impervious body.

But wait. There was a time he tasted deeper anguish.

No. Please. That is locked away—eternal sanity demanded it. But the horrific images descend once again.

> *The loved one weeps in agony, precious flesh is torn over and over as Rapha's heart feels every rip of the whip, every trickle of spittle, every curse thrown like a poisoned spear. And there, in the crazed mob, everywhere he looks, the twisted, beautiful, triumphant, mocking face of one who was once a brother.*

Rapha's earth-crusted hands clutch at his ears but the laughter grows, filling every recess of his soul, stealing every hope and joyful memory.

A joyful memory?

In a flash Rapha is there; catapulted through eons of space and time, before the purity of the garden, back through countless ages to a fresh hilltop lit by a younger, more optimistic sun. He and Luc preferred the plunging cliffs dropping to unseen depths below. Somehow, a spiral dive carried more of a thrill when performed in a temporal world.

"There's something about this place," Luc's eyes flitted from tree to mountain and stream as he stretched golden arms wide as if to embrace the early morning's glow filtering through droplets of mist. "It's not as grand as our *flawless, hallowed domain* but the appeal is undeniable."

Rapha had ignored the note of restlessness in that melodic voice, choosing to enjoy fresh air laced with flowered perfume and the spiced musk of fertile soil. In the countless years of their friendship, he had learned Luc's passions could flash with the slightest provocation, but usually, if Rapha allowed Luc to give vent to his emotions, the darker frame of mind would pass. And, a visit to this, their favorite retreat, was usually the perfect remedy, a change of pace and a different rhythm that put celestial matters into perspective. With a sigh Rapha settled back into thick green with one arm behind his head to contemplate the crisp blue above. Yes. This was just what Luc needed, a deep breath of contentment.

"Listen!" Luc crouched down as a biped creature struggled into view on the steep slope below. It was bent forward as if sniffing the wind, its hair-covered body tense, heavy brow shading deep-set eyes that scanned its surroundings. "What do you suppose it's thinking?" Luc questioned. "Does that puny mind delve beyond putting one pathetic foot in front of the other or is it merely contemplating which part of its putrid body to scratch next?"

This new creature, standing somewhat upright and possessing intelligence beyond Earth's other inhabitants, had stirred Luc's ire. Rapha could not understand why these beings, known as "man," so inferior to angelic structure, should irritate his friend so.

Rapha studied the perfect planes of the face beside him as Luc observed the creature with disdain and declared, “Do you realize it can’t live without water? A stiff wind could blow it off this cliff and that’s it. The young are even more vulnerable—tiny, squirming things one breath away from oblivion!” A mournful expression shadowed the handsome face. “I’d be doing a favor to end such a pathetic existence….” He raised an arm as if to summon a whirlwind.

“No!” Rapha was accustomed to Luc’s teasing but something in his friend’s expression warned him the humor had taken on a malicious tone.

Luc resisted Rapha’s restraining arm, “Just a small puff… oh please… it will know the thrill of flight as it plummets to the ground!”

“We are not to influence them,” Rapha was alarmed at Luc’s narrowed eyes and the hard lines of repulsion that marred the beautiful face. “You know the command….”

Luc burst into laughter, eyes glittering with the triumph of disrupting his stoic friend’s calm demeanor. “As if I would dare defy Adonai!” Relief flooded Rapha as the shadow disappeared from Luc’s face. Ah… this was his beloved, teasing Lucifer.

“However….” Luc observed the squat creature, now scratching and snuffling under a bush, “he must have something to record on his cave wall.”

Without further discourse, Luc drew himself up to a height rivaling the tall evergreens, revealing himself in all his celestial glory. His body flared like lightning and a whirlwind of smoke rushed up from the ground, causing the bright hair cascading about his shoulders to flow up and out creating both a crown and mantle. With eyes of fire he flung a lightning bolt across the valley as the man creature screamed in fright and threw himself beneath the bush. When Luc turned his smoking gaze toward the trembling being, Rapha moved quickly. Expanding to equal Luc's stature, his own muscular body rising thirty feet into the air, he took one step that resounded across the valley like a clap of thunder and placed himself between Luc and the frightened man creature that howled in terror then ran, fell, and rolled back down the rocky slope.

Luc reduced himself to his original proportions and fell back on the plush turf laughing, unfazed by the menacing regard of his friend who sunk back to a mere eight feet tall.

"Adonai will know."

"Oh, I'm *counting* on it!" Luc's eyes flashed with anger. "I've told Him these pathetic men will never develop if left to their own slow, cognitive abilities. Besides, you've just helped me initiate worship! That creature will grunt stories of his brush with 'the gods' for the rest of his life! He'll be esteemed and honored. I've done him a favor…."

"You have disobeyed Adonai!"

"I'm showing Him I can *think for myself!*" Luc roared with a pent-up fury that drove Rapha backwards to shatter the rock wall behind him and send another resounding crash across the valley.

Finally, all was quiet. Rapha looked up from the mound of shattered rock toward Luc whose face registered vague surprise at his own violence. There was regret, but no apology. "Admit it, Rapha. You have doubts as well. How long will Adonai keep us slaves to His will? He plots to dishonor us, the greatest of His creation, yet we continue to bow and scrape and—"

"Silence!" Rapha's voice thundered across the valley cutting off Luc's tirade. He had never controlled his friend by force but the words against Adonai were an insult he would not endure.

Enraged, Luc fixed mute but murderous eyes on him as Rapha continued, struggling to remember how Adonai maintained the celestial court without anger. "Adonai has given nothing but honor and power to us. You shame Him, and yourself, with these words."

Finally Luc's tongue was loosened, dripping with bitterness. "Shame? You want shame? Continue blindly following orders until you find yourself nursemaid to the mud creatures, *my friend*!" In a split second Luc launched himself off the precipice and, like a glorious phoenix, traced an arc of fire through blushing, sun-kissed clouds.

Rapha's mind skipped immediately to a more recent memory.

It was another day atop Luc's favorite mountain. When Rapha appeared, Luc was tracing a lazy finger in the air to swirl a dark cloud in the sky above him. "You heard?"

Rapha allowed a tight smile, "How could I not? Your anger still resounds through the cosmos."

Luc sneered, "Gabriel. Michael. *'Thank you, Adonai!'*" he mocked, *"'We will honor and obey.'"* A spasm of fury flicked across Luc's features, "They grovel while Adonai humiliates…."

"No! They were chosen because they refuse to stir contention about what they do not understand…."

"Unlike me." Luc finished, his eyes piercing, his hands clenched into fists. "I, who have been closer to Adonai's counsel than any other; I knew this was coming. I warned you. I understand all too well."

"And make assumptions based on a glimpse of His plans."

"Assumptions?" Luc's volume rose, "What more is there to know? Adonai announced it. He plans to elevate these *creatures*," Luc spat the word, "to give them dominion over this place. Can you honestly say that is no insult to us, His servants of light, His firstborn?"

"You mean insult to *you*, Adonai's favored."

"Yes. Insult to me. If anyone should be offered dominion it is I. I, who have been Adonai's most trusted, the morning star of all His creation, not some vile creature of dust!"

"But you told me Adonai will dwell within them. They will be children of the Most High in every sense and one day His highest purpose will be realized through one of them—" But Rapha's words were cut off by a whizzing blow and his mouth tasted earth from the chunk of mountain that had hit him. Immediately he transformed into his transparent body but Luc was one step ahead. Cords of light were flung 'round Rapha's chest and were tightening their painful grip even as Lucifer, arms outstretched, summoned a continuing barrage of rocks and trees as he spun in the air like a malevolent cyclone.

"NOOO! Adonai has betrayed me!" Luc screamed over the tumult of his storm, "He says *I* am not ready to rule! He gives authority to Michael, to Gabriel, to these, these *animals*…."

Rapha dodged and blocked Luc's projectiles as he struggled to contain his own rising rage. "Please," he shouted, gritting his teeth in the effort to escape the grip of Lucifer's bonds. "Come with me. Adonai will explain any misunderstanding."

But his words only stoked Luc's rage. "You're a fool, Rapha!" Luc screamed. "You had your chance. Twice Adonai has betrayed us while you, *my friend*, stood silent!" Rapha discerned other bright figures descending to Luc. Grief, anger and pain gripped him as he recognized the faces of those whose power now ripped his being. There was Aegeus and Epiron and, a shudder ran through Rapha's body as he saw mighty Zelneus, one he thought forever faithful to Adonai, adding his strength to the assault, drawing molten rock from deep in the Earth to turn the swirling madness into a firestorm.

With a burst of power, Rapha flung off his bindings, and answering cords of golden light whipped from him toward his attackers. But these were angelic brothers who knew his strength—and there were too many. As they added their power to Lucifer's, immense rocks shoved and jostled, breaking the surface of ground that had been solid only seconds before but now roiled like a storm tossed sea, opening immense jaws to consume him.

As Rapha fell beneath his angelic brother's fury, their relentless attack piercing and shredding with blinding pain, despair stole his will to fight. They had shielded their thoughts and planned this attack. Now they used the mighty gifts of Adonai, power given to create beauty, to destroy.

"Abba Adonai," Rapha gasped, the weight of his friends' betrayal heavier than the mountain of rock and their binding power bearing down upon him. Immediately the sweet fragrance of Adonai, usually only experienced before the throne, wrapped its comfort around Rapha's battered form.

"Do not resist."

As Adonai's command filled the crushing darkness, peace like a fast-opening bloom pressed out from Rapha's soul and enveloped him. He relaxed, trusting, as the weight bore down and curses of his brother angels tore at him in the same way their fury smote the ground. However, Rapha had never felt more immersed in Adonai, so the burial was sweet. He saw a glimmer before his eyes, a reflection of his own ebbing fire and, with trembling fingers, wrenched it from the rock. It was a large gem. Rapha cupped it to his breast, its smooth, unyielding surface his only tangible companion, as his last feeble thread of consciousness was severed.

Then came the melting, the sifting, the re-molding; all within Adonai's very being. No grief could exist there. In Adonai only wholeness and light wrapped Rapha in peace. He drank deeply of the goodness—unfathomable, sweet, all encompassing, freeing. There, hidden in Adonai's embrace, Rapha slept.

Chapter Two

Rebellion

Rapha woke to celestial war.

Many had joined Lucifer's rebellion. Heartbreak and devastation infiltrated the fabric of the heavenlies threatening to strip creation from its foundation, attempting to topple the very throne of Adonai. Finally Lucifer, the instigator and accuser, stood before the assembly proclaiming Adonai's treachery.

Into the midst of this firestorm of severed trust strode Rapha, his eyes and voice aglow with faith in Adonai. In ages past Lucifer had ruled in the celestial court, his arguments the most compelling, his voice and mannerisms irresistible. But that day belonged to Rapha. Many who were prepared to cast their lot with Lucifer hearkened to the authority of Rapha's testimony, moved to repentance by his absolute trust in Adonai's goodness, while those who had remained faithful were ignited with renewed passion.

Even as Rapha spoke, flowing with eloquence, joyfully describing his rebirth, he could feel Lucifer seethe. Lucifer had been certain of victory, now Rapha could sense the shift as thousands hearkened to his words, "There is no room in Adonai's goodness for deception or betrayal," Rapha stated. With a surge of bliss, he felt Adonai's pleasure.

It was at that moment Lucifer did the unthinkable. He attacked Rapha before the very throne of Adonai. Rapha's words were cut off by searing pain as he realized a shard of light was protruding from his chest.

But Michael was prepared. While Rapha crumpled, eyes wide with disbelief, Michael's forces, scattered strategically throughout the faithful and treacherous, leapt to action.

The brawl that ensued was decisive, not in determining a victor but in revealing loyalties. When it seemed every hand was raised in violence toward a brother, Adonai spoke one word.

"Peace."

The heavenly inhabitants froze.

If the moment had not been tragic—and painful for Rapha who wrenched the shard from his chest—Rapha would have thought it comical to behold his celestial brothers caught in suspended animation, expressions of anger and surprise etched on their faces, bodies arrested in various violent postures.

"Samael," Adonai addressed Lucifer who had one hand on Michael's throat while the other grasped a jagged bolt of light aimed directly at Adonai's throne. **"Observe what your pride has done."**

Lucifer's body shuddered as his hands were forced to his sides and the bolt of light dissipated. Finally, his tongue was loosed and he said through clenched teeth. "I *hate* that. *Never* call me that. I am Lucifer, the bright morning star!"

"Even in this moment, when all is brought to the brink of ruin, you consider only yourself."

"Someone must watch out for my interests, *as You once did*."

"Your lack of faith separates us."

"My lack of.... Do you hear this?" Lucifer spoke to the motionless witnesses around him, "Adonai betrays us. Then he would lay the blame at *my* feet!"

"Enough."

Once more Lucifer was mute though his eyes continued to flash with fury.

"Two choices are before you this day. Either repent of your rebellion and remain or… go."

When Lucifer was once more released he spun, a blur of raging light, to fling cords of power, power that would have destroyed his defenseless brothers but for the sphere encasing him, a buffer from Adonai. Abruptly Lucifer stopped, stricken senseless by his own poison.

There would be no repentance. That day Lucifer and his followers, fully one-third of the celestial population, were banished.

Heartbreak infiltrated the heavenlies as longstanding friendships were severed.

It was not long before Lucifer's forces felt the poverty of their new existence outside Adonai's favor. Like fish gasping out of water, their bodies longed for His presence though they had not realized their need until they were deprived. A few threw themselves on Adonai's mercy and accepted their sentence, an age of witnessing the ongoing drama trapped as watchers in the sky. But the rest believed Lucifer's lies, that Adonai had goaded them to this place of desperation and rejoiced in their pain. Their hatred and hopelessness drove them to greater evil. They raged throughout the cosmos defacing all in their path, joining Lucifer in venting their fury. Galaxies were thrown out of alignment and whole planets were destroyed or rendered lifeless due to their scorching blasts.

Rapha and the other loyal celestials were dispatched to restore order. At every turn they were ambushed as Lucifer and his followers became adept at this colossal game of hide-and-seek, burrowing deep into planets to continue their destruction like unstoppable termites, devouring in darkness. Wars raged on distant planets as Lucifer tried to ensure no outpost of safety remained for Adonai's prophecy of creation's future redeemer. Even Rapha, battlescarred and weary of the struggle, had moments of doubt as Lucifer's destructive lust swept the cosmos and verdant planets were reduced to dust-shrouded tombs.

Michael, the leader of heaven's forces, also adapted as he learned to listen to Adonai's quiet leading rather than rush headlong in reaction to Lucifer's wrongs. To this end he relied heavily on Rapha whose ear was attuned to Adonai's direction. Time and again they surprised Lucifer's troops, having foreknowledge of his plans before they were put into action. Finally, heaven's forces began to have the upper hand and the sphere of Lucifer's influence began to constrict.

But Lucifer would not accept defeat. When he realized the noose tightening around his position he lashed out, driving his faithful hordes to madness as he screamed defiance and proclaimed the righteousness of their struggle.

How the heavens crashed with frightful flashings and rumblings. To the inhabitants of Earth, it appeared the end had come, as day and night strange flares lit the sky. Finally, the tide turned. Within Lucifer's own hosts mutiny erupted and as the rebel forces fought among themselves, Michael's troops surrounded them, cutting off Lucifer's escape by forging an impenetrable net of heaven's unified power.

Even then, bound, defeated and delivered before Adonai's throne, Lucifer was defiant. "Is this how you treat your *free* citizens? Do you see, you blind beggars serving this tyrant?" Once more Lucifer was silenced. As he stood looking as if his tongue had sealed his lips, Adonai spoke.

"We will now hear the charges."

Angel after angel stepped forward to state Lucifer's offenses, even some who had joined him in his rampage across the heavenlies. Finally Adonai asked, **"Will any stand to defend the accused?"**

All was quiet. Still Lucifer held his head high to stare at those who had spoken against him.

Suddenly, every eye was drawn to Adonai's throne where, in the center of holiness, the bright purity grew blindingly brighter until the brilliance pressed forward as if to engulf all. Just when Rapha felt his being crushed by overwhelming bliss, the orb of holiness contracted, compressing back to the throne, yet increasing in its intensity. Immediately the tension vanished and a dim shape became visible. To Rapha it appeared five darker points were emerging from the center of Adonai's being. Gradually the shape became discernable—two arms swinging free, two feet striding, a bright robe covering the torso, and hair that flowed to the shoulders. But light did not pass through. Rapha pondered this fact. This being was clothed in light, he even glowed with Adonai's radiance, but He was not of the same fiber as the surrounding celestials.

This relatively small someone strode until he stood before the throne within arm's reach of Lucifer.

"I will speak for him," the One said.

A jolt of joy coursed through Rapha. He had heard only five words from the man's mouth, yet Rapha *knew* him. How could this be?

Lucifer stared at the white-robed figure and, with a hand over his mouth as if stifling a laugh he said, "Is this my only friend? How pathetic."

But the One before the throne ignored him. **"Father, Samael is your child. Whatever offenses he has committed, and they are many, let them fall on me."**

Lucifer gasped, "*Father*? Is this... No."

The man continued, **"My flesh and blood alone can restore him to holiness."**

"Your flesh and blood?" Lucifer spat. "This… *thing* is not worthy to stand in my presence!" Lucifer's voice rose and his slander became more and more vile while the man stood, quiet and calm.

"Silence." Adonai's voice boomed from the throne. **"This is my Son in whom I am well pleased."**

A collective gasp resounded.

Lucifer stared up and down the small figure as if searching for a hint of greatness. In fact, Rapha could feel every eye fixed on the man, such a contrast to celestial splendor. This was the One—fully God and fully man. The prophecy stood before their eyes.

"So this is what all the fuss was about?" Lucifer sneered, "How disappointing." But his body betrayed the condescending tone with tremors of fury.

The man before the throne turned to face Lucifer. **"Will you accept Our gift, Samael?"**

"I am the Morning Star, the brightest and greatest of all creation! I have no need of your *beggar's rations*," Lucifer proclaimed.

Once again the voice from the throne filled their ears. **"At any time, Samael, my servant stands ready to restore you."**

"Restore? Him?" Lucifer laughed but his eyes remained deadly, "To what? Could I too be ugly and dress poorly?"

Though many celestial voices murmured with anger and Michael grumbled at Rapha's side, the voice from the throne remained steady. **"Since you reject restoration, your sentence is set. No more will you have access to the heavens. You will be confined to one planet just like those you destroyed."**

"That's not fair! I am a citizen of the stars. It is my *right*...."

Adonai's voice continued and Lucifer stopped speaking, his expression intent, as if straining to hear something better.

"Make your choice. Where will you abide?"

Rapha watched the thoughts play across Lucifer's face. If a loophole were available, no matter how obscure, Lucifer would find it.

"Just to make things clear," Lucifer said, "will I dwell alone?"

"No. I will not hinder those who choose to accompany you."

Lucifer smirked, "I choose Earth."

"No!" Michael shouted from the crowd. "He chooses Earth to hinder prophecy."

"But, if the Most High wants to go back on His *word*...." Lucifer said.

Michael made a move toward Lucifer and Rapha laid a restraining hand on his shoulder.

"But," Lucifer's brow furrowed with concern, "am I correct in assuming I will maintain my other powers? After all, I must not be left to the *mercy* of my enemies."

"Yes. Your other powers will remain."

"But, Adonai," Michael interjected again, "with all due respect, he *must* be stripped of his powers or he will destroy Earth."

"Understand, Samael," Adonai addressed Lucifer, **"you are tied to the fate of Earth. To destroy her is to destroy yourself."**

Lucifer's eyes narrowed, shrewd and calculating, "I will, of course, be the most powerful being there."

"No. Authority over Earth is given to another."

"To what? To this *son* of yours?" Lucifer hissed. "He will have no authority over *me!"*

But the trial was over. Lucifer, still screaming threats and defiance, was ushered from Adonai's presence and the edict was put into effect. He and those loyal to him were confined to Earth and stripped of their access to the heavens.

As Rapha and the other celestials began the task of mending the scars of war, he could not help but shudder as he considered the fate of the tiny planet that now played host to a raging outcast angel. Perhaps Lucifer would be tamed by having his wings clipped?

Michael laughed when they discussed that possibility. Rapha agreed, but he did not have the heart to laugh.

Later, when all was relatively peaceful once again, Rapha sought Luc upon Earth, delving deep until he found himself returning to the place of his own unmaking. In these depths, a slight remnant of Adonai's fragrance clung to the cavern walls. And there, in the very hole where Rapha had known both an end and a beginning, huddled Lucifer, his beautiful hands clutching like talons at his once-glorious hair that now hung about him like tangled vines. A heavy scent of grief enshrouded him as well as… could it be… fear?

"No matter how high I fly or how deeply I delve You are there," Luc's voice was a hoarse whisper, "and yet I am banished from Your presence… and yet… You. Are. *Everywhere*!" Luc's hands gripped at his glowing arms as if to wrench them from his body.

"You mock me. I can feel it. You sit on your golden throne and laugh at the morning star that grovels in the dirt like… like a creature of dust!" A moan shook Luc's frame. "Why? Why do You delight to dishonor me? What was my superior intelligence for if not to discover Your plan? Surely You knew I could not be fooled?" A gasp of pain escaped his lips. "Surely this was Your plan all along, to lift me high in order to crush me."

Rapha could remain silent no longer. "Never. Adonai grieves. All heaven grieves the loss of bright Lucifer."

Luc spun, crouching low as if ready to spring, "What? Now you are Adonai's spy; relishing my pain to perform it as a jest before His throne?"

"I came of my own accord, Lucifer," Rapha knelt to Luc's level. "This has gone too far. Adonai will yet forgive…."

"Forgive?" Lucifer spat in disgust, "He should ask *my* forgiveness! He spins His webs of deception while those too simple… too *cowardly—*" his accusing gaze swept Rapha, "blindly sing His praises."

"To trust Adonai's love is the only true wisdom…"

"Don't quote me your brainwashed rhetoric! *'The fear of the Lord is the beginning of wisdom,'"* Luc's eyes opened wide as his hands mouthed the air like puppets, "Blah, bull-ah, bull-ah! The Great Adonai's wisdom has *failed*! He has set a course for *our* disgrace and destruction! I strive to protect you and the rest of my brothers yet *I am banished*! And you, *my friend*, stood silent."

"I am still your friend, Luc. You are the one set on destruction. If I did not care I would not be here. Do you really think I desire burial beneath another mountain?"

Rapha caught a fleeting glimpse of humor in the poison-filled eyes as Luc shrugged with grudging admiration, "Yes. I thought we'd at least crush the fight out of you but it only buried you that much deeper in Adonai's debt with your touching tale of rebirth." He sneered, "Thanks to you and your *passionate* testimony of Adonai's *love,* Phineas betrayed me. I suppose I shouldn't be surprised when Adonai has managed to turn even you against me."

"I am not against you, but I stand with the Most High."

"Even now you can join me, old friend," Luc's eyes widened. "We will prove Adonai's error together. Perhaps with you on our side Gabriel could be influenced. We are strong, Rapha. We will break Adonai's grip over us…."

The words continued as Rapha studied the earnest, perfect face before him. So, one-third of heaven's hosts were not enough? How had he been so blind to Luc's ambition? But even defeated and banished, Lucifer's words wielded truth, appealing to their angelic fraternity, begging him not to end their ancient friendship. Rapha had been buried beneath a mountain by Lucifer's fury yet still he felt the pull, the yearning to join the noble venture to wrest their fate once and for all from the controlling hands of Adonai.

A smile crept over Rapha's features even as Lucifer spoke of war.

> *The hands of Adonai... the gentle, healing, creating, pure presence of his Lord... the unspeakable joy of pulsing with Adonai's power... the sense of losing his identity in that fathomless sweetness... emerging empty yet bursting with fulfillment.*

The compelling voice ceased as Lucifer realized the tension between them was gone. His eyes narrowed, "Even now Adonai whispers His lies to you. I'd recognize that vacant expression anywhere. Rapha! *You must think for yourself*!"

"I choose to be single-minded. If it does not please Adonai, I do not think it."

"But Rapha! Brother!" Luc reached toward him with graceful hands. "Don't you see? Perhaps this *is* Adonai's plan. We are ready to rule but we must shake off our fear of Him. No one rules Him. To be *like* Adonai, no one can rule us!"

"*You* do not wish to rule us?"

In the split-second's pause, Lucifer shut his eyes and a spasm of pain played across his features. The sadness in his eyes when he opened them was truly heartbreaking.

"I would… *lead* my brothers to greater glory."

Rapha fought the sudden urge to let out an explosive "Ha!" like Michael. Instead he took a steadying breath to say, "And how would you deal with those who oppose you—uproot another mountain?"

"I *tried* to persuade you…." Lucifer began.

"Your own actions prove you are not ready to rule." Rage flamed in Lucifer's eyes and Rapha fought to keep his own voice steady. "Please, humble yourself. Adonai's ways, His timing, His methods are perfect. The more you struggle against Him the more you destroy yourself!"

"Humble myself? He does not need my help to do that. I who was at Adonai's right hand am left to grovel with filth!" A deadly resolve filled Lucifer's face, "But I promise, though it take an eternity, one day Adonai will bow to *me*."

The rumble started deep beneath their feet and grew closer until the cavern over their heads began to collapse.

"What, Adonai?" Lucifer shouted. "Would You, my creator, destroy your beloved? Go ahead and prove you are a selfish, vengeful God who maintains your throne by force rather than love!" His voice, Lucifer's voice which had been able to coax the entire celestial court to glorious, perfection of song, which had been his greatest gift bestowed by his Creator, now screamed to match the deafening noise, *"Go ahead and crush me! I will never stop! You have rejected me? I. Defy. You!"*

Eyes bulging, Lucifer continued to rage, taunting and ridiculing the great Creator, commanding Adonai to prove His superiority.

Soon the rumbling ceased and Lucifer laughed in triumph, "Oh, that's right. You're so holy and *long-suffering*. Your *righteousness* stays your hand." He cackled with glee and strutted to place a talon grip on Rapha's shoulders.

Lucifer's face was hardly recognizable. The peace and confidence was replaced by hatred, and his beauty was lost beneath rage that flickered across his features like tongues of fire. Rapha stood his ground as Lucifer pulled him close to whisper. "Be assured, old friend, *I* am hampered by no such weakness." He kissed Rapha's cheek, then, with a burst of fire that exploded the rock around them, he vanished.

All heaven waited. Surely Lucifer's rebellion would not go unanswered.

But the surface of the land in that ancient age resumed its cycles—life and death, bloom and fade—as heavenly order was restored, more cherished by its inhabitants than ever, even though a threat was growing in the hidden shadows. Soon, what began as inconceivable rumor became undeniable.

Lucifer and his followers were corrupting the fabric of Adonai's creation.

Rapha stumbled upon proof of this depravity in a forest glade from which rumors had risen. Woodland creatures did not add their chatter here. He felt the void of sweet breeze carrying the scent of fertile soil and woodland blooms; this ground was wounded, tainted, diseased. Dis-ease—the word fit. The air pulsed with a reek that choked the flow of life. Never before had a locale so repulsed Rapha, yet the inner, compelling force of Adonai willed him forward through an increasing stench that rose through fissures in the earth's scarred skin.

To Rapha, accustomed to heaven's breath, these sensations clawed at his sanity as he probed his surroundings with senses that far outstripped the wariest prey. Never before had those senses been such a curse. Faint but piercing cries assaulted his ears, cries of such despair and agony they drove him with a gasp to his knees toward the buried pestilence that wrapped round his being like poison tentacles. Eyes shut to shield against the horror, he clung to the lifeline of Adonai, feeling a gentle, sweet infusion of strength to face what horrors lay in store.

And he had only to open his eyes to find them.

A tiny humanoid foot, no longer than his thumbnail, lay half-hidden and quivering upon a bed of decaying leaves. With a trembling hand, Rapha parted the debris and a moan escaped his ancient lips.

Though the foot was that of an embryonic manchild, the rest appeared comprised of the spare parts of other species—feline ears, primate torso, reptilian skin on its upper body while some type of fur covered the lower half that ended with one human leg and foot. But Rapha's horror was not due to its unnatural design but rather to what had been done *to* it. One leg and arm had been removed. The rest of its body was mutilated with diabolical, exploratory precision. The miniature talons on its remaining hand were clenched so tight that blood pooled beneath the self-inflicted piercings on its palm.

Worst of all, the creature was still alive.

Rapha scooped the remains into his hands, careful to dig beneath its bed of leaves to keep the beast cushioned, and cupped it to his breast. When a large tear fell from Rapha's cheek to steam upward from exposed organs, the creature shuddered, and its nocturnally round eyes fluttered open to hold Rapha's gaze, twisting a barbed knife deep into the angel's soul. He did not want to see into the creature's mind but those large eyes held his, a gateway to horrors visited upon helplessness.

Rapha gasped in pain with the memories of ripping, of piercing, of twisted, powerful faces with no remorse for the torture they inflicted. Rage engulfed him. He knew those faces… trusted, beloved brothers whose eyes now mirrored the ruthless ambition of Lucifer.

Down, down he was pulled into the madness of the creature's mind, choking on memories of chambers thick with death, fear, endless pain, and the poison of despair.

He wrenched his mind free and held the creature to his breast. When he felt a feeble claw clutch his chest he cried out in the language of the heavens, *"Adonai! Ah! El Dai-ine!"*

How could Adonai know and yet… do nothing?

Rapha looked down through a haze of his own confusion and met that same emotion in the creature's eyes. Their lives had been worlds apart and yet they shared this moment, the same thought… why… how?

Mercy demanded he should kill the creature, end its torture.

He could not do it. Instead, Rapha sat in the leaves, oblivious to all but the spasms of his tiny ward whose heart continued to beat even as its blood poured into his palm. His vigil continued until the creature, its large eyes probing and questioning to the very end, shuddered a last wracking breath and grew still.

Rapha remained, lost in darkness despite a persistent sun piercing the forest's canopy.

As if from a great distance, he became aware of a roar, a sound that carried such rage and grief that all nature trembled. Slowly, Rapha realized the sound came from his own mouth opened wide in agony as he too longed to know the release of death. It was the first time a mortal end seemed welcome. It would not be the last.

"Ah. I see you found my gift."

Rapha had been so consumed by confusion, grief, and despair, Lucifer's arrival had gone unnoticed. His old friend was watching with an obscene, rapturous expression.

As Lucifer's voice ripped through him, stirring old wounds and raking across new devastation, Rapha succumbed to emotion and summoned his angelic forces, who began to appear, their pure light surrounding the fallen angel who crouched on a fire-scarred hillock, staring down on Rapha's torment with shining eyes. Except for the voice, Rapha would hardly have known him. Angelic beings do not age but Lucifer had always been a "youthful" presence, eager and teasing. Now, rather than light, his face bore deep shadows and the eager expression had been transformed to unquenchable greed. And Rapha's pain was his feast.

The desire to erase Lucifer's mocking smile shoved Rapha's grief aside. How he lusted to channel his rage toward Lucifer and his followers. Visions of blasting through soil and rock to destroy every trace of death, stench and corruption were a dizzying wine. Rapha could taste revenge on his tongue… and he savored it.

But even in this moment, Adonai's will flowed clearly into Rapha's mind.

"This is not the hour of retribution."

Now came the real test as Rapha faced his greatest temptation. What Lucifer deserved was clear, but what Adonai asked…. How could holiness allow this abomination to go unanswered?

Lucifer's mocking laughter cut through Rapha's turmoil. "Adonai demands mercy, right? But you, mighty warrior, desire justice. How long will you serve such *weakness*?" The question ended in a hiss.

Righteous fury was almost Rapha's undoing. Never had he been more vulnerable than at that moment, longing to rip Lucifer in exactly the way the tiny creature had suffered. Then he looked down at its mangled body still cradled in his hands. The compassion that overwhelmed him, straight from Adonai's heart, cooled the heat of revenge. The words Adonai implanted in Rapha's consciousness made no sense, but they carried reassurance.

"This very seed will one day hasten his defeat."

No, Rapha would not strike with physical force this day. But he could not resist goading his enemy just once. Looking up, he fixed the peace of Adonai on Lucifer like a laser, held that malicious gaze for one eternal second—and smiled. A flicker of uncertainty stirred in Lucifer's eyes.

Rapha opened a single thought to Lucifer as he disappeared with the creature still cradled to his breast:

"You always did *hate secrets."*

Chapter Three

A Fresh Start

Again evil's menace grew. Why did Adonai refuse to destroy the roots of perversion? Surely He could discern only too well Lucifer's desire to corrupt… everything. Was it pity for the victims of Lucifer's experiments that kept Adonai from destroying every hidden hold? Could Adonai remain holy *and* defeat evil? When Rapha could not understand he grieved and found unity with the heart of his Maker.

For the man creatures, things went from bad to worse. Lucifer's experiments became more sophisticated as he refined the art of corruption. New manipulated beasts erupted from the bowels of the earth.

Reptiles, the sleek, dominant hunters of the period, began increasing in size and ferocity. Most simply grew in height and girth but not intelligence, their lumbering forms multiplying across the earth's surface. But some of the species developed a particular taste for humans. Life on earth became a constant struggle to survive for early man. Men lacked the size, strength and cold-blooded focus of their foe that was drawn to their warmth even in darkness. Thus it appeared the roots of mankind would be erased. But the man creatures displayed a surprising ability to adapt, a fact Lucifer underestimated; a fact that would serve them well in the days to come.

Rapha was there in the celestial court when Lucifer was granted an audience and appeared with a contingent of his fallen brothers. Lucifer's words of greeting were gracious, all according to protocol, but it did not take long for his true purpose to be revealed.

"I come with a proposition, Oh Most High."

"Yes, my child." Lucifer flinched at the address. **"State your thoughts."**

"I offer peace." The attending celestials murmured in surprise. "Let us make an end of death and war. From this day forward my motto with the man beings is 'Live and let live.'" Lucifer raised a magnanimous arm and smiled at his former compatriots.

"And what do you gain?"

"What do I gain? It is enough to know our conflict would be at an end."

"Speak your desire, Samael."

Lucifer grimaced once again but when he spoke his voice was steady, even cheerful. "My desire is to heal, to take the hands of my celestial family and, together, return creation to her former glory, beginning with Earth." With a flick of a finger Lucifer opened a porthole in the heavenlies and the assembly beheld the blue-green planet, peaceful from a distance, but as they watched, he brought their view closer until glimpses of war, pain and devastation—a weeping child, a sleeping woman unaware a gigantic reptile hovered above her, man slaying man, the injured, sick, naked, and starving populace of Earth paraded before their eyes. Lucifer's accusing gaze swept the faces of those gathered.

"State your requirement," Adonai's calm voice broke the hypnotic hold of the horrific images.

"Nothing much, actually quite trivial." Lucifer shrugged and put a hand to his head as if recalling a fleeting thought. "Ah, yes! Celestial stewardship over earth."

The uproar was immediate and Lucifer's entourage formed a protective circle around their leader while Michael's angry voice rose above the rest, "With you in charge, no doubt!"

"Actually," Lucifer continued, "I would join my angelic brothers in this errand of peace and restoration. Men are not prepared for this task. It requires celestial wisdom and power. We would show them the way."

Michael burst forth with an explosive laugh.

"Yes, Michael. Something you would like to share?"

Michael's massive, muscular form shouldered through the crowd, "Adonai, he dares to come before your throne with a lie!"

"Unlike others," Lucifer continued without so much as a glance in Michael's direction, "I seek to heal division, even to work side by side with those of a more… unforgiving nature."

Michael gave a snort of disgust.

"And if your request is denied?"

"The best interests of earth, of *Your* creation, are at stake."

"You knew you would be denied and your plan is already at work."

Lucifer chuckled. "It's just impossible to surprise You." He shrugged and swept a hand toward his companions, "Of course, I cannot accept all the credit for our plan, but I stand prepared to aid earth, *if* given the ability to do so."

Rapha recognized his old friend's expression of triumph. Compromise had never been in Lucifer's vocabulary. It was absolute victory or nothing.

"I cannot grant your desire, Samael."

"I had a feeling you'd say that, always faithful to your word." Lucifer shook his head and sighed.

"Tell your brothers your plan."

"Well, you already know, and why should I alarm them since, if You are true to form, You will not intervene."

But Michael, with lightning-quick temper and reflexes, already held Lucifer's throat. "You *will* obey the command."

Lucifer sneered, "Predictable as always, Michael. *You* I will enjoy telling. *If* you please," he tapped the hand at his throat with a dainty finger and smiled into Michael's glare. The hand at the fallen angel's throat was grudgingly removed but Michael's grip on Lucifer's shoulder remained. Lucifer smiled into Michael's angry face as if relishing a delicious secret.

"Earth will be destroyed," Lucifer announced with wide-eyed innocence. "There now, we'll have nothing more to fight about. We'll be *best* of friends again."

"You lie!" Michael said.

Lucifer turned his attention back to the throne, "Would you like to revise your answer, Oh Most High?"

"I see the end of all things, Samael, yet I choose holiness. It would be well for you to do the same."

Lucifer inclined his head and his cohorts sprang into action, closing tighter around him. "I am not given dominion over earth but I retain some power. An oversight on your part?"

The rebels' fire blazed, blinding in its combined strength. Michael was also caught in their midst as their sphere grew tighter and brighter.

But Rapha was determined to retrieve Michael who struggled in vain as Lucifer cackled with ecstasy.

"No, brother!" Gabriel's urgent voice was in Rapha's ear and his strong arms grasped him as Rapha dove toward Michael.

Immediately Rapha's momentum was increased a hundredfold and he was sucked toward Lucifer.

"Yes, *brother.* Join us," Lucifer's face was ecstatic in welcome.

They whirled, spinning and increasing to piercing brightness until, with a breathless, split-second's silence, even Lucifer's laughter stopped and all was black.

Rapha felt his being shatter and collapse as he and the other celestials caught in Lucifer's vortex exploded through the porthole and plummeted toward Earth.

Even at such a moment, Adonai's strength flowed through Rapha, calming, giving hope and direction. He sensed unity with Gabriel and Michael whose thoughts also centered on the Most High even as the rebel angels enfolding them shrieked hatred and targeted Earth's core.

Cords of trust and love linked Rapha, Gabriel, and Michael, an even stronger link than the fire engulfing them. They felt the burst of surprise from Lucifer when the three of them pulled the cluster of celestials tighter still. They felt his resistance as they willed their light to revolve in the opposite direction of Lucifer and his minions, every rotation grating against the rebels' collective will. Then they heard his howl of rage as the celestial fireball burst asunder short of Lucifer's target to scatter plummeting points of light across land and sea.

Rapha knew one instant of vague satisfaction before his being was splintered as by myriad shards of molten glass.

He had no way of knowing how much time had passed when he came to with liquid fire before his eyes. He had impacted on dry ground. That much Rapha remembered. But the searing acid engulfing him was real.

Had Earth been destroyed? Had all been reduced to swirling elements without form?

"No," Adonai's calm voice assured him. And Rapha was not alone. Strong arms were lifting him; familiar voices were speaking to him. His last view of earth as one of his brothers sped him toward the heavens was a blur of smoke, fire, and flood with thousands of bright points of light—the attending, faithful celestials—working amidst the devastation.

The pain from countless screaming souls smote the last of Rapha's waning strength and he knew no more.

In the following days, as Rapha recovered, the stench of death rose from the land while ash rained filth from above. Panic and horror reigned as land and sea traded places and foundational stones ground together forcing jagged pinnacles skyward. Huge tidal waves capsized forests and mountains and many of the ocean's inhabitants were marooned in shallow pools or stranded on dry land. Magnetic forces clawed for stability and the earth's rotation tilted as if threatening to fall out of its appointed path in the cosmos.

But there were survivors. With celestial assistance and man's knowledge of caves and deep-water sources, discovered as they had fled Lucifer's monster lizards, a ragtag remnant of mankind remained to defy insurmountable odds.

The huge reptiles, however, did not fare so well. Stranded on the surface where sustaining plants withered and the temperature plummeted, the giant predators starved, their ice- and ash-covered carcasses the largest among the tombstones dotting earth's strange new landscape where the titanic forces of displaced seas formed giant swells of ice on Earth's new polar axes.

But, despite an unrecognizable terrain and skewed forces of nature, Earth's life force continued to pulse, feeble but constant, beneath the shroud of death.

The stain of immortal flesh, Lucifer's triumph, could not be destroyed, but the planet's natural forces, made more violent due to its injuries, served to bury this corruption far beneath rock, soil, and water, out of harm's way—for a time.

But Lucifer was nothing if not persistent. His experiments continued even as earth limped toward renewal and many centuries of relative peace.

Earth's inhabitants began creeping out of hiding as air and water flowed clean once again. As before, fierce creatures made life a constant battle, but the deeper aim of their manipulator was taking form in Lucifer's hidden holds.

Rumors reached Rapha's ears of new horrors, of creatures possessing both the intelligence of humanity and the ferocity of beasts. On occasion they erupted to fuel the night terrors of those who inhabited the yet fertile land and sea. With the passing years these skirmishes grew in scope and intensity. Roots of myth and legend were born while mankind became more and more like the beasts they fought.

Finally, Lucifer's new strategy was unveiled.

No longer would the fallen angel refrain from defying Adonai's primary celestial edict, a law established from the beginning of all things—**"Celestials will not join their flesh to that of mankind."**

But if earthly flesh and blood were required for earthly dominion, so be it. The rebels would acquire it.

All heaven grieved when descendants of "the gods" began appearing as lords of Earth's various tribes. What use did the children of men have for an unseen creator when these glorious beings, a feast for earthly senses, could be worshiped?

These lords were a diabolical combination of glorified beast and man. Whatever creature was most feared in a tribe, the lord would appear who claimed dominion over it. They possessed the physical attributes of man and beast, yet were larger, stronger, wiser. For one culture the lord resembled man and snake, for another, a man-lion, while yet another bowed before a man-dragon.

Mankind was eager to seek the favor of these gods. Who else would give them the knowledge and tools of war necessary to survive?

Thus the leaders of men swore allegiance to these glorious beings. In return they received knowledge, power, wealth, and the means to destroy the beasts that plagued them. These "shining ones" received whatever they demanded. Their requests were simple. They merely desired earth women as their mates.

So Lucifer's goal was achieved with mankind's eager acquiescence. The cities of men became glorious wonders of architecture while commerce, art, and science attained astonishing heights through wisdom handed down from the gods.

And the celestial offspring! Never had there been men of such stature, beauty, and strength. In that golden age following the defeat of the evil beasts, men knew ease and safety. Their edifices rose higher, their tables overflowed with the fat of the land and their pride soared.

But not all were deceived. Some prophets spoke of catastrophe to come but few listened. Who would dare oppose the sons of gods? Indeed, any who tried paid the price of that folly with their lives.

However, as celestial offspring flourished, mankind began to realize their error. They watched these saviors become the oppressors; their tyranny, cruelty, and disdain for those of inferior blood established the reigning law of the land: Might is right.

Rapha and heaven's allies were busy sustaining those who called on Adonai. From the sprawling cities came a steady trickle of refugees seeking escape and communion with their Maker. Among these remnants of human kind were others, a manipulated and mixed species of beast, human, and angelic blood. They were a motley crew but they had one thing in common: a deep desire for truth and love. There were even beasts of hideous visage that possessed this hunger for purity, as if holiness was an anomaly Lucifer could not predict or destroy. Finally, Rapha understood Adonai's patient unwillingness to destroy the seeds of goodness along with the wicked.

But the bloodbath was inevitable. When the shining star of earth's cities sank into the earth and was buried beneath floodwaters, a result of Lucifer's massive lairs beneath it, Lucifer's servants fanned the grief and outrage, aiming it toward those who professed belief in the One True God. "They have been tunneling beneath our cities like rats!" his servants proclaimed. "They weaken our foundations of unity and power!"

The faithful sought refuge as Lucifer's forces gave relentless pursuit, scarring the land with their engines of war.

When wasting disease swept the land, another result of joining earthly and celestial flesh, it was yet another opportunity to blame the followers of Adonai.

"This is the judgment of their cruel God!" Lucifer's hordes screamed. "His prophets gave warnings, now Adonai has brought His plagues upon us!" So the hatred for and slaughter of those who professed fealty to the One True God raged stronger than ever.

Finally, no pocket of purity could be found on earth. Soil, air, water and flesh were corrupt. The only good dwelt within the hearts of those who sought Adonai. As these faithful ones endured torture, starvation, and death of all they loved, Rapha and his celestials ushered most of them one by one out of their diseased flesh and into paradise.

It was a wonder creation could resist as long as it did.

When earth could take no more, the spontaneous collapse was mirrored in all life. Structure was swallowed in chaos, harmony gave way to strife, and life finally succumbed to death. The earth, sickened to its core, vomited ash and fumes into the sky. The sun's light turned a sickening sepia, then gray, until, finally, choking darkness settled over the land.

Through this horror, Rapha and his allies strove to preserve the seeds of faithfulness. Lucifer too preserved a remnant of his kingdom. So, in vast, hidden realms, separate yet still sharing earth's hospitality, seeds of righteousness and evil dug deep to survive.

Thus the earth's surface lay fallow while the carnage of battle and catastrophe decayed. Again, what was of earth was reabsorbed. But the leavings of immortality remained, an indestructible poison to add to the stores of former celestial corruption. Down through rock and soil this distilled toxin seeped, transformed but still indestructible. These caches were hidden but not forgotten. The day would come when mankind would possess the will and means to draw forth this poison once more. But that day was far in earth's future.

> *And the earth was shapeless and void and darkness covered the face of the deep. (Gen. 1:2)*

Chapter Four

Grace

When the hand of Adonai reached to stir away the smoke and fumes, a deafening celestial cheer shook the heavens while the earth roared and rumbled to greet her Maker. Pure power coursed through Rapha's frame, renewing him as completely as the freshly formed mountain ranges and lush valleys that rejoiced to hear the Maker's long awaited summons. The scent of warmed soil and life-sustaining flora rose to heaven, the sweet incense of Earth's gratitude.

The land once again felt the hoofs and pads of life teeming across grass-covered slopes, the swirl of fins through sun-warmed streams, and the stir of feathers on the wind as the leaves of tall trees and the chatter of waters answered Adonai's laughter. Earth was pulsing with the life's blood of its creator.

The scent of new life intoxicated Rapha. Atop a fragrant hill he dug his hands into fresh, fertile soil, all the more rich for its years of disuse, and swore he could feel Earth's heartbeat throbbing through his fingers, sharing with him an almost unbearable joy. It had been too long. He had not realized how much he missed the simple stability of Earth's rhythm.

That was it! The ebb and flow was addictive to a tired soul that had experienced too much. Perhaps the enemy still plotted revenge for ancient grievances, but the birds, flowers, and padding wildlife were free of it. Evil had no hold on fresh, earthly thoughts.

With a rumbling laugh Rapha flung his arms wide and felt the updraft of warmth rising from the sun-teased mountain lake far below. If it weren't a talent he already possessed, that was a day to teach a body how to fly! Vast expanses of vivid greens and blues with vibrant splashes of crimson, gold, and purple spread before him, a flawless canvas kissed with the Master's bold perfection.

Feeling newborn himself, Rapha stooped to grasp a shining stone. He studied flashing depths as it fractured, bent and multiplied the sunlight into dozens of glimmering rays. The substance was rare, composed of carbon, compressed and crushed in grinding darkness. Even to Rapha it felt ancient. This gem had survived the wars and cataclysms of the planet's past while those stresses had molded and purified it into a thing of beauty and strength. Soon enough it would be coveted for its beauty. But on this day, it too deserved the chance to fly. With a childish whoop Rapha flung it high, toward the sun's light, where it seemed to hang a moment, flashing, then began its plummet to join the clear, shining depths of liquid emerald in the lake below.

As the gem fell to the water with a distant splash a familiar voice said, "Careful. You might harm a witty, bitty fish!"

In the fraction of an instant before Rapha turned to face his ancient foe, the virgin air around the mountain was stripped of its virtue. Iridescent light pierced the lingering morning mist even as a choking darkness of deception clutched Rapha's mind. His spirit responded to the presence of all that is unholy while his eyes were dazzled by splendor. Fragrant vapors encircled Luc's image and formed a majestic train. He stood, proud and beautiful, his perfect body and diadem-encircled brow proclaiming him the unrivalled Lord of Earth even as the true, depraved image in Rapha's mind snarled, fangs dripping gore.

"Aw, Rapha. So serious! Not even a 'My Lucifer, you're looking well?' But you've missed me, I can tell." The image changed. The majestic glow faded until he was simply Luc, Rapha's old friend with the impish gleam in his eye. This less elaborate illusion more effectively masked evil and Rapha struggled to recall the repellant specter as he felt his heart drawn to ancient, innocent days.

"Well, well. That was quite entertaining. *'Let there be LIGHT!'"* Luc made childish thundering noises and broad gestures with his arms before collapsing in a fit of giggles onto the green turf. "And they say *I* have a flare for drama."

The sight of Lucifer taking on the form of his once beloved friend laid wide the ancient wound but Rapha harbored no illusions of a tearful reconciliation. "To what do I owe this honor?"

"Do I detect sarcasm? I'm so *proud* of you!"

When Rapha gave no answer, Lucifer hopped to his feet.

"I merely want to convey my deepest gratitude to Adonai for my lovely new home," he gestured with his arm as if the fresh beauty was for his pleasure alone.

When Rapha again remained silent, Lucifer frowned. "You could at least be polite…."

"I have not attempted to destroy you."

All gentility was dropped as Lucifer's eyes glittered with malice. "Attempted, indeed. You have no idea the power at my command. With a flick of my hand all could be laid waste once more."

"Yes, your *gratitude* is overwhelming."

"More sarcasm? Aw, how did such a pretty angel get so jaded?"

"Perhaps it is the shrieks that rise to Adonai's ears from those you torture." Rapha felt the fury those cries ignited when Adonai withheld permission to destroy Lucifer and his strongholds. "Perhaps it is the ongoing disbelief that one who had all heaven and earth laid at his feet could yet be dissatisfied...."

Lucifer cut him off with a hiss. "All heaven and earth laid at my feet in order to steal it away!" The intensity of his gaze sought to strip the thoughts from Rapha's mind. "Do you think I cannot perceive Adonai's schemes? Do you think I cower in fear of almighty retribution? While He has rested, *I* have grown strong. No more do I await Adonai's pleasure. I *take* what is mine!"

"And promptly bring it to ruin."

"And prove Adonai's *impotence*!" Lucifer smiled as Rapha winced. "It goads you, doesn't it old friend? You have strained at heaven's leash desiring to save a few pitiful beasts. Ah! If only you had cared so deeply for our angelic brothers, I never would have had to resort to drastic measures...."

"Do not blame your depravity on me!"

"New talents arise when one is betrayed."

Rapha studied the accusing eyes, realizing Lucifer actually believed his own lies. "*Adonai* was betrayed. He is constantly provoked and grieved, yet He remains pure."

"Not caring that his inaction tortures *you*."

With diabolical precision Lucifer had found the chink. Sensing vulnerability, he aimed to deepen the wound, his voice a razor-thin whisper.

"Is it really long-suffering holiness, or is the Almighty *afraid of failure*?"

Without a conscious thought Rapha's anger flashed, slamming Lucifer through tall evergreens, leaving a wide, torn path in his wake. Even as rumbles and cracks of crashing trees continued, Lucifer's laughter echoed back through that corridor of destruction, growing nearer as he glided back into sight, small forms floating into his outstretched arms. Soon Rapha could discern the mangled bodies of squirrels, birds and reptiles held close to Lucifer's bosom. He strode to Rapha and dropped the still twitching carnage at his feet.

"Look who drew first blood. So promptly you bring Adonai's creation to ruin."

Speechless, Rapha slipped to the ground, horrified by the result of his rage. He lifted each body, gently separating fur from feather and scale among the bloodied mass, hardly noticing when five large, evil-eyed angels settled around him. Normally he would have summoned his own contingent but the pain displayed before him was his fault. A deep, guilty part of him hoped to receive the pounding he deserved when he felt the force of their combined wills paralyze his body. He didn't even resist when crushed forward into the blood of the maimed creatures.

Lucifer's voice was in his ear. "Ooh, you're in trouble now. Wait 'til Daddy hears about this." Reaching toward the mound of dead and dying, Lucifer plucked up a tiny, struggling rabbit. Too late, Rapha realized his intent and fought against invisible bonds as, with one sharp twist, Lucifer detached one of the rabbit's legs, relishing its pain-filled shriek and Rapha's mute struggle.

"This is a momentous occasion. A proud angel is taught humility." Lucifer squatted beside Rapha and shoved the writhing bunny into his face. "Take note little beast. This is the first to shed innocent blood in Adonai's new world." With a gentle caress, he held the mangled creature close. Then, gazing into Rapha's eyes, he squeezed tighter and tighter, his gaze never wavering through the cracking of tiny bones and terrified shrieks until, finally, the mound of fur ceased twitching.

Lucifer tossed the limp form into Rapha's face, then brought forth the severed leg and pressed it against the angel's mouth. "Here. Kiss it. Perhaps it will bring me luck."

As Lucifer stood to leave, Rapha felt his body and tongue released but had no will to fight. With the blood still warm on his lips and proof of his foolishness displayed before him, he remained kneeling, his spirit as broken as the animals' bodies.

"Remember this position," Lucifer stated from above. "I know I will."

With that, Rapha was once more alone atop the mountain. If not for the suffering before him, he might have crawled away in shame. Even with countless years of experiencing Adonai's fathomless love, his faith in the face of such guilt failed. But he could not abandon the innocence he had helped to crush.

"Please, Adonai," he whispered, "come and heal."

At first, the only difference was a new scent. Instead of the metallic smell of blood, there was a fragrance of sweet, honey-filled blooms and a particular type of fruit that grew only before Adonai's throne. All was borne on a breeze of such unreasonable love that Rapha felt he could slip into glorious delirium if he took one deep breath. As it was, he kept his breathing shallow. He was unworthy of such a gift.

Then someone touched his shoulder. Warmth flooded his being and the sweet scent took physical form in his mouth, becoming the purest nectar that flowed over his tongue. But the bitterness of guilt welled up to repel this glorious intruder.

"Please," a soft voice with the magnitude of a surging ocean spoke, **"to heal them,** you **must first be healed."**

The kindness of that voice was a wedge to the vault of his pain. A trickle of purity slipped inside exposing the venom that sought to infiltrate every fiber of his being. The deep shadows were no match for that piercing light. Yet still Rapha resisted. He did not deserve absolution, much less this absolute bliss offered freely to his tortured soul. Besides, there was a question to be answered.

With his head still bowed, Rapha asked, "I sense the presence of Adonai, but He cannot dwell with impurity. Who are you?"

Rather than words, Rapha heard the most unexpected sound. Laughter. With a warm updraft the soil sighed, a flock of graceful birds took flight, the branches of surrounding trees waved as if applauding and, deep underground, Rapha felt the murmur of earth's bones straining closer. Even the whimpers of the suffering animals hushed. Surprised, Rapha looked up.

It was the man who had offered restoration to Lucifer so long ago before Adonai's throne. In contrast to Lucifer's glory, the man bore a rough garment and unremarkable features. However, Rapha sensed distilled power as if the sun's radiation were compressed into an earthen vessel. Rapha's sadness and guilt could not exist before those eyes that peered unhindered into the core of his being and pulsed with delight. The power was soft and malleable, like water, trickling into every hidden place but capable of breaking the proudest rock with its patient assault.

As a mother might tend a messy child, the stranger lifted the edge of his sleeve to Rapha's mouth and wiped away the blood. Rapha blinked in amazement as the garment absorbed the stain, leaving only snowy whiteness in its wake.

His senses probed into fathomless confidence and unbreakable love. Questions pulled at his mind but they too bowed, swallowed in this One who embodied the meaning of all things.

The familiar stranger breathed across the animals. One by one every wound healed and the shy creatures crept forward to nuzzle, perch, scamper, and slither to their heart's delight. Once again, creation was gifted with His laughter. This time Rapha, awed that his failure was transformed into this moment of joy, also laughed.

He stared in wonder at the humble, human profile that contained the sum of Adonai's character, discovering delight in the paradox. Why couple earthly flesh with divinity? Then again, at his lowest moment, this One provided what Rapha needed; not the Almighty surrounded in blinding holiness, but this Holy One choosing to wrap Himself in vulnerability.

Ultimate power *choosing* humility? Yes, that would be inconceivable to Lucifer.

But, wasn't this One destined to appear thousands of years in humanity's future?

The Son of Man addressed the unspoken query. **"What I will do is already recorded in eternity. That moment is as the pinnacle of this mountain. Those on either side can look up, ponder, and climb toward its height."**

Even as Rapha grappled with this concept, he noticed something odd. The tiny, abused hare struggled on only three legs as it tried to climb into the lap of its healer.

Once again the man answered his thoughts. **"This small one is a sign to all creation."** As He spoke, the three-legged creature stepped timidly onto His palm, drawing Rapha's attention to a scarred gash in the Holy One's hand. As He drew the animal to His breast, Rapha noted a matching wound on the back of the other hand as well.

The soothing voice continued, **"This age will be well-acquainted with corruption and cruelty, yet the greatest beauty and strength will thrive in that environment. Adonai will never leave them comfortless."** He placed a kiss on the animal's head, then set it upon the ground. As if understanding its purpose, the creature hopped toward the forest without looking back.

Rapha pondered the Holy One's words as he watched the small outline merge with shadows. When he turned toward his mysterious companion, he discovered the man was gone. There were two spots of bruised grass where His knees had rested and, as Rapha watched, they filled with water as if an underground spring had been tapped. When the puddles overflowed, they began to trickle in opposite directions down each side of the mountain's face. Rapha raised himself to hover above the ground and watch each shallow stream become a widening river. Within moments they were digging deep grooves in solid rock and splashing to the valley below, their force carving twin canyons that rejoined for the journey to the sea.

In the pounding waters, Rapha heard echoes of the Holy One's laughter.

Chapter Five

All Things New

That was a glorious dawn. With Adonai's leading, the loyal celestial forces combined their talents to create an abode worthy of His presence. In a lush valley they planted and nurtured a verdant garden. In its midst they wove, crafted and spoke until a dazzling reflection of heaven's glory sparkled in Earth's crown.

How Rapha's heart swelled with hope and joy as he surveyed their accomplishment. As far as he could see he beheld glimmering waters, ranging, peaceful wildlife, vibrant color and even the smooth stone walls of terraced gardens and quiet halls. All was arranged in perfect harmony to the sun's path across the sky and the nightly dance of lesser lights. In the day the sun's warmth coaxed forth fertility, producing sustenance from every hanging bough, while night brought a gentle mist that drove away all thirst.

Rapha paused to drink deeply of the fragrance embracing this blessed valley. The air nourished his soul, overflowing with a richness combining the best of heaven and earth, bringing to mind the Holy One who had removed his stain. As always, when Rapha recalled that horrible, beautiful day, he would shut his eyes to bask in the memory of the Chosen One's touch and ponder the mystery of Adonai's plan. It was just outside his understanding but the tiny bit that had been revealed was enough to cement his trust in Adonai's wisdom.

He had but to secure the last section of encircling wall, and this perfect dwelling, this protected garden of Adonai's holiness, would be ready to receive its inhabitants. Rapha felt the familiar thrill course through him when he considered that the beings dwelling here would be direct ancestors of God in the flesh. He could not wait to meet these glorious creatures! As his mind wandered in breathtaking visions of a long and peaceful collaboration between heaven and earth, a tiny monkey scrambled up to take its customary seat on Rapha's shoulder. Many animals knew Rapha, even some destined to dwell outside the garden's walls, and often he conducted his work while a great cat purred against his leg or a curious bird attempted to nest in the warmth of his hair. But this little one had decided Rapha was his personal assistant to reach the juiciest fruit without having to expend the energy of climbing. Rapha had grown fond of the monkey's chatter even though his garments often bore the stains of ripened fruit. The creature would shriek with delight whenever Rapha displayed his angelic abilities, whether in moving gigantic stones to add to the wall or speaking Adonai's eternal words of protection to prevent its breaching.

He knew the latter threat was greatest. Already hints of Lucifer's corruption infiltrated the surrounding lands where creatures knew fear before taking their first breath. One would think the fallen angel's ambition would be satisfied with access to the rest of the planet, both surface and subterranean, but Rapha wasted no time believing Lucifer would allow the virgin purity of this land to remain. Although his secret monstrosities thrived and creation cowered before his cruelty, Rapha could feel the dark angel bending his thoughts to pierce this one bastion of Adonai's presence, pressing close on all sides as if to steal the garden's acreage one inch at a time.

But such was Lucifer's way—to ruin what he touched and covet what was out of his reach.

"Hey! Watch it, Emeth." The angel addressed his persistent shoulder ornament when a chunk of Rapha's long hair became entwined in a bite of banana. With a shriek, the monkey abandoned his perch and the uneaten fruit to leap from Rapha's shoulder and streak away into the trees. The call to entice the frightened animal back died on his lips when he beheld Lucifer lounging atop the wall, surveying the protected valley.

"You really should be careful about naming them. It's a waste of time to become attached to something so… vulnerable," he looked into Rapha's eyes as he continued. "Shame he had to run. Were you aware the baby tree-swingers can scream in a tone that's inaudible to mortal ears?"

A raging fury shoved aside Rapha's contentment, "We have heard the echoes of your depravity. You are not welcome here. Be gone!"

Lucifer's face registered an almost vulgar bliss. "That glorious, pent-up emotion—like a ripe volcano." His eyes sparkled, "Ah, my friend. Your talents are sorely wasted. What you could accomplish without a leash!"

"I am nothing without my Creator—*just like you*." Adonai forgive him, the insult felt so good. For a few tense moments, the celestial beings regarded one another; each striving for dominance until visible sparks flew between them.

Finally Lucifer broke off with a sneer. "I did not come to bandy words with a messenger boy. There are terms to discuss," Lucifer leaned forward and enunciated the next words carefully, "regarding my residence here."

Rapha did not even try to hide his horror as Lucifer, glowing with satisfaction, added, "Tell Adonai I demand an audience."

With that, he disappeared, leaving the scent of putrefaction in his wake.

After a moment's dumbfounded hesitation, Rapha also melted from Earth's realm. He needed an audience of his own with the Most High.

When the glory of Adonai overshadowed the mountain in the center of the garden, called Eden, meaning source of life, Rapha and the celestials were summoned to the wide valley in the garden's center to attend this next glorious dawn, the creation of Earth's steward.

A hush filled the valley as celestial and terrestrial alike gazed on Adonai, their Maker and source of all that is whole and good. Spontaneous joy swept the assembly and every being knelt. But that was not sufficient. Such love flowed from Him, even angelic eyes closed, unable to bear the untamed purity of the relentless, scorching bliss.

Rapha heard the moan of his soul. How he longed to rush to that purity even if it meant the end of his existence. Every being in that valley wept, whether tears of earthly moisture or angelic light that seeped from their mouths clothed in song; all offered the core of their essence back to the Maker of all.

It was a perfect blend of two realms joined to honor their Lord. If he listened carefully, Rapha could discern the individual notes of hound, lion, bear, cricket, bird and even the dolphins' laughter, but together with angelic harmony the completion of that symphony made him gasp with wonder and fulfillment. On and on the melodies flowed, building to frightening intensity, then descending like a bird diving out of the sky to a synchronous rumble that extended far beneath their feet into Earth's core.

As if the ground groaned and writhed, a wave of power flowed from the mountains surrounding the valley and rushed in. For an instant the diapason ceased, echoing the breathless anticipation of the watchers who strained toward the valley's center, answering the unspoken will of their Maker to reveal what was hidden.

"Come forth!" The voice of The Almighty echoed through heaven and earth.

Immediately a glowing mound like a pulsing star emerged, a miniature sun announcing the dawn of a new day. Up it rose in the nighttime sky, hanging before their eyes in the center of that constellation which signals the birth of a king, eclipsing the light of stars and moon with its brilliance.

Such holiness and solemnity filled that moment, the world stilled its turning, pausing to synchronize with eternity. Finally, the newborn brilliance descended to Adonai and its light was lost in His glory.

Again voices lifted in song, ebbing and flowing with a mighty wind that scattered throughout the valley in dancing cyclones that gathered the various hues for the Master's canvas.

The rainbow of Earth's elements flowed into Adonai's glory as the creation song continued, flowing with the will of Adonai. Sometimes the melody was heartbreakingly sweet, sometimes overwhelming in intensity, but always the latest movement fit perfectly with the desire of Rapha's heart, and pulsed in one accord with all creation straining to fulfill the Maker's pleasure.

At last the wind was silent and the glory parted. There was Adonai with a manchild cupped to his breast. Perhaps a child on the cusp of manliness, but a child nonetheless. It seemed all creation stood on tiptoe to study this one, so small in Adonai's glory, yet the hope of all.

Was there anything remarkable about him? Granted, he was well formed, long of limb and fair of features with thick, dark hair that trailed past his shoulders but....

Then Adonai spoke and light infused the being in His arms. **"Into this man I breathe My essence. My life shall flow in his blood. My spirit shall abide in his soul. His body shall be My temple on Earth."**

The most basic elements of life—fire, water, wind, and soil—strained forward, leaning toward this epochal moment as the Creator leaned over His created and kissed him. The action was completed in a split second but the next moment stretched taut with anticipation as all creation held its breath. Slowly the manchild was lit from within, growing brighter as they watched until his body was encased in a garment of light. Finally, the young man's eyes fluttered and his mouth opened—in a wide yawn. Adonai laughed and spontaneous celebration erupted. The ground shook, flowers rained from overhanging boughs and streaks of light fell from the sky as if the stars longed for a glimpse.

Silence. Along with every celestial and earthly eye, Rapha stared. Yes. Here was a king. His frame was coltish and his eyes full of questions, more boy than man, but embraced in Adonai's glory, he was breathtaking.

Adonai spoke, **"You will be called Adam, the father of those in whom My spirit shall dwell. You are given dominion over all on Earth. What you say shall be established, from the naming of each according to their holy design to protecting the sacred trust given you."**

And, for the first time, Adam looked around at his kingdom, his wide eyes filling with recognition as they settled on his furred, feathered and scaled subjects. Finally, the young man opened his mouth to speak.

He grasped a fold of Adonai's robe, "You *will* help me?"

Again Adonai laughed, and this time creation joined in with a deafening noise of cheers, bays, howls, and roars that shook the mountain's foundation. In the midst of this cacophony man and Creator carried on a private conversation. In the manchild's eyes Rapha recognized the adoration for the Heavenly Father he too had felt after his rebirth.

A shiver of protectiveness for such innocence shook him to the core. In his heart, Rapha committed himself before Adonai to the preservation of this alliance between heaven and earth. As earthly creation wept with joy and the celestial host glowed ever brighter, their song of gratitude flowing like a shimmering mist toward their Maker and his new creation, Rapha realized Adam stared at him as if to say, "He's told me so much about you."

When the young man smiled, Rapha choked with emotion on his song. *"Yes,"* the angel's heart replied to his Maker's prompting, *"I will look after him."*

Soon, Rapha's duties as chief architect of the human's training required undivided attention and constant reliance on Adonai's wisdom. He had never voiced his expectations of what this heavenly yet earthly creature would resemble, but in every aspect Adam was a surprise.

The manchild was all freshness, enthusiasm, boundless energy and, admittedly, harder to keep under control than Rapha's chattering friend, Emeth. Rapha learned if he wanted Adam to concentrate on a given task he must first run the boy up a steep mountain, initiate a game of cheetah-tag or at least challenge him to a swim race. Only when Adam was puffing and blowing from exertion would he finally remain still long enough to listen to stories of ancient history or learn the many varieties, uses, and care of the surrounding plants, herbs, trees, and fruits.

How Rapha grew to cherish the boy's enthusiasm since it filled him with fresh appreciation for Adonai's attention to detail. Rapha could not help but absorb Adam's joy as the young man discovered the garden's riches for the first time, meeting each animal, climbing every accommodating tree and questioning Rapha about *everything*—until the angel quipped his immortal ears would fall off due to overuse.

Sure there was a title for each species of animal but Adam's primary edict was to give each a *name*—that word that captured their essence as well as their special function in the grand scheme of the garden's community. Rapha and the other angels, each possessing their own area of expertise, aided Adam in this quest. For burrowing creatures he sought Eldad; for nocturnal ones, Jadon; for inhabitants of the water, both fresh and salt, he questioned Perseus, an adventurous sort who would place Adam on his shoulders and dive, utilizing his command of water to create an air bubble around Adam's head to allow for their lengthy excursions.

Therefore, the garden's inhabitants developed a routine. Morning's first light would find Adam diving into the churning waters of the waterfall, streaking toward the rushing, deep pool below, past cataracts of opalescent turquoise and emerald. Adam insisted on races and other water contests, and the angels humored him. To dry himself, he would race to the top of Eden's highest peak, surefooted as the mountain goats that scattered from his approach. At their favorite perch, cradled by the sun-warmed rocks at their back and reclining against an accommodating mountain lion that demanded they scratch his ears "just so," Rapha would explain the synchronous workings of the universe—from the tiniest creeping creature to the farthest visible star—describing how Adam was to be caretaker of this small corner called Earth.

Mealtimes were ongoing for the human. The angels often teased Adam that his strongest muscles were those in his jaws since he was always either chewing or talking. From nuts to fruits that hung down in their path, Adam constantly partook. He gave no thought to a need for food since he dwelled in such abundance. Occasionally, Rapha and a few of the other angels would eat with Adam, enjoying the camaraderie even though their angelic bodies did not require the sustenance.

The afternoon hours were Rapha's favorite, usually a time he had Adam all to himself. It was then that Adam grew calm, relaxing in the sleepy atmosphere of napping animals. This was when they discussed the morning's discoveries and Adam attempted to discern what Adonai would want him to learn from his adventures. In these quiet hours the active young man's body and mind grew receptive to Rapha's leading, partly because his favorite time of day approached and he wanted to ready himself for his appointment with Adonai.

Rapha treasured images of Adam's earnest face imprinted by leafy shadows as the boy laughed about the antics of the dolphins or grew reflective as he absorbed ancient tales. His favorite stories were the fables Rapha would weave about the various animals that sprawled around them, each with an aspect of Adonai's personality encoded in their instinctive behavior. Adam would interrupt with a burst of laughter in response to the squirrels' tenacity, or the pride of the lion, so aware of his mane's crowning glory. Rapha was trying to warn his young charge of the dangers of vanity (Adam was extremely aware of his own flowing hair) but the young man was blissfully blind to this shortcoming.

Later, as the shadows lengthened, they would walk together to the appointed place as a fragrant stillness descended over the garden. Rapha was always amused by Adam's sudden attention to hygiene, bathing the dirt from his body and asking Rapha's assistance with his hair, whereas the rest of the day the boy was content to wrestle in the grass and leaves with the bears and wolf cubs. But Adonai was the center of the young man's existence, which was as it should be.

Then would come the golden hours of Eden. The physical glory of Adonai would descend to His waiting creation. How Rapha loved the moment when the blinding brightness dimmed by slow degrees until every eye could gaze on Adonai's much-simplified form. The next moment, what would begin as a tentative creeping forward would become a veritable stampede of adoring beings, as all were drawn with the force of a central star on orbiting planets.

Indeed, although Adonai became an approachable form, every element was transformed by His presence. The air pulsed with His power, the ground underfoot hummed with it, the waters would steam and swell as hidden openings in the earth's pores released life-giving, cleansing vapors. It was a daily restoration and healing as the planet nestled in the bosom of its Creator.

Then Adam, the usually cocksure manchild, would approach. Rapha's heart swelled with pride every time he beheld the awe of those meetings when Adam collapsed at Adonai's feet. The Holy One would raise him up (Rapha believed that touch also strengthened the man to stand in His presence) then manchild and Creator would stroll, arm in arm, through the garden's deepening shadows that drew back in wonder at His approach.

At all times Adam's body was clothed in light, but in those precious hours with Adonai, he would shine even brighter. The reflected and absorbed radiance of his Creator made him rival the glow of the celestial host who hovered close, witnesses to this extraordinary communion.

Ah, the beauty of those hours! Much of the time Adonai spoke only to Adam but the celestial host was always nearby, ever attendant to His summons. On the occasions when Rapha joined the discussions, he felt a soaring sense of destiny and purpose—not to mention humility—at the role he was honored to play in this pivotal moment in history.

Yes, Adam was receiving training to fulfill his monumental task but, after those moments with Adonai, his gaze was so firmly fixed on the precious beauty of that relationship, even governing the world became trivial in comparison.

The transformation of Adam's countenance in Adonai's presence was breathtaking. He became both more innocent and more kingly as the intensity of his expression was more glorious than the most noble crown, and his ardent love for his Maker clothed him in radiance that would have made garments wrought of pure gold appear as filthy rags.

And later, when the sun was tucked away for the night, Adonai instituted a sacred rite between parent and child: the bedtime story. With His power dimmed, He would draw Adam close and together they would ponder the dazzling points of light in the sky, as the greatest power in the universe became chief bard and storyteller. The Maker wove simple tales of undying love, of ancient battles, of past mistakes and future threat, of the riches of loyalty, and the poverty of becoming a slave to ambition.

In these moments Rapha fulfilled the role of scribe, recording these tales in long, fluid strokes, sometimes having to blot a tear that fell onto smooth parchment, as his immortal soul struggled to fathom the paradox of Adonai's magnified glory presented in such a humble form.

One particular night, when the boy had quizzed Adonai about why all the animals had mates and for what purpose, the fateful question arose, "So where are the angels' mates?"

"Their wholeness is complete in My presence. A mate is the other half of a whole."

"But they are not like me, are they?" Adam's gaze brushed across Rapha's reclining form. Their differences had been downplayed and the angelic form dimmed for dwelling in Eden, but those differences could not be denied when Rapha's body steamed even as it streaked through the water in their morning swims. And it was impossible to hide the fact his kind never hungered or slept. As with all earth creatures, Adam obeyed a pattern of night and day, waking and resting, and his sustenance came from the soil from which he was formed; while the celestial beings were restored by the sun's light filtering through earth's canopy and their daily sojourn in heaven's halls to bask in the glory of their Maker.

Adam's thoughtful gaze searched the night sky as if he were hesitant to speak his mind. Finally, he swallowed with an audible gulp, took a deep breath, and blurted a bit too loudly, "Will I have a mate?"

He squared his shoulders as if bracing for disappointment and raced on, "I know I'm given everything I could possibly need… and You must think me ungrateful to still desire…."

His words were silenced when Adonai laid a hand to his cheek, **"I wondered, child, when you would ask."**

Adam's jaw dropped, "But... I thought it was faithless of me to still long for… when the world is laid at my feet."

Adonai's soft chuckle summoned a warm breeze to ruffle Adam's hair. **"Foolish boy. Who made you? Who placed those longings in your heart? The longing is not wrong. Only if it reveals a distrust of My love can it lead to evil."**

Adam's eyes were wide with wonder.

"So?" Adonai prompted.

With a dazzling smile, Adam almost shouted his enthusiastic request, "Please Adonai, Most High Creator of all things, Joy of my heart, He who embodies all bliss…."

"Child," Adonai smiled as a solitary streak of light arced overhead, **"will you make your request before this age is spent?"**

One deep breath, then Adam's heart overflowed. "Please, may I have a she-man—uh, a mate?"

"Of course."

Overwhelmed, Adam fell back against a lion's side, disturbing the king of beast's slumber. The great cat gave a low growl but Adam remained, gazing at the stars as the lion's tail flicked a warning across his face. With a start he sat upright. "When?"

"Well, perhaps I should ask Rapha's opinion. Oh venerable tutor," Adonai turned to Rapha with a mischievous gleam in His eye, **"are you pleased with your student's progress?"**

"He makes good progress. However," Rapha's brow furrowed, "he remains easily distracted."

"Hey!"

"With a 'she-man' trotting around I doubt I would ever again have his undivided attention."

The Maker nodded and rubbed His chin, **"Perhaps the granting of this desire should wait until he exhibits more maturity."**

"I *am* mature!" Adam's voice cracked in protest.

They continued discussing Adam's fate, ignoring the young man's agitated state. **"Perhaps if you turn his studies to the mapping of stars he would learn patience."**

"I AM patient!" Adam's hand slapped the lion's side who, with lightning reflex, enveloped him with velveted paws. With yelps, growls, and screeches, the wolves, bears, and monkeys joined the fray, overjoyed at the prospect of a late-night tussle.

As the menagerie's cacophony blended with the laughter of God, angel, and man, the bright streaks in the nighttime sky multiplied until the heavens were alight with sparkling rain. Soon Adam and the animals were distracted from their fight by the streaks of brilliance and lay in a jumble on the ground, faces upturned to the dazzling display. One of the wolves howled in appreciation and more laughter echoed into the night.

Even in that golden moment, Rapha felt malevolent eyes watching. He almost turned to seek the source of the hate-filled current probing the back of his skull but Adonai's kind regard stopped him. A simple phrase stilled Rapha's mind, **"Never let him steal the NOW."**

Obeying that command, he kept his back to the evil presence, feeling Lucifer's anger at being ignored, and focused instead on etching that moment's beauty on his heart, even as it was captured with a thought onto the parchment in his hand.

Chapter Six

Begin Again

Rapha stood, peering down into turquoise depths. With a sudden intake of breath he hovered a couple feet off the ground and moved over the water for a better view of dark shadows flitting in the seabed's rocky terrain. For a moment, as he lost sight of the drama unfolding below, a flicker of fear crossed his mind.

Ah! There was Adam rising to the surface, a mere thirty feet below. But wait. Rapha focused on the large shadow looming out of the depths in Adam's wake. *It could not be!* Mocking laughter floated across the water, drawing Rapha's gaze to an outcropping where Lucifer lounged, enjoying an excellent view of Adam's plight, with Emeth, Rapha's monkey friend, perched on his shoulder.

If that creature was what Rapha thought it was, Adam didn't stand a chance of out-swimming it. Rapha dove. Immediately the scene sprang to life with a piercing shriek, a rush of warm current and the flash of a long scaled body shooting past. Rapha strove to overtake them; his only thought was to come between monster and prey.

He had to give the boy credit as the frantic flight wove through submerged forests that forced the massive body to slow its pursuit. Finally, Adam led it into a maze with twisting corridors and, after coming dangerously close to snapping off the boy's retreating feet, the creature was caught before a hole too small for its passage. Rapha saw Adam streak to the surface and, feeling relief course through his frame, he moved to follow, careful to rise slowly lest his shining form attract the monster's attention like a flickering lure.

Just as Rapha broke the surface, Adam dove back in and streaked past. What was the boy doing? Obviously, Adam was determined to *not* leave well enough alone. In his hand, Rapha spied a long, thick branch. Did he expect to duel the beast?

But Adam was aiming for a point several yards behind the confused creature. The young man's intent dawned over Rapha as he saw Adam wedge the stick beneath a large boulder and attempt to topple it from its precarious perch. He swam to Adam's aid and, with their combined efforts, the huge rock shifted and fell. With a final roll it settled into place, blocking the creature's corridor of escape.

Once again Adam shot to the surface and Rapha followed, thankful their morning's adventure was over.

"That was cutting it a bit close, don't you think," Rapha began his lecture as soon as he clambered onto a sunny rock. Yet Adam grabbed an armful of surface plants, took a deep breath and dove again. "Adam!" He yelled as the boy's shape disappeared once again into the depths. Rapha carried on a mumbled, frustrated, one-sided conversation as he stood to re-enter the water. Curious, he shot a glance where he had spied Lucifer earlier, but fallen angel and monkey were nowhere to be seen.

He dove to where their guest mucked the water, attacking the rock over and over in attempts to free itself. Through the murky cloud, Rapha saw Adam with an arm poked into the hole of the makeshift cage. The young man was yanked forward and almost through while Rapha froze, fully expecting to see a pool of red join the expanding cloud of silt—but all grew still and

Adam withdrew an unscathed arm. Rapha swam closer until his glow lit the interior of the large, rocky chamber. There curled the beast, munching the plants Adam had provided and keeping a wary, luminescent eye on its benefactor.

After several more trips to the surface for Adam to secure more of the plants the beast favored, Adam and Rapha emerged to flop onto the sun-warmed rock. Adam's formidable lung capacity had been sorely tried by their exertion but the expression on his face as he gasped for air was exultant.

"He's one of the ancient ones isn't he!" Adam proclaimed. "He's magnificent! Did you see the size of those teeth?"

"They would not be so exciting from the inside."

"That was *amazing*!" Adam's enthusiasm soared. "I thought they were just legend! And then whoosh! There he was staring right at me!"

"He was sent to kill you… or at least to test you."

"How do you know that? He probably survived in some hidden cave all these years and…."

"Lucifer was here to watch the show."

"Lucifer! THE Lucifer? Where?" Adam craned his neck to look everywhere at once. "What does he look like?"

"Your fascination is disturbing…."

"I'm not fascinated. It's just…." Adam knew he was denying the obvious, "Aw Rapha, you must admit he's a legend too. He must be pretty powerful to have… I mean, *war* against *Adonai*."

Rapha remained silent. Finally he sighed, "Perhaps I have been too careful. Trying to protect you, I have left too much to your active imagination."

"I understand." Adam's young face flushed as he hurried to protest the accusation of ignorance. "You've told me his history."

"Yes, but cursory knowledge does not acquaint you with the horrors of which he is capable. Your heart has not been destroyed in his quest for power." A niggling foreknowledge in Rapha's mind added a disturbing *yet.*

"What else do I need to know? He's the enemy of Adonai and therefore he's my enemy."

How could Rapha convince Adam of a hideous, consuming ambition that would stop at nothing to achieve dominance? How could he explain such hatred when the protected manchild had no point of reference?

"What? I should fear him? Why should I fear the one Adonai defeated?" He searched Rapha's face, striving to read his tutor's thoughts. "Wait," Adam's eyes narrowed in concentration. "Why is he allowed here? If he was defeated, why does he still roam free?"

In truth, Rapha had wondered the same thing. When Lucifer had boasted of his residence in the garden, Rapha had immediately sought Adonai. Just short of formal protest, he had made his thoughts on the matter known—as if they were ever hidden—and in answer he had been offered only two words: ***"Trust me."***

As Adonai's calm command had filled his mind, it had happened. There were no words to describe the merest flash of Adonai's burden. Rapha, whose body was created to never fade, suddenly felt crippled, blind, and naked, shredded before the enormity of horrors past and those yet to come. A searing stripping of his sanity overwhelmed him in grief-drenched agony. Blessedly, the connection had halted as quickly as it had begun. Then, like warm, healing oil, Adonai's voice had flowed through his being.

"Understanding would destroy you. Please trust."

Now Adam was asking him to explain the unexplainable.

With a deep breath, Rapha said, "He is allowed here because it is his lawful right."

"But Adonai created all things, including eternal law. Why would He knowingly allow…."

"I don't know!"

Rapha immediately regretted his outburst. Never before had he revealed vulnerability, thinking it would lessen Adam's confidence in him.

"Good."

Stunned, Rapha looked at Adam.

"I'm glad you don't know everything. It's no fun to be with someone who *always* knows, who's *always* under control. I think," Adam hesitated, understanding dawning on his face, "I think that's why I sometimes try to drive you crazy."

Rapha smiled, "You are very good at it. Diving foolishly into Lucifer's traps…."

"You can blame Lucifer all you want but this whole thing was your fault," Adam accused.

"*My* fault?"

"If you hadn't hidden the stone so well, I might never have disturbed the beast."

"Well, at least you showed *some* wisdom by abandoning our game when it meant a choice between life or being devoured."

With a smug smile, Adam reached into a crevice beside him and withdrew a large diamond.

Rapha tossed back his head for a laugh. As an eternal being, surprise was a rare commodity. It felt good.

"My turn!" Adam dove back into the water.

For a moment Rapha breathed deep, enjoying the beauty surrounding him. The sun's warmth filtering through the azure sky soothed him. He needed to laugh more. The joy in Adam's face when he had sensed Rapha's approval had also been a ray of sunshine. Instead of feeding Adam's cockiness, the thing he had been trying to avoid by limiting praise, Rapha had sensed an eagerness to please that had been lacking in their relationship. The day was indeed full of surprises when an old angel was learning something new.

Deep in his soul he knew this time was limited. He was under no delusions. Lucifer was biding his time, looking for an opportunity to tarnish this perfect corner of the world. Somehow, rather than bringing panic, the thought made Rapha determined to infuse as much joy into what remained as possible—as much joy *and* as much preparation. As far as was within his power, when the test came, his student would be ready.

For now, the boy's greatest weakness was a steadfast belief in his own invincibility. Rapha peered into the water's crystalline depths but could not spy Adam. Would the lad really be foolhardy enough to… yes. He saw Adam shoot out the narrow hole where the creature was trapped.

"Ah, well," Rapha commented to himself as he prepared to seek the diamond, most likely hidden in the beast's teeth, "maybe when the creature claims a chunk of Adam's flesh and bone the boy will finally learn caution."

Later, he would wince at the prophecy of those words.

The next morning, Rapha gave up trying to teach the boy a blessed thing. By midday, Adam was beside himself with anticipation, chattering and cavorting around Rapha in a manner that once more brought to mind the excitable Emeth. Indeed Rapha could not have felt more harried if the manchild had been climbing back and forth over his head as the little monkey was wont to do.

"But Adonai laughed! He actually *laughed* as He gave hints of when but He wouldn't tell me!" A fresh wave of restlessness struck Adam and he climbed up the nearest tree where he proceeded to dangle upside down while his barrage of chatter continued. "All He would say is that it would be 'soon' and I would be 'summoned' when it was time. What do I do with that? Does 'soon' mean a day, several weeks? Anyway, I couldn't sleep and I can't eat, so hopefully 'soon' will mean...."

"By the way," Rapha studied his fingernails with casual ease as he broke in, "it is time."

With a thud, Adam landed headfirst. "What?" He sat up rubbing his head with a look of terror. "What does that mean, 'It's time'? That Adonai wants to discuss things more, that there's unfinished work on the shelter? What?"

Once again Rapha was surprised. Why should the fulfillment of his heart's desire frighten the lad? Wasn't this what he had been begging for and talking about for weeks? Why did he now look prepared to flee? The angel could only guess it had something to do with being young and inexperienced. Rapha could relate very little on either count.

As it was, he could not resist exploiting this turn of events. It seemed due payback for the countless times Adam had harassed him. The particular morning the young man had organized the tree-dwellers to ambush Rapha with a barrage of fruit projectiles sprang to mind. Some of the chimpanzees had enjoyed the game so much they still shook the trees with their laughter whenever he passed.

"When I say 'It is time' I refer to several things, starting with 'It is time for you to come down out of the tree.' Once again you are being a bad example for the primates." As he spoke, Rapha offered a hand to assist Adam to his feet. "But since you have already fulfilled the first directive, we will move on to the second—the issue of your appearance. Adonai has decreed you should care for and understand the animals, not smell like them. So, it is time for you to bathe!"

With that, Rapha flung the astonished young man over his shoulder and covered the short distance to the water's edge. As if Adam weighed no more than a skipping stone, the angel tossed him high and far over the water, then threw back his head with a roar of laughter as Adam flailed in mid-air and landed with a spread-eagle slap that routed several gliding flocks of waterfowl.

When Adam sputtered to the surface with a disgruntled "Hey!" Rapha ignored the boy's protests.

"Now come here. It is time to cleanse that bird's nest you call hair."

With the sun's light filtering through the trees overhead, Adam's hair shone as if he too were woven of light rather than earth. "So, are we going to meet her?" His appearance may have been kingly but the tremor in his voice belied Adam's nervousness.

"No," Rapha said as he worked drops of fragrant oil through Adam's tangle-free, debris-free mane.

Adam whirled to grip the angel's muscular shoulders, his hands at the height of his own head to do so. "What do you mean, 'No'?"

He was tempted to continue teasing but Adam's emotions were so strong on this point Rapha felt it would be cruel.

"I am afraid that person does not yet exist."

"What?" Adam searched the angel's face. Rapha could be evasive but he never lied. "Look! I've been scrubbed within an inch of my life, not to mention I endured your raking that, that *thing* through my hair until my scalp fairly bleeds, only for you to tell me she doesn't exist?"

"Adonai wishes to secure the proper substance with which to knit her form."

"But, is she not to be like me? I was fashioned from earth. I see no shortage of that particular substance, so what else is needed?"

"She will be formed of something nearer to you than the earth." Rapha began leading the way with the confused manchild following.

"What could possibly be nearer? Will she be formed of the air I breathe, the water I drink? Neither seems a hardy enough substance."

"Yes, she will contain those substances, just as you do, but her seed, the core of her existence, will be unique from any other creature on earth."

Wondering why Adam's footfalls had ceased, Rapha called over his shoulder, "Come! Adonai expects us." When the boy remained unmoving, locked in a fog of misery, the angel retraced his steps.

Adam's voice broke with grief. "I thought Adonai understood. I desire someone like me, more similar to me than any other creature He's ever created, someone who sleeps when I sleep and hungers and dreams and longs to feel my touch more than any other. I sometimes feel this longing will reach up to swallow me like, like the gaping jaws of that creature trapped in the rocks."

Rapha reached to place a hand on the boy's shoulder. "Adam, think. Who is the most unique creature in the garden?"

"I am the only one without another like me."

"Now place your hand here," Rapha guided Adam's palm to lay it flat on the boy's chest. "Do you feel that?"

As the rhythmic throb of his own heart pounded against his hand, Adam gave a slow nod.

"The seed of your mate can feel the life flowing through you as well. Adonai will use *you* to create her."

Adam struggled with this mystery. "But the seeds you showed me, the ones that grew from the ground and began to flower, when I dug down to see what had happened to them, they had burst. Will Adonai put me in the ground until I burst so she may live?"

Rapha smiled and spoke gently. "Adam, does that sound like Adonai? No, you will not be destroyed so she may live."

Again Adam followed in Rapha's long strides. Curiosity still permeated the air but for the moment the boy seemed content to know she would be a part of him and that he would not have to burst to accomplish this. However, with the desperation Adam had exhibited, Rapha felt certain the boy would gladly sacrifice an arm and a leg if it meant he would gain his mate.

That evening, once again in the valley of his making, Adam approached his Maker with emotions overflowing in every direction. Rapha was used to sensing the boy's moods; in fact it was solely for Adam's understanding that words were ever required. But the moment Adonai appeared and beckoned the manchild forth, the intensity of feeling flowing through Adam's frame was so strong even Rapha's knees felt weak in empathy. He wondered how the human was able to remain upright as his emotions surged from excitement to fear, anticipation, dread, and an overriding determination to hold these feelings in check in order to not make a fool of himself. Though Rapha sensed a gnawing uncertainty, his respect for the boy soared, knowing he was getting a glimpse of the kingliness inherent in Adam.

When the Maker asked the manchild once more to state his heart's desire, Adam's voice was firm as he requested a helpmeet in his likeness.

"Are you prepared to lay down your life so she may live?"

His voice shook only slightly as he answered, "You gave me life. It is Yours, O Adonai, to take as You will."

Adonai's answer was a whispered, **"Well spoken, my son."**

The boy's eyes never left those of his Maker as a thick, sparkling mist rose from the ground at Adam's feet. The love and trust between them brought a lump to Rapha's throat. Although Adam remained unsure of his fate, he had placed himself in Adonai's hands. Rapha had beheld countless glorious beginnings in creation but the beauty of that moment eclipsed them all. As Adam's eyes closed in slumber and he swooned to the ground, the Maker's hand was there to cushion his fall.

In spontaneous praise, celestial voices sang of Adonai's glories, His triumphs, His faithfulness, His goodness and His unfathomable love. All creation joined the song, caught up in irresistible joy, straining with one mind to see Adonai's desire fulfilled. The voices blended as one, piercing and harmonious, gentle and cacophonous, soaring to the heavens, swirling the thick mist surrounding Creator and created. Then a new melody rose, similar but more undulating than man's creation song with its booms and triumphant crescendo. This was a gentler movement, more subtle and varied with a relentless, steady rhythm that supported and carried the original melody. Mysterious and ephemeral, it seemed to echo the diamond glow of the stars that slowly appeared one by one as if summoned to sparkle in syncronous resonance.

Through tears of joy, Rapha was aware of Adonai bending over the human. With the flash of a piercing point of light, a line of bright red appeared in Adam's side. Through the flesh, a slender bone was withdrawn. Again the piercing light flashed and the flesh mended.

An overriding rhythm began to pulse at Rapha's feet, a swoosh and throb that grew stronger and nearer with creation's every breath, so compelling every living being aligned with the magnetic force drawing this power from the earth's womb. With one smooth movement, Adonai scooped a hand into soft, fertile soil. As if drawing forth a tiny germ of a living star, His hand now cradled a pulsing brilliance smaller than Adam's fist.

For a brief moment, the Maker held the light close to His chest as if unwilling to let it go. Then he brought the light to His mouth for a gentle kiss and whispered words none present could overhear. As His hands moved to place the light within the curve of Adam's bone, a shining tear fell from His eye. As that tear joined with the light, it became shrouded in deep red flesh, shading its light and buffering its pulse.

The Creator laid flesh and bone in a hollow depression before him and bent low, covering life's seed and calling forth Earth's elements to converge. A thunderous clap echoed through earth and sky and a blinding glow engulfed the very spot where the seed lay while a sparkling flow bubbled up to fill the hallowed depression. To Rapha, the swell appeared infused with liquid gold that swirled in the glimmering fluid like living starlight, diving to entwine and flow, leaving bits behind every time it embraced the brighter glow in its center. From the earth's pores, various hues arose, from vibrant and daring to muted pastels, providing pigment for the Master Craftsman's canvas. The glory of Adonai filled the valley.

As an indiscernible shape took form in the liquid light, all creation shifted forward, straining to behold the work of Adonai's fingers. The melody grew soothing and peaceful although the air seemed ready to explode with anticipation. In the midst of the lullaby, a surprising duet began. The sweet trill of a nightingale rose, calling forth peaceful repose even as the lament of a she-wolf sounded a restless summons to the heavens, stirring the blood with an untamed fierceness.

The two voices continued, dancing in a fragrant breeze that shushed the night. All paused to breathe deep. The passing perfume was a draught of exotic nectars of the sweetest fruit and most alluring blossoms coupled with an earthy, nut-flavored spice. It was a heady, healing, stirring yet simple scent of which Rapha felt he could never tire. It seemed woven of such varied and subtle bouquets that, if he were given unlimited time to peel back its composition, he could never plumb the depths of its mysteries.

Then a strange wonder occurred. Rapha was accustomed to the distinct characteristics of the temporal and the eternal, since daily he passed through the veil between them, but in that one shining instant, the two converged. Time was suspended as eternity sealed and sanctified the moment. It was a joining of opposite realms, knit together and destined to strain at the fabric of their confinement, and that very struggle was a key ingredient in the Master's plan.

Again all was hushed. The glow at Adonai's feet grew dim, and restfulness descended on Earth's witnesses. The fullness of that silence was profound. Rapha felt oddly detached yet acutely aware of every detail as he was lost in the importance of that moment, woven into the flow of eternity.

As if waking from a dream, animals and celestial beings began to stir. A lion roared. Adam stretched before gazing with a dazed expression to ponder the surrounding spectators. His eyes widened with remembrance of the occasion and his head snapped to aim a questioning look toward Adonai.

The Maker laughed and again all creation responded with joy. **"Patience, son,"** the soothing voice said. **"All is well."**

Sensing the summons, Rapha stepped forward to lead Adam to a quiet place to recover. The boy was reluctant to depart, curious to delve into the new mystery at Adonai's feet, but he obeyed Rapha's prompting, even as the assembled crowd began to disperse.

Once again, sleep was elusive for Adam. Late into the night he lay awake, staring at the stars, asking Rapha to repeat all that had occurred, then gazing toward the place where Adonai's glory continued to hover. Just before dawn, the exhausted manchild slept. His final words before drifting into slumber were, "Just think. Hereafter, she will keep me company at night."

Rapha supposed he should have felt insulted to be so quickly discarded, but this was as it should be.

One thing Rapha knew with certainty. Everything was about to change.

Chapter Seven

She

Adam sat bolt upright as the first shaft of light filtered through the trees to illumine the hallowed spot where Adonai had hovered, but no trace of his Maker or the new creation lingered. With a cry of dismay the boy leapt to his feet. "Where are they?"

Rapha stretched, a pleasant habit he had acquired from the human. "All is well. But come, refresh yourself. There is much to do."

Adam took little notice of the beautiful breakfast of fruit and nutmeats Rapha had prepared complete with his favorite drink of coconut milk straight from the shell.

"Did you see her? Where did they go? When will I meet her?" The questions were peppered throughout their meal and continued as the sun marched high into the sky, but Rapha's response was guarded. In truth, Rapha had glimpsed the dainty human when his Master had at last drawn her from the earth's womb, but Adonai had hidden her in His shadow and taken her to a secret place. Rapha could only guess that her experience at present would be similar to his reawakening—surrounded by light and love, immersed in Adonai's wholeness and unaware of anything but bliss. Soon enough Adam's curiosity would be satisfied, but at present the angel appealed to the boy to calm himself and concentrate on making the first impression of her new home as tranquil and beautiful as possible.

In all honesty, the only element threatening to spoil the picture was Adam's impatience. Thus Rapha kept his young charge busy fetching rare fruits from obscure locales—from succulent melons that thrived in the tallest trees on the highest summit, to the delicate roots and berries only accessible by braving a path down a rugged cliff. After accomplishing these quests, Adam was grateful for another bath and polish, submitting like a lamb to Rapha's massage of his sore muscles and another raking of his hair.

"Take note, Adam. Your mate will appreciate the ability to coax muscles to relaxation."

"My mate. That sounds so strange." The boy fell silent a moment. "I'm not ready, am I," he said with unexpected humility. "There's so much I don't know, so much I need to learn about how to care for her." His eyes widened. "What if she doesn't like me? I saw the she-lion box her mate yesterday and they tumbled about growling and biting."

Rapha smiled. He too had been aware of the lions' amour. In fact, the entire valley had heard them. They were nothing if not enthusiastic. "Actually, it is precisely because she likes him a great deal that she enjoys vexing him into a wrestling match. It is all part of their game of seduction."

Then, of course, Rapha had to describe that concept.

"That sounds fun," Adam finally said, his expression bemused. "I'm glad they enjoyed it." His cheek took on a slight flush as he glanced down, suddenly shy, "Will my mate want to, um, wrestle?"

Rapha had been awaiting just such an opportunity. "Understand, I have never had a mate, but I have observed that, as each cares for the needs of the other, the wrestling is a natural outgrowth of their affection...."

"And I hope she loves to climb and run and swim," Adam cut in with his unbroken thread of thought. "Do she-men enjoy those things? Will she think me foolish to play duck-and-throw with the monkeys?" Adam recalled the shrieking protest when a well-aimed kumquat had caught one of his opponents unawares, and he laughed aloud at the memory. "Who wouldn't enjoy that? I'll just have to make sure they don't resort to coconuts...."

The angel sighed. Very soon the boy's attention would be so captured by the thought of mating he would find it difficult to think of anything else. Already Adam's voice was beginning to deepen and the coltishness of his body was fading. This conversation could not be put off any longer. Adam's destiny dictated that the act of joining would signify far more than a mere coupling to produce offspring. Since sexual corruption had been the enemy's weapon of choice in ages past, the purity of Adonai's chosen would provide a tempting target.

"Adam," Rapha interrupted the boy's rambling, "soon you will experience physical love with your mate, the joy of which will make other activities pale in comparison. This gift represents your spirit intertwined with Adonai," the angel continued to speak, introducing Adam to this precious gift freely given from the Father's hand.

For two interminable days Rapha endured Adam's mounting excitement and impatience. In addition to teaching Adam some of the finer details of metalwork and refining of gems, he continued efforts to exhaust him so the boy could cease his questioning and feverish activity for a blessed few hours each night. To this end he decided to work on Adam's diving skills. Diving would be just the ticket; the flowing, calming depths of blue soothed his young charge like nothing else.

At first Adam had resisted, far too distracted by the impending introduction to his mate and unwilling to sully his glossy tresses—due more to his disdain for Rapha's raking than to vanity—but when Rapha had pointed out the male birds who strutted their bright plumage to capture female attention, the boy had cooperated.

"Besides," Rapha instructed as they made their way to massive outcroppings of rock protruding over a crystalline pool, "a being who continues to strive for further accomplishment is far more interesting than one who merely sits and awaits desire's fulfillment. Which will she prefer, a preening boy or a dazzling diver who takes her breath away?"

Adam's acquiescence was half-hearted, "Alright! Let's make this quick. I will still need to gather the fresh flowers you insist upon when we receive the summons."

Ignoring the less than optimistic attitude, Rapha began with the basics of body control required to achieve the most graceful entry into the water. When the morning was still young, Adam had perfected a virtually splashless, arching swan dive. Not content with such tame accomplishments, he rushed to increase his repertoire.

Soon Rapha was concerned that his efforts had been *too* successful. From simple, graceful dives five feet above the water's surface, Adam's innate athleticism and penchant for thrills drove him higher to attempt twists, spirals, and flips that caused Rapha to stand at water's edge, muscles taut for quick flight if the human's head aimed for the rocks. How could he blame him? Rapha knew the thrill of plunging headlong into thin air.

Yes, his primary objective of exhausting the lad was accomplished as Adam flopped to Adonai's side that evening, calm enough to receive the Master's wisdom; but the other goal, the one uppermost in *Adam's* mind, was also fulfilled: the manchild was beautiful in flight!

In fact, on the morning of the third day, a new set of wide eyes followed the laughing boy's progress. Her hand never released its hold on her Creator's. This was simply an invisible visit to view her future, but as shafts of golden morning light glimmered like liquid diamonds on the glistening body that leapt to slice the turquoise water, her heart also felt the thrill of flight. And when the young man jumped from the water to toss back dripping ribbons of black hair revealing long-lashed eyes in his handsome face, she gave Adonai's hand an involuntary squeeze, signifying her agreement with the Creator's assessment of His creation; it was good… *very* good.

Rapha did not turn to stare—this visit was hidden from Adam—but the tutor could not ignore the pleasure flowing from his Creator. He was glad this was the female's first glimpse of her intended. The young man was unaware of the stunning picture he made climbing to the heights, then abandoning himself to the earth's pull. Rapha had a sneaking suspicion, due to the excited squawks and myriad bright wings, the flocks of birds in attendance were more than mere coincidence. If they had gathered for a tutorial on the laws of attraction they were not disappointed. The male displayed himself to his best advantage and the female gasped each time he dove, eyes shining with admiration.

In the blink of an eye, the esteemed audience was gone and finally Rapha received the silent, anticipated call. In response to the shouted announcement of, "It's time!" Adam, perched in a handstand on the highest ledge, lost focus and slipped, thwacking his head and tumbling with a splat!

The injury was trivial, a small lump on the head, but when Rapha divulged the news of their visitors, Adam panicked. "She saw that? Great! Already I play the fool!"

He had planned to prolong the boy's agony but with the fatalism of youth Adam proclaimed he could "never" face her now. Rapha, pitying the mortified young man, explained the actual moment of her departure. Ah! Then! It was as if the sun rose again to honor the athletic hero. Insecurity fled, replaced by exuberance and a demand for Rapha to recall the girl's every reaction. Luckily, since the tutor had not actually looked at her, there was not much to relate beyond the fact she had witnessed only his most dazzling dives. This brought satisfaction bordering on conceit. What was it about this human that kept him swinging between extremes?

However, though the young man continued the shift from incessant questioning to a dazed state requiring a firm shake to bring him into the here and now, they managed to gather a brilliant bouquet of flowers with the perfect message encoded in the choice of each bloom, to complete the daintily wrought crown (the gems would be added later for their marriage ceremony) *and* to make Adam gloriously presentable, even fragrant, by the appointed time.

At the final moment, when Adam was to step into the clearing in full view of the celestials and the magnificence of Adonai, the young man's courage waned. In truth, Rapha could not blame him. The array of heaven's court, though a fractional representation of the entire celestial realm, was daunting. Just like Rapha, their true glory was veiled, but there was no denying the undercurrent of immense power radiating among the glittering assembly.

Adam stopped, staring at the path he was to tread through these amazing beings. In a hoarse whisper he said, "Couldn't we do this some other way, perhaps a private meeting by the lake?"

"This is what Adonai has decreed."

"But it's hard enough trying not to do anything foolish in front of her; now there's a crowd of angels as well?"

"Maybe your fear of appearing foolish is the very reason Adonai laid this path at your feet." Rapha plumbed the depths of his experience for the proper words. "To achieve your desire, you must first conquer your fear. To conquer fear, Adonai must be your only focus. Thus you are no longer a slave to fear; you achieve your desire, *and* gain freedom from your greatest weakness. This is why Adonai's path leads through hardship. As you draw closer to your heavenly Father, the heart's desire aligns with Him. It is when you try to circumvent the narrow path that aims for His heart that desire becomes destructive." There. Rapha smiled, grateful for wisdom to share with his pupil in the hour of need.

Adam's gaze was fixed on the brightest spot straight ahead, the flower-strewn expanse where Adonai awaited him. "So is she standing behind Him? I don't see her." The boy turned to Rapha, "Oh. Did you say something?"

Rapha had to chuckle. So much for imparting wisdom. But, since Adam was giving him a split second's attention, Rapha added, "Just keep your eyes fixed on Adonai."

Relief flooded Adam's features. He turned toward the assembly, locked eyes with his Creator—and took on the countenance of a king.

When every eye turned to view the first ruler of Adonai's new age, it seemed the boy grew in stature. Even to Rapha who was familiar with the many facets of the boy's personality, a new serenity and purpose suffused Adam's countenance. He was no longer simply the energetic, irrepressible manchild. A quiet strength flowed from him along with something more, something intangible but as real as the trees that leaned close, reaching toward him as if recognizing his destiny. Finally, when Rapha tore his eyes from the boy, he discovered the source of this elusive substance. Favor from the Most High flowed toward Adam, crowning the boy with majesty. Adam's body was at all times encased with radiance but now that steady glow was lit from within as well, an answering glory fanned to dazzling brilliance that left no doubt—this was Adonai's anointed. Through this joining of earth and heaven, age-old prophecies would come to pass.

With all eyes on the young man, Rapha almost missed it—a nagging hatred that clashed with the purity of the moment—but it was there, a veiled stench borne on the fragrant breeze. Lucifer, too, was in attendance. Rapha shoved the hateful thought aside. Nothing should tarnish this moment.

Adam continued down the long corridor, eyes fixed on his goal. In the young face, no trace of fear remained. In fact, the expression in his eyes spoke so clearly of absolute love and trust that Rapha felt an unexpected lump in his throat. Radiating with Adonai's love, the boy was breathtaking. The angel felt a wave of awe to be chosen to influence such a remarkable being.

Then Adam stood before the throne. When he knelt and bowed his face to the ground, the glorious assembly followed suit.

"Rise, my son," the compassionate voice poured out like mighty waters, **"what is your desire?"**

"You know my deepest thoughts, O Adonai. I desire my mate, she who would remain by my side, who would govern with me; she who would be made complete by joining her life to mine even as I am completed by joining my life to hers.

She who would be the deepest expression on this earth of your lovingkindness toward me."

Rapha's brow raised as the boy's eloquence flowed. Had Adam composed that heartfelt speech when he tossed and turned so long into the night?

But that question was forgotten as someone appeared beside the Father, one who shone so bright it seemed a separate ray of light was emanating from the Lord's essence. A lithe form with hair like windswept clouds on a starry night came into focus, clothed in shimmering threads of light spun finer than a spider's web.

The most striking feature was her eyes. Rapha discerned a keen intelligence and inquisitive nature that overcame her shyness as she peered back at her spectators. However, it was evident she was seeking *him.*

When she saw the manchild, a smile lit her features that made even Rapha, the creature of light positioned farthest from this tender meeting, burn brighter—as something deep inside, some care-encrusted core, melted.

Adam stood unmoving, his face turned away from Rapha's vantage point, but he must have looked stunned because Adonai prompted, **"Do not forget to breathe, son."**

A wave of chuckles flowed through the crowd and Adam, as if released from a spell, remembered the gifts he bore. "Um… oh! These are for you," he stepped up and placed the enormous bouquet into her arms. Suddenly eloquence returned. "They *were* the most beautiful things in the garden… until now."

Rapha would not have thought it possible but, at the young man's words, the womanchild glowed brighter and her smile grew even more dazzling. She said nothing (later Rapha was to realize how unusual this was). However, her expression communicated more than the most lyrical poem.

When Adam put a hand to his chest where his life's rhythm was felt most strongly, and then held his palm toward her, she copied the movement and fitted her hand to his. As they stood, unified by the light of Adonai, it was as if the observers no longer existed. There was only Adonai, the man and the woman, an interwoven cord of three, the Maker's plan for their future. Rapha could not foresee, in that moment brimming with promise, the horrible path required for that promise to be fulfilled.

Adam's voice cracked a bit as he broke the silence, "So, what do I call you?"

"Adam," Adonai answered with a hint of a smile in His voice, **"we are leaving that up to you."**

Again, Adam's face betrayed uncertainty but after a moment's pause he said, "Then, *officially,* I will call you 'Woman' because you were drawn forth from me. Will that do?" He addressed the girl.

She smiled and brought his hand to her heart. "I was taken from your side but now, I will never leave it."

A murmur of approval swept the crowd.

Rapha walked toward the throne, the dainty, golden circlet shining in his hands. The memory of that slow walk was to remain so clear even thousands of years later. As he was swept up in the overflow of their gratitude toward Adonai, Rapha felt—there was no other way to describe it—*younger*.

Adam's hands shook as he took the crown and reached to place it on her gleaming head. Her crown for him was heavier but still simple, an interwoven circle of three golden vines that slipped down on his forehead, as yet a bit large for his brow.

Then Adonai spoke. **"These tokens are a testament to the authority I bestow. If you feel unprepared to rule... good: I am here to instruct and guide you and these faithful of the celestial host are vessels of My knowledge as well. In**

this place, the one thing you need—wisdom—is ripe for the taking."

Then He addressed the assembly, **"This man and woman are the first fruits of this new age. Honor them as my anointed ones. Stand with them and protect them. Their welfare affects all life and through their offspring all creation is restored."**

Again the Maker addressed the young man and woman who continued to sneak glances at each other. **"Today, you are betrothed. You see in each other the promise of future fulfillment. You will grow and learn together. Then, when you are prepared to rule, the two shall become one flesh. Until then you will learn of your calling to lay down your own lives to ensure the welfare of all things, from the least to the greatest. Abide in Me and your joy shall be secure."**

Then the young man and woman turned toward the assembly and the entire valley broke into celebration. Chattering birds took flight, large mammals trumpeted and roared, smaller creatures scampered and shrieked in a joyous symphony.

In the midst of this celebration, the piercing light of Adonai lit upon Lucifer, crouching atop a carved pillar like an eager bird of prey. With a hiss, the fallen angel disappeared.

Chapter Eight

It Is Good

Rapha is staring with unseeing eyes toward distant fires and sounds of chaos. How he has wished through thousands of painful years he could have stopped time to hold them in that place of innocence. All too soon the purity of those days was a golden phantom to taunt him with what might have been.

Although—he cannot help but smile—they did *have good times.*

With the addition of the female, Adam's education took flight. Her appetite for learning was voracious and her curiosity was unrelenting. Oh the hundreds of questions she asked every day!

"Why do we have to eat and you don't?" "What makes the honeybee want to sip from the flowers when he could fly over the hills and see so much more?" "How do the stars stay up in the sky?" "How high would I have to fly to touch them?" "Have you ever touched them?" "Why don't we have a tail to help us climb trees?" "Where does the sun go at night?"

And she was forever digging. The girl had an innate curiosity about hidden things; the roots of flowers and trees, rocks under soil, little creatures that lived beneath logs and small, quick beings that thrived in the dark quiet of cool caverns.

On the surface, Adam appeared to attend more than ever to his studies, but actually he was distracted. As her finger traced the words on the scrolls, Adam nudged closer so her hair brushed his cheek. As they stood pondering the path of the moon that rose even though the sun was yet high in the sky, Adam's attention wandered. With a grin, Rapha grasped the young man's head, turning it toward a lunar view once again.

Rapha was their constant tutor and chaperone but he knew his angelic approval was no longer the one most coveted by Adam. Now the young man was spurred on by a driving competition with the female. Her admiration, next to that of Adonai, was his most treasured reward. Each of the young humans had their strengths; he excelled in narrative detail while she was able to grasp deeper meaning behind a story; he was the faster swimmer and runner but she had the greater stamina; she was the one the animals sought for comfort while Adam was prized for rambunctious play; but they each strove to improve where the other excelled. She inspired his former unenthusiastic study of things that grew out of the ground while he encouraged her interest in the cosmos.

Rapha was fascinated by their complementary personalities. She had a gentling influence on the boy when he desired to test his physical limits since she was sure to attempt whatever he did; and he made her laugh when she tended to take herself too seriously. It was a perfect blend, with each encouraging the other toward balance and wholeness. It gave them vulnerability and strength, helping Rapha understand why Adonai would take the risk of making two separate beings so interdependent. In fact, it even caused him to question if the angels' wholeness could be viewed as weakness in the grand scheme of things. Perhaps if Lucifer had been a bit vulnerable, his pride might not have been his undoing?

Their discussions about history became fascinating. The two humans brought fresh perspective to tales experienced and retold by Rapha for millennia.

But sometimes the discussion hit a little too close to danger for Rapha's comfort. The memory of their inquisitive young faces as the angel attempted to describe how his physiognomy differed from theirs was so clear the conversation could have taken place yesterday. That day the young humans had raced up their favorite summit to join the angel by the clear mountain stream for another history lesson. Usually the climb helped to curb some of their energetic nature but this time she had won the race and Adam was accusing her of foul play. The interchange was creating anything *but* a teachable moment.

"You just don't want to admit I beat you fair and square," she laughed, tossing her hair back from flushed cheeks.

"You cheated!" Adam stated. In truth, he was too stirred by her flashing eyes and smile to even care about the race. "You tripped and I slowed to help you. If you hadn't let go of that branch at the perfect moment to knock me down—"

"There! You admit it!" She poked Adam's shoulder. "You were already losing or you would not have seen me trip."

"I was being chivalrous by letting you keep up," he returned the poke.

"Besides, it just goes to show what Rapha says, 'the race doesn't always go to the merely swift,'" she paraphrased liberally to goad him. "Strategy is more important than might."

"So you admit you cheated!" He leaned into her face, inhaling the scent of honeysuckle and herbed oils.

"I never said that!" her hand had been trailing in the stream in preparation for a drink, but she decided on a better use. With a flick of her fingers the water splashed in his face, transforming the smug expression as excitement lit his handsome features.

In an instant the splash had turned into a full-blown water free-for-all.

It was both amusing and alarming to view the sexual tension between the young man and woman when they still had no real grasp of where it was leading. No stretching of Rapha's angelic emotional probing was necessary to recognize the obvious. If left to their own devices, this innocent tussle would follow the natural course of the lions' wrestling match.

One of his most important directives was to prevent such an occurrence until Adonai proclaimed the proper time, therefore Rapha placed himself between the youthful combatants, breaking the inevitable force that drew the ocean to the shore. He was rewarded for his efforts by becoming their mutual target. He endured the soaking for a moment, then shut down the assault by summoning a strong wave that swept them both off their feet.

Soon the dripping, bedraggled trio flopped to the grass in the warm sun, the humans wringing water from their hair while Rapha shook his head as the heat of his body reduced liquid to steam. Soon he was dry while they continued to drip.

Luckily, this difference triggered her incessant curiosity and shifted the focus of the moment. Unfortunately, Rapha ever after questioned whether his answers could have been delivered in a way less inclined to intrigue.

"So what, exactly, are you made of?" The girl watched the steam rise above Rapha, fascination in her penetrating gaze.

"I am a creature of light and spirit," Rapha answered.

"But I can't grasp a ray of sunlight. How are we able to touch you?" She reached to squeeze his arm.

"All matter can be reduced to a flimsier substance; and all matter, if condensed to a high enough degree, can be solid."

Something about that answer intrigued Adam enough to take his focus off the girl. "So when you go away, are you becoming a flimsier substance?"

"I suppose it could be viewed that way."

"Can you teach us to do that?"

"It is much more difficult to reduce earth to a malleable state…." before Rapha could finish, another question was fired, this time by the girl.

"Is it difficult for you to become… solid again?"

"It has always been a simple concept for me…."

"Can you teach us to do that?"

"That ability is not part of Adonai's plan for…."

"It must be amazing. Are you aware of everything while you're, um, malleable?"

"The core of my being, my spirit, remains intact, therefore I have no lapse in…."

The girl leapt to her feet and spread her arms wide, "How wonderful to feel so free!"

"The feeling of freedom does not rely on my material state."

Adam cut in, pondering a different aspect. "Are there females like you?"

That caught the girl's attention. She stopped spinning, her eyes riveted on Rapha.

"Ah! There's a difficult question… actually, no."

"Have you never requested a mate? As you told me, Adonai will give you whatever you ask…"

"…in accordance with His will," Rapha finished, hoping the conversation could be steered from the rocky shoal that lay ahead. "Adonai guides our desires and…."

"Why have you never requested a female?" Her voice was steady as her eyes searched his.

"Please understand, while we look similar in elemental ways our… requirements… are dissimilar." Rapha sighed. He was handling this poorly. "Like the animals that surround you, you and Adam will one day have offspring. Due to our unchanging nature, there is no need for celestials to reproduce."

"So, in your… society… I am *unnecessary*."

There it was. The conversation capsized. "That word is inaccurate in this context…."

She didn't miss a beat, "Then aid my *inaccuracy*. What word would fit?"

The edge in her voice was heartbreaking. He hated the fact that his answers had wounded her, but how could he explain something he hardly understood himself? "Please, perhaps these questions should be directed to Adonai…."

"Why? The question is simple. Am I only necessary for bearing offspring?"

"No! Adonai created you to strengthen mankind," if only he had stopped right there, the moment might have been salvaged, "and… and for you to be—strengthened together." Rapha raked a frustrated hand through his hair. Why couldn't he make any sense while those wide eyes were fixed on him?

"So Adam was incomplete without me?"

"Well, no. And yes. I mean, you are both complete, but it is a matter of—fulfillment." There. That sounded better. "And reproduction, of course."

"Will we ever be more like you? Will we ever be able to become—malleable—and perhaps fly?"

If Rapha's own emotional state had not been so jumbled he might have read her intent. But he was so glad the conversation had landed on safer ground, he unwittingly ensnared himself. "If mankind grows in harmony with Adonai, nothing will be impossible…."

"And one day my kind will no longer be necessary for offspring?"

"What? No! That is not what I meant…."

But she had added the known facts and assumed the inevitable. "So it's only because Adam is less… developed… that I am needed."

Rapha rushed to redeem the moment. "I am discovering daily the wisdom of Adonai's plan in creating two individuals who complement and strengthen each other," he rushed on, though he could tell that her jumbled thoughts were not absorbing his words. "I often wonder if our angelic… completeness… might even be viewed as a weakness… and whether interdependence is actually a strength…."

Adam jumped in, "I would never want to be without you. If being like a celestial means leaving you behind I will remain as I am." His hopes to score points with his tender speech were dashed.

"That is ridiculous, Adam. Do you think I would thwart Adonai's plan?"

"No! That's not what I meant…" He spluttered, echoing Rapha's predicament.

The girl jumped to her feet and started walking away. After one helpless look at each other they clambered to join her, but she stopped, rolling her eyes in frustration. "Please, I want to be alone."

She pushed through the trees as Rapha and Adam stood blinking. When the angel probed the girl's emotions he encountered confusion; she desired to be alone and yet was lonely. He walked to the black leopard that usually shadowed her. Rousing the cat from slumber he held the animal's gaze, communicating his request, then watched the sleek animal follow the girl's path. Hopefully, by sending the cat he had provided a subtle presence that would soothe her. Besides, he had noticed a natural aversion among the animals to Lucifer's presence and, while he didn't want to voice his fears to Adam, he felt better knowing the animal's instincts would accompany her. But just to be safe, Rapha kept his awareness open to the girl. If she felt threatened in any way, he would know it.

In a few moments his watchfulness relaxed. She was with the Maker. He could feel the hard knot of hurt unravel as her confusion disappeared.

He took note of the words that finally brought peace to her heart.

"My wholeness—justice and mercy, love and discipline, beauty, and might—is too great, too complex, to be present only in man. Your offspring will better understand Me and the reflection of My holiness is more complete, when the two become one."

Their conversation continued, deepening her understanding of her destiny, of the balance and strength she would contribute. Like the tiny roots that hold the soil together and yet keep it broken and fertile, she was indispensable.

"Thank you, Adonai," Rapha exhaled with relief and passed on the news to Adam who celebrated by climbing the cliff. For Adam, emotions required a physical outlet.

Later that day, their delicate balance restored, Rapha watched as the young man and woman made their way to the evening's rendezvous with Adonai. Each brought a gift, something that was most precious to them. On the girl's forearm perched a large, brightly plumed parrot, which she had succeeded in teaching several words and phrases. With pride she brought the bird forth, encouraging it with rewards of seeds to show off its skills as the animals pressed around their Maker, nuzzling His hands, climbing on His shoulders or leaning as close as possible with unabashed adoration. Each brought something—a piece of fruit, a rock, a flower—whatever they deemed most valuable.

Even the trees leaned closer and a shower of blossoms fell on the path creating a confetti-strewn carpet for His feet. A large, lumbering sea turtle with a mollusk held in its hooked mouth moved as quickly as its bulky body would allow, inching closer and closer, vying for attention. One female chimp chattered, her voice rising in volume until Adonai turned toward her and laid a hand to her wrinkled, brown face. With unblinking trust she swung her baby from her back and, with the slightest glance of longing toward her child, she held it toward Adonai.

A hush fell among the animals as the large, bright hands cradled the baby and the Maker snuggled it closer to deliver a kiss to its forehead. Adonai whispered in its ear, gave one more hug, then His eyes fell on the mother who looked on with brimming eyes. The smile He gave her was blinding; each one present was rendered speechless by the intensity of love that flowed between them.

"This shall not be forgotten," His words radiated throughout the clearing. He reached an arm toward the mother who chattered and leapt to His side. Absolute silence prevailed except in the circle of His arms where the breathtaking drama was taking place. He held them close for a moment as tears ran down His cheeks. The mother whimpered and nestled closer while the baby appeared stupefied, one tiny hand grasping a fold of His robe.

"The gift is received, a living sacrifice, holy and eternal." With another kiss, He knelt to place the mother on the ground and then handed the baby back into her arms. As Adonai turned to attend to others, both chimps continued to glow, encased in His light.

Adam had yet to present his gift, the large diamond he and Rapha had used for their game, polished to a brilliant sheen. Now he hesitated. But Adonai beckoned to him and the boy stepped forward to bow and offer his sacrifice. Rapha sensed that Adam had hoped to increase his gift's importance with a pompous presentation, but all it accomplished was to accentuate the contrast between his offering of a gem when the simpler creature had handed over her heart.

However, Adonai embraced the boy, and then held the precious stone aloft. Stars of light danced, transforming the clearing into a magical, glittering prism. A lion cub pounced and chased the points of light and the girl laughed at its play and even joined the pursuit. While the other creatures were distracted by the game, Adam knelt, a grateful smile lighting up his face. "Thank you, Adonai, for transforming my gift into something that brings joy to all."

The Maker's reply was inaudible but crystal clear to Rapha as it was written onto the boy's heart. **"I am not greedy. I only desire that My good gifts never separate us."**

Adam's eyes were drawn to the laughing girl, desire and love etched on his features. When he looked back into Adonai's eyes, he could not hold the penetrating gaze for long.

Rapha shuddered. Lucifer would be seeking just such a weakness, just such a chink in Adam's armor. He met the Maker's eye. Yes, they would address this at the earliest opportunity.

The next day, Rapha tried to prepare them for the inevitable—an encounter with Lucifer.

The two young people were climbing a huge tree, grappling for handholds in their ongoing efforts to outdo each other. The girl was able to climb higher, her lesser weight making it possible to navigate the topmost branches. To deepen the drama of the moment she let go and inched along the thin branch, hands held out for balance.

"Okay, I'm very impressed. Now stop," Adam's voice had a commanding edge.

Rapha sensed the girl was pleased with Adam's concern. In fact, her present mood bordered on giddiness as she wavered and her foot slipped. In truth, the little faker was in no danger and had the balance of a cat, but she loved to tease and could not help bursting into giggles when Adam gasped and crouched on his branch as if prepared to dive to her rescue.

Rapha climbed to join them, not shaking a single branch or leaf with his passage.

"What a showoff!" the girl pronounced. "But it is nice to know with Rapha around someone would catch me if I actually *did* fall."

"Still, perhaps it's wise to not push the limits." Adam's voice sounded a bit pompous even to Rapha.

The girl snorted, "This from the one who slipped this morning attempting three back flips from the highest ledge! You seemed awfully grateful to have an angel on hand."

"It was worth it to hear you scream my name," he took on a feminine tone, "Oh! *Adam*!"

The girl blushed. "Well, now you know how it feels." She stole a glance at him through lowered lashes.

Adam's heart pounded so hard Rapha could feel it throb through the branch where he perched. Heaven help them if the girl ever realized the true extent of the power she possessed.

Eager to change the subject, she looked out to the lands that stretched beyond their domain on the other side of the garden's wall. "Just how far does the land go? Does it end where the sky begins?"

"No. If you were to stand at that place, you would see yet more land stretching to another point that seems to reach the sky, then another, then another, following a gentle curve until finally, after many, many times, you would end up right back here."

The girl's brow puckered a moment, then she laughed, "You're teasing, right? Can you imagine animals on the other side standing upside down?"

"Just because you cannot imagine something does not make it false," Rapha said.

"Alright," her eyes took on a calculating gleam. "Take me flying. Show me the other side."

"Hey! She's not going anywhere without me!" Adam protested.

"We are not allowed to take you outside these walls."

"So," she said with a pout, "we'll never get to explore what's out there?"

"I do not perceive everything Adonai has in store."

She pondered a loophole. "We can just dig down until we reach it! We need never go outside the wall!"

Rapha smiled. If only things were so simple. "Do you see how far it is until the earth and sky meet?" He gestured toward the horizon, "Could you dig that far?"

"Well…." she hated to admit defeat. "If we worked long and hard enough…."

"Through solid rock?"

"Oh." Even her irrepressible will could see his logic.

Adam said, "I don't see why we should be so desperate to explore the outside. Look around. We could explore for years and never see everything within these walls. Besides, is there another place in all the earth as beautiful as this?"

"No. Adonai has seen to your every need and desire. He has even provided those who can answer your questions about the outside."

"So what *is* out there?" she asked as her hungry eyes scanned the horizon.

"The rest of creation; the other men, animals, birds of the air, inhabitants of the water, and things that grow from the ground. These, as you can see, are not the only trees; and every animal has those of its kind outside the garden."

"Then why were we separated from them, these other men and animals? Do these walls hold us *in* or keep something bad out?"

Rapha regarded her a moment as he sent a silent plea to Adonai for wisdom. "Actually, the greatest threat is also within these walls."

That got their attention. Both young people stared at him until a light dawned in her head. "Oh. I remember. You said we are our own worst enemy when we, uh," she scrunched her forehead, "'want what Adonai has not put in our reach' or something like that."

"No, it was, *'led astray by their evil desires,'* and you were talking about what caused the wars between God and His creation." Adam shot a satisfied smile her way.

"Good. You listened. But that is not the enemy to which I refer."

"The creature in the lake?" The boy wondered, unable to conceive anything more dangerous than that.

"This evil one desires to discover your greatest weakness and lure you to destroy yourself," Rapha said. "He will manipulate your highest aspiration and make it your master." As Rapha's description continued, the sun dimmed and the joyful chirp and chatter around them grew silent. "Then he will devour you as slowly and excruciatingly as possible, feeding on your tortured mind and soul until life becomes a constant torment."

Rapha hated the effect of his words on the young faces before him. Revulsion shadowed their brows but there was also, playing across their faces, something which concerned him much more—a gleam of fascination. Words like "torment" and "devour" had no context for them. Even the larger animals in the garden feasted on plants, nutmeats, and fruit. None were prey. How could they comprehend Lucifer when they could not even grasp the words to describe him?

"Do you speak of Lucifer?" Adam's voice was low, almost reverent. When Rapha nodded they both leaned closer.

"Is it true he can bend others to his will just by the sound of his voice?" her eyes blazed with curiosity.

"He makes what serves *him* best sound best for all," Rapha answered. "He is very… seductive."

"But you used that word when describing mating," Adam blurted. Immediately a deeper red lit his cheeks, and his eyes, when he turned to her, were warm with anticipation.

"Alright you two. Pay attention," Rapha said with mock severity. "The word 'seduce' can also imply 'tempting to do wrong.'"

Their brows furrowed in tandem. The young people had no experience with falsehood or trickery beyond a friendly jest. How could he make them understand?

"Outside these walls," Rapha began, "animals and humans devour each other, the strong prey on the weak and… horrible things happen."

"No. Adonai would never allow it," the girl stated.

"Understand. This is not what Adonai created. Long ago, Lucifer *seduced* mankind. He tricked them. They *chose* his corruption in return for power."

"But why didn't Adonai stop him?" Adam asked.

"What? *Force* Lucifer to obedience? Is that Adonai's way?"

"Well, no, but Adonai knows everything, right? Why would He create Lucifer when he knew he would cause so much trouble?"

"What Adonai created was good. Lucifer was His beloved child, like you."

Adam's mouth gaped. "No. I would *never* be Adonai's enemy."

"There was a time I would not have believed it of Lucifer," Rapha said, his face twisting with grief at the memory of that glorious head resting against Adonai's breast.

"How did it happen?" The girl's voice was no more than a whisper.

How did one answer a question like that? How could young, simple minds understand emotions that took eons to evolve? Rapha took a deep breath and plunged ahead. "Lucifer could not conceive of a love that is truly endless. He resented anyone and anything that gained Adonai's favor—as if that regard stole from *him*."

"But how could he dwell with Adonai and yet not understand Him?"

"It is never that simple," Rapha answered, surprised by a rush of defensiveness on Lucifer's behalf. "Undisciplined passion turns to contempt. Lucifer demanded what Adonai could not give. He demanded what he was not ready to handle. It began as an offense that Lucifer regarded as betrayal. Over time he became a slave to his lust, rage, and revenge."

"That's horrible," the girl's eyes were moist with tears.

"Do not pity him," Rapha said. "Lucifer is powerful. His hatred for Adonai overshadows all. He would feel no pity for you. He would fill you with poison and revel in your pain. He would rejoice in the agony this would bring to Adonai."

"But *why* is he allowed here?" Adam asked.

The angel swept a hand toward the view of their home as he tried to make them understand what still baffled him. "Adonai keeps no prisoner. He holds all He loves with an open hand—even those who hate Him."

Anger flooded Adam's face. Even without his gift of reading thoughts, Rapha could have read the boy's emotions loud and clear as Adam digested those words, his eyes gazing 'round at the beauty of the garden until they came to rest on the young woman beside him. The thought of Lucifer dwelling so close did not concern the boy… until he considered *her*.

"What good are walls if evil is shut in with us?" Adam asked.

Rapha gazed across the outlands, mulling distant memories. "Even in paradise, evil can thrive." He sighed and faced them, "I, too, struggle with these questions. Adonai's ways are mysterious but what seems foolish to me has always proved to be His deepest wisdom. Nevertheless, you are free to ask Him. He has often told me, ***'Deep faith is evidenced more in honest questions than in blind acceptance.'*** Even if you are not ready for the answer, He will not forget. He always honors a request for wisdom."

Adam grabbed a piece of golden fruit but rather than eat it, he gave vent to his frustration and flung it far and high, over the garden wall. They did not see where it landed but its passing roused a vibrant flock of birds that squawked their protest and flapped away over the wall only to wheel about in the sky and return to the garden's peaceful shade. Rapha watched his young charges, hoping the birds' wisdom was not lost on them.

But the girl had had enough seriousness for one day. Suddenly she clambered down, goading Adam, "You're so good at diving. If I get too far ahead you can just *fall* to beat me!"

"Perhaps I should name you 'Vexing' since you're so good at it," Adam retorted as he dodged the branch she released with precision toward his head.

As their laughing voices retreated Rapha shut his eyes and shuddered at the icy wind that pierced his soul. "Yes, Adonai," Rapha whispered, "he comes."

But late that night as the girl slumbered, Adam stared at the stars, pondering their patterns. Rapha sensed an unfamiliar emotion in the boy: fear. He was moved by pity to go to Adam but Adonai's silent direction forbade it, **"Let it drive him to Me."**

So in the deepest watch of the night, Adam leapt from his bed and made his way to the river. With the swift-moving water bubbling over stones that echoed back the sparkle of myriad points of starlight, Adam paced on the bank muttering, grabbing stones, and flinging them into the dark waters.

"Show yourself!" the boy finally shouted to the night. "I know you're here, watching and waiting. I can feel your hatred. I know you want to hurt us, to hurt her. I am not afraid of you!" Adam spun as if expecting an attack but no one was there.

As Adam continued his rant, calling to Lucifer, even taunting him, a shadowy figure appeared in the half-light.

After a few moments, a quiet voice came from the cloaked form. **"What do you seek?"**

Adam gasped and spun to face the man, his body coiled and ready to fight. "Are you my enemy?"

"No," the quiet voice replied.

Adam studied the speaker who was bathed in the radiance reflected from Adam's body but the man's face remained in shadow due to the long piece of cloth that draped over his head.

"Lucifer would lie. How can I believe you?"

"You must discern," the man said. **"Your eyes and ears can be deceived but your heart sees truth."**

"My heart does not have eyes. How can it see?"

"Seek the memory of communion with Adonai. That is your foundation and your confidence. That is where your vision is clear."

Adam was quiet a moment. "But I've been told Lucifer would say anything to make me believe him."

The man did not answer.

Adam's brow furrowed with concentration even as he kept a wary eye on the visitor. "Why do you hide your face?"

"I am hidden from eyes that do not see."

"Uncover your face and I will see just fine," Adam leapt toward the man and grabbed for the concealing length of cloth—but a fire flashed, and for a split second the night was brighter than day. When all was dark and silent again, Adam was dumb, blind, and trembling at the man's feet.

Adam's shoulders began to shake and a sob broke from his mouth.

"My child, why do you fear?" The man's voice was gentle and when he touched Adam, the boy's tongue was loosed.

"I do not have the power to fight you. I do not have the power to, to protect *her*."

"You do not lack power. What you lack is humility. A humble man would ask the Father for whatever he needs, and receive it."

Adam's head shot up. "Then I will ask the Father for power."

"And you would still be defeated," the man's quiet voice stated.

"You lie! Adonai has power over everything."

"And Adonai obeys His own law. Authority is given according to law."

"Authority? Does this authority give power?"

"Yes. It is the right to rule."

"Then that is what I need. I will *humbly* ask the Father for authority."

"It is already yours."

"But, I am helpless before you."

"Your authority is of this Earth. It does not extend to Me."

Adam's eyes narrowed. "Tell me who you are."

"As you have said, words could deceive. Come closer, child."

But Adam remained unmoving.

"Tell me, how can you decide which trees in the garden provide what is good to eat?"

"Easy," Adam said, "I see the fruit."

"And that is how you should decide if you can trust me."

"I do not see any branches or leaves on you."

"My words and actions are my fruit. If I draw you closer to the Father, I am a good tree."

Adam squatted down, still wary, and watched as the man gathered kindling to add to a small mound of wood. In a few moments a cheerful blaze crackled and the man brought forth a simple meal of fruit and nuts wrapped in savory leaves along with small cakes of what appeared to be several types of grain pressed together. He laid the cakes on a flat rock among the glowing embers.

When the man took a seat on a log and reached to stir the fire with a stick, for just a moment it flared and chased every shadow from his features. Adam's jaw dropped and he stared. Rapha felt the boy's surge of excitement.

"I know your eyes," Adam whispered.

The man met Adam's gaze and smiled. **"Will you come and eat?"**

In answer, Adam inched closer and eased onto a rock within the circle of warm light.

The man poured water into a shallow bowl, **"To wash away the dust,"** he said, then returned to his seat to tend the cakes.

But Adam continued to stare, "I see Adonai in you."

"Come, there is much to discuss."

Adam moved as if in a dream to dip his hands into the water. "Please, tell me who you are."

"I AM the Word of Adonai made flesh."

The blank look on Adam's face plainly showed he did not comprehend.

"I AM truth. I AM life. To know Me is to know Adonai."

"But I *know* Adonai. Why did I not recognize you?"

"Because eyes are blind when clouded by fear," the man said, then poured more water, this time into a small wooden vessel. He handed it to Adam who, without hesitation, put it to his lips.

Immediately he gave an exclamation of surprise, "This is not water!"

"No. This is the fruit of My vine. Drink it and you will never thirst."

Adam took a small sip. "It is wonderful," he said, and then tilted his head to one side and peered once again at the man. "But Adonai is complete; He has no need of a body." His eyes lit with suspicion once again, "He is the one true God. How can He be split in two?"

The man reached above him for a piece of fruit. **"You see this fruit. It is whole and yet it has three parts."**

Adam nodded but his eyes were still narrowed.

The man broke open the fruit and its aroma filled the air. **"Three separate and distinct parts—skin, flesh and seed—but all part of the whole. You also, like Adonai, are a union of three—spirit, soul, and body."**

"Yes, but why would Adonai separate the three?"

"The Father and I are One. Even in this humble form I AM complete. However, from me you will learn how to lead what is broken back to holiness."

To Rapha, it seemed Adam absorbed the man's words and melted in response. His shoulders sagged and his radiant face was bowed. "You remind me of my true purpose. Adonai has told me that through me the whole Earth will be blessed. Forgive me. I have been thinking only of her," Adam's shoulders slumped and a sigh escaped his lips, "of myself."

"Well said." The man reached up to lay the hood of his cloak around his shoulders. **"Come here, my child."** He extended a hand toward Adam who crept nearer to sit at the man's feet. **"Rapha,"** his smile was wide as he addressed the angel, **"now that he believes I am not Lucifer, there are things to discuss."**

Rapha stepped out of the shadows as Adam and the man shared their meal. Mostly the conversation dealt with Adam's role in the earth and how his authority, awarded by Adonai, was what Lucifer truly desired.

"He would corrupt everything again if given the chance. He desires to bring pain to Adonai by bringing pain to His creation. Yes, Lucifer is here and he is seeking a weakness.

You must not listen to him. He is beautiful and he knows how to twist truth to his purposes. Do not listen to his words. Do not desire his fruit. It is poison. To be like him will seem irresistible; so do not even look upon him. And do not think a sample of what he offers will be safe. With just a taste of his corruption your body will know death, and then all creation will fall under his authority.

"Look around you, Adam. All is laid at your feet. This one thing only, Lucifer's corruption, the fruit of his tree, is forbidden."

The man spoke with Adam until a brilliant strip of sunlight peeked over the horizon. Then he leaned toward the boy and kissed him on the forehead. Rapha smiled, his own heart overflowing with the look of bliss on Adam's face.

Immediately, the man was gone.

The next day, while Adam slept, the girl decided to do some exploring on her own. She dug with fervor, exposing a fascinating, hidden world just beneath the grass and moss. Rapha lounged, unseen, high in a neighboring tree. Of late his anxiety had grown so he tried to keep an eye on the young people even when they desired privacy. When they bathed or took care of other private matters he retreated, but at all times he stayed attuned to their emotions. Even during their slumber he remained alert, knowing the enemy's preference for vulnerability. Unbeknownst to his charges, other angels also formed a protective circle during those hours.

One other factor had heightened Rapha's watchfulness. Adam and his betrothed were coming of age. Adams body was thickening, his voice changing and the peach fuzz on his cheeks darkening. The girl also had come to maturity. The scent of her blood on the wind was unmistakable. This development, other than sending her to bathe more often, had caused little disturbance to her daily routine, but to Rapha, so well acquainted with Lucifer's ways, it felt like a red flag waved above the trees, marking her location.

Later, when Adam came through the bushes, his eyes still puffy from sleep, the young woman smiled a greeting from the pit she had dug and brushed the hair from her face, leaving a dark smudge on her forehead.

"I need to talk to you," Adam announced in a serious tone.

"Look at this! I can't even get to the bottom of these roots! They go down so much deeper than the ones by the river. It's just like Rapha said. The water is harder to reach so their roots are longer."

Adam's face lost a bit of concern for heavier matters as he watched her back where her dazzling garment dipped below her shoulders that strained at the earth, but he shook his head to clear it and addressed her again, "Please, this is important."

"I'm listening," she replied, then grabbed at something and proudly extracted a tiny green lizard.

"Listen!" Adam commanded and reached for her hands. She watched with a pout as the startled lizard ran away, but she soon realized that Adam still held her hands. For a moment they both stared at the joining until Adam grinned and opened her soil-encrusted palms. "They're very… um… dirty," he murmured as he brought her hands to his lips.

Rapha watched from his high perch, observing what human eyes could not see, a magnetic intertwining of their souls. But the expressions of alert, breathless fascination said it all. Their bodies longed to follow suit. Rapha hoped he would not have to intervene should their attraction prove overwhelming.

Eyes wide, the girl pulled her hands away and slapped them together a few times. "So what's so important?"

Adam looked away from her body, from the compelling garment of light that followed her gentle curves. He clenched his eyes shut and took a deep breath as if to shake away the cloud from his mind caused by gazing at her. When he spoke again, his voice was stern. "I have spoken to Adonai about Lucifer. He said to stay away from him. We… cannot have anything to do with him, especially we cannot *touch* him, or we'll die." So the message was a bit befuddled. At the moment, Adam was feeling proprietary; he didn't want her touching *anyone* but himself.

She returned to her digging, a bit perplexed. "It feels strange." She slapped at the soil. "I don't see what's so scary about one banished angel. Doesn't Adonai trust our judgment at all?"

Adam watched her back as she dug. Finally, he wiped a hand across his forehead, leaving a brown streak to match hers, and turned to move away through the trees.

She prattled on. "After all, he *lost*, right? And what does *'we will die'* even mean?" She looked over her shoulder to discover she was alone. "Adam? Where are you?"

Chapter Nine

Sabotage

It was several hours later when Rapha sought Adam. The young man, like the young woman in her moment of crisis, had taken his frustration to Adonai and, once again, the Maker's words had brought order from confusion. With the sun at its highest point in the sky, Adam perched in the trees, a bemused expression on his face. For a few moments after Rapha joined him, the boy was silent.

Rapha could not recall the last time he had been first to speak. Sensing the boy's emotions, he broke the silence with the rhetorical question, "You are pleased with Adonai's gift?"

Adam sputtered a moment as if he had lost the gift of speech. "All I could say was, 'Thank you.' I am so amazed by what Adonai has created, the joy that will be ours when she and I… when we are joined." Adam paused. "I believe her rightful name is 'Glory' since that is what Adonai says she is. He said her well-being and joy are my glory. As I care for her in the same way Adonai cares for me, she will be like this well-tended garden, rewarding my life and offspring with sustenance, protection, and joy."

Then Adam spread his arms wide as if to embrace all of creation. "She is my 'Glory'!" he shouted to the heavens. "She is Adonai's precious gift. As I honor her above all creation our joy shall be like the sun, rising in the sky until all are blessed by its light!"

Adam was so giddy he almost fell from his perch. He flailed and grabbed at the branch on which he sat to regain his balance and began to laugh. The young man's joy was infectious. Soon Rapha too was laughing as Adam shook the entire tree with his mirth… nearly losing his balance once more.

"Perhaps her name should be 'Wine' since even the thought of her has intoxicated you," Rapha teased, causing Adam's laughter to explode once again. "Or 'Hyena' because she makes you sound like one of them."

As they continued the mindless jests, tears streamed from Adam's eyes and Rapha was swept with a hilarious drunkenness, the likes of which he had never experienced in his eons of existence. A glimpse of the power of mankind's melding with Adonai pierced his consciousness. By discovering the Maker's goodness like the petals of an unfolding flower, humans drank richly of each revealed aspect of His fathomless personality. In this way, ignorance was a blessing, like discovering treasures around every corner. Rapha understood Adonai's immense power, love and holiness—had understood for time immemorial—but when was the last time he had been drunk with joy about it?

But even in this moment, Rapha felt Lucifer's piercing gaze upon him. Lucifer's jealousy was a choking vapor paralyzing his mind even as Adam's joy made his soul take flight. Rapha felt his being would be ripped in two by the warring emotions.

A malicious chuckle filled his heart and Lucifer's unbidden message accosted his mind. *"Timing, old friend. That's all. Simple timing."*

The young woman moved with swift strokes through clear turquoise depths. How she treasured the quiet, pre-dawn moments when she could melt into the water and flow with the swishings, flutterings and murmurings of a gently waking world. Adam still slept. Again he had conversed with Adonai late into the evening, long after she had succumbed to slumber.

The conversations with their Maker were always fascinating. He had a way of making the complex and confusing simple. Often she and Adam would cry out something like, "Oh! I understand..." or, "Of course! Why didn't I see that?" as He opened their minds and wove truth from the rough fibers of their knowledge.

Her reaction to this knowledge differed from Adam's. While discovery would excite the boy and cause him to beg for more, she would sit back and ponder, turning the wisdom this way and that in her mind, taking what was revealed and polishing it until, a few moments later, she broke her silence with a provocative question.

Just last evening when she had brought up her discoveries about the tree roots, that they will continue to dig until they reach water, Adonai had pointed to the largest tree on their mountain, the very one she and Adam had climbed with Rapha. He had described the years of patient growth that had taken those mighty roots through solid rock until, if they cut away the face of the mountain, they would be able to follow those stubborn tendrils down into the mountain's very core. **"No mere wind or rushing water will topple it. In fact, its roots reach even deeper and wider into the ground than the branches reach into the sky."**

Adam had talked about the long skinny birches and the fat berry bushes, asking if their roots resembled what was seen. As Adonai explained how each tree and bush balanced underground what was needed above, the girl's mind had developed a wrinkle right down its center. Adam, noticing her silence, had teased her, "Don't worry, Glory. You can start digging first thing in the morning. The roots will wait."

But she had locked eyes with her Maker, almost afraid of the outcome of her thoughts. "Do the trees outside this garden, those that have to dig deeper for water, have deeper roots?"

"That is the natural way of things, is it not?" He had answered.

It was just enough to encourage her to venture forward, "You have often compared *us,* me and Adam, to a tender young tree You nurture and protect."

Adonai had nodded.

"You have also said the trees have to get stronger before they can bear the fruit that feeds many."

In that tense moment, it had seemed to her all creation, even Adonai, leaned in to hear her conclusion. The bold adventurer in her stood ready to beat a path through uncharted trails, but there was also a pampered princess, a side of herself she had never acknowledged, who wanted to shut her eyes to truth.

Glory's next words were almost a whisper. "But what of a tree that has constant water and never leans into a fierce wind and is… protected from all harm?" Her eyes were fixed on her clenched hands. "Would that tree be strong or would its roots be shallow?"

She had gazed into those all-knowing eyes and found the painful answer. She had begun to weep. In her short, glorious life she had known no pain or lack, yet now she felt, through those eyes, a connection with bitter grief. Glory had drawn as close to Adonai as possible and buried her face in His chest. She had no idea how long she remained, feeling like her heavy heart was exiting through her eyes. Eventually she had become aware that Adam was weeping on the Master's other side. Adam also understood. She and Adam were that tree. Their roots had to be strong, digging down into unshakeable rock, to fulfill their destiny. They had known nothing but joy and laughter. What was this grief flowing through them from Adonai? Was He warning them? Preparing them?

But Glory had felt ushered into a much deeper knowledge of their Maker and therefore she could not regret the pain. Nestling in His side and sharing the emotions of His heart made the moment not just bearable but beautiful.

Rapha was attuned to Glory as he entered the garden's workshop, the sweet fragrance of grapevines and flowering vines greeting him as he brought out the golden crowns, the same crowns that had sealed their betrothal and would now grace their shining heads as they were wed. He had only to set the gems that would glitter like colorful stars as Adam and Glory stood before the garden's inhabitants and the attending celestial hosts. He had arrived early to his post, eager to complete preparations. As soon as Adam woke, Rapha would share the good news with them—"Today is the day!"—but for now he would let the young man sleep and allow the young woman, Glory, her moment of tranquility and privacy.

Glory's emotions at the moment were a bit befuddled—she was both sad and fulfilled—but she still flowed with Adonai's presence, numbed yet enlivened as she marveled anew at colors, sounds, and fragrances that were present yesterday but overnight had gained intensity and loveliness. Rapha would not delve beyond that sense of her basic emotions. If there was a new revelation she chose to share with him, he wanted to hear it from her lips. He had discovered he enjoyed surprises.

Rapha had only observed the conversation last evening. Adonai had shut the angel's inner senses to the young people; certain things should be kept between the Maker and His children. Thus the angel had retreated to the circle of celestial hosts awaiting their Lord's will, while something miraculous occurred. Rapha's senses might have been blocked but his eyes were not. The beauty of the two humans melting into Adonai's being was breathtaking.

In those eternal moments, a paradigm shift had occurred. Rapha could not pinpoint exactly *what* had changed; he could only identify its effects. There was crystal clarity to the atmosphere that put him on high alert, yet it seemed born of acceptance, like heated gold that cools and conforms to the Master's plan. He had returned at the appointed time to the celestial court to bask in his Maker's love, his heart overflowing with gratitude for Earth's bright future and the perfection of Adonai's plan.

Glory dove deep, loving the caress of peaceful waters that soothed her muscles and renewed her overextended senses. Crying was a new sensation, cleansing yet exhausting, and deep recesses of her body ached with fulfillment and melancholy that escaped her understanding. However, she was at peace, like a rite of passage had been completed. Or was it just beginning? Regardless, Glory felt less… young than she had yesterday morning. But it was more than worth it. She would treasure those timeless moments with their Maker forever. Whatever it had cost was paid back in dazzling proportions.

She finished her swim and sat for a moment in the arc of waterfall where the cascade was gentle. From a little shelf behind the curtain of water she brought forth the covered stone bowls of toiletries Rapha had taught her to concoct. Their clean fragrance as she set aside stone lids and applied combinations of the garden's fruits and oils to her skin and hair were like a concentrated day in Eden, fresh and freeing, teeming with the best Adonai and Earth had to offer.

A swim to her favorite sunning rock rinsed away the excess. Glory then dried Rapha-style by lying in the sun's early-morning rays, the glow which always emanated from her body, warming, covering, and protecting her like a diaphanous raiment as she fingered her long curls into place. Beside her, a slender tree flourished, spreading its canopy of scarlet blossoms overhead, its decorative bower a gift from Adam who had coaxed the branches to lean over her favorite perch. Her thoughts turned the young man's way accompanied by nervous flutterings in her stomach. Somehow, drawing nearer to Adonai had deepened her attachment to Adam as well. She recalled one of their early lessons where Rapha had illustrated how a third point added above the two points of a line created a triangle. Glory saw their relationship with Adonai that way. Moving closer to their Maker also heightened intimacy with her intended and gave a new dimension of substance to their relationship. She recalled the feeling of falling asleep last night cradled in Adonai's arms with her fingers entwined in Adam's. He had pressed her palm to his lips, unashamed of moistening them with his tears.

Knowing it would make him smile, she chose one perfect scarlet bloom and secured it in her curls.

The metaphors rolled as Rapha continued his work on the crowns that symbolized the humans' destiny. When they were joined physically, their offspring would be the first fruits of Adonai's new order, a people to shine in His hand, lighting the darkness like stars on a moonless night.

"The sooner the better," Rapha mumbled, recalling the devastation outside these walls as he selected the centerpiece of Adam's crown—a large, flawless diamond. He held it in place as he wove golden strands around the circlet, tamping the metal to affix the gem. He would continue this process, tapping, stretching, and molding until the crown would be ablaze with flawless stones.

As he worked he considered the effort required to complete even one of the precious gems.

The largest of diamonds, the central diadem, had been with Rapha during his burial by Lucifer and his fellow traitors. With the last of his physical strength he had reached toward the glow, wresting it from solid rock, and cupped it to his breast even as he had felt his own being tucked into Adonai. When he had woken, the gem was still in his hand. He had broken away the remaining dullness and carefully polished the diamond, treasuring it as a promise of hope during his darkest hour. He could think of no more fitting treasure to grace the brow of the promised one who would restore creation to its Maker.

As for the gold, the intense heating and purifying process had seemed endless. But he was creating a treasure to last millennia, not a bauble; therefore he had punished the precious substance until purity alone remained.

His tiny hammer stopped mid-swing. The Holy One was speaking to his heart.

"Rapha. Do you see?"

Yes. Adam and Glory were the treasure. Earth had been swept clean, purified, in order to bring them forth. They were the diadem, purified by Adonai's loving hand.

An icy fear capsized his thoughts. *No!* He clapped his hands over his ears in a vain attempt to waylay the hideous train of thought, too harsh to bear. With a tremendous force of will he shoved down the growing dread and focused on one question, *"When?"*

He tried to convince himself that the pounding and purifying process was far off in the future, perhaps a trial that distant generations would have to endure in order to help renew their commitment to Adonai. But the unwelcome answer inserted into his soul was no comfort.

Sheep, water fowl, and a myriad supply of four and two-legged creatures gathered at the water's edge, tokens of a waking garden, as the girl poured water into a depression on the rock's surface and studied her reflection. She smoothed a stubborn curl behind one ear but, as if possessing a will of its own, it soon reasserted itself, poking out at an awkward angle. Finally, she repositioned the flower directly on that troublesome area and gave a satisfied nod. A brilliant blue and green bird she and Adam had dubbed "Strut" hopped up beside her, a bright yellow tuft waving above his inquisitive black eyes. She reached for its head, gently stroking the golden protrusion to make it lie flat. "I can fix that."

Glory giggled as he shook his head free and then… strutted… as if to say, "But the chicks love it!"

A snowy white lamb trotted forward, requesting its customary morning audience. She scooped it into her lap, nuzzling her face into its silky wool as it bleated with contentment. Of all the animals in the garden this one held a special place in her heart. It could not climb like the monkeys, or roar to shake the ground, or fly, or dazzle with any exceptional talent, but it would relax in her arms, not demanding food or belly rubs or even a romp, and gaze at her with trusting eyes, content simply to breathe in her presence.

Glory loved all the animals and enjoyed their chatter, rambunctious play, and antics, but this one was her special pet—so much so that Adam had decided she alone should determine its name. *Grace*. That was what she called the sweet friend who had no special talents to speak of but could soothe her mind with its quiet snuggles.

Bathed in sunshine with the lamb's squeezable warmth nestled in her arms, she thought again of the precious hours with her Maker when questions ceased, preparations for their destiny halted, and only that moment mattered. It was better than the joy of laughing, playing, eating, or learning all rolled into one. And last night, getting to share such closeness with Adonai *and* Adam had been the most beautiful experience of all. In fact, she would not have been surprised if she had been able to fly like the angels, since she could not imagine feeling any more "malleable" than the way her heart had melted.

What an amazing unity the three of them shared! Together with Adonai, they were to rule creation, bringing a new start and fresh hope to the whole world. But there was still so much to learn. They had only scratched the surface of the angels' knowledge and, although she and Adam were eager enough, Glory could not imagine how long it would take them to prepare for the task.

The lamb, Grace, broke her reverie with a calm bleat.

She looked down at the lamb and laughed, "It's easy enough for you. All you're concerned about is which patch of grass to chew next!"

As Grace held her gaze she saw something flicker in the innocent depths of its eyes, some knowledge or instinct that surpassed her own wisdom as if to say, *"We are together. What else matters?"*

A mournful whimper sounded from behind her and she turned to see a tiny monkey holding up a crushed front paw. Bright crimson drops fell to the grass at his feet. The girl stared in horror. She had seen blood, she had even experienced pain but she had never beheld terror.

"Come here, baby." She held out a hand but it backed away, eyes wide and wary. That was another first. She set aside the lamb, "What happened?" As she took a step closer the creature hissed at her, baring sharp teeth. The next moment it appeared penitent as it licked its abused limb. That did it. She *had* to try to help. When the monkey took off through the trees, she was hard pressed to keep it in sight.

Rapha had been so distracted by the alarming turn of his thoughts; he had relaxed his focus on Glory. He probed carefully, expecting to discover tranquility but was dismayed to encounter confusion. He wanted to assure himself her emotion was fleeting and harmless, but something about the subtlety and timing felt all too familiar. The sky was just as blue, the trees still waved in the breeze, but something. Was. Wrong. He bolted from his work, taking no notice of the clatter of precious gems across the hewn stones. This present unrest bore Lucifer's signature. As he raced toward Glory's bathing pool he summoned the angelic hosts. The response was sluggish. Something was hindering their communication. This was the moment, just as the sun peeked over the edge of the world, that signaled the changing of the guard. Fresh celestial forces were indeed arriving, so why did his summons not bring their ready response?

Rapha emerged from the arched shelter of the garden's workshop just as he heard it… or rather did not hear. The birds. Their songs had stopped. Then came one, harsh "skrawk!"

A buzzard? Here?

He crashed into the clearing where Adam still reclined under the flower-canopied bower of standing stones. "Has Glory returned?" Rapha tried to keep his voice steady but the boy must have read something in his demeanor.

"Why? What's going on?"

Without a word, Rapha turned to make his way toward the bathing pool. The urgency in his heart made him desire to fly but

Glory's trail would be easier to locate and follow on the ground. Even so Adam, still wiping sleep from his eyes, had to scramble to keep up with the angel's long stride.

They broke through the thick foliage surrounding the pool to a tranquil scene, but not her. There was something in the air, something besides the girl's bathing oils, something that brought horrific memories to mind—a faint but unmistakable metallic smell, a smell that settled on his tongue with the memories of swords coated with its slick stickiness—a smell accompanied by the scents of fear and cruelty. Rapha's concern escalated to panic.

Just then an angry roar erupted from the lioness at the water's edge as her mate shook his mane and charged. The two fell to the ground, claws and teeth bared. This was *not* a moment of passion. Adam ran toward the enraged pair to break up the fight but the lions turned on him, snarling and roaring. What had gotten into them? Rapha materialized between them with a flash of light and the startled pair ran away.

The smell was overpowering where the lions had been. Rapha looked down. There were drops of fresh blood on the grass at his feet. He knelt to pluck a crimson-stained blade and, with trembling fingers, held it up to a shaft of light. For Rapha, all sound ceased. The disturbed rhythm of nature and the anxious breathing of the young man at his side were outside his universe as he studied the bright red against green, delving deep into its molecular structure. With a rush he retreated from the tunnel of his sight with a sigh of relief. What the scent had hinted, his sight confirmed; this blood was not human.

Adam's questions came in a torrent. "What's going on? What is that? Blood?" Then the young man was reaching to grasp his shoulders, "Rapha! *Where is she*?"

"Come." The angel shook off Adam's hand and ran, chasing the mingled scent of fragrant oils, fresh blood, and fear.

Chapter Ten

Corruption

Time and again, just as Glory came close enough to reach for the injured animal, it would dart away. It seemed eager for her to follow, trotting on its hind legs but never running fast enough to get out of sight, and even making frequent stops to ensure she still followed. But the animal's fear was genuine. The only time she had beheld such panic was on Adam's face as he had plummeted head-over-heels during a botched dive.

Her concern for the monkey was so great Glory did not even realize when she entered a part of the garden she had never visited before. And when the monkey dropped out of sight, she did not hesitate but boldly pushed aside bushes to reveal a wide, overgrown, stone path. As the monkey's chatter echoed back, a glorious fragrance of flowers and spices—a scent that made her heart race and chills of excitement run through her body—assaulted her senses.

"What's going on?" Adam asked. "Is it Lucifer?"

"I'm not sure."

"Is she hurt?" The still developing young voice caught on a stifled sob.

With a wave of compassion, Rapha drew his attention from her trail. "I do not detect pain in her. It appears Glory is following an injured creature." The relief that flooded Adam's features smote the angel with guilt. He knew the girl's path led toward far worse than physical peril. Taking a deep breath, he voiced his fears. "The creature Glory follows, apparently a young monkey, is terrified. Great power is required to bring terror to this place. And only great evil would desire it."

The relief fled. "Go, go, go! Let's find her!" The boy shoved ahead.

"Wait! I am better equipped to follow her trail. You could destroy the signs of her passage."

Adam whipped around with an accusing glare, "It seems with an enemy such as this our teaching would have included such knowledge!"

A deep grief smote Rapha's heart as he recognized the trademark of Lucifer's handiwork. The discord hung between them like a stench as he said, "Come. We must hurry."

Glory had never seen anything so... old. Walls of stone—stones that bore a dark sheen as if countless hands had stroked them—rose on either side and formed a lofty, vine-coated arc that was four, maybe five times higher than she could reach. She stumbled in the dim light and put out a palm to keep from falling. A shock of raw power almost threw her to the ground. Glory recalled the feeling of placing her hand in Adonai's, sensing a controlled might that was far beyond her comprehension. That power had been dazzling, stupefying, and overwhelming yet… kind. The stones in this ancient place spoke of a power with no such safeguards. It was raw, dangerous—and thrilling, like the beast that daily beat against its stone prison in their lake.

The monkey's voice echoed toward her, rising to a shriek. As Glory forged ahead a breath-like wind brushed her cheek and lifted the crimson flower from her hair. She did not even notice as it floated to the ground.

Rapha was at a dead end. Glory's scent disappeared into thin air at the edge of a precipice. Unless she had sprouted wings, his angelic senses were fooling him. Again and again their efforts had been slowed by her elusive trail that had led over solid rock and through shallow streams.

This was taking too long! Hopelessness gripped his heart as he realized his connection to Glory's thoughts had been cut. She must be deep in Lucifer's web. Rapha was failing in every way. He had relaxed his guard and now, when the real test came, he could not even follow a trail that was quickly growing cold.

"What now?" Adam's voice broke through Rapha's mental flogging.

How could he admit he hadn't a clue?

The enticing scent was growing stronger. Glory felt her senses relaxing, growing fuzzy and warm and... muddled. Why was she here? Oh yes! There was that monkey... the familiar little face peeked out from the next corner where sparkling, colorful light glimmered against another massive arched entryway. She had to get a closer look.

Rapha paced at the ravine's edge, studying the air where Glory's slight scent lingered as if willing it to divulge its secrets. It was so hard to focus his thoughts. The other angelic forces were still not responding to his summons. When he turned his thoughts to them he encountered a hodgepodge of distress. It would seem the young woman's trail was not the only challenge in the garden this morning.

But another fact disturbed him even more. When he called to Adonai, he encountered silence. Was his guilt shutting off communication, or was his Master silent for a purpose?

As Glory rounded the corner, the dazzling lights softened to a caressing glow and she gazed around at the enormous courtyard that opened to the sky… and gasped. The feast of sights, sounds, smells, and delicious sensations overflowed her senses. The air caressed her skin as a musky, intoxicating scent compelled her forward, awakening her appetite and curiosity. Glory was excited and yet she wanted to shut her eyes and inhale the bliss. But her eyes were wide with wonder and her mouth gaped as she beheld immense birds with glorious plumage that strutted with other majestic animals she had never beheld, in a vibrant garden of gigantic flowers and fruits—all three and four times the size of those in the rest of the garden. Most of the animals were a combination of those she recognized, but some had a surprising feature or ability, such as the horse with a sharp horn protruding out of the center of its head or another with massive wings tucked along its body. There were others that sported wings. A monkey swooped, cackling, through the air while an enormous feathered creature as *large* as a horse yet possessing beak and claws, regarded her with unblinking eyes from a high ledge beside a mighty waterfall rushing over multi-hued stones that appeared to glow from within.

Glory blinked and stared. In the deep pool below, large forms flitted among glimmering rocks and submerged flora. Suddenly she realized that wide, tilted eyes were regarding her from—was that a *human* face?

She stepped closer, peering through the sparkling water, mesmerized by the timid creature who cowered behind a spray of underwater foliage as if it too could not believe its eyes. Suddenly the creature shook its head and waved an arm as if shooing her away, in the process exposing the upper portion of its body—the smooth skin and breasts of a human female. Glory gasped and stumbled to her knees in shock, splashing the water's surface and startling the creature that flashed out of sight, displaying the bottom half of its body—the grey, sleek tail of a large fish. With a swirl of shimmering hair, the creature flitted away through swaying seaweed and out of sight.

Rapha put a hand on a large tree trunk, bent his head to its bark and spoke in a quiet voice.

"Are you talking to the tree? Can it tell you what happened?"

With a sigh the angel pushed. Slowly the tree bent, giving way with surprising ease. Loud pops and groans echoed through the forest until, seemingly in slow motion, it fell with a mighty crash, massive roots exposed, forming a bridge across the chasm.

"Why did you do that? There's no way she's over there unless she flew."

Without a word, Rapha walked across, sidestepping and swinging around large branches. Adam followed, casting wary glances toward the jagged rocks far below. "Are you sure about this?"

Rapha hopped off the trunk and scanned the ground. The scent was once again unmistakable. There it was. A bright patch of blood and several broken branches on a flowering bush showed evidence of a crash landing while, in the intertwining branches over their heads, he spied a thick vine.

The truth was evident to Adam as well. The creature had crossed on the thin treetop branches and Glory had followed, swinging over on an accommodating vine—a vine that just happened to be in the perfect place and of the perfect length and thickness. What were the odds?

Yes indeed, this plot was well planned, and by someone who knew Glory's nature, that her daring was outweighed only by her compassion.

With the trail clear once again, Rapha began to run.

"But why should the tree suffer? You could have just flown us across."

"If there is need for escape, the path will now be prepared."

"Escape?" *Glory* was all that mattered.

She felt bereft at the mysterious creature's disappearance. Glory would dearly have enjoyed another female to talk to… *if* it could talk.

All at once the aroma grew even stronger and she sighed, drinking in its richness as a flurry of bright, fluttering… *somethings…* rose around her like a colorful, living veil. She gasped with delight and spun in an attempt to study every glittering wing. She glimpsed tiny faces… and legs… and arms among the flurry and sparkle.

"I have never seen anything more beautiful." A melodic voice settled around her like a caress.

She knew even before she looked. The one who had spoken was the will behind all the loveliness. Glory turned toward the center of the open expanse where an enormous tree towered up, higher than the gigantic walls of the courtyard. As she watched, draping vines that hung from the tree parted, revealing what appeared to be a blazing star. Its blinding brightness caused Glory to bring up a hand to shield her eyes.

"My apologies, dear one," the melodious voice spoke again. *"Please, take what I give you."*

Something flew toward her from the midst of the brightness—a winged fire that came to hover over her head. Once more Glory had the impression of a face among the wings and luminous eyes that peered back at her, mirroring her solemn fascination. As it swayed, dazzling her eyes, Glory's mouth gaped open in wonder and a drop of flame fell on her tongue. Instead of burning, its sweetness flooded into her mouth and spread throughout her body until her entire being pulsed with its warmth. The brightness lost no intensity but her eyes changed, absorbing and reflecting the light in a new way. When she once more looked toward the brightness at the base of the tree she found herself gazing straight into the prismatic eyes of a being so marvelous Glory gasped with delight.

It was a woman with flowing, golden hair, her transparent garment clinging to her ample bosom and trailing onto the blossom-strewn grass. Glory felt lightheaded and her knees buckled as the woman's brilliance came into focus like the glimmer of a perfect sun peeking over the world's rim to set morning mists aflame.

The power of speech left her. This being, now at the center of undulating lights of every hue known to nature—and a few *un*known—smiled. In that smile Glory saw the promise of fulfillment of her every dream. She had not realized she was unfulfilled before, but that would now be remedied as well; she could learn to desire what she truly deserved.

As Glory watched, she felt her ambitions melt and transform. She could think of nothing more glorious than to be just like… her. This glowing being was much more than female; this was the epitome of feminine aspiration, the ultimate wisdom and beauty complete with luscious curves, flowing, lustrous hair, and… more. Here was a being who would make a devoted slave of all who beheld her and receive nothing but admiration and gratitude in return. Until Glory beheld this marvelous being, she had had no idea what the word "woman" meant. This was the ultimate female—a goddess for the ages.

A chatter at her feet reminded Glory of the reason she had entered here.

"Yes, my pet. Come," the gorgeous being reached one graceful, tapered hand toward the monkey who ventured toward her, keeping its face averted as if the sight of her hurt him. A few paces from the raised, curtained platform where the woman lounged, the monkey began to hover above the ground. Its terrified shriek was silenced with a wave of her hand and a glazed expression replaced the terror in its eyes. It floated to the woman's outstretched hand and she cupped it to her bosom with endearing tones before placing a kiss on its forehead. Immediately, the mangled paw straightened and, to Glory's wondering eyes, all traces of the wound disappeared.

"There now little friend, be relieved of your pain." With another wave, the monkey floated back to the ground. Its confusion vanished when it realized the source of its pain was gone, and it chattered and scampered about on all fours. Then the woman reached toward a feast-laden table Glory had previously overlooked. The woman tossed a tidbit to the monkey who grabbed the treat and ran.

Tinkling laughter filled the air and echoed back from the ancient walls, *"Ah, there is gratitude for you. He will be back when he hungers once again."*

Then those eyes were once more turned her way, *"And what is your desire, my pet?"*

The only coherent thought in Glory's mind was, *"I will be happy to just look at you,"* but the woman's gaze probed deeper.

"Ah! The young man. Of course." She leaned forward, sending forth another wave of intoxicating perfume. *"I could teach you how to fascinate your Adam for all eternity!"*

Glory's eyes widened and her face grew hot as shocking images of being with Adam flooded her mind. Oh my! This was territory they had never covered with Rapha.

The voluptuous woman settled back into her silken cushions with a satisfied smile.

As Rapha followed Glory's trail through trees and onto a stone pathway overrun with cascading vines, he carried on a muttered, one-sided conversation with his Maker. "No, Adonai! It is too soon. She is not ready!"

But could one ever be ready to face creation's great deceiver? Lucifer was so adept at spinning beauty around his vile ambitions that many of the wisest of all creation had been seduced into serving him. What chance did the girl truly have?

The wave of darkness that enveloped him with that thought brought his swift-moving feet to an abrupt standstill so that Adam, breathlessly keeping pace with the angel's long stride, bounced off Rapha's broad back and landed in a surprised heap.

"What is it?" Adam hopped up to look where Rapha stared.

Despair, guilt and hopelessness were an impenetrable wall. Every defeat, every horror of his dealings with the fallen angel replayed in his mind with a new, hideous insistence. *"As it was before, it shall be again. And* this time *your heart will never recover."*

An image flashed into his mind. Adam and Glory cowered in fear, their eyes feral, their bodies bloodied and mud-spattered. A cry of pain escaped his lips.

Adam's hand shook his shoulder. "Rapha! Move! She is in danger."

But Rapha mumbled. "He will wrap himself in her deepest desires." His hands trembled and he gripped his head as if he could crush the horrors from his mind. "He will make her most noble ambitions her greatest weakness. He will take your love for each other and use it to torture…."

"There is no time for this! Go!" Adam gave Rapha a hard shove.

The boy's action shook away despair's hold. As Rapha stumbled forward he scanned their surroundings. Yes. There, high in the rocks, three malevolent pairs of eyes regarded them. He had been so intent upon pursuit he had stumbled into their sinister ambush.

Suddenly a coconut smacked the largest enemy directly on his nose and Adam, another coconut already in his hand, shouted in a commanding voice, *"Be gone! All creation spews you from this place!"*

And it happened just as he said. A fierce wind rose around them, the towering trees bent and grasped the fallen celestial beings, and leaves were stuffed in their mouths preventing a counter command as regal birds descended to grasp them in huge talons and remove them from the garden.

Rapha had to stare at the kingly young man beside him. The boy had grown in stature. Power hummed around him as he stood, eyes ablaze, hair flying about his body like a majestic robe. The holiness of Adonai shone, encased in the earthly body but burning fiercely through every pore and rising from the earth beneath their feet, eager to obey the master's voice. Joy and hope coursed through the angel's frame. Ah yes! Lucifer was not going to like this one bit.

The two continued on the ancient path as if their feet had sprouted wings.

Chapter Eleven
The Fallen Angel

Glory's voice trembled as she asked, "Who are you?"

"Who do you want me to be?" The woman's purr was soft, hypnotizing. *"There is too much of me to be known by only one name. Do you wish to call me Melkor or Athena? Perhaps you would prefer Lilith? Or"*—the woman leaned forward conspiratorially—*"how fun it would be for you to give me a new name, a secret shared only between us."*

"Lilith is beautiful," the girl said, meaning both the name and the person before her.

"So, I will be Lilith and... what shall we call you, dear one?"

"Adam has named me 'Glory' but now that I have seen you, I no longer think I deserve that name."

"My dear, it is a most fitting title, for that is exactly what you are."

The compliment brought a flush of pink to the young woman's cheek.

"And that is what I will call you, my Glory, my queen. Long have I looked for your coming." The one called Lilith knelt.

The girl gaped in wonder. Queen? This glorious creature would serve *her*? "Please. Get up. There is no need for that."

"Oh, my Glory, do you not know? You and the young man are Adonai's chosen to rule the earth."

"Well, yes. We know. But surely it is not necessary for you to bow."

The woman's charming laugh showered down around her with another kiss of a heavenly scent. *"How sweet!"* The woman stood and the girl's eyes widened. Through the shimmering, multi-hued mist that shrouded her form, the woman's voluptuous body was evident in tantalizing glimpses of rounded breasts and curves that defied imagination.

The young woman could not help but stare. Yes! She needed this captivating power. Hardly realizing it, she took a step closer.

"Please reveal Glory's path," Adam stated calmly. The dense, ivy-strewn branches drew back and he and Rapha stepped through unhindered. Rapha marveled at the boy's newfound confidence, amazed at how easily he had stepped into his authority without a shred of selfishness or pride. Once again, Adonai's wisdom prevailed. The boy was becoming a man due to his love for another.

But when the monstrous stone monument to Lucifer's pride came into view, Adam's faith quailed. Lifting his eyes to graceful arches and enormous columns he stopped. "What is this place?"

"Lucifer's first order of business on earth was to build a home worthy of his… magnificence. This is all that remains… above ground. In former days, his dwelling spread the length and breadth of this land."

"Why would Adonai build our home so close?"

A bitter laugh escaped Rapha's lips, "Your coming was prophesied long before. It is always Lucifer's way to build obstacles to block Adonai's plan. This land was chosen by the Most High; therefore Lucifer rushed to establish *his* kingdom first."

Rapha watched as the terrible truth flooded Adam's mind.

Adam and Glory were Adonai's chosen.

Their offspring were to bring all creation back into harmony.

Their joining was planned for this very day; therefore Lucifer would try to....

Adam's gaze locked with Rapha's.

Without another word, Adam sprang from the trees and started sprinting.

The magnetic pull grew stronger with every inch she advanced toward this one called Lilith. Surely her beauty was so devastating Glory would be consumed by its power. Power. It throbbed over, under, around, and through her. Unlike Adonai's and even Rapha's power, this was displayed in mind-numbing proportions. With the thought of Adonai her mind returned to those amazing hours spent with Him during the night. He was the creator of all things yet He was humble enough to hold the humans while they wept. It was almost comical to imagine this amazing creature wiping another's tears.

Glory was unaware she was standing still until the woman said with another melodic laugh, *"Come, my dear. There is so much to learn."*

When the girl looked back into those eyes she saw—or did she imagine—a hint of impatience. Lilith's arm was stretched toward her, the long, graceful fingertips mere inches from her own, while the incredible eyes were fixed on her hand. Glory snatched her hand away and tucked it behind her back, at that moment, unsure why. A bolt of pain shot through her arm as if the attraction were a living thing that hated being denied. Her eyes opened wide in surprise and, for an instant, Lilith's image flickered like a reflection on waters stirred by a passing breeze. Emboldened by pain, Glory searched the woman's visage. Again, the feminine loveliness seemed to fluctuate.

"Do you know Lucifer?"

A slow smile spread across Lilith's beautiful face. *"So bright! What a jewel you would be to any crown!"* Once more the one called Lilith laughed and a shower of brilliant petals floated from above, settling on the girl's hair and shoulders and forming a bright carpet around her. Through the falling blooms, the girl watched the woman turn away, still laughing. As the floral shower continued, the petals washed away the femininity from Lilith's form. In the place of curves, glimmering jewels winking from various body parts and flowing hair, a new landscape emerged—raw, virile, decidedly masculine.

It was the ultimate torture. Rapha could once again sense the girl's emotions and physical sensations, but his way was blocked. On either side of the wide path, fierce stone creatures marked the entrance to Lucifer's domain. To add insult, a golden parchment appeared before his eyes and hovered, an ancient script aflame, reiterating the agreement between Lucifer and Adonai. "Adam!" Rapha shouted to the boy who turned with a *What now?* expression. "It is forbidden for me to enter!"

Adam retraced his steps and studied the flame-inscribed scroll but was unable to decipher the language. "What does it say?"

"In its simplest terms, Lucifer cannot have access to the humans elsewhere and Adonai's forces may not enter."

With a confident shrug, Adam pointed at the hovering document and declared in a commanding voice. “I decree this agreement null. Adonai’s forces may enter!”

A shudder ran through the ground as a sulphur-laced wind rushed from all directions to converge in a whirling gale around man and angel. Cackling laughter spun around them and the fiery scroll vanished with a flash.

“There!” Adam declared and stretched a decisive hand toward Rapha.

“I cannot. If I break the decree, the protection of the garden’s walls will no longer repel Lucifer’s forces.” Rapha did not add that those forces would have free reign soon enough if the young woman disobeyed the law given to her and Adam—that they must not partake of Lucifer’s poison, his fruit of corruption.

“Rapha! Please! I will see to the rest of the garden when she is safe.”

“No. If we love Adonai, we obey Him.”

“But Adonai is gracious. If we break His decree, He will forgive.”

“Yes, but the consequences cannot be avoided. His laws are for our good even when we do not yet understand His….”

“I *understand* there is no time for argument. Come!” Adam exerted his newly discovered authority and, with a shock, the angel felt compelled to obey. With an angry mental shove Rapha lashed back, knocking Adam to the ground.

Sensing the gravity of this lesson, Rapha prayed the young man would heed his words. “If we disobey, we serve evil’s purpose. If Lucifer finds the issue that will bring disobedience, he will use it again and again, forging a chain to enslave.”

“I cannot leave her here!”

“Then you must go on alone.”

To Rapha, this was a momentous circumstance. He sensed a parting of ways, painful but inescapable. Adam was now a man, ready to risk himself for his beloved and take on the responsibilities of a king.

Realizing his angelic friend would not budge, Adam stepped back through the gate marking Lucifer's domain and grasped Rapha's broad shoulders.

Rapha bowed until celestial and human forehead touched, and said, "As lies within my power, I speak the eternal wisdom of Adonai upon you. May your body and spirit remain secure in Him until next we meet."

With a reassuring squeeze to his friend's arms, Adam then turned to sprint toward the monstrous arched entrance. The sound of his footsteps reverberating from the surrounding walls filled Rapha's heart with grief.

Not only had her host's appearance changed, their surroundings too had transformed. In place of flowering bowers and sumptuous furnishings, the ancient tree's trailing vines were heavy with glowing fruit and its low-hanging boughs now released a musky scent. But all this was practically unnoticed due to the amazing creature who commanded her attention. Nothing could have prepared her for the devastation of that sight. Every element of his appearance promised fulfillment of her wildest dreams and anticipation of desires as yet undiscovered.

Glory's eyes were wide, her body poised to run, "You… *are* Lucifer."

He opened his hands toward her. *"Please forgive me. I merely wanted to avoid startling you. I thought a feminine form would be less… frightening."*

"I am not frightened," Glory declared, though her voice quavered.

"As befits a queen," he inclined his head approvingly, turned toward the feast displayed beside him, selected two golden goblets, and filled them with a dark, red liquid.

She could not help staring at his magnificent body, rippling with power and grace. Like the feminine image, his masculinity was evident through provocative, rainbow mists. Her mind once more beheld the visions that had caused her pulse to race and her cheek to flame—the visions of her and Adam melting into one flesh. Only this time, while her image remained, Adam's had been replaced... by this angel before her.

"Please, refresh yourself." He held the goblet toward her but she shook her head, knowing her trembling body would find the hand-to-mouth movement impossible.

"You do not trust what I would give you?"

Again Glory shook her head, her hands clasped behind her back even while they longed to touch him. Not only was he beautiful, he also aroused her curiosity. He was different from the other angels who presented themselves in a form very similar to humans. His skin appeared almost molten, glowing and fluid—yet somehow solid. Would his skin (if she could call it that) burn her? Would it feel like thick water, or smooth and hot like the crowns when they had passed from Rapha's hands? Or would it be a new, unspeakable sensation?

He was talking again. It was difficult to understand his words because his voice affected her so, both soothing and dangerous. He connected to something much deeper than auditory response—as if his speech probed every nook of her existence and molded into the perfect shape to fulfill her. How she wanted to drown in the pleasure! But no. She had been warned about... something.

"You are wise to be cautious, dear Glory. The warnings of a trusted counselor should not be cast aside lightly. You have a loyal soul. That is good."

When his iridescent eyes turned to regard her with admiration, intense heat rose from her toes. How she longed to touch him. But another desire was even stronger.

How she longed for *him* to touch *her*.

The feeling shocked her pristine body so she clapped her hands over her ears and shut her eyes tight, seeking respite from his overwhelming presence. Even then Lucifer's image was burned on her eyelids, cast in dark relief but breathtaking nonetheless, and his scent still muddled her thoughts.

"Run!" Rapha commanded the girl with all the force of his will though he felt his thoughts bounce back from a mighty barrier. *"RUN!"* he shouted his plea to the wind, hoping sound could break through where the spirit had failed.

An icy blast swirled around Glory's feet that, seemingly of their own accord, started to move away although every facet of her being rebelled.

If only she had not tripped over something at that very moment. If only she had kept her eyes shut and her hands over her ears, even if it meant crashing to the ground and rolling in a blind, broken heap. But Glory's hands and eyes betrayed her, reaching out to break her fall and opening to see what blocked her path.

It was long and firm, colorful and glowing, round like an enormous tree root but… then it slithered, sliding through the grass at her feet.

Rapha's hopes soared when he sensed her desire turn to fright. Yes. Glory was resisting. She was fleeing. She was… *fascinated*. No! What new evil was this?

"Run!" He commanded again but the cry was caught and shoved down his throat by a hate-filled deluge that roiled from the aperture before him.

Chapter Twelve

A Choice

Adam's efforts were thwarted at every turn. Tall tunnels of stone, lit by sunlight that poured down from square holes set high in the walls, were suddenly plunged into darkness; then when he thought he had discovered another path—some opening that beckoned with better light or perhaps a long line of stones set one on top of the other like a chiseled mountainside—the new path would lead to a solid stone wall or even to a narrow, ascending series of carved stones that would bring him to yet another blocked passage. Many times his heart would leap with hope and he would run toward an opening only to find the sight vanished when he drew near and came upon yet another solid barrier.

When he once again smacked into solid stone where an opening had been seconds before, he beat his fists on the unyielding wall and commanded, *"Open and show me the way to Glory!"* The rocks moaned with a sound of pain and anger and—he could not believe his eyes—the walls around him expanded as if taking a deep breath in hopes of crushing him! An accompanying rage stole the air from his lungs and beat upon his senses while a dark malice pressed down, driving him to the hard floor.

The thing was thicker than Glory's waist as it glided, a shifting, shining iridescence, like a wide stream of reflective water that retained its shape outside its banks in order to curve around her. She followed an array of dappled, luminous golds, greens, pinks, purples, and patches where the colors seemed to bend before her eyes—from deep blue to black or snowy white transforming to bronze. It was, simply, a captivating, astonishing entity. But she had not yet learned the meaning of astonishment. Her eyes traced the unbelievable length of this mysterious… something… until it widened and rose into the air. Were those wings intertwined in the high branches of the tree? Higher and higher the incredible sight drew her gaze until, finally, there they were, shining with an inner fire and staring, unblinking, back at her—eyes—frightening, beautiful, and brimming with intelligence.

Then, when she felt her heart would burst, it spoke.

"She fears because she does not understand," it said in a low, soothing voice. Then it stepped away from the tree—on strong, well-formed legs.

When Glory fell backwards in astonishment, it reached for her, its wings unfolding above like a diaphanous canopy.

No longer needing the guise of a humble tutor, Rapha's body glowed like a powerful flame and he rose into the air, a beacon to his forces. The bright beings appeared around him, several bearing the marks of heavy combat. Their tidings were grim. Enemy forces surrounded the garden's borders on all sides, waiting. Unfortunately, Rapha knew exactly what they were waiting for.

When he felt he was drawing his last breath, Adam gasped, "Please, Adonai! Help me!"

The pressure immediately lifted, his dark surroundings melted away, and he blinked in the warm, green light of a pleasant glade. At its center, the trunk of a huge, smooth tree rose up, branching into myriad limbs that climbed high to flow in every direction, bursting into clusters of bright leaves and flowering smaller branches, each bending toward the ground, heavy with fruit. A movement at the foot of the tree drew his attention where he saw a man digging in the soil while a snowy white lamb dozed beside him.

A surge of frustration overtook Adam. This place was lovely and peaceful and already its wholesome fragrance had renewed his strength, but *why had Adonai not taken him to Glory?*

He ran toward the man who remained, calmly digging in the dirt. "Please," Adam shouted, "You must help me."

The man turned to him and Adam recognized the Holy One who had instructed him through the night. Rather than answer, the man motioned for him to sit down.

"But there is no time! Even now she could be…" Adam's protests died on his lips. The man was looking at him. In those eyes Adam saw empathy, peace, joy, compassion, boundless love, unfathomable pain, and even… hope. In fact, in that momentary connection, Adam felt he could look in those eyes and find everything he would ever need, never again requiring rest, food, drink, or instruction. He knew he was gazing upon the source of all things.

"Come and drink," the man said, offering the familiar cup to Adam.

"Please," Adam said, "come with me. We have to save her."

The man's gaze was sad. **"I am unable to break the agreement."**

"I thought you had power over heaven and earth. What good are you if she remains in danger?" Adam shoved the cup away causing some of the liquid to splash to the ground. "Are you as *impotent* against him as Rapha?"

In an instant, Adam had to shield his face and throw himself to the ground. The man's appearance was blindingly bright but the eyes were still clear, piercing into Adam's innermost being. As if a veil had hidden them, a vast host of bright, celestial beings stretched in every direction, a multitude of witnesses to this moment. Suddenly, the fate of one man and woman seemed insignificant in the presence of such glory. Despair seized his soul and Adam bowed his head, trembling at the Holy One's feet.

A gentle hand touched his shoulder. Adam opened tear-filled eyes to find the brilliant light was gone. The man lifted Adam's chin and, with the sleeve of his garment, wiped away the dirt and tears. No sooner was the robe blemished with Adam's filth than it was once again snow white.

"Understand, son of earth, if I break the laws that knit all creation, I become like the fallen one, putting creation under his power."

"But what of Glory?" Adam's voice was a tortured whisper, "I care more for her than all creation combined."

"That is both your strength and your weakness. The evil one knows this."

"Please show me the way to her. Time is passing."

"This moment is enough."

"Enough for what? You speak in riddles when Glory is in danger!"

"Her greatest danger lies in your decision."

"There is no decision. I have to help her any way I can!"

"How you choose to do this affects all that is and will be."

Adam dropped his head into his hands, "How I wish that weight could pass from me. The reward of her smile every day would be enough."

"There was a time Adonai's favor was enough."

That stung, reminding him Glory existed due to Adonai's love. "But she is more precious to me than my own body."

"More precious than the One who created her?"

Guilt assailed him. Now that the issue was laid bare, he could not look in the Holy One's eyes. "She is my flesh and bone," Adam whispered to the earth from which he was formed.

"Adonai knew the danger when He gave such a precious gift, but His nature is to give."

The Holy One's voice was full of compassion, giving Adam the courage to look up. "Please. I must go to her."

"But I AM what she needs. Hear my words, trust me, and you will have power over evil."

Glory was frozen with horror as an arm—so like those of tiny lizards but one hundred times the size—came near. Was it going to crush her? Pick her up like a ripe fruit and eat her? Even in that terrifying moment, she could not help but admire the intricate markings around its eyes and triangular nose as well as its luminous skin that glowed from within like a pulsing, flawless jewel. It was a reptile, like those she saw every day in the garden, but transformed into a superior being that stood before her with majestic grace. It paused before her wide eyes, its huge hand still outstretched… to assist her? As if she was about to plunge into icy waters, she gulped and reached for the finger that was as large as her forearm.

The hand looked damp due to its sheen, but it was surprisingly dry, cool, and smooth. Glory stared at that hand and gave it a quick squeeze, as if to prove she was not dreaming, before releasing it in haste with a mumbled apology as soon as she scrambled to her feet. She wanted to ask so many questions as her eyes raced to take in the creature's entire length, but all Glory accomplished was another gasp.

It, too, studied her, sweeping its unblinking gaze the length of Glory's body and returning to her eyes as if measuring her intelligence. Finally it said, "*This* is the new order?" in a voice disarmingly refined and most assuredly feminine.

Was she weighed in the balance and found wanting? Glory had no time to decide before Lucifer's voice once again flowed over and through her.

"Yes. This is Adonai's most glorious creation. 'Glory' is an appropriate name, wouldn't you agree?"

"A definite improvement." The amazing being smiled—at least she thought it did—the expression seemed to soften before a forked tongue flicked her way.

"Glory, allow me to introduce Ra-el, Empress of this humble domain."

The amazing creature gave a subtle nod of acknowledgement.

"You, my dear, have glorious possibilities before you." Ra-el spoke with exaggerated sibilance. Each word was melodic and lilting, their gentle beauty soothing Glory's pounding heart even as the unblinking gaze held her spellbound.

The young woman simply nodded.

"'What?' you may ask, 'could be more glorious than being queen of the world?'" Ra-el drew herself up to her full height, displaying the shimmering, muscular expanse of her underbelly, and spreading the membranous wings. "Yes, I am beautiful to behold. But consider; if Lucifer had remained obedient to the Maker's plan, my years would have been spent shuffling through the dust, unable to speak or reason." Again the beautiful eyes with the long, narrow pupils sought hers. "If not for Lucifer, that is where I would be to this day."

Glory attempted to process what she was hearing; the words were so beautiful it took intense effort to decipher their meaning. Was Ra-el saying Lucifer was helpful and Adonai was stingy?

"No! Adonai has never shown anything but love!" The words that burst from Glory's lips sounded coarse in comparison.

The two glorious beings shared a pitying look. Once again, Lucifer spoke. *"You see only what He wants you to see. Why do you think you dwell within walls? Adonai would say they are for your protection, when their purpose is to keep you blind."*

"That is not true," Glory's mind was grasping for reason. "We receive constant instruction. Our tutor tells us about life outside the walls," again she moved toward the exit.

"Ah! Rapha. Your trusted tutor. I am sure he would want to give his version of history—leaving out the part where he shed innocent blood."

The shock of that statement froze her.

Lucifer gave a dismissive gesture with his hand. *"Ask him yourself. He will not deny it."*

Glory stood, wounded and confused. If what she was hearing was true, even a bit true, whom could she trust?

Lucifer, as if reading her thoughts, continued, *"I can understand why you would not trust me, 'Lucifer! His very voice is evil!'"* He echoed Rapha's serious tones perfectly. *"But what if he keeps you from me so you will remain content in your cage?"*

She winced and shut her eyes, wanting to hide from the cruel statement even as it struck a discordant note of truth. Thus Glory missed her host's look of triumph.

As Rapha sensed Glory's mounting confusion and vulnerability, an inferno of rage mounted within him. Visions of storming the stronghold assaulted his mind again and again. He had never felt so strong in protective love for another and yet so horribly exposed. Glory and Adam had become his own heart beating outside his body. He would gladly give up his place beside Adonai if only they could be spared the devastation Lucifer desired.

He longed with every fiber of his being to give in to the power of his emotions. He was capable of rending the stones of that fortress with his thoughts. Wasn't this the appropriate time to utilize that might? But the memory of the last time he had succumbed to rage smote him. That would be exactly what Lucifer expected—and most likely what he *desired.*

With a silent command Rapha's eyes swept his surroundings and clusters of opposing celestial beings became visible, perched high on the towers, watching from the trees like eager vultures. Yes, they were hoping for a frontal assault. That was what they understood.

Another sharp pain pierced his heart as he felt the bond of the girl's trust in him begin to crumble. "No, Adonai. Please, no." He whispered as he knelt, desperate to hear and obey his Maker's will.

A comforting hand was on his shoulder. He looked up to discover the One who had restored him on that horrible day when a flash of his angelic power had resulted in death and devastation. Large tears ran down the Holy One's face. At His appearance, the rogue celestial beings took flight.

"Please, refresh yourself." Her host extended an array of monstrously large fruits but the girl declined, her heart too much in turmoil to be tempted. *"What?"* He laughed disarmingly.

"Will the grapes wrap their vines around you and pull you down to darkness? Will the apples bite back? Ah! Look here. This cluster is angry for having been plucked!"

She responded with a shy smile. When Lucifer smiled back, her knees once again felt unable to support her and she looked away, an intense heat flushing her cheeks.

Glory could feel his eyes searching her. *"I do not want to frighten you."* His voice was soft and low, a caress that made her lean forward to savor every word. *"I know you believe I am a monster."*

She looked up to negate that statement and the force of his presence made the words lodge in her throat. He was so beautiful and his eyes… oh! His eyes stroked her soul, convincing her no one ever had or ever could understand, as he alone understood, what an amazing creature she was. She could not look away. Possibly, she was not even breathing. All that mattered was the connection between them. That would be her sustenance.

"Give me your hand." He held his out to her and she looked at it. His hand was the most exquisite, desirable thing she had ever seen. The skin appeared golden and silky, yet firm and—she discovered she was jealous of that skin because it clothed the perfect hills and valleys that traveled up his arms to his muscular shoulders and across his chest and down to—she gasped. Her eyes had followed her mind with a will of their own. Once more she felt heat rush to her face.

She wanted to look anywhere else but he filled her entire vision and inserted a thought directly to her mind. *"Take my hand and* everything *else is yours."*

"I cannot!" she shrieked and the rest of her body rebelled against the words. "Adam!" Her mouth spoke again though she could hardly recall the owner of that name. "Adam said… I mustn't." The words were painful to pronounce.

Lucifer turned away to hide his triumphant smile. So the man had tried to warn her about him? Such efforts were futile. Very soon the war would be won. It was all too easy.

And you, Rapha? In his mind he taunted the faithful angel whose presence hung about Glory like an evaporating morning mist. *Your efforts are just as foolish. She is a ripe fruit longing to be plucked, and you are powerless to stop me.*

How he wanted to laugh and dance! He was drunk on the power of pain from a threefold source: the man's fear and helplessness, Rapha's impotence, and, the most satisfying of all, the grief of Adonai! If just being close to his victory brought such satisfaction, surely he would explode when…. He breathed in her desire. It emanated from her, intoxicating and satisfying. He would teach her. He would mold her to his hand. He would open her eyes to wonders she could never imagine. He would delve deep into her soul and draw out every treasure Adonai had buried there. With every discovery, every exquisite pleasure, he would possess her more and more completely. Then the *real* fun would begin.

Do you hear me, Adonai? His hatred flung the thought toward his Maker. *I will savor her torment because, with every pain, every betrayal, every breath of despair, every time she cries out begging for death, You will* feel *it."*

He glanced toward the radiant, pure young woman. How he was going to enjoy devouring her. And this time he would draw forth sons worthy of him, the perfect army to overthrow Adonai's dominion!

He looked toward Ra-el, the towering queen of the past age. If *that* could be manipulated from Adonai's original creation, he could not wait to see the heights that would be attained through humans!

Ra-el flinched and Lucifer reveled in her jealousy. *No matter.* He aimed the hateful thought her way, *your usefulness has passed.* He directed another lust-filled wave toward the girl, whose eyes glazed as her young body trembled. *You have been replaced.*

But, he had one more task for his former queen. Ra-el's powerful will ground against his and her eyes narrowed to slits—she had always been a formidable delight! But with one flick of his thoughts he forced her compliance, and through clenched jaws, Ra-el spoke.

"Woman, the delights in store for you are beyond compare. You were told you would die if you touched Lucifer, but I tell you, you will surely not die but instead will gain understanding. I should know. I would be nothing without him." The hateful glare from the creature would have slain a lesser being, but it only served to heighten Lucifer's ecstasy.

With another casual toss of Lucifer's thoughts, Ra-el's wings fell once, and she began to rise, her malice boiling in the cauldron of her heart into a poisonous bile. How she longed to strike at him! His delight soared as she rose and flew toward the high wall. The combination of the girl's desire and the ancient one's hatred formed a dizzying elixir. All that intensity was aimed *toward him*. Good or bad, as long as he was the focus of their idolatry, he had achieved his goal.

Glory's eyes were closed as she wandered in a fantastic dream. Lucifer, like a vapor on the wind, appeared behind her. She was his for the taking! His desires were within his grasp! Just one last obstacle to overcome.

"Look at yourself. Open your eyes to what I see in you," Lucifer whispered.

The girl sighed with delight at the pleasure of his voice and her eyes were quick to do his bidding. Suspended in the air before her was a sparkling vision of herself, robed and crowned, as all creation groveled at her feet, captivated by her wisdom and beauty. Lucifer stood beside this glorious creature, devouring her with his eyes. But something was missing.

"Adonai," the girl whispered.

"Adonai has hidden the truth from you." Lucifer's hand was suspended above her head, manipulating her thoughts like puppet strings. *"Where does He dwell when He is not with you? Where do your faithful teachers go every day? Have they ever offered to take you with them? Have they ever offered to* make you one of them*?"*

Those words were devastating. Adonai had always been the core of her existence, but was He keeping something from her? With that thought came a rush of anger. Did the heavenly hosts believe she and Adam were not good enough? Did Rapha want to "keep them in their place?"

Lucifer's voice flowed once more. *"Look around at my handiwork. The horse does not envy the eagle's flight, the owl possesses the lion's strength. But Adonai would say they are an abomination."* When he spoke again it was with a near sob of longing. *"Ah, the plans I have for mankind. They would share celestial glory, would enjoy knowledge of wonders far beyond this earthly realm.*

"You are called 'Glory' and that is what you will bring to all creation. Your deepest longing is to heal the strife, and end the pain of all the Earth. That is my greatest desire as well. It can be done without forsaking those outside these walls. Our combined power will heal their pain. Join with me. When celestial and earthly are one, there will be no more envy, no more reason for war. The peace of our garden will belong to all."

Lucifer stepped away with a heartbroken expression, *"My compassion was my undoing. Other celestials were willing to allow mankind to remain ignorant, but I longed to... teach them to fly!"* At that moment the huge, owl-like, horse-sized creature swooped from its perch with a screech, soared low over their heads, then began to circle higher and higher into the deep blue of the cloudless sky.

Glory gazed toward the creature's graceful arc, her breath coming in sharp, pain-filled gasps. As the longing played across her features, Lucifer reached a hand toward her hair but when his fingers touched the barrier of light a painful jolt threw him backwards. With lightning speed he masked his fury. By the time she turned toward him, he had managed a pitying smile.

"Adonai has even surrounded you in His might to protect you because He knows flesh of the Earth is vulnerable. If you join with me, your body will no longer be weak. You and your offspring would take on invincible, celestial strength."

He took a step toward her, focusing all his will against that forbidding barrier of light. Sparks flew between them. The tension was fascinating, pure white holding back a fractured array. He laughed, *"Ah well, Adonai insulates His children even when their desires contradict His."* With a gracious shrug he strolled toward the feast and reached once more for the silver goblets with the shimmering, red liquid. *"We will share a drink. You will agree to ponder my offer and I will try to be patient. It is probably for the best. A decision this momentous should not be rushed."*

Lucifer held a goblet toward Glory. She hesitated, searching his face for one eternal moment. Then she lifted her eyes skyward where the soaring creature was just disappearing into the light of the sun.

With a trembling hand, she reached for the proffered goblet. When her fingers brushed his, a tongue of fire flared from the cup.

The Holy One beside Rapha doubled over with a moan and lost his footing for a moment as a low rumble spread out beneath them. **"The veil is torn. The deceiver will deal the fatal blow."** With tears flowing down his cheeks, He turned to grasp Rapha by the shoulders. **"Only blood will cleanse his corruption. All creation will groan under his slavery, but Adonai has numbered the years of his dominion."**

His eyes fixed on Rapha with deep compassion. **"Never give up hope, son of light. Adonai will not leave them, or you, comfortless."**

Then he was gone.

Chapter Thirteen

Pain

Glory jumped back and looked around as if expecting something to appear and devour her but the scene around them had not changed. When she raised her stricken eyes to Lucifer she encountered his kind smile.

"Do not fear. You are not dead. In fact, with just one touch from the Morning Star, you are more breathtaking than ever."

She looked down at her own body and gasped. Her simple garment of light had been transformed into a sparkling prism that scattered beams of multi-hued brilliance.

Fascinated, she held up a hand to study the colorful glow.

"Your Maker misled you because He does not want a thought in your head that does not come from Him." Lucifer's voice was quiet and soothing as he glided behind her and reached for her outstretched hand. *"Look how our hands fit together."* Her small hand somehow rested perfectly in his.

Adam felt Earth's tremor and, in panic, looked to the Holy One Whose eyes revealed pain but no surprise as a shower of green leaves began to fall from above, covering the ground with a bright emerald carpet.

"Is this because of Glory? Please, take me to her!"

"To help her, you must abide in me."

"I cannot sit here and do nothing!"

The Holy One shuddered and his face betrayed a momentary spasm of pain. When he opened his clenched fists, each palm bore a bright, freshly torn wound. As Adam stared, horrified, the man's entire being became blood-drenched and disfigured, covered in angry welts, rips, and filth. Adam recoiled from the grotesque sight as the man, through swollen, bleeding lips, whispered, **"Go to Glory. But you are not the One who will save her."**

Beside the disfigured man, the lamb bleated and nuzzled the abused hand. Quivering with pain, the man opened his arms and the lamb climbed onto his lap where bright drops of blood began to stain its snowy wool.

With a start, Adam realized he was once more prostrate before a stone wall.

The girl's eyes were wide as a strangled gasp caught in her throat. Lucifer was behind her, one hand gripping her hair so tightly she could not breathe while his other arm was around her waist, crushing her against his body.

He was hissing words, his breath scorching her ear. *"You are mine. You will never be free of me. I own your past, present and future."*

The words continued but she could not hear them over her own screams as something terrible sliced into her soul.

Fire, ice, and pain.

She was flailing, every ounce of her strength straining to break Lucifer's ever-tightening grip. His hands burned through skin, through bone and into her core, infiltrating and stripping her soul while his mantra pounded through her being.

"You are mine. You will never *be free. You are mine. You will never be free."*

Then the pain blazed, consuming her from the inside out. Surely she was dying. Please, if death would stop the pain, let her die! "Adonai!" she screamed, and everything went dark.

The enemy forces doubled and then tripled, yet still they waited, sneering and taunting Rapha and the others who had answered his summons—a pitifully small, war-weary crew.

Rapha tried to focus on the battle around him but, now that the connection to Adam and the young woman's thoughts had been reestablished, the clarity of their emotions—the sights, smells, even physical sensations—was so intense Rapha felt he was living this horrible scene through their eyes. When he tried to escape, to lessen the connection, it was relentless.

For the second time, Battue, one of his generals, was shaking his shoulder. "Fearsome creatures are erupting from the caves, sir," his fellow angel's words continued. But Battue's voice was a distant shout across a storm-tossed sea of pain. "The walls are breached…." Battue continued his report, but Rapha was frozen by Glory's horror.

"Aaaah!" Rapha fell to his knees, clutching his head as Lucifer's intended torture, the relentless image of his triumph, ripped through Rapha's soul.

Glory opened her eyes to find she was lying on the flat stones of the courtyard. Her body throbbed with pain and her nose was filled with a sickly sweet smell. She was shaking so hard her teeth chattered. She sat up, aching with every movement, realizing her face had been in a puddle of red, that most of her body was stained with it, and that something red was oozing from her, mixing with the liquid of the spilled goblet.

"I am dying," she whispered.

Despair engulfed her and she collapsed into the cold, unyielding floor.

Cruel laughter echoed around her. *"No my Glory. You are not dying. That is just one of Adonai's many lies. You are honored above all creation."*

She pulled herself out of the sticky, red goo once again as his voice continued.

"You will bear my offspring, the most magnificent beings that ever have been or will be."

Glory looked up to the cliffs and trees to the fantastical creatures gazing on her with unblinking eyes. She stood on trembling limbs and moved toward the flowing water with a dazed expression, her teeth still chattering as she tried unsuccessfully to untangle her matted hair.

As Lucifer cackled and cursed Adonai, Glory stumbled into the water and, with trembling hands, began to bathe.

Behind her, a flock of squawking birds descended from the huge, overhanging tree and began pecking at the red-stained stones.

The path was well lit and strewn with blossoms that drifted down from overhanging branches, but Adam could have found her by scent alone. The air was laden with her essence as if the sweetest core of her existence was calling out to him on the breeze.

When he entered the vast chamber he stopped, confounded by the serene scene before him. The girl lounged on a low couch while a magnificent being piled lush fruit onto a gleaming platter. He turned to greet the newcomer with delight. *"Ah! Adam! At last we meet. I, as you have guessed, am Lucifer."*

But Adam could only look at Glory who stared back at him with wounded eyes. "What happened?" Adam demanded, but Glory just looked down so he directed the inquiry to Lucifer.

Lucifer's eyes gleamed as his gaze caressed the young woman. *"I have simply opened her eyes—to who she is, who she can be, what Adonai has been hiding from both of you."*

Adam strode to place himself between them. "You lie! Adonai hides nothing from us!"

Mocking laughter echoed around him. *"He makes you the caretaker of this entire world, keeps you in a gilded cage, cut off from the depraved state outside your walls, yet you would say He hides nothing!"* Again Lucifer chortled with arrogance while Adam's face flushed with anger and his shoulders slumped under the weight of Lucifer's mockery.

In desperation Adam turned to Glory. "Come with me. Leave this place." He reached for the girl's hand but the colorful light enshrouding her was a fortress he could not penetrate. To add to his frustration, she did not reach back. Glory just sat there, imploring him to stop as tears ran down her cheeks. Again and again he beat against the barrier but all he accomplished was bloodied knuckles.

"Ahem, if I might be allowed to interject. That's not going to work." Lucifer's cheerful voice said. *"Glory is now my mate. She belongs to a different realm... mine."*

"No! She is of *my* flesh and bone! She belongs with me!" Adam turned and rushed at Lucifer but his attempts once again proved futile.

Lucifer chuckled as he manipulated Adam's destructive thoughts. The boy's panicked mind was especially vulnerable. He would enjoy one more mental stab before progressing to the next phase of his plan.

When Adam peered at the girl through tear-stained eyes, he beheld Lucifer's mirage. Glory stretched, languid, exposing a tantalizing glimpse of her body through the colorful mist as she directed a private smile toward—Lucifer. The apparent betrayal stoked an inferno of jealous rage. Suddenly, all the anger he had directed toward Adonai and Lucifer was focused with piercing accuracy toward *her*.

Glory blinked with shock. "Adam?"

Lucifer sighed with satisfaction. Toying with his victims before devouring them was one of his greatest pleasures—second only to relishing Adonai's heartbreak in those moments.

Adam turned his back on the girl and stood to face the enemy. "Exactly what *gift* did you give her?"

"I gave Glory what you could not, what Adonai and that pious tutor would *not give her. Look around. My way is to lift creation out of the mundane, to teach the earthbound to fly, to make the weak strong. With you, she would bear offspring fit only to grovel through dirt all their days. Adonai would make her a slave, a lowly servant barred from the heavens; but I bridged that gap. Just look at her. Have you ever seen anything more lovely?"*

"She… mated with you?" Adam's voice was a strangled whisper and all color drained from his face.

"Adam! Please! I didn't mean to. There was this enormous s… serpent and I st… stumbled over it and, and it told me…."

Adam sneered. "Where is this *enormous serpent*?" His eyes took in Lucifer's magnificent form. "I *see* the serpent that convinced you. I doubt any talking was necessary."

The girl burst into heartrending sobs. "Please, Adam. Do not hate me. I never meant to hurt you."

Lucifer watched them, licking his lips with anticipation. The girl's powers of persuasion were formidable indeed, the desperate eyes, the lovely breasts heaving with sobs, the imploring reach of her hands toward the boy. Lucifer practiced the graceful hand gesture. He'd have to remember that. Well, his work was done. All he had to do was sit back and watch the girl's performance. The boy didn't have a chance.

Rapha wept even as they organized the defense. Much more than water and air was corrupted this day. The very seed of mankind was on the verge of ruin. For ages to come earth and light, mortal and immortal, would strive in their flesh. *"Please, Adonai!"* Rapha's heart cried out, *"Surely You can intervene! Or give me permission to storm the fortress—the boy's flesh remains uncorrupted but he is caught in the snare. Please!"*

But Adonai was silent. There were no words to answer Rapha's plea—just grief. As evil beings flooded the garden, the angel strove to prepare his forces for attack, but a greater war raged in his heart. He knew Lucifer had allowed his connection to the humans' thoughts and emotions in order to torment and goad him to intervene. He knew also that to allow emotions to dictate his actions was exactly what Lucifer desired, but his love for the young man and woman defied logic.

There was Michael! The Warring Angel's presence gave Rapha hope. As enemy forces retreated, muttering, before Michael's fierce countenance and his accompanying band of heaven's most fearsome warriors, Rapha rushed to his side. "New orders, sir?"

The pained look of compassion in the chiseled face did not bode well. Michael placed a hand on Rapha's shoulder, "We come to remove corruption from the garden."

"But not to prevent it?" Rapha interjected, though the answer was evident in Michael's face. "If the man and woman are evicted, *I go with them*." The words burst from his heart but even as they left his tongue, he realized their implication.

Michael's penetrating gaze held his. "You would bind yourself to their fate?" Astonishment was etched in the ancient eyes. "Adonai warned me that you might choose this path but I could not believe it. He told me, 'a father would do no less for his children.'"

For one eternal instant the two angels regarded one another, then a hint of a smile lit Michael's face. "This should make things interesting," he murmured. "You do know the barrier is removed. To step through that entrance is to join their corruption." Michael's eyes searched his face. "Are you sure, brother?"

Words were unnecessary. In that brief moment Rapha and Michael shared their silent farewells amidst the myriad ties and memories they had experienced through the ages since their dawn.

Finally Michael said, "We will make the performance convincing."

Rapha wanted to throw his arms around the formidable angel and weep with gratitude but he knew they were being watched. Subterfuge was not his specialty but he would do his best.

"I will not leave them!" Rapha wrenched his shoulder from Michael's grasp. "There is no time to spare!"

He turned to step through the opening but Michael's massive form barred the way.

"You would *force* obedience?" Rapha shouted, "That has never been Adonai's way. Or are *you* in charge of heaven now?"

The hoots and catcalls of opposing forces underscored their playacting. Finally, Rapha, with a wink, wielded a flash of power he had never utilized against any but the fallen of their brethren and melted from Michael's grasp only to reappear at the fortress's entrance. He noted the grief, mingled with a gleam of respect in Michael's eyes, which mirrored his own. As he turned away, the mighty warrior's parting thought filled his mind.

Adonai's heart is with you, brother.

"Go, Adam. I do not deserve you. Leave this place!"

Lucifer growled. Glory's selfless plea was unexpected. Not to worry. One more moment's manipulation would win him the world.

"Yes, Adam. Go. You still have more ribs. I am sure Adonai could easily whip up a new mate." Lucifer's silky voice encouraged him.

The girl shut her eyes as fresh tears spilled down. The thought of Adam mating with another was too much.

"I *will not* abandon you," Adam whispered. Glory opened her eyes to find him kneeling before her as close as the shimmering light would allow.

"But you forget, son of Earth, she belongs with me now. She is my flesh and bone," Lucifer taunted. *"But there is still a way you can be with her, if you possess sufficient courage,"* he ended with a shrug as if Adam's choice mattered little.

The love in Adam's eyes warmed Glory, announcing loud and clear she was worth fighting for, dying for if necessary. "What must I do?"

"It is really not such a horrible fate. You simply need some of my fire in you," Lucifer tilted his head as if searching for the perfect phrase, *"to restore compatibility. Does it seem to you to have done her any harm?"*

Adam threw her an inquiring look.

Glory's body was quivering and she clenched her jaws to still her chattering teeth. She reached toward Adam but the light surrounding him repelled her. For an instant he saw panic in her face and then she turned away again, breathing deeply, clasping her hands tightly together. "Why did I touch Lucifer? Because I wanted to fly, because I wanted to speed the fulfillment of my highest calling and destiny—*our* highest calling and destiny—to heal creation's wounds."

She looked up at Adam, sobbing. "But now I know, even if wings sprouted from my shoulders and I shot high into the sky, I would… ache… for you."

Then she collapsed back onto the couch, her shoulders heaving as she wept.

"Please, Glory, I will be with you." Adam reached toward her but the barrier flared once again. His fists dropped into his lap and his head fell forward in surrender.

Then Adam rose and turned toward Lucifer.

"Do not worry, dear boy." Lucifer's body wavered, flickered and refocused with voluptuous, alluring femininity. His next words flowed with Lilith's caressing voice. *"You will only scream with pleasure."*

Adam, startled but determined, took one hesitant step forward. The glow around Lilith expanded and then surrounded him. Adam's body relaxed, his eyes closed, bliss etched across his features as he took a deep, shuddering breath. When he opened his eyes, Lilith was directly before him, a dazzling smile on her lips, and one graceful hand held out in invitation.

Slowly, Adam reached for Lilith's fingers, deaf to the sound of Glory's screams, "Adam! NOOO!"

Glory jumped up from the couch and threw herself against the dazzling barrier, tears streaming down her face. "Adam! Stop!"

Although Adam appeared deaf to her pleas, Lucifer/Lilith did not ignore the young woman. She turned toward Glory with a victorious smile as she took the dazed young man beneath her.

The ground thundered and shook. Enemy forces descended and the sky grew dark with swirling fumes that rained fire and ash. Now Rapha knew. He was too late. Nonetheless, he flew to them, melting through solid walls and casting aside opposing forces like leaves in the wind. All the while, Lucifer's triumphant cackling echoed in his ears.

Adam was thrown to the ground covered with red, oozing welts, wounds from the woman's claw-like nails. Finally Glory could get to him. She reached to push Adam's hair from his bleeding face but he turned away, too ashamed to even look at her.

Lucifer stood and stretched, shrugging off the feminine persona as he licked his lips, tasting Adam's blood that lingered there. A loud crash sounded behind him but he did not even turn to look as Rapha arrived, moaning as he took in the sordid scene. *"Mmmm. Salty."* Lucifer said, *"Makes me want something sweet... again. Care to join me, Rapha?"*

Rapha knew it was useless, but his rage flashed forth, grinding uselessly against Lucifer who laughed, *"You fool! All authority is mine now!"*

Adam's eyes appealed to the helpless tutor. His arms were pinned to his sides and he fell to the ground, paralyzed, facing the nightmare of Lucifer's blood-smeared hands reaching for Glory.

"It is only fair you observe her performance as well, Adam. I do believe she could teach you a thing or two."

Suddenly, the fallen angel stopped to wipe at the blood on his hands with a look of confused surprise. Again he pushed at the stains, but instead of disappearing they spread, creeping up his arms toward his neck, burning like trails of molten lava with an audible sizzling sound on his perfect skin, continuing their relentless journey over his body's flawless landscape. Lucifer's eyes widened as the fire marched toward his groin and he shrieked, doubling over as the flames engulfed his entire body.

When the light encasing Adam and Glory faded, Rapha sprang forward and grabbed the two humans. As they ran through the structure's twisting corridors, Lucifer's agonized screams faded behind them.

Chapter Fourteen

Allies

Rapha knew he would have to repent for the delight he took in Lucifer's pain. The fallen angel had visited agony on so many. Now, through stealing what was forbidden, Lucifer was learning true physical pain for the first time and thus his angelic body would forever be marked by this transgression—one more giant step away from the purity for which he was formed.

When Rapha led Adam and Glory through the monstrous arch and into the courtyard that now rang with the cacophony of vicious battle, they gagged on fumes roiling up from the ground as if the rot of a millennia had been loosed. Through the noxious haze, a shaft of sunlight pierced through. Glory shrieked. There was no need to ask the cause of her fright. They could now see clearly that all illumination was gone from her and from Adam. No heavenly radiance, no glowing colors. Nothing.

She looked around in horror and her arms flailed in a vain attempt to cover her body but there was no time for modesty. Their world had gone mad.

Fire and chaos greeted them. Horrors rained from the sky and crawled from the belly of the Earth bringing turmoil in their wake. In their terror, formerly gentle creatures ripped and tore, their bodies resembling more and more the accursed beasts trained for death as enemy forces spurred more bloodshed. Time and again Glory wanted to assist the frightened, wounded animals but Rapha drove them on without rest, until they came to a small cave where he left them a moment to spy out the path ahead.

When he returned to collect them, the humans were sewing together leaves to cover their bodies. Their attempts to hide their nakedness moved him to pity. For one short hour Adam had tasted his authority over creation only to experience complete humiliation before that hour was through. Therefore, even as a growing threat haunted his heart, Rapha humored their feeble attempts by grabbing one of the sharp needles from the prickly bush at the mouth of the cave and joining their efforts.

He wanted to say something to encourage them, to dismiss the fear and bring peace, but there was nothing to say. On and on they stitched, aware of the futility of the gesture, too shocked for conversation, too mortified to look at one other, but somehow the mundane task was calming. As they donned their garments, Adam finally spoke.

"Thank you," he muttered. It was two words and Adam's eyes were averted, but it was something.

Glory was so stunned she appeared unaware of her surroundings. Perhaps that was for the best. They could not afford the luxury of emotional collapse.

Rapha longed to gather them into his arms and comfort them but the urgent sense of danger made him press on at a greater pace. His fellow angels were summoning him. The sooner he could get the young man and woman into the midst of allies, the better.

On they journeyed past indescribable horrors and into familiar territory now rendered unrecognizable by earthquakes, falling ash, and bloodshed. Over and over Rapha saved their lives, not just because enraged animals prowled and the ground might split at their feet, but because Adam and Glory seemed too distraught to save themselves.

Strangely enough, when they did cross paths with enemy forces, they were allowed to pass unmolested. Stranger still was their encounter with a vicious, flying reptile that had circled lower and lower until it landed in a small clearing, blocking their path. Two others had joined it, obviously anticipating a feast. Rapha summoned reinforcements and braced himself for a fight, but when the ringleader came close and sniffed the wind blowing past the man and woman, it retreated, rose quickly into the smoke-filled sky on membranous wings, and immediately its companions followed.

Rapha had no time to ponder the occurrence since his brother angels' summons was increasingly urgent. In fact, several from the bedraggled angelic host had already gathered in the center of the garden where, although defenses had fallen, enemy forces were still refusing to approach, repelled by Adonai's fragrance which still lingered so strongly there.

The last frantic push past carcasses of well-loved animal companions was more than the humans could bear so that by the time they joined the circle of angelic hosts, Adam and Glory simply fell to the ground in a near-catatonic state, lost in the horrors they had witnessed.

Rapha peered around the circle at the solemn faces of his celestial brothers, sensing an animosity directed toward the humans.

Battue was the first to speak. "It is good they are with you. We can more easily accomplish… unpleasant duties."

"The entire day has been unpleasant. To what do you refer?" Rapha inquired, turning to stand in front of Adam and Glory.

"We were sent to eradicate evil from the garden. They are carriers of Lucifer's corruption, and thus they must be eliminated."

Adam put a protective arm around Glory who gazed blankly at the accusing celestials, her face devoid of emotion.

"They are not your concern." Rapha was shocked by the deadly intent in several faces and sifted through the surrounding thoughts, seeking support. "I will take complete responsibility for…."

"You are no longer in charge," Battue shouted, cutting him off. "You abandoned your responsibilities when you entered Lucifer's domain."

"I could not abandon *them*!" He detected a hint of empathy beneath Battue's harshness. He had been reluctant to oppose Rapha but others had convinced him of this present course. *Ah. There it was.* The deepest resentment flowed from the tight-knit threesome led by Phineas, a stalwart, reliable warrior, but not someone Rapha desired as an enemy. Phineas' dark, angry eyes returned his gaze. "Speak your mind, brother," Rapha said.

"There is no other choice." Phineas replied as several others nodded agreement. "Will you deny their bodies were joined with Lucifer? Will you suggest another way to eradicate corruption? You know death alone will suffice."

"This judgment is not ours to apply. We must await Adonai's specific instructions—"

Phineas interrupted. "Have we learned nothing? If we allow this… thing to survive, all creation will once again destroy itself. Lucifer will have his way—again!"

Battue motioned to Phineas who reluctantly yielded to his authority. "Rapha, wiping out evil now will prevent an age of bloodshed. We all wish it could be otherwise. We had such high hopes and have grown so fond of the humans, but Lucifer's plan must not succeed. If I were corrupted by Lucifer's seed, I would gladly sacrifice myself to...."

"But it is *not* you!" The pious prose was grating on Rapha. "And it is not for you to decide whether another member of Adonai's creation is not worthy to live. He will give us *His* counsel; *we* will not advise *Him*...."

"Do *not* quote Adonai's ways to us," Phineas reprimanded. "You have become so enmeshed with the humans, the truth is hidden from you!"

"No, I see the truth all too clearly, Phineas. You would end their lives because they threaten what you see as the proper order of things. You prefer a world where humans are kept in their place, unable to comprehend Adonai's ways, with no longing for what they are missing."

A breathless silence hovered. Rapha had just implied that Phineas' views were in league with Lucifer. They remembered well Phineas' history, that he had once almost joined Lucifer's cause. Every angel crouched, ready for attack, as Phineas' face twisted with fury.

"How dare you accuse me when you stand aligned with evil!" Phineas, flanked by his supporters, advanced toward Rapha as Battue leapt between them.

"NO!" The young woman's voice cried out. "Please! Don't. I will not resist, but let Adam and Rapha go."

The angels stopped, stunned. There stood the woman, filthy, shamed and bloodstained but (how could it be?) she looked every inch a queen. And when Adam leapt to her side, the sun's rays, sepia-toned from the smoke-filled haze, reflected off the white stone behind him, creating a halo of gold atop his head.

That was all the distraction Rapha required. He enveloped the humans in his arms. For a split second, they heard a corresponding outcry from the surrounding angels, then nothing but the sound of rushing water. Immediately Rapha was hit with a wave of exhaustion from the effort of shifting the three of them through space. He fell to his knees as Adam and the girl blinked in amazement to find themselves in a small cavern behind a waterfall.

This was her first time becoming "malleable" and the girl was too heartbroken to care. She realized this was the very spot where she had bathed just a few hours before, but a cataclysmic transformation had occurred. That girl who swam in the early morning light and placed a flower in her hair… was no more.

The freshness was gone. The air smelled strange. Even the sound of splashing water carried a thud instead of a happy sparkle. The light was dim, glowing with a strange, reddish tinge. Maybe that was why the water pouring down before their eyes looked pink rather than clear. She reached a hand toward the splashing fall that had always been so refreshing, but now recoiled as the first drop touched her skin. How could water *feel* wrong?

Then she looked *through* the falling curtain, down to the pool—and screamed. Immediately Rapha's hand was over her mouth, squelching the sound.

Bodies were everywhere. Some were their enemies but most were remains of beloved animal friends. And not just bodies, but mangled body parts were strewn as far as she could see, the aftermath of mindless slaughter, the work of those who destroyed for the pleasure of it.

Glory was gasping, then she was on her knees, wretching until her stomach expelled its contents.

As she tore her gaze from the bloody panorama and wiped a trembling hand across her lips, her eyes met Rapha's. And there sat Adam, weeping.

"Why didn't you let them kill me?" She spat the words as Rapha winced at the harsh tone of her voice. "That would make it simple. Adonai could just make another woman. You'd like that, wouldn't you?" She addressed Adam, "Maybe this time He could do things right—wider hips, bigger breasts… perhaps someone who *enjoys playing rough*."

Adam's mouth went white at the edges and he flinched as if her words were physical blows. "I came after *you*. What I did, I did *for you*." His voice sounded dead, hollow. "Why didn't you tell me what he had done?"

She flushed and turned away.

"And why are there no marks on *you*? Is that because you did not resist?"

It was Glory's turn to flinch as if Adam had struck her. "I saw you!" she hissed. "You loved every single blow, every single thrill of… that… that… creature's…." Her hands were over her face as if to hide from the spectacle replaying in her mind.

"Please, stop," Rapha pleaded. "This is Lucifer's way. He tricks and seduces then divides. Resist the evil desiring to consume you…."

"It is far too late for instruction, *friend*," Adam flung the accusation at Rapha, his shame and helplessness lashing out like a whip. "Go!" He rushed toward Rapha. "Do not look at us. Go back to your place of glory with Adonai. Go fly with your angel friends who hate us! Go tell our story to some other stupid boy who believes he is Adonai's gift to creation!"

Rapha, filled with anguish, wanted to scream. Adam, with wild eyes and face flushed with rage, looked and sounded just like… Lucifer.

"You are fools," Glory's voice was quiet but it carried even more venom. "Fools!" she screamed. "You are free! You are both free. I am Lucifer's now. His seed is in me." She fell to her knees, bowing her face to the damp rock. "Failed. Failed," she said over and over as she scraped her hands across the stone until the fingertips bled.

Rapha rushed to her but Glory shoved him away, her hands leaving red stains on his chest. He spoke kindly, told them again of Adonai's love, of His word that cannot be broken, but Adam and Glory were deaf to Rapha—she, intent on punishing her body; he, lost in desperation.

With growing dread, Rapha realized the direction of Adam's thoughts. "No," he said. "Adam, do not do this." He put a hand to Adam's chest as the young man moved toward Glory.

Adam shook himself free. "Lucifer will not steal her from me. This was to be our day of joining. So it shall be."

Glory froze and looked up at Adam through matted, mucked hair, her eyes puffy and feral. "You will not touch me."

When Adam grabbed her shoulders and pulled her to her feet, Glory exploded with violence, kicking, punching, and scratching in desperation. Again and again Rapha bullied his way between them, but neither would stop. Both craved the abuse. Both welcomed the pain that numbed their torment and guilt.

In the blink of an eye Rapha was gone, streaking through the sky to escape. Yet there was no escape.

The doors of heaven were closed to him. He had thrown in his lot with the humans. The enormity of that decision hit home. There was nowhere to hide from evil's consequences. Over the churning ocean waters he fled, but turmoil sped before him, infecting every intertwined cell of creation, from the depths below to the far-flung heavens that rained fearsome fire and blotted out the stars—a constant reminder of Adonai's divine story.

Still he heard their words, felt their accusations, their guilt and despair ripping at the perfection their Maker had intended.

Through it all Lucifer's maniacal laughter continued, exulting in Adonai's pain.

It was early evening when Rapha felt the summons. **"Where are you?"** his Maker called.

"Lost," was Rapha's reply.

"You are never lost if I know where you are. Come."

So Rapha limped back, wanting to shut his eyes to the devastation that had been wrought in the world in a single day, but feeling it was his penance to view what might have been prevented if he had somehow been wiser, had acted more quickly, had not run away....

The Garden was destroyed. Streams flowed red with blood. Birds, other than scavengers enjoying a carrion feast, had flown. The joyful chatter of life was replaced with sounds of mourning—whimpers, roars and fearful silence.

In the midst of this horror, Adonai stood, his holiness revealing evil in stark relief. Enemy forces had fled at his approach, loathsome creatures of darkness had slunk back to their hidden caves but left behind the carnage of their partially consumed victims. Adonai's celestial forces were assembled, but so different from the glorious celebrations of past days. Today they were bedraggled and reeked of the evil that had vomited forth from Earth's abyss. Today, they mourned with one voice the loss of this one bastion of purity. Today, they watered the tainted soil with their tears.

But someone was missing.

"Adam, where are you?" Adonai's call echoed throughout the Garden. Every creature within the walls came. Even if maimed, blind, or with the blood of a victim yet dripping from their mouths, the Garden's inhabitants walked, flew, hopped, crawled, or at least willed their broken body in the direction of

The Maker's voice—but not the man and woman. Over and over Adonai called, wooing them with a His gentle voice, but they did not come.

Rapha could feel their shame. He knew where they cowered.

"Bring them," his Maker requested.

Adonai's will moved Rapha to the mouth of a shallow cave. "Come, my friends," he called. The only answer he received was a despairing wail of anguish. Further into the gloom he ventured, the glow from his body causing shadows to recede. "Adam?" He spoke softly, sensing their fragile grip on sanity.

"Please, we cannot go to Him like this. Beg Him to forget us." The broken rasp of a whisper echoed from the damp walls.

"You do not have the luxury of cowering in disgrace, Adam. You are His son."

"I am not fit to die here. I feel this body withering. We go to seek a place where our tainted blood will not infect the ground, where our flesh will be devoured by the birds of the air and our bones will lie, exposed in shame for all time."

Rapha allowed a sad smile as Adam's prose brought to mind the eloquent speech the boy had delivered on the day of Glory's creation. Even in his despair poetry poured from his lips.

But when his warm light fell on them, the smile was replaced by a heartbroken moan. The girl's eyes were glazed with shock as her grimy fingers plucked at her scant, torn leaf covering as if somewhere in her diseased mind she remembered a thing called dignity. Adam cowered close beside her, his face turned toward the cave wall, his nude body coated with wounds, new scratches and bruises mixed with several layers of filth. Adam, hope of the world, and the woman created as his mate, had torn at each other like vicious dogs.

Perhaps Adam was right. Perhaps they were beyond hope, so far fallen from Adonai's intended glory there was nothing left but to crawl away and rot. There was silence in Rapha's heart. He knelt in the dirt as hot tears coursed down his cheeks. He reached a hand toward Adam but the boy cringed as if expecting a blow. For long moments Rapha sat, inhaling their hopelessness as the steady drip, drip of water somewhere in the dark recesses combined with the occasional plink of tears onto the cave's rocky floor.

Then his heart spoke with Adonai's gentle voice and, in his exhaustion and despair, he did not even think. He simply opened his mouth and let their Maker address them.

"My children. I AM with you. I could never forsake you. Wherever you go I AM there. Whatever you do, I have seen. My love is more constant than the stars, more reliable than the rising sun. My plan will come to pass. I have spoken; it is accomplished. I make a way where there is no way. When it is impossible, I break through. You have failed. But My love cannot fail. My word cannot be broken. Come."

A faint breeze of hope stirred in their hearts. It was just enough to lift their heads. Without a word they consented to follow Rapha from the cave. At a shallow pool by the cave's entrance they bathed, their eyes averted from each other, as Rapha added fresh leaves to their abused garments. But, although washed and clothed, nothing could cleanse the haunted, hunted expression from their eyes that still proclaimed their disgrace.

They refused Rapha's offer to expedite the journey to their Maker. "No." Adam stood firm. "I will have no part of angelic ways. I am a creature of Earth. I will walk."

Every step was torture. Everywhere they looked another heartbreaking scene awaited. They choked and coughed in the poisonous fumes that continued to rise from Earth's open wounds.

They tried not to cower when they beheld the decapitated and maimed, but soon they became numb, walking through this hell with pale young faces that grew older by the minute.

Only once did Rapha intervene. By a stream, a young lion had cornered a man-like creature with broken membranous wings. The creature still lived though its breath came in gurgling gasps. Rapha ran forward, chasing the lion into the shadows.

When it beheld Rapha, the winged creature hurled a string of curses at him and then made a sound they presumed to be a laugh. "We have won, foul servant of Adonai. You can keep us captive in your pits no longer while you coddle the man creatures." It coughed, spewing a stream of dark blood onto the ground, and its eyes rolled back, barely retaining consciousness.

Rapha knelt beside the creature, "You are dying. What is your final request?"

The fangs were bared with a hideous smile and it replied, "I want to die ripping your flesh."

When Rapha reached toward its fangs, the yellow eyes widened in surprise but, as if afraid the offer wouldn't last, it bit and shook Rapha's forearm, giving in to blood lust. Rapha winced but placed his other hand on the creature's brow to stroke the bloodied hair from its eyes.

The creature released its hold and stared at Rapha. "Why?" It rasped.

"You deserve to see a touch of Adonai's love before you die."

Suddenly the confusion was replaced by another spasm of pain and the yellow eyes grew still. The creature was dead. Rapha gently closed the eyelids and stepped away. With a wave of his hand, a ball of fire consumed the body. Soon even the bones were gone. Only a scorched patch of ground remained.

They continued walking.

"Why?" Adam finally spoke, gazing at Rapha with new respect.

"I chased the lion away out of pity, for both creatures. The lion's flesh would have rejected the tainted blood and would have begun to devour itself, but not before it had passed the corruption to many others. As for the unnatural creature, it never asked to be manipulated for evil purposes."

"But your arm," the girl reached toward his mangled limb.

"Do not touch it. The fangs were poisonous."

"What will it do to you?" Adam inquired.

Rapha was touched by their concern. Their world was destroyed yet still they had the capacity to care. Indeed, his injury seemed to be the healthiest medicine for them, the antidote to self-absorption. "I will take it to Adonai."

"If the poison becomes a part of you, what can be done?" The girl's welfare was tied to this question as well. Rapha sensed the weakness she felt spreading through her body.

"I do not know exactly what Adonai will do, but I trust His love."

"But what does He employ to remove corruption? Surely you have seen the process many times."

Rapha hesitated. How would they continue to hope if he told them the truth? However, they deserved a straight answer. "Fire and water. But, as you have seen, the seeds of corruption remain. Many of the heavenly host believe Adonai erred by not making the destruction complete, but He hates to destroy."

Glory was silent a moment, coming to her own painful conclusions. "So, the corrupted flesh on Earth was burned like you burned that creature?"

"Yes, but that does not completely destroy evil. The smoke carries it on the wind. Water is needed to wash it away. Even then it remains, seeping down into the soil, infecting the land."

“Corruption remains—even after fire and floods? Then where is the hope?” She was filled with despair.

“The hope is in Adonai. His very existence is impossible, therefore the impossible does not stop Him.” Rapha’s encouraging words were lost on them. The humans trudged on, certain they marched to their own doom.

Chapter Fifteen

Justice and Mercy

As they drew near the appointed place, the air became solemn and still. On all sides now they beheld the garden's bedraggled, wounded occupants drawn, just like them, toward Adonai's presence.

Then they felt His gaze and their sorrow was complete as His purity flayed their souls which had never known anything but acceptance and love in His presence. Now the scent and sight of His holiness repelled them.

The man and woman were so ashamed they did not even try to look at Adonai. If they had, they might have found courage. His every gesture and expression poured forth only heartbroken compassion and grief. His eyes were molten love—with righteous anger, yet determined to save and restore. Although His creation lay in tatters at His feet, not a trace of hopelessness or despair bowed His shoulders.

"Why did you not come when I called?"

Adonai's voice was gentle but to their guilty ears His words were vindictive and full of judgment. Adam was trembling as every instinct screamed for him to run away. His voice cracked with adolescent nervousness, "We were ashamed b… because we were naked."

"I created you. Is anything hidden from Me? Who taught you to be ashamed of your nakedness, to hide in fear from Me?"

Neither could answer. Each felt the eyes of countless wounded creatures and heavenly hosts bearing down, driving them to the ground with guilt.

"My child, I gave one directive, one command you were to obey, to avoid the fruit of the evil one. Did you disobey that command?"

His words sliced across the young man's heart. In that moment, Adam finally understood the horror of possible separation from his Maker. He had never realized how Adonai was more important than the air he breathed until he found himself suffocating in panic. "Please, Oh Most High, I would not ever have dreamed of disobeying you, but the… the woman you gave me, she convinced me to listen to the evil one."

As he blamed Glory, Adam glanced into his Creator's eyes… then looked away, more ashamed than ever.

"Woman, the man has accused you of leading him into evil. What do you say?"

Glory was finally feeling something besides shame as anger flooded her being. Here, before Adonai and the assembled host, Adam had laid the blame for evil's triumph at her feet. Tears stung her eyes as she realized she stood alone to defend herself. "Lord, I wanted to run away, but a monstrous serpent charmed and ensnared me. It lied to me and convinced me to heed the evil one."

"Where is the serpent?"

"*I* never saw a serpent…" Adam began but stopped when *it* came into view.

Tall and mesmerizing, it was escorted forward by two angels. The gorgeous creature held its head high, forcing all assembled to acknowledge its queenly bearing. A dull roar of murmurs and exclamations accompanied her progress toward Adonai's throne.

"Handmaiden of evil, long have we heard rumors of your service to the fallen one. Do you deny these accusations?"

When she opened her mouth to speak, the soothing, honeyed tones of her words caused a hush to fall over the assembly. None could resist a longing to do her bidding. The master of seduction had honed her talents for innumerable years; every inflection was music to the ears, every movement a graceful dance.

"Creator of All, I deny nothing."

A shocked silence followed as the creature continued.

"The fault for this evil lies with me, so should their curse of death be mine. Long have I served one whose promises wrapped me in cords of slavery. Long have I believed he loved me. I obeyed his every command, eager to bring ruin to Your kingdom. But I have been deceived. Today I finally understand his treachery. He can love only himself. I come before you, Maker of all that is good, throwing myself on Your mercy."

And then, accompanied by gasps, she bent her astounding frame until she was prostrate, her beautiful face and proud eyes pressed to the ground at Adonai's feet.

Adonai knelt until His head was beside hers, **"Dear one, this day you have displayed the greatest faith. You have known nothing but deception and hatred but you have come, without any claim of your own goodness, to seek mercy. You believe the truth as soon as it is before you. Your requests are heard and fulfilled."**

When she lifted her head, a tremendous transformation had occurred. Gone was the pride and studied seduction. In its place were eyes that shone with love for the One who knelt with her.

"I know I can never repair the wrong I have caused, but I am Yours, completely and forever."

"Are you ready to trust Me, even though the road ahead will be harsh?"

"Anything," she stated simply, and then awaited her sentence with eyes that held His with a boldness born of adoration.

"Are you willing to relinquish the very thing that lifted you beyond your intended station?"

"I fear its release, but it galls me. Long has this body warred within, torturing me even in my slumber."

"Are you willing, you who have ruled, to lay aside your glory and exist for an age as one accursed, one who hides in fear from the realm of humans?"

"Yes, only please allow me and my descendants to be found blameless at the end of that age."

"Because you offer yourself willingly, your descendants will not be cut off. Your flesh will no longer be in turmoil. I will this day heal you of your corruption. However, you will no longer walk, but will move in the dust of the ground. Mankind will despise you, believing you to be cursed even though you accept the brunt of their shame. A natural enmity will exist between your seed and the seed of the woman but you will not be left defenseless because man's fear will be your shield. You will be the very symbol of those accursed and rejected but you will also represent the healing of all mankind.

"Know this dear one, I will be with you in your shame. I too choose to lay aside my glory and submit to mankind's contempt. I too am lifted up as the curse that heals their flesh—and yours. Do not despair. You will never be parted from Me and at the end of this age your sacrifice will be made known."

"Then my sentence is far too kind, for to be cast from Your presence for all eternity would be just."

Those were the last words she ever spoke. The transformation was so smooth and seamless, each in attendance wondered at first if their eyes were simply dazzled, but they watched as the shapely legs receded into the long sinuous body, the wings shriveled and her size diminished until she was merely a large—albeit beautiful—snake lying before her Maker Who reached a hand toward her. Hesitantly, she arched her strong body and began to wrap around His arm. And there she rested a moment, storing up His warmth. Then Adonai lifted her high and all the assembly stared, struck dumb by the boundless trust and severe mercy displayed before them.

Their parting was painful to behold. As she moved slowly down his arm, Adonai's tears flowed, both anointing her body and preparing her path at His feet.

The humans' shame consumed them. This creature, carefully bred and groomed by Lucifer's hand, had proven that her faith actually outstripped theirs. The thought of being reduced to a dumb animal that would slide through dust for the rest of its days terrified them. Glory wondered, if the serpent's faith and bravery were rewarded thus, perhaps something worse awaited them? As the snake's length slid by, the girl recoiled as if the curse would rub off on her. The snake, in reaction to her sudden movement, drew back sharply and held her gaze, forked tongue tasting her fear, unblinking eyes reading her revulsion.

"Go your way, child," Adonai's voice soothed the snake. **"Seek the hidden places. In the quiet you will find rest."**

The snake relaxed her stance and resumed her newfound mode of travel, the unexpected, graceful, side-to-side movement, already a miracle to behold.

The wide, horrified eyes of the man and woman followed her progress. They moved closer together and clasped hands.

"Woman," Adonai's eyes were boring into her soul, **"because you chose to hearken to the serpent's lies and thus took Lucifer's fruit unto your loins, the joy of motherhood will bring deep pain. Also, your union with Adam, intended to comfort and fulfill, will bring great turmoil to your heart."**

Glory simply nodded her head, her eyes never leaving the ground at her feet.

"Adam, since you hearkened to the woman and joined her sin, your life of ease is over. Providing sustenance and protection for your family will be a grievous and time-consuming effort. Your days will be spent struggling against the thorns now planted among your offspring, and, at the end of your days, your bodies will die, once more becoming one with the earth from which they came."

There, before Adonai's purity, Adam and Glory wept.

Rapha, still bonded to their emotions, had reason, even in that horrible moment, to be proud of his protégés. What was torturing their hearts was not their sentence of hard work and future conflict but the grief in Adonai's voice. They knew they had caused that pain. All that they had endured—their shame and torture at Lucifer's hands, the animals' mutilation, and their own desecration—paled in the light of the suffering they had caused Him.

Adonai spoke again, words that seemed increasingly painful for Him to utter.

"These things are only the natural outgrowth of your sin. Nothing will atone for it but death. However, you shall not be the One to pay that price. I have decreed that through you the whole Earth shall be restored. That restoration will include you as well. Until that day, you shall look ahead to

your hope. Until that day when My Holy One shall spill His life's blood in your stead, a grievous but necessary practice must be employed to fulfill the requirement of blood, or you will indeed be subject to the evil one."

Once more their Maker knelt. As if on cue, a young lamb trotted forth and leapt into His arms. The girl gave a soft cry of recognition, realizing this was Grace, the lamb she had held at the beginning of this horrific day. With heartrending tenderness, Adonai held the animal close, burying His face in the lush, white wool. Tears rolled down His cheeks and dripped to disappear into that snowy softness. **"A volunteer among the animals offers its life to ensure the humans will fulfill their calling."** The words caught in His throat and the lamb gave one bleat before He continued, a bittersweet smile illuminating His features as He gazed into its eyes. **"There is no greater love than that displayed by this innocent one giving his life for the life of a friend. He will forever be aligned with My own life's blood, pledged to cleanse all creation."**

A shudder ran through the entire assembly as a haughty voice broke the holy moment and Lucifer appeared, his perfect visage marred by angry blue welts that traced an intricate pattern over every inch of his golden skin. *"How touching! Adonai and His pets have gathered to congratulate me!"*

"Samael," Adonai addressed Lucifer by his ancient name. **"Where have you come from and what have you been doing?"**

"Oh Most Exalted One," his voice dripped razor-edged sarcasm, *"while I always enjoy our conversations, today I* am *in a bit of a hurry, so I'd appreciate just getting down to it. Ruling the world is so time-consuming. I am here to claim my prize... es."* He surveyed the young man and woman with eager malice.

"Then today is your day indeed, because your prize is the goal for which you have aimed for many ages past. In place of the humans, I give you—Myself. In Adam's line shall come one who is born of my Holy Spirit. I shall live in him, fully God and fully man. He will offer his life for the lives of mankind. He will willingly lay aside his authority and die at your hands."

Lucifer paused, contemplating this unbelievable offer as a gasp resounded from those assembled. *"If You were anyone else, I would accuse You of lying but... You can't do that... can You?*

"Let me get this straight," he reiterated. *"You will place in this man's progeny one who will be—You—in the flesh, and You will allow me to destroy this 'Son of Man,' thus claiming my right to Your blood?"*

"Yes."

"And in the meantime, I have the right to move things along on Earth the way I see fit?"

"Yes."

"Well! This sounds like fun—for me."

"But, the man and woman and all their descendants who bring themselves under the protection of my promised blood *YOU WILL NOT TOUCH.*"

Lucifer flinched ever so slightly before those blazing, holy eyes. *"Agreed, especially since a lion's share of those descendants will be mine,"* he smiled possessively at the young woman. *"And, as is Your habit, they will have free choice of their allegiance."*

Glory shuddered and lifted exhausted eyes to her Maker who regarded her with compassion.

"I will be with you," He whispered.

"Yes, yes, that is sweet, but we need to bind this contract," Lucifer's harsh voice broke the moment. *"I cannot have* their

blood and you don't have earthly blood yet so how are we to satisfy my terms today because—I demand blood. Now!"

Wordlessly, Adonai handed the lamb to Lucifer. It did not struggle when placed into the evil one's grasp. Lucifer laughed. *"Do you truly expect them to cower behind the blood of a mere animal?"*

"Their sins are conferred onto the head of this innocent victim and My Spirit binds with that accursed flesh. The knife is plunged into My heart. In this way, you will have the pleasure of spilling My blood repeatedly until the Son of Man becomes that sacrifice."

Lucifer's scarred features lit with giddy joy at the power of causing Adonai pain. He wasted no more time but turned toward the assembly, the silent lamb held over his head as he savored this moment of triumph he would enjoy over and over throughout the age to come.

"I accept Adonai's terms—His life for the life of the humans. This innocent blood is mine! The Earth is mine to command! This age belongs to me!"

He brought the lamb down and looked at it with disdain. Finally the animal struggled as its pure body joined to sin. Desperately it craned its neck, trying to see its Maker, but Adonai had turned away. With one swift movement, Lucifer brought the lamb's neck to his mouth—and bit. Glory cried out, appalled Adonai did not intervene. But her Maker was doubled over, grief and pain etching his face while Lucifer ripped and tore the flesh of the tiny creature, reveling in the fact that all creation stared in horror. In a matter of seconds the lamb, drained of life, was tossed to the ground, reduced to mere skin and bone, while Lucifer stood proudly displaying his blood-drenched face… but his moment of triumph was cut short.

"Be gone! The innocent blood staining you fulfills the human's debt. Your claim on their flesh is broken."

But Lucifer stepped toward the couple. Adonai remained bent with agony so the fallen angel seized the opportunity for one last intimidation. *"It has been a pleasure, lovely one,"* he towered over Glory. *"Just think. We are one. What grows in you—is mine."* He reached out a blood-soaked hand and touched her stomach.

But Glory's eyes stared with new boldness into his. "Your price of blood has been paid. You have no right to me."

A familiar burning sizzled his skin and the lamb's blood burst into flame, searing his blood-soaked chest, face and arms. With a scream Lucifer reeled backwards into the crowd while animals and celestial beings leapt out of his path. As he moved away, the flames slowly subsided. When he reached the tree line, the fire was quenched but fresh wounds remained; the skin hanging from his face and torso resembled tattered parchment. He pointed a scorched finger at the Most High. *"That lamb's blood covers them with—YOU!"*

Adam leapt toward Lucifer. "Yes! So please stand still. I would like to see that fire again."

But the fallen angel disappeared, leaving behind only the stench of charred flesh.

However, the horror of his handiwork remained. The girl was already on her knees with the remains of Grace clutched to her chest, oblivious to the blood that now soaked her garments. "This little one's death was my fault. It should be my blood staining these stones, not his!" Heart-wrenching sobs tore from her breast as she rocked back and forth with the lamb's ravaged body.

"Yes, dear one. This is death. This is what you and the man have loosed upon creation. But the grief you feel is

penitence--unselfish, and restorative. Receive it as a gift from My hand, evidence of your redemption. Guard your unity with me, always remembering the price paid, the selflessness that represents My blood."

Adam was bent over Glory, reaching toward her with unsure hands. He too was crushed by failure. He had failed as her protector. He had failed as steward of the animals. Glancing up through unshed tears he observed the lions stalking away. In fact, a mass exodus was now taking place. It appeared all the species had chosen to look after themselves. Birds, reptiles, primates, amphibians—all were moving away. How could he blame them? He had betrayed their trust and ushered bloodshed into the garden. In truth, there was a longing in his heart to join them, to just leave this hotbed of responsibility and commitment, to roam free in the world, free to look only after himself, free of Lucifer's threats, free from seeing the constant reminder of his failure every day in her beautiful face.

But wait. Not all were leaving. Close by he beheld a sight that finally brought tears. The sheep, those who had just beheld the death of their own, remained, their peaceful eyes convicting him for his thoughts of escape.

"They will remain with those who honor the blood of their first martyr." Adonai declared. **"They commit themselves to the day mankind is restored as ruler of all creation. Until then, you will need their blood to renew the protection against Lucifer's claim."**

A growling and yapping drew his attention; a pair of dogs were at odds about their loyalties, the female moving closer to the humans while the male nipped at her, encouraging her to follow the retreating crowd. Finally, she turned, bared dangerous teeth and bit his ear. When he howled in pain she released him, and trotted to Adam where the tawny creature sat regally at the man's feet to survey the sad procession.

When Adam placed a hand on her shaggy head, she gave him an adoring look, her tongue lolling from the side of her panting mouth.

"Why does she choose to remain?" Adam asked.

"To put it simply, she likes you," Adonai answered. **"And she dislikes Lucifer so much she is willing to stand with anyone opposed to him. If only all could understand life's choices so clearly."**

When she actually sighed and leaned against Adam's leg, content in her choice, Adam stroked her head and wept. "I will call you Eden, in remembrance of the paradise that once was."

"Come, dear one, the day's work is not yet done."

An angel stepped forward to present a knife that appeared to be wrought of blazing light. Adonai lifted it high and announced, **"Through death, this body is returned to righteousness and is pure in My hands. I sever the skin from the bone just as one day I will forever sever the connection between you and the evil one."** The knife flashed with precision to remove the precious lamb's skin. The girl began sobbing again as she beheld the ghastly process. Blessedly, it was over quickly and the bones were given to the angel who had presented the knife.

"These bones will remain in the midst of the garden, covered with the soil where the lamb's blood was shed, an everlasting witness to his sacrifice.

"What he has done will continue to provide for you in a sun-scorched land. His skin will cover your shame, his wool will keep you warm and the oil therein will both soothe and heal. This covering will serve as a constant reminder to you and your enemies that you dwell under the protection of My covenant."

As He worked, the heat from His hand tempered the hide. Soon, it was soft, supple and dry. Adonai wove and shaped beautiful garments to cover the man and woman, including sturdy protection for their feet. There was no shortage even though the generous garments covered all but their faces. In the Maker's hands, the small lamb's sacrifice became more than enough.

Only yesterday, the light of His holiness shielded their bodies. The synchronicity with their Maker had been disrupted yet Adonai had ensured they were beautifully and sufficiently clothed for the next phase of that painful day.

"Children, give me your hands."

Trembling with fear, the humans reached toward their Maker. Did their sin, after all, require the sacrifice of a limb?

"You are husband and wife. You are one flesh—one in body, mind, and spirit. Cleave to each other. Comfort one another. From this day forth your allegiance is first to Me but then, before all earthly ties, you are sworn to each other. To protect the integrity of this joining is to protect your own flesh. Choose to sow life in every word, every thought, every action, and this union will bring blessing, healing, strength, and joy throughout the years to come. Choose to rip at the fabric of this union and you destroy your own heart.

"For this reason a man will leave his father and mother and cleave to his wife, and the two shall become one flesh."

Then Adonai addressed the young woman. **"From this day forth, you are named Eve, because you will be called the mother of all humanity. With this great honor comes the tremendous responsibility to teach your offspring My ways; tell them that I nurture and protect, that My love will remain steadfast even when they choose evil, that My heart never stops yearning for my children even when they want to hide from Me. Teach them that even when they choose the hard**

road of discipline, I long to hold them close and absorb their pain. Their joys shall be your joy, their pains shall pierce your heart. But, as you abide in Me, the strength for this task will flow, and you too will gain understanding of My love."

Then He turned to Adam. **"You are the first they will call 'father.' You are the first they will see as strong. As you defend their lives and work to provide their needs, may you commit yourself to the more important task of defending their hearts. Through you they will learn faithfulness, fearlessness, and the true meekness of honoring their heavenly Father above and before all else. Through you they will see the balance of strength that readily bows to holiness. Through you they will see themselves as worthy of My love. Nurture them. Rejoice over them. Be ready with encouragement and slow to anger. In this way they will learn self-control. As you remain grafted in Me, My virtues will overflow to your children."**

Thus Rapha witnessed the long-awaited ceremony unifying the young woman and Adam, so different from the joyous occasion he had envisioned. But the day was not yet done. The man and woman could no longer dwell in the atmosphere of Adonai's holiness.

As their young, shattered minds were still trying to absorb these precepts, Adonai spoke words that further pierced their hearts. **"From this day forth I will not be seen by you. No longer will we enjoy the unhindered relationship of our days in this blessed place. As long as you remain encased in earthly flesh, your desire for the fullness of My presence cannot be completely fulfilled. Allow this hunger and longing to drive you to seek Me. This ongoing struggle will strengthen you to stand firm in evil days. So you will thrive when all around you is swallowed in death."**

As those final words hung in the air, Adam and his mate faded from Rapha's sight. He could no longer see them but he felt their confusion when they realized their eyes no longer beheld Adonai. Where Adonai had been remained the large red orb of a sun that slipped behind the horizon as they stood, hands clasped, hearts sore with shock and grief. Finally, in the deepening twilight, they gazed at the unfamiliar copse of trees that surrounded them. Wordlessly they sat, huddled together, hearts too heavy to move, until they finally nodded off in exhaustion. When the moon was high in the sky, its silver light peeked between protective branches to behold the man and woman, arms wrapped tightly around one another as their minds wandered into sweet dreams of their Garden of Eden and the bliss their world would never know again.

Chapter Sixteen

Out of the Womb

So long ago but the memory was fresh.

For one moment more, Rapha was before his Maker and his celestial family, his heart breaking but resolved. Theirs was a farewell without words. He remembered the eyes, full of love and compassion and another emotion not typical among his celestial brothers—regret.

Rapha could feel himself changing. The core of his being was cooling, his light was going out. Or was it being veiled? There was no time to ponder as the eyes of Adonai filled his vision and the Holy One's thoughts flooded his being.

"Yours, Rapha, son of light, is a difficult path. Your choice is to accompany the man and woman into banishment. Therefore, throughout this age, you will remain among men, angelic in understanding and unfading in body. You, of all my celestial forces, will learn the ways of men from the inside, as one of them. But you will also drink deeper of their pain. You will be a stranger in a strange land, equipped to guide, teach, and protect those who are crucial to My plan of redemption. Your body will obey the natural laws of Earth, yet many of your angelic gifts will remain. Take heed, though, that these gifts are used only at My specific direction."

Love. Pure love flooded Rapha's being. Heat passed through. A flash and it was done. His body rearranged, conformed to another rhythm, another realm. He was a bird now being suited to thrive beneath crashing waves, but the memory of flight would endure.

Then Rapha was moving, it must be north, since the lowering sun was on his left. Adonai and the celestials were removed from his sight but Adonai's words continued to fill his mind.

"By choosing to serve mankind, you become part of their fate, to know My love through the knowledge of good and evil. Always remember, I Am with you through the pain."

Solid ground was beneath Rapha and he was alone, at least he could not discern any companions with his altered eyes. The sunlight was fading. He looked down at his own body to discover woolen and leather raiment much like that created for Adam and Eve, as well as leather coverings for his feet. The need for clothing would take getting used to, since light had been his only garment since time immemorial.

Now he would require food, water, shelter—a whole new set of needs.

And his body was… tired. The concept of requiring sleep had always intrigued him. His questions in that regard would soon be answered.

He wrapped the garment tighter, discovering the upper part would pull up to cover his head. So he lay upon the ground, too exhausted to move.

With the last of his strength on that fateful day he probed the world with his thoughts. The shared consciousness of heavenly hosts was lost. He gasped as a wave of loneliness flooded his body. Like a starving newborn babe he groped for Adonai, at last sensing an answer to his heart's cry as his soul was immediately cradled in peace.

But what of Adam and Eve?

He stretched his senses again, almost afraid to learn the truth. Then Rapha sighed with huge relief. Though it was difficult, and untold miles stood between him and his former students, the ability to connect to their thoughts remained. There were Adam and Eve, their minds as muddled and their hearts as broken as his.

The effort had drained the last of his strength.

Just then he heard rustling in the bushes followed by a bleat and a sharp woof. A moment later the fuzzy muzzle of the dog, Eden, was sniffing Rapha's ear as several warm, wooly bodies gathered close in the darkness.

With a breath of thanks to Adonai, Rapha, estranged son of the heavens, slept.

It was a brutal awakening for Adam and Eve. Their bodies ached; their hearts were numb, and their minds reeled as they tried to grasp the reality of their new circumstances. However, practical matters forced immediate action. A quick survey of the surrounding area yielded the discovery of a clear stream and a cave that would provide temporary shelter, a pressing need made obvious by several large paw prints close to where they had slept. It was so strange to think they would need to defend themselves against wildlife, those creatures with which they had formerly dwelt in peace.

The surrounding trees, while not as verdant as those within the garden, yielded nuts and berries. Also, the girl's knowledge of roots and herbs yielded several edible plants in the vicinity.

Feeding themselves, while requiring attention they were unaccustomed to, at least was possible.

They were not entirely bereft—except for company. Their social life in the garden had been abundant. The many personalities and fascinating areas of expertise among the angels had provided constant mental stimulation, and the wildlife in attendance had ensured their lives overflowed with color, laughter, and affection. Beyond all this, with their Heavenly Father's visits they had lived entirely fulfilled, in peace and effortless love. Now, they had only each other.

For the first few weeks, they spoke hardly a word. They scarcely had the energy. Adam had decided a house of stone afforded the most reliable protection, so his days were spent gathering and transporting them to their home's intended site, a glen nestled in the arms of the mountain range, close to the stream and with a gorgeous view of the valley beyond. Their home would face the rising sun. From the position of nighttime stars he had surmised their former dwelling lay in that direction. It was a painful memory, but he felt compelled to remind himself on a daily basis that it had once been real.

Eve moved in a fog of sadness through her tasks. Her heart ached for her former friends and the creatures she had loved. But most of all she felt the loss of those precious early evening hours reclining in the arms of Adonai. The mornings were busy as she dug for the dense clay Adam required to fill chinks between the stones of their dwelling and gathered the roots, nuts and berries for their daily food. Their hard work left little time for reminiscence but she was finding it increasingly difficult to work without pause as Adam was wont to do. Her tears would flow without warning at the sight of a pert bird cocking a bright eye her way or a wary fox skimming the edge of their glen, its tiny pup tagging behind. In those moments homesickness would consume her and memories would flow, complete with the smell of warm sun on the flank of the sleek jaguar that used to recline with her in the afternoon, suffering itself to be used as her pillow.

And something was happening in her body. She was especially achy in the mornings and her appetite, which had always been voracious, was waning. Often when she did force herself to eat, she would later sneak away because she felt the recent meal warring inside and forcing its way back up. She felt as if her body desired to rid itself of something that did not belong there. She could only surmise it was the result of the death Adonai had warned was their lot outside the garden.

Adam did not complain as he worked tirelessly on their new home. Of course, he never told her anything, just pounded and hauled with fervor from first light until he fell into the stream in the evening to wash away the day's grime, ate their scant rations with gusto, and then wrapped himself in his woolen blanket and slept without moving until dawn.

She guessed he must despise the sight of her and held her responsible for their difficulties. She could not blame him. Anyway, from what she spied in the clear water when she bathed, she did not feel worthy of his gaze. Her flat stomach and supple, muscular legs, used to constant running and climbing, were becoming a bit soft—along with her eyes that cried too much and looked sad even when dry. Her breasts were even getting puffy. Perhaps *that* part he would appreciate—*if* he ever took notice. But his words were few. "Yes," "No," "Thank you." And that was on a talkative day.

So the afternoon when she dug beside the water, scooping the dense clay into her baskets woven from the large leaves that grew along the river, her emotions were one tiny straw from collapse. That straw occurred when some of the clay lodged under one fingernail of her work-worn hands. As she placed the throbbing fingers in the cool water, the rough skin mocked her. Her nails and hands had been perfection—Adam had told her so—now they were like the rest of her; puffy and scraped free of her former beauty.

She studied her reflection, hating what she saw. No wonder he never looked at her. That sniveling, frightened coward was a disgrace. Ignoring the protest from her abused fingers she scooped a handful of the stubborn clay and launched it directly at those eyes, and the image scattered in a satisfying chaos of ripples. More! With both hands she dug and threw, rage overflowing unchecked in a heavy, muddy downpour. Again and again she grabbed and hurled, moans bubbling up from the abscess of her heart. She could never return. Adonai had rejected her. She was alone and without hope—unloved and unneeded—friendless and pathetic. Then she grabbed a stick to strike at all she had soiled—leaves, ground, water—all received the brunt of her rage until her surroundings at last resembled her emotions… shredded, bruised, and filthy.

And that was how Adam found his beautiful Eve, on her knees in the mud, sobbing with a grief that tore away the scars encasing his own heart. With bumbling fingers he lifted her muddy hair away from her face and gazed into her eyes to see her desperate need of him, a need that answered back from his own heart's famine.

Together they wept and mourned, melding together in their grief, exposing their hearts and finding healing in shared pain. Then they removed their soiled garments and plunged into the shallow waters to scrub each other's hair and aching muscles until, finally, the flowing water ran clean and they remembered how to smile.

And together they discovered the beauty of owning only one set of clothing. As their damp garments warmed in the sun, they finally found the beauty of love for which their Creator had molded them, a passion and tenderness that made them feel, for one shining moment, that they were back in Eden where they could ask for nothing more.

Chapter Seventeen

Sacrifice

Their simple home continued to take shape. Day by day they became more of a team, looking after the other's needs and actually enjoying the hard work of scraping an existence from the stubborn land. They had a decent store of nuts gathered, but the berries were scant and shriveled, and a chill they had never known was in the air. Eve had cultivated a small plot of her favorite roots and greens, but a morning came when the tender leaves were dark, stiff and cold. What was happening?

The animals were on the move. Daily now flocks of birds flew overhead and herds of hoofed creatures moved hurriedly southward as if outrunning some evil of which the humans were unaware. Should they follow? Adam tried to keep his worries to himself, but their accustomed food sources were exhausted and the air grew ever colder. Also, his mate's belly was swelling day by day. He had observed the ways of the animals enough to know what was happening. She had a baby growing inside her. They spoke of this a bit but both felt unprepared. Their only comfort came from the fact the animals surrounding them seemed able to raise their young. Surely they would know what to do when the time came—right?

Daily Adam's fear mounted as their rations waned but, amazingly, Eve was content. She was fascinated with the miracle taking place within her body and would cry out in astonishment and grab Adam's hand to share the movement when her belly moved of its own accord. Like the mother birds, she prepared their home, continuing to fill the chinks with clay to make it snug and laying aside whatever she could gather of the scant food.

One morning Adam rose early, gazing with tenderness on the girl-woman who slept on in the pre-dawn light. He had been taught so much about how to manage animals and nature, but how could that knowledge aid him when he simply needed to keep food in their mouths? How he wished for Adonai's limitless wisdom that he had enjoyed in the garden. He recalled their conversations. They usually followed a simple line. He would ask a question and the Maker would answer, sometimes with another leading question, sometimes with a story.

"How I need You, Adonai," he intoned without thinking. "I can't believe You have forgotten us or didn't have a plan for our survival here. You know everything. You are so kind and good. It is just so much harder to believe in You when I can't see You every day. But I know You. You would not want her to be hungry. You would show me a way if You could. I know You hear me, but how do I hear You?

He recalled the words Adonai had spoken when He had joined them as man and wife. How did that go?

"For this reason a man shall leave his father and mother and cleave to his wife and the two shall become one flesh."

At the time Adam had not understood the meaning. Now those words made sense. He and Eve had finally become true mates when ties with their old life were severed and they were forced to rely on each other. There had been nowhere to run when their pain had bubbled over. They were forced to trust each other with their vulnerability and therefore they had melted into one—just as surely as two mounds of precious metal became one when Rapha had placed them in fire.

So this was part of Adonai's plan? No, Adonai could not intend evil, it was not in His nature, but He had known. He had known everything that was to come. He had even known their love would flourish outside the safety and ease of the garden. So, could Adam surmise that Adonai's plan was still unfolding according to its purpose? Could he hope that he and Eve had not completely failed? Hope warmed him. Was Adonai so powerful He could even work beauty from their utter failure?

That thought almost choked him. Shouldn't he hold that failure close to remain truly sorry for it? Wasn't it his future to dwell in that failure forever? He could not fix it, he could not turn back time and undo it, but was it possible he needed to let it go?

He hopped to his feet, pacing as the rim of morning sun blazed out to greet him. He caught his breath at its beauty. Overhead a flock of ducks flew east and appeared to be swallowed by its brightness just as a fresh breeze, like a kiss blown from Adonai's mouth, brushed his cheek.

He recalled another conversation with Adonai when he had questioned why the sun appeared and disappeared each day. ***"It is a picture of my love, that my mercy is new every morning, that no matter how dark the night may be, a new day awaits and my love is renewed."***

Those words had carried little meaning for a young man wrapped in the lap of luxury and contentment but now he grasped them like a lifeline. Adonai's love was new every morning. Every day He offered a fresh start—even for a cocky manchild who had to lose everything to realize how much he had.

Then it hit him. He felt renewed much like he had after lounging in Adonai's arms in Eden. He had asked and Adonai had answered! All the words from their many conversations were in his heart, just waiting for him. They were like the seeds placed in the ground, hidden but taking root, growing in secret until finally their meaning broke through the soil of his stubborn mind. Gratitude flooded his being and he cast himself to the ground. Adonai was here, unseen but still present, still available to give counsel and comfort.

Hardly realizing why he did it, Adam started gathering stones and placing them one on top of the other. He wanted to remember this moment. He wanted to have a visible reminder of his first conversation with his Maker outside the garden.

The sun continued to climb, chasing away the night's chill as Adam, sweat trickling into his eyes, continued his backbreaking task, invigorated by Adonai's presence. For the first time in several moons, his heart felt light and… filled—in the way only Adonai could fill it. He had thought he would never have that sensation again.

His conversation with the Almighty continued as his muscles strained, groaned and rejoiced. Amazingly, Adonai felt just as near in his work as He did in Adam's repose. His whole body wanted to dance and—and—*fly!* But his feet were rooted to earth so his hands worked while his soul soared.

There were still questions and practical matters to address. How was he to feed his mate? He had seen their store of nuts and dried berries. Only one handful of each remained. He paused in his work to push the drenched locks from his forehead.

"Do you bring a sacrifice for Adonai?"

The voice startled him and Adam spun to face the speaker. The morning sun was in his eyes but he made out the figure of a man outlined in the brightness.

"Who are you, Lord?"

"I AM His Word that sustains you," the puzzling answer flowed over Adam's trembling body and he fell face down to the ground.

"Do you bring a sacrifice?" the shining One asked again.

"We have only a handful of nuts and berries…"

"Bring what you have," came the gentle request.

Adam's forehead wrinkled in confusion, "Surely You dwell in Adonai's abundance, and our scant offering cannot compare."

"What you have is sufficient."

There did not seem anything else to say so Adam ran to the shelter to retrieve the last of their rations, nearly bowling over the still groggy Eve. "He's here! He is on the hill! Come and see!" His excitement was so great he almost forgot their tiny store of food. But when he checked the basket, not a single crumb remained.

"Where is the food?" Adam asked.

Eve's face flushed with guilt. "While I slept, I dreamed of feasting in Eden. When I woke I was so hungry. I tried to wait for you but you were gone so long…."

"But He said to bring it. Now we have no sacrifice."

"I'm sorry. I was just so hungry," her eyes welled with tears.

Adam pulled her into his arms. "All will be well even if we are empty-handed. But come, He is waiting."

"Who? What is his name?"

"I don't know."

"Then how do you know he is good?"

"When you meet Him you will see."

"What did he look like? What did he say?" Her questions would have continued if the trek up the hill had not made it difficult to breathe as she wrestled with her own clumsiness.

Thus the trip back went much slower than Adam desired and a few sharp words flew between them before they finally crested the hill and she beheld—a pile of stones. Adam searched and called while Eve, hungry and tired, slumped against Adam's stone monstrosity. So this is where he had been all morning. "Adam, you must be exhausted. Perhaps you fell asleep and dreamed."

"No! He was—" Adam froze as the man's last words rang out in his heart, ***"Whatever you have is sufficient."*** And there was his precious Eve, hair tousled and cheeks rosy from exertion, leaning against his monument to Adonai. She was the only thing in his life of any worth, the only thing worthy of his Lord. For the second time that morning he fell to his knees.

"What is it?" Eve rushed to his side, frightened by the horror on his face, but he did not answer; he just clung to her. Finally, when he did speak, the words were not for her.

"But what else is there?" He gasped, the loneliness of his life without her already consuming him. Clearly, he pictured the baby monkey when they were in the garden and the mother's trust as she handed him to Adonai. The gift was accepted and then returned. Perhaps Adonai would be gracious? Just as quickly, he remembered the lamb. Adonai had given no guarantees. He was simply asking obedience.

Adam's body trembled as the war raged inside. A picture of Eve's lifeless body stretched upon the stones assaulted his mind. How could Adonai require this of him? Was this the price of his sin, to lose what he loved and spend his days in grief? Did he really want to be joined to such a bloodthirsty God?

No. Adonai was kind and generous and it was His love that had created Eve. Without Adonai, there would be no life. It came to this. This was the moment that separated bone from sinew. This was the crisis of his heart. Over and over he had failed the test. Over and over he had come up against the wall of his will versus Adonai's. Would he serve himself or his Maker? From this defining moment on, who would be Lord?

He wept with so much remorse it seemed his life's blood would drain away with the tears. Good. Better him than her, the one who had become the center of his world.

"There! Look!" He heard Adonai's command as the wound was ripped aside to view the disease. Words spoken by his Master in the garden flowed through him, ***"My gifts are to be held with an open hand. Whatever is not entrusted to My keeping will turn to poison. The enemy prowls to discover and exploit that weakness."***

Through tortured eyes he looked up and cupped her cheek in his hand. "I have to give you back."

He did not need to explain. His torment had forewarned her. Amazingly, she was not frightened—but could she be as brave as the lamb? It seemed such a cruel thing to ask when they had at last found the wonder of Adonai's intended love. "Why?"

"It is my fault because I have put you before my devotion to Adonai."

"If that's the case, I am guilty of the same offense," her eyes flashed with anger. "Should we *not* love so Adonai remains unoffended?"

"No. He once told me that to love best, we must love Him first, for only His love is unending. Only in that way will the love remain pure because we show our trust most with what we treasure." The words were correct, but they cut in a way he had never imagined.

"But what of the life growing in me?" She placed his hand on her swollen belly, "The child kicks as if fighting for life."

He had no answer as the frantic movement beat against his hand. Then, grasping at a thread of hope, he offered, "Adonai breathed life into you once. Perhaps He plans to do so again."

She laughed through tears. "If Adonai, the giver of life, decides to take it back, does He really need my permission? He could take it before my next breath. The lamb took my place once. Adonai has proven His faithfulness when I did not deserve it. Shouldn't I trust Him again, even when I don't understand?"

The fear in her eyes fled. "I don't see any reason to wait." She gulped, "How?"

"The stones. I… I saw you… l-laying on the stones."

She strode to the monument that reached her chest in height and tried to climb onto it but her swollen form was cumbersome. Finally, she turned her back and attempted to clamber up. When she almost pitched forward, Adam was there to steady her. "Yes, I mustn't get hurt!" But her laugh was hollow. With a kiss to his forehead she lay back on the stones with her hand still holding tight to his.

And they waited. A sweet breeze blew across them, filled with the spiced scent of Adonai's embrace. Stillness grew in Adam's heart, a peace that made no sense whatsoever.

"I-am-given," Eve whispered in a groggy voice. Suddenly her hand tightened on his and she cried out as if in pain. Then she was still. Deathly still.

"Eve?" Adam squeezed her fingers. No response. He reached for her cheek then drew his hand away in dismay and gazed at her face. He laid his head on her chest and was silent a moment but soon his shoulders shook with sobs and he buried his face in her neck. "My Eve, my love," Adam choked out as he gathered her into his arms and rocked, wailing with grief.

"I have come to claim what is mine."

Adam paused and looked up through tear-drenched hair to see Lucifer, a glow encircling his head and a golden garment draping his body. *"So nice of you to present my mate so conveniently."* The mocking voice continued. *"And you've taken such good care of my seed. How kind!"*

"You are too late," Adam spoke in a toneless voice. "She is given."

"What is that supposed to mean? Sacrifice? Don't tell me the Great One's developed a taste for blood!"

"He asked, we gave. It is over. Now go away."

"But... but what about my seed?" Lucifer sputtered. *"She is mine by right! I was first! What is inside of her* is mine*!"*

Adam chuckled as fresh tears spilled and he brought her palm to his cheek. "I am so glad she is dead rather than in your clutches. Thanks be to Adonai for His wisdom."

"Then I will remove my seed from her body!" Lucifer strode toward Eve, his hand outstretched, clawlike fingers contorting and grasping as if to will the inhabitant of Eve's body out of hiding.

But Adam's voice carried authority in his grief. "You will not touch her! *All* is given. All. Is. Adonai's!"

There was a mighty flash of light and a roaring flame enveloped Lucifer as he emitted a high, piercing shriek and disappeared. All was silent once more.

Adam sat staring where Lucifer had vanished, astonished at what his eyes had just beheld.

But the strange events of that day were not over. A voice spoke, bringing once again the contented breeze of paradise. **"Well done! Your trust and obedience are a pleasing fragrance to your heavenly Father."**

Adam looked to where the man, looking like a bit of the sun had come for a visit, once again reclined on the rock. As before, the brightness of His form made it difficult to make out His features but His voice was filled with joy.

"Rejoice! This day your enemy's plans are thwarted. Adonai accepts the sacrifice of your greatest treasure."

“Does she know,” Adam looked to the peaceful smile on Eve’s still features, “that we did something right?” He stroked her cold cheek.

“She is held in Adonai’s embrace. There is no deeper joy.”

The man came toward Adam, **“However, the heartache of offering the blood of the beloved as a sacrifice for sin is not something the Father asks of his children. He asks it only of Himself. Receive back the gift given, renewed and restored through your faith.”**

Then the shining man placed a hand on Eve’s head. The heavenly glow encased her body and was absorbed. Immediately her chest rose with a deep breath and her eyes fluttered open. She gazed at the man before her, joy flooding in. “It’s You!” she exclaimed.

The man laughed, **“Yes, dear one. But you are not the lamb, so rise.”** He assisted Eve down from the altar, and then placed her hand in Adam’s.

Adam looked at Eve’s hand in his, then hungrily drank in every feature of her face before hugging and spinning her as he whooped with joy and she laughed, returning his eager kisses. Finally they stopped and Adam placed her feet on the ground as they turned toward their heavenly visitor with sheepish expressions.

“Thank you,” Adam said, stealing glances toward Eve’s flushed cheeks and glowing eyes. “I do not deserve such joy.”

The heavenly messenger laughed, then said, **“All heaven rejoices with you. However,”** when he continued, his voice was gentle, **“your task today is unfinished. The covenant of Eden must be renewed with blood until the promised One is given. As the priest of your household, Adam, this task is yours.”**

“But I have no lamb to give,” Adam said.

"Adonai provides the lamb."

No sooner was the word spoken than the provision appeared. A young lamb trotted into view, a stout yearling, and, with a plaintive bleat, it started up the hill, its hooves clicking against the rocky ground, until it stood between the two parties.

"You must bind him and place him on the altar," the man's voice continued. **"Approach, son of man, and receive the tools of sacrifice."**

Adam crossed to take a golden bowl from the shining hands. Inside was a length of rope and a sharp knife. Tears already glimmered on Eve's cheeks but she moved forward to take the lamb's head in her hands, stroking and kissing it. "I am so sorry," she murmured. "Thank you."

Soon, the lamb was bound and lay quietly upon the altar. Adam recalled the scene of sacrifice in the garden and repeated Adonai's words. "Our sins are conferred onto this innocent one. Adonai's spirit binds with this accursed flesh, thus the knife is plunged into His heart; the blood that flows is His divine blood."

As before, this was the first time the animal struggled. According to instruction, the knife rose, glimmering in Adam's trembling hand, and plunged into the lamb's heart. Through his tears, Adam allowed the blood, set aside as holy unto Adonai, to flow into the bowl as their divine visitor directed.

When all was complete the man said, **"Step away."**

Adam and Eve complied and when fire from heaven enveloped the altar, they trembled with fear and fell to their knees. Then, when the terrifying rain ceased, both saw in the smoke that rose to the sky, the disfigured form of a man, dripping streams of blood from countless cruel wounds, arms outstretched, muscles straining with torturous pain, eyes peering through the smoke until his gaze locked with theirs. The torn lips gave a smile of recognition and moved with unheard words, then his body was wracked with one final spasm of pain and the man's head fell forward. The vision billowed upward with the rising smoke, and faded.

They were speechless; eyes still locked on the smoke that rose heavenward, a swiftly building monolith, until it began to spread, reaching swiftly to the north and south horizons and beyond. Finally, where horizontal and vertical met, the sun's rays shot out.

"Adam, dip your hands in the bowl."

Adam walked to the stones and the golden bowl where he had drained the lamb's blood, surprised to discover the liquid was clear. In fact, it seemed a shame to stain it with his bloodied hands, but he plunged them into the sparkling fluid and watched the red stains disappear without a trace.

"Now eat what the Lord has set aside as your portion," the man instructed.

Adam hesitated, eyeing the lamb that sizzled and smoked on the stones that still glowed from the firestorm. "I… am not accustomed…. In the garden Lucifer consumed the lamb and—"

"Fire burned him," the Holy One finished the thought. **"It will not be so for you whose stain is cleansed. When you eat the lamb's flesh, you partake of his death and cleansing through fire. In this way, you are one with his death and yet you live."**

"Might Eve be allowed to share the portion with me?"

"No, it is the priest's job to eat of the sacrificed lamb. Trust Adonai. When all is accomplished to fulfill the covenant, provision is made for those in your care."

As Adam chewed slowly, the Holy One continued, **"This sacrament is to be observed as a reminder to you and your**

descendants of Adonai's steadfast love. In this way, the evil one is defeated in your flesh until the sacrifice that heals all is given."

With those final words, the light of the man's presence began to fade until Adam and Eve were left staring where His eyes had been, an after-image of peace and joy wreathed in fire.

Thus they remained on the hilltop beside the blackened altar while the crossbeams of smoke continued to rise above their heads.

Finally, as the sun edged toward the western horizon, Adam and Eve made their way back down the mountain, arms entwined.

"Did it hurt?" Adam asked.

"On the altar?"

"You cried out as if in pain."

Eve smiled and her head fell against Adam's shoulder, "It was too beautiful, too… fulfilling. I was absolutely free, no fear, I couldn't even imagine the word. Even now I can't imagine ever needing anything ever again. I am not even hungry!" She laughed.

"Did you really die?"

"I can't be sure," Eve replied, a bemused expression on her face. "I was aware of all that happened but I was so peaceful there was no desire to move and no need to even breathe. It was like," she paused, eyes squinted in concentration, "like those times I fell asleep in Adonai's arms. It was pure bliss. I wanted to laugh when Lucifer spoke because I felt so… so free."

Later, an exhausted but joyful Adam whispered, "Thank you," to his Maker as he drifted to sleep with Eve nestled in his arms.

Far away a pair of piercing eyes had beheld the rising smoke. The long-awaited sign was given. If he kept his face toward the northern star, he should reach them by daybreak. Hopefully that would be soon enough.

Chapter Eighteen

Attack

The night was a suffocating, velvet blackness when Adam woke with a start. A distant, bloodcurdling howl drifted in on a cold breeze. Closer at hand, something large and snarling pounded the earth with its footsteps accompanied by the explosive groans and crashes of trees ripped from the ground.

"What is it?" Eve's frightened voice whispered as Adam slipped from the warmth of their shared woolen cloaks to peer into the darkness. He had no answer. No animal in their region was strong enough to tear up trees and certainly nothing in his experience could explain that hulking, black shape that stood staring toward their dwelling with glowing eyes.

Cold fear flowed through his body.

"I AM His Word that sustains you," the Holy One had said.

Adam tried to recall more of Adonai's words, any words, but when he looked back at those glowing eyes, holiness felt extinct. A putrid stench blew across his skin and swirled through the confines of their shelter, bringing panic in its wake. They were trapped here! How could he defend Eve against this monstrosity? Perhaps the only hope was for him to draw the creature away.

He inched toward the door but Eve's hand clasped his arm with surprising strength. "What are you doing?" When he whispered his intentions her nails bit into his skin. "No! We are stronger together. It is the enemy's way to separate us because then his job is easy."

"If it comes to fighting, you will only be a hindrance…."

"Do you really think *that* will be defeated by strength?" she hissed. "Look at it. Why do you think it just *happened* to show up after our sacrifice?" Her volume rose as she heard and believed her own words. "Lucifer wants us to believe we are vulnerable. Nothing can touch us and *nothing* is going to ruin Adonai's plan!"

She moved in the dark to find the golden bowl that still contained the remains of the lamb's blood. "*This* is why we have nothing to fear. Lucifer knows this. Perhaps we need to remind him."

She strode to the entrance of their shelter and, with her bare hands, dipped and spread the liquid around the opening. Then she placed her still-dripping hands on Adam's head and ended by applying it to her own head and the portion of her clothing that covered her belly. "There!" she announced to the darkness, "The blood of the lamb is mightier than evil!"

The night erupted with anger. Snarls and howls were all around them. Evidently the monster in the trees had not come alone. If Eve had not stopped him from going out into the night…. Adam broke out in a cold sweat as he considered that possibility. He spared another cautious glance out of the shelter and, from the position of the stars, surmised darkness was only three-quarters complete. With that quick glance he also detected at least five more pairs of glowing eyes. Eyes of that sort were made for darkness but retreated during daylight. How would he and Eve survive until the sun? Furthermore, what were they to do the next night? And the next?

"Human!" The harsh voice made Adam's skin crawl. "Give us what belongs to our master and you will live."

Eve stepped to Adam's side. "Nothing here belongs to your master, so go!"

The speaker's guttural laughter was joined by a chorus of hisses and growls, "The pretty one thinks to defy the master of this world! You are his. Your flesh is joined to his. What grows in you is his!"

Eve wanted to shout more brave words, but the accusations replayed those horrible moments of abuse at Lucifer's hands. She was there again, trapped, defiled, and stripped of innocence with his hate-filled breath in her ears.

"Yes, woman," the monster replied, enjoying her thoughts, "you know. You belong to the Lord Lucifer. There is no escape."

"You would call Adonai a liar?" Adam shouted. "The lamb's blood cancels Lucifer's claim."

Again their unseen opponent laughed. "Woman, you have been joined to this world's ruler. Why do you grovel with this maggot in his hole of stone? Come quickly and my master will be merciful to *it*."

Another round of appreciation erupted in the darkness and Adam's bravery quailed. How could they stand against such forces? Where were the troops of celestials coming to their aid? Had Adonai ritually cleansed them so their spirits could join Him when these servants of evil consumed their flesh? Okay, maybe just *his* flesh since Lucifer obviously still had use for Eve. With that thought, he reached for his mate in the dark and pulled her close. Her fate would be worse than death. "Get the knife," he whispered. "It came from Adonai's hand. Protect yourself with it."

Again the enemy in the dark read his thoughts. "You would dare to defy us? You are nothing! We come from long lines of kings with knowledge you cannot imagine! Our master honors the lowly human to graft her into his glorious lineage. Choose resistance and we will *take* what is his."

Adam could tell the vile being *hoped* to shed blood. They had not come to talk, they had come to feed. Indeed, they were sounding more impatient by the second.

"Adonai help us," Eve breathed.

"Adonai is weak!" Their opponent shouted to a chorus of snarls and clatter of metal. "His creation is taken from Him! He sits in heaven and allows it! He will stay there as we rip your flesh!"

The air was stifling and the patch of night stars was obliterated as the enormous creature rose to the height of the trees. There was something familiar about its elongated, sinuous silhouette. When a membranous wing unfurled against the night sky, Adam gasped in recognition and declared, "We have met one like you before. Wasn't it your queen who bowed to Adonai and begged release from Lucifer's slavery?"

Silence. Then an angry hiss, "Human! Adonai murdered our queen for her mingled blood. You defile her memory!"

No!" Adam shouted. "She lives and chose to honor Adonai by casting off her royalty."

"You lie!" The bloodthirsty snarls broke out again. "The Lord Lucifer said…."

"*Lucifer* lies! You know this." Then came a flash of inspiration, "Did he promise that you would rule, yet you are his slaves? Did he say that you would be superior to all creation yet your bodies fade day by day? Even now he uses you to do what he cannot! Or did he fail to tell you about the fire from heaven that repelled him today?"

The creature screamed with rage and fear once more clutched Adam's heart. He had seen the mocking, proud Lucifer fall today when.... Adam searched his mind. Something he had said in his grief had carried tremendous power. What was it?

"Lucifer will devour you! He has raised us! He has given power!" The mob closed in. An overwhelming smell of death descended.

"Adonai, deliver us!" Eve whispered although she could see no hope. She clutched the knife to her heart.

"Surrender to us, humans. You are defeated. There is no escape." The evil voice droned on.

"Adonai!" It was the only sound Adam could force from his mouth but his voice was weak, drowned in a sea of hatred. Perhaps the knife had come to their possession for this moment. He was overwhelmed with the ease with which they could die, cheating evil of that pleasure. An image of him driving the sharp blade into their hearts blazed in his mind. Was this Adonai's directive? His hand groped toward Eve, reaching for the blade, but a piercing pain screamed through his being and he yelped as his hand was pinned against her with the sharp knife. His hand had stopped her from piercing her own throat!

With the pain of the blade came clarity.

"We smell your blood, human. Finish it!" The voice quivered with anticipation.

"Why have you not done it yourself?" Adam gritted the words as he yanked the knife from his hand. "Does the blood of the lamb repel you? Are we so close yet out of your reach?"

Suddenly, the words Adam had spoken on the hilltop spilled out in rage from Eve's lips, "YOU WILL NOT TOUCH US! ALL IS GIVEN! ALL IS ADONAI'S!"

Instantly, a flash of light behind the murderous warriors interrupted their shrieks of rage. The enemy forces were blinded by the piercing glare that flooded the woods and reflected off the wet stain on the entrance of their dwelling. Adam and Eve blinked at each other in amazement to discover their own brows lit with what seemed to be flames. Their astonishment continued as they looked back towards the spectacle of their enemies lit from behind by what appeared to be stars approaching through the trees. The gnarled, armored bodies of their enemies crushed together, heads whipping from side to side, arms upraised as if to deflect mighty blows, swords flailing as they stared with horror at a blinding light advancing on all sides. Shrieks of pain and fear erupted from the confused hordes as they began to cut down their own.

There was no time to question. Adam gripped the knife tight in his hand and ran toward the still-dazed leader even though the creature's form was a living nightmare, alive with carved symbols etched in the iridescent flesh that towered high above Adam's head. With a mighty leap that made Adam feel for a moment as if his feet had wings, he bounded up and plunged the flaming knife high into the reptile's body. A terrifying, gurgling scream hissed from the monster's lips as the blade pierced the thick hide. The sound of their champion's pain drove the blinded warriors into an even greater panic and they fell to stabbing, biting, and tearing one another. Adam leapt aside as the leader's enormous body whipped, convulsed, and, with wings flailing and clawed arms grasping, fell to the ground, crushing several of his troops in the process. All the while the light in the woods grew brighter and Lucifer's groping, blinded servants continued their self-destruction.

Eve remained in the doorway with the golden, flame-filled bowl in her hands, ready to repel any who approached. But there was no need. The sources of light caused such fear among the enemy that they continued to drive themselves against their own swords.

As Adam returned to her side, she noticed one creature in those fearsome ranks that held her gaze even as it dodged and ducked the swords around him. Obviously, the light did not blind this one.

As gray daylight began to silhouette the branches of the trees, they beheld a most welcome sight. A huge, shaggy shape came bounding through the trees, toppling injured enemies in its path—its joyful, ferocious baying echoing off the arms of the mountains around them. A moment later it ran straight at the humans. Reflexively, Adam stepped in front of his pregnant mate but the bedraggled beast slid to a halt, barking and quivering from the tip of a muck-crusted nose to the end of a matted tail. Adam and Eve laughed and reached to caress the ears of the animal that, crazed with delight in their presence, proceeded to lick every inch of them she could reach.

She was hardly recognizable beneath the grime but it was the dog Adam had named Eden, who had elected to join them on that heartbreaking last day in the garden. They had no idea how the faithful beast had found them, but her delight in being united with them was the perfect balm to chase away the remaining darkness from their hearts.

But this was not the end of happy reunions. Along with the bright heavenly hosts who continued to herd the remnants of their enemy into a tighter, snarling circle, another figure was seen picking his way through the dead and wounded. Eve was laughing at Eden's antics as she reared up on her hind legs to place massive paws on Adam's shoulders while the young man stumbled under the dog's weight, when she spied the mysterious stranger. He was not one of the enemies. In fact, the heavenly army appeared to treat him with utmost deference although he was quite ragged in appearance and did not blaze with their inner fire. There was something familiar about the way this one moved, though his shoulders were stooped with fatigue and his hair and clothing were caked with mud. Then Eve caught the glimmer of a keen eye beneath the lank hair and she gasped. Following her gaze, Adam peered at the stranger then whooped with joy and bounded through the trees, embracing him with an exuberance that rivaled the dog's greeting. Eve also trotted to him with open arms as quickly as her awkward frame would allow.

"Rapha!" she screamed with delight. "How did you… where have you… why aren't you…." she stammered, too many questions filling her mind to voice just one.

For his part, Rapha held the young people at arm's length, drinking in the sight of them. "You are well," he whispered, relief and joy etched on his tired features.

"Excuse me, sir," one of the celestials addressed Rapha. "One of the enemy bears the mark of Adonai. What are your orders?"

Rapha turned to Adam. "Well?"

But Adam appeared lost in wonder as he clapped Rapha on the back, laughing as a cloud of dust rose from Rapha's garment. "I am discovering friends everywhere I look. One more will be welcome."

The angel led them to a spot a bit removed from the other defeated hosts to where a deformed man creature sat, quiet and composed, though his bulbous eyes peered in wonder from his fierce, spiked helmet. When he spied Rapha and Adam he put his face to the ground.

"Masters, I swear to serve you as long as I live. And if I am to be slain, it would be an honor for my blood to be spilled by your hand."

Rapha blinked in astonishment. He studied the creature, taking in the bent body and the scent of evil that clung to its thick hide. But, yes, the mark of Adonai was in his eyes. “Who are you?” Rapha asked.

“Who I was is past. May I never again hear that name. From this day forth, I will answer only to the name you would bestow—if I live.”

Rapha stared into eyes resigned to death, yet filled with peace. The hand of Adonai had grown long indeed. “How can this be?” he spoke his thought aloud.

“I was there,” the man answered. “On the day you showed mercy to my friend, Lak, I watched your kindness.” His large eyes, gleaming with unshed tears, searched their faces. “Since that moment, I have questioned everything I was ever taught.”

Adam gasped, “Do you speak of the creature who died? The one who bit my friend here?”

“Yes. His *name* was Lak.” The man’s eyes flashed with a touch of defiance. “But I saw you that day,” the man continued, “and your mate, and your friend.” He gazed into their eyes in turn. “I could not understand why you would treat an enemy with kindness. I had never beheld anything so… beautiful.” He looked down, blinking hard as the muscles in his face fought for command of powerful emotions. “Something happened inside of me. I have had dreams of a man with kind eyes and a white garment who says Adonai… l-loves me.”

Celestials and evil forces within earshot of such a statement gasped, and two swarthy beings dove for the man, growling obscenities. But the aggressors fell back when Adam flourished the knife that still glowed like a red-hot ember.

After much deliberation, it was decided the remaining enemy forces would be marched by the heavenly hosts far away to a land that would support them with plenty of food and water.

As for this one who swore allegiance, Rapha said he would take responsibility.

For his part, the man was grateful *not* to be handed over to the tender mercies of his former people.

Later, the scene in their camp was humble but serene as they savored the sweetness of good company and plentiful food procured from the rations left by their fallen foes.

When Adam and Eve retreated to their stone dwelling, Eden took up her post at the entrance while Rapha and their new ally kept watch by the fire, their low voices blending with the music of an occasional lamb's bleat. These friendly sounds were a lullaby as Adam wrapped his arms around his exhausted wife and slept more deeply than he had since their days in the garden.

Chapter Nineteen

Family

When Eve woke the next morning, she discovered Adam's absence and the presence of a delicious aroma in the air. Beside their pallet a simple but tasty breakfast of fresh goat milk and some sort of ground, sweet paste was arranged with dried fruit and a spongy, bland but pleasant substance on a mat woven of green reeds. With a squeal of delight, she devoured the meal with gusto, discovering the spongy stuff was wonderful eaten with the sweet paste. For the first time in at least two moons, her hunger was satisfied. Even the babe in her womb stretched luxuriously, making her stomach appear lumpy and misshapen.

With a sigh she parted the folds of her garment to peer at her swelling physique. How much larger would she grow? For that matter, how much larger *could* she grow? She was not entirely ignorant of the process of birthing young—she had witnessed the event repeatedly among the animals—but she did not recall any who carried their babies inside ever getting *this* large. And the babe was so active! Just how many arms and legs could it possibly have?

A jolt of fear shot down her spine. Lucifer proudly claimed that what was inside her belonged to him. Perhaps what grew unseen resembled some of the frightening creatures in his service?

That thought almost cost her the breakfast.

She placed a trembling hand against the hard swell that strained and stretched her smooth skin. Immediately her belly jostled as if every part of the babe competed for the warmth of her touch. She giggled and pushed against what must be a foot pressing against her rib. "Stop that!" she commanded, and shoved the offending limb, but the pressure only increased as if the stranger within was excited by her undivided attention.

In that moment she knew. Sight unseen, this child already owned her heart. It was part of her. Even if it emerged with horns on its head, cloven hoofs and wings, she would devote her life to protecting and loving it.

Having resolved that question, she splashed her face with cool water provided in a stone bowl just inside the door. It was a strange sensation to hear voices since for so long she had heard no conversation whatsoever unless it was hers and Adam's. For a moment she paused, enjoying the sound of soft laughter, the chatter of birds, and the homey scent of a campfire, such a far cry from the harrowing experiences of the night. Bracing herself for whatever traces of battle she might face and swallowing hard (there was no way she was going to waste that wonderful breakfast) she pulled back the covering and peeked out.

But the ground outside their dwelling was spotless; scrubbed, scraped and covered with fresh dirt. Not a broken branch, trace of blood, or any other sign of battle remained except for the thin column of smoke from the distant fire. For her breakfast's sake, she was *very* grateful it was distant.

Adam and their new ally were so deep in conversation they did not even notice her, so she took the opportunity to study this interesting specimen.

Obviously, some of the markings she had spied on his body the night before had been added for battle because his skin, which had appeared reptilian, was simply pale, hairy and rough. He was small in stature, due partly to his stooped posture and the way he kept his head tucked. His clothing, now that the barbed armor was removed, was simple and functional, a tunic of animal skin that fell to knobby, scarred knees and coverings for his feet, tooled in a method unknown to her. His face, though free of grotesque markings, was still disconcerting with the bulbous eyes, a large nose that protruded at an odd angle and deep grooves around his eyes and mouth as if his face knew only how to scowl. His hands sported pointed nails. Eden didn't seem to mind this fact as she lay beside him, belly exposed, enjoying a good scratch.

It was the dog, in fact, that gave Eve away, lifting its shaggy head and running to nuzzle her hands. Adam too leapt to his feet and greeted her with a joyous smile, looking just for a moment like the carefree boy she once knew in the garden.

Their guest, however, busied himself dusting off a wooden seat and laying a plush, black covering upon it. Then he stepped away with an outstretched hand. Eve was suddenly shy. She had almost forgotten what it felt like to be treated like a queen. She sank into the chair, enjoying the relief to her tired back. "Thank you!" She fingered the covering. "Is this fur?"

"Yes, my… highness," he stammered, unsure how to address her. "It is from a rare animal that thrives in frigid water. The fur is highly prized among my… former people."

Pulling back the fur she studied the simple construction of a wide, split log carved to fit perfectly into two smaller logs that served to hold the seat and back in place while also providing armrests. "Did you make this?"

He nodded but kept his eyes downcast.

"And do I have you to thank for the food as well?"

Again he nodded then hastened to add, "But your mate brought it to you." Light, almost colorless eyes flicked her way.

"Well, it was wonderful."

He acknowledged her with another nod but remained standing, head bowed. Eve's eyes implored Adam to intervene.

"Have a seat, friend," Adam gestured toward the spot where their guest had reclined before but instead the man knelt, hands clutched upon his knees.

"How did you make the wood so straight and smooth?" Eve asked to break the awkward silence. "I thought those outside the garden were unskilled, more accustomed to warfare than artistry."

"Is that what you were taught?" A grim smile played about his lips.

Eve stammered, "Actually, I guess that is what I assumed since your… people… do not serve Adonai."

Again his eyes met her gaze only for an instant. "Our heritage and history are proud, and our cities were the greatest ever beheld and our artistry, unsurpassed. Though we dwelt in deep, hidden places many years, we remember."

Eve was immediately alert, leaning forward with an eager light in her eyes.

"Make yourself comfortable, friend." Adam said with a smile as he settled back with his hands behind his head. "Your jaws will have to work just as hard as your body did throughout the night."

After a playful swat to Adam's arm Eve's questioning began in earnest, "You say your people dwelt in deep, hidden places. Why?"

"Our ancient writings and tales told around our campfires record that Adonai wished to destroy us. Thus he sent a barrage of stars from the sky. The few who survived did so by escaping to caverns far below the surface."

At these words anger flashed across Eve's features and she squirmed in her chair. But if the man noticed her discomfort, he gave no indication.

"The most magnificent of our cities," he continued, "a great center of art and wisdom that shone like a jewel on the edge of an azure sea, collapsed and was swallowed into the depths."

"Rapha told us that story," Eve interjected, "but he said that men followed evil counsel, delving too deep beneath the city and building such gigantic structures that the foundations were unable to support them."

The man was quiet a moment as a muscle twitched in his jaw. "That may be true but you will forgive me if I repeat our history in the only manner I have known."

"Please continue," Adam encouraged.

"As floodwaters rose and fire rained from the sky, tall, shining men came to lead the survivors to deep caverns. For untold generations, more than a thousand years, our people struggled to survive, always holding to the promise given by the shining messengers that a day would come when we would once more dwell beneath the warmth of the sun.

"So we have longed for the day we could wreak vengeance against the cruelty of He who reigns over the heavens."

"But," Eve's brow furrowed with confusion, "the messengers who saved your people, didn't they say they served Adonai?"

"All I know is what was told to my father and his fathers before him, that it was the gods we… my people… serve who saved us."

"Well, Rapha will give you the true account since he was there when it happened." Eve tossed out this bit of information with a shrug while their guest's eyes widened with disbelief.

"Who is this Ra-fa?" he asked. "He must be aged indeed if he claims knowledge of ancient events."

“What do you mean, ‘Who is he?’ You two hauled and cleaned together until the sun was high,” Adam informed him.

“You and Rapha did all this?” Eve gestured toward the night’s battlefield that now bore no trace of bloodshed. “You must be so tired.”

But the man’s eyes remained on Adam, “The… tall one who spoke with phantoms that transported the slain?”

“Phantoms?” Adam questioned, “Do you refer to the celestial hosts who aided us in battle?”

“I *mean* the unseen ones who struck terror to our forces and who keep watch even now,” he said. “I feel their eyes on me.”

“Where?” Eve peered around the glade.

“Can you not smell them?”

“*Smell* them?” Eve laughed. “Why would I need to smell what I can see?”

“You *see* them?” His eyes widened in horror.

“Of course. Didn’t you see them during the battle?”

“No. I heard words shouted in your dwelling, my eyes were robbed of sight and fear descended like thick smoke. My mind was gripped by madness. Then… it happened.” He gazed at his clenched hands, lost in thought.

“What?” Adam prompted.

“I recalled the kindness of your friend while Lak lay dying and I cried out, ‘Adonai, have mercy!’ Immediately, the darkness was gone. I looked around to discover my companions attacking each other. After that, I dodged their blades and wondered… how much I have been taught is a lie.”

Eve was still stuck on another mystery, “If you cannot see them, how can you see Rapha? He *is* one of the celestials.”

“That I cannot tell you but he is as clear to me as you are.“

As Eve pondered this, Adam turned to practical matters, “What are your plans now? Will you return to your people?”

After a moment's silence, the man responded, "They are dead to me and I to them. I can never return."

"But don't you have a mate or young of your own there?" Adam inquired.

Pain flashed in the man's eyes, "No."

"What hap—" Adam began, but Eve placed a cautioning hand on Adam's arm.

"What shall we call you?" she asked.

"It matters not. Where I go there will be no need of a name."

"Why should you go?"

At last the man's pale eyes met her gaze. "I may not understand Adonai's ways but there is something here, something I have no right to be a part of. I smell it, I feel it in the air, I see it when you look at each other and I sense the heavenly ones watching, expecting the evil of my heritage to infect this… this," he gestured around him, "*purity*."

Eve laughed, "If you are seeing something pure, it is only by the forgiveness of Adonai." She met his gaze with a smile. "We too have memories of evil but… what was that part about the sun rising," she prompted Adam.

"Adonai's mercy is new every morning, just like the sun rising on a new day."

Rapha watched their discourse, hidden in the branches of a nearby tree. While many talents such as flight and the ability to shift through time and space were no longer at his disposal, he was still a master of stealth. Although he read no deception in the man's countenance, he had to be sure. Thus he delved into the man's thoughts.

The man searched their carefree faces. Had he ever looked like that? No. His earliest memories were of strife and secrets and manipulations. When he was yet a child, he had been taught to fight. That was his inbred station among his people—he caught himself—his former people—a society ruled by one law: "The strong survive."

After a lifetime of winning at that game he had discovered there was nothing to live for. His family was gone and he had become as twisted and hopeless as those around him.

At the thought of family a door slammed in the man's mind as if that was a subject he refused to discuss even with himself. Thus with a soldier's discipline he turned from too-painful memories toward a former companion. Into the man's mind came the image of a winged, fanged man-beast, the one called Lak.

He had found a friend of sorts in Lak. He didn't trust the strange creature at first—the differing breeds had a deep hatred for each other—but once a tentative alliance was forged between them, he had found Lak to be a loyal and indispensable ally in battle.

Their strange bond was one of shared hate—for their leaders who ruled by fear, for their fellow warriors willing to betray for an extra ration of mind-numbing drink, for their putrid existence hiding in dark places like maggots.

He and Lak also shared a deep hatred for the others.

Once more an image jumped to the fore of the man's mind; men and beasts, women and children, with a much different way of life, a gentle, peaceful existence where they worshipped the one called Adonai. These strange beings clung to old writings that told of the "high God's" love and of His plan to restore their world to peace and plenty. Bloody memories of attacking and pillaging these people flooded the man's mind along with just a tinge of longing to understand their peaceful existence, even if it was based on the lie of love.

But his and Lak's deepest hatred was reserved for Adonai, the one who, according to their lore, had attempted to exterminate his people. It was He who was responsible for the loss of their privileged existence and devastation of their mighty cities.

Over and over they had heard the dogma that stoked their rage. "Adonai despises you. Adonai sees you as an abomination. We must ascend to the heavens and wrest power from His hands!"

Then, on the day of their great victory in Eden, he had witnessed a power that shook that hatred: undeserved kindness exhibited by a servant of Adonai. As he had wandered, grieving the loss of Lak, the closest thing he had ever had to a brother, he had breathed air laced with the essence of that kindness, had drunk from an untainted stream, and had tasted fruit so sweet it brought tears to his eyes.

And a question had taken root in the darkness of his poisoned mind.

"Is Adonai good?"

Since that day, he had been struggling in a world turned upside down. He began to sift through what he had accepted as fact and found he was increasingly repulsed by his people's practices, their deceit and constant grasping for power, the darkness of their minds that feasted on cruelty, their worship that had stolen his reason for living.

The past night's events had confirmed it.

He could never go back.

"We could use your help," Adam was saying, "if you're willing to stay."

The man gaped in disbelief. "I come during the night to destroy you and in the morning, though you do not even know my name, you invite me to stay?"

"That can be changed. What shall we call you?" Eve responded. "You have to at least stay long enough to give me the secret of your breakfast. It was delicious."

Thus the man without a home found himself chatting in the warmth of a bright new day about different ways to prepare dried fruits. As Rapha observed the scene, he had to smile. The night before, the battle-scarred man had overflowed with heartache even as he had worked to erase the stench of violence. Now, hope was dawning in his eyes.

Adonai never ceased to amaze Rapha. The Maker's ability to reach into the deepest evil and draw out a faithful heart was breathtaking. In this emotionally charred individual, Rapha sensed loyalty and a resilience that was, honestly, lacking in the young man and woman who were used to a life of abundance. He would learn knowledge of Adonai and they would learn keys to survive in a hostile world.

It was an efficient arrangement—profound, yet so typical of his Master.

Chapter Twenty

Birth

The coming days were taut with brooding hostility. Their new friend, whom they dubbed Kal, a reversal of his slain friend's name, warned them the defeat would not go unanswered. Although they had the forces of heaven on their side, even Rapha cautioned against remaining in one place for long. Thus their little band of outcasts began a nomadic existence.

Thanks to the livestock Rapha had brought from Eden, they never lacked fresh goat and sheep's milk, as well as wool and oil. Kal's knowledge of herbs, edible roots, and the location of seasonal nuts and fruits, further ensured their survival. It was he who taught them to harvest fish eggs, a food he insisted would be healthful for Eve and the baby in her womb. She balked at the taste but trusted his advice, having to admit the strange, salty clusters supplied a surge of energy for her growing frame.

But after two cycles of the moon of constant travel, a morning dawned when Eve could not walk. Her time was near. Adam and Rapha did what they could to make her comfortable, piling the woolen blankets beneath her and bathing her brow, but the process was slow.

Kal went about his duties seeing to the needs of the livestock and keeping watch for enemies but his gaze returned to the shelter of animal skins that had formerly housed one of his generals during battle. Smoke from the fire Adam stoked to ensure Eve's warmth rose from the center of the shelter. When he heard the young woman cry out in pain he busied himself gathering the leaves and petals of a certain flower known for its calming properties. When mixed with water warmed over the fire it would provide a measure of relief for the young woman. Although, as he told Rapha with a grim laugh, "Perhaps the relief will be mine since it gives me something to do."

He also confessed to Rapha the rumors about the babe Eve carried and his concerns about the imminent birth. "As a rule, women joined to the gods do not survive the birth process. But Eve is physically superior to the women among my people. Perhaps this will aid her." He grew quiet after this observation. Finally he had looked up at Rapha with the grim statement, "The Prince of Evil will never stop trying to reclaim his own."

Therefore Kal had taken to talking to Adonai and His unseen servants as he went about his duties tending the animals and keeping watch. Although he could not see them, Kal sensed the celestial presence and, as he sheared a ram, milked an ewe, or kept watch in the deep of night, he would invoke Adonai's protection or remind the wind of the covenant of blood that marked them. He was under no delusions. He could smell evil on that wind. Watching. Waiting.

Kal had been taught the power of words. Their rituals and incantations had been much more than mere tradition. Those practices, their smokes and dances and offerings, had been their pledge of devotion to "the gods," enslaving them body, mind, and spirit. He now saw them for what they were, attempts by the usurper to be worshipped as only Adonai deserved. Therefore, Kal, with a need to express his newfound freedom, created new dances to honor Adonai and new mantras for chanting as he went about his work.

Rapha smiled when he came upon Kal performing a vigorous dance in the moonlight or muttering under his breath as if engrossed in deep conversation with the sheep. The strange man's heartfelt worship was pleasing to Adonai who studied the intentions of the heart. Also, these ongoing practices were having their effect. Rapha sensed the growing numbers of celestials encamping around them and the sweet essence of Adonai's presence that flowed through and around Kal, cleansing the wounds of his past even as it protected the present.

In Kal, Rapha discovered a fascinating dichotomy. The swarthy man was full of knowledge, yet was eager to learn the ways of purity. His presence was a constant reminder of Adonai's grace and restorative power. Daily, Rapha marveled that such a pure heart proceeded from the very midst of Lucifer's earthly domain.

Rapha also discovered deep friendship with the little man. To Kal he spoke of his past life with unlimited access to Adonai. Rapha loved the way Kal's eyes would glow as he soaked in the tales of Adonai's kindness and holiness. At every opportunity Kal would ask questions about history, eager to dispel the lies of his past.

And the favor of the Most High rested on him. In time, even Rapha felt a twinge of envy for Adonai's relationship with that humble man. This aspect was also part of the mystery of Kal's character. He viewed himself as nothing, therefore he possessed no ego to pollute Adonai's thoughts. In turn his life was like a tree transplanted from poisonous waters to a pure flow that transformed the source of his existence. His countenance even became pleasing as bitter lines were erased and the knots in his soul unraveled, allowing his frame to straighten—although he would laugh when Eve ventured to call him handsome.

How Rapha grew to love the sound of Kal's voice, raspy from too many years smoking a special blend of tranquilizing herbs native to his people. Among his adopted family, that cheerful, hoarse crooning meant all was well: The flocks were accounted for and no enemies plagued their borders.

If Rapha came upon Kal in low spirits, he sensed this was due to the family Kal had lost, an event Kal chose not to divulge. But Eve's state was a constant painful reminder to Kal. Rapha tried not to pry but sometimes the image of a stout woman with a wide smile and abundant curly, dark hair was too strong to ignore. Rapha even knew her name, Eliana, a name that shoved forward in Kal's mind whenever he heard Eve's laughter. But the former angel wanted Kal to divulge his past out of trust and friendship. Thus, Rapha respectfully shut the mental door on Kal's privacy.

But Rapha was glad to have another in their company to watch and pray. While Adam and Eve trusted Adonai, the abundance of the garden had not prepared them for surviving, much less thriving, in a hostile environment.

He could feel the darkness blowing around their small camp, testing the perimeter, seeking a chink in their defenses, sifting Adonai's law to find a loophole—brooding, malicious, determined. Thus Kal's vigilance was most welcome and his knowledge of enemy strategy was the perfect balance to Adam and Eve's wholesome but sometimes complacent trust in Adonai's protection.

Perhaps due to the loneliness of their existence and their mutual sense of loss, their small company of four developed into a strong, interdependent community—even, in the truest sense of the word, a family—with Kal fulfilling the role of eccentric grandfather, with his stories that enlivened conversations around the fire and passed on indispensable information about their enemy.

But on the morn of Eve's travail, Kal's voice was a whisper lest he disturb her, and his darting eyes swept the horizon for signs of trouble. All night his unease had been growing, and, just like Eden, the faithful dog that stood at his side bristling from head to toe, he was on guard.

Rapha too had spent a sleepless night, hearing every moan of discomfort that escaped Eve's lips and echoing the sentiment of Kal's endless supplications to Adonai. In his less glorified form the lack of rest made him edgy. For several moons he had observed the girl's expanding frame, her delicate beauty stretched beyond what he thought possible. That she had remained mobile until they reached this wide land devoid of stones or trees that could hide their enemies was a miracle. The rolling, grassy slopes and fresh water could feed their flocks for as long as was necessary.

Over and over Rapha sifted Adonai's prophecy, searching for assurance that Eve would survive the ordeal but he found no guarantees. He had finally concluded the wisest course of action was to worship and pray like Kal. With words, Adonai had set all things in motion. With their words, he and Kal would call forth Adonai's best for Eve and for all those to come.

As the sun marched across the sky, clouds built in the west. Higher and higher they rose until, with the sun at its zenith, they turned the bright day to dusk.

Rapha did not need to see the celestial realm to realize the clash taking place in the heavenlies. With a flash, a streak of blinding light split the sky, striking the tree beside the prostrate Kal—whose fervent supplications simply rose in volume to combat the rush of punishing wind. Without skipping a beat in his prayers, the stalwart man hopped to his feet and raced to lead the flocks to a low-lying shelter of trees, with Eden's barking and herding assistance.

At first, Rapha did not hear the rising wail over the sound of the storm, rather he responded to the crashing tidal wave of grief. As he sprinted toward the shelter the sound of Adam's voice rose, a prolonged, primal, "NOOOOO!" colliding with the storm's fury.

He threw aside the flap of the battered shelter and entered a nightmare.

Blood. It was everywhere: on Adam's hands as he cradled the still form of his wife, coating the woolen blankets on which she lay and pooling on the ground around her. Death. He could smell it pressing in, draining life from the motionless young woman.

"It happened so suddenly," Adam stammered. "I think s-something… tore… inside. Sh… she… screamed."

"Kal!" Rapha called, but the little man was already outside having seen Rapha running toward the shelter. "Clean water. Lots. In the large skins."

One did not live as long as Rapha without learning the birthing process. After cleaning his hands with water and wine he assessed the situation. Gently probing, he confirmed his fears. The head of the baby was huge and pressed uselessly against the fully dilated opening. He bared Eve's stomach, all the while explaining to Adam what must be done and continuing his dialogue with Adonai. Taking the sacrificial knife, he once again utilized the wine and, instructing Adam to grip his wife lest she struggle, he cut.

His ancient heart quailed as Eve came to and shrieked while Adam whispered assurance and strove to keep her still. Rapha steadied his hands and shut his ears, his only goal to complete the process as quickly as possible. Continuing through the layers of skin, muscle and membrane, he once again probed… and froze.

Too many limbs. No time to ponder. There was the head. He lifted the bloody babe up. It was huge but perfectly formed with large eyes that blinked once before its mouth opened wide with a lusty wail. In carefully extracting the remainder of the body from Eve's still form—luckily she had lost consciousness again—he encountered resistance. The cord was tangled around the foot of the baby he held along with… a hand... from another.

Rapha disengaged the first baby's foot and handed it to Adam before calling, "KAL!"

Instantly the little man was beside him, dousing with wine and lending assistance. Again Rapha probed, located the head and lifted. The second blood-covered body emerged but, even through the muck, the color was wrong. The long cord was wrapped around its neck.

The next moment stretched endlessly as Rapha removed the afterbirth, cut the cords and swabbed. Two lives were waning before his eyes.

"Pray!" he commanded as his own tongue slipped into his native language, a dialect reserved for unhindered communication with his Maker. All the while his heart, mind and hands raced with lightning speed, the flow of life-giving words continued from his lips, pausing only when he placed his mouth over the mouth and nose of the second babe and breathed short puffs, gently inflating the tiny lungs, then sucking and spitting until those passageways were cleared and the child breathed of its own accord. When the second babe joined the chorus of cries, he began the painstaking process of stitching Eve's womb and staunching the flow of her blood. Utilizing a strong, thin line of intestinal skin, a by-product from their last sacrificial lamb, he stitched with his crude needle fashioned from the sharp leaf of a nearby bush. How Rapha prayed, never pausing in the battle for the young woman's life that raged with more fury than the wind that threatened to wrench their shelter from the ground.

As Rapha tied off the first layer of stitches and began on the second, the wind died. Peace descended. Eve's eyes fluttered and she smiled at Adam who stroked her forehead and murmured endearments as he placed the first baby into her arms.

Eve was barely coherent, for which Rapha was grateful as his fingers continued their deft manipulation of thread and needle. The wonder and relief as she gazed upon her baby also worked as an excellent distraction between her gasps of pain.

However, while the war was no longer beating against the confines of their shelter, it raged stronger than ever inside the minds of those surrounding Rapha. Adam's struggle was understandable as he supported his wife, stroking the hair from her brow even as he strove against feelings of revulsion toward the babe in his arms, the perfectly formed, eerily aware baby boy who gazed with innocence from thick-lashed eyes of prismatic beauty. The iridescent glow was unmistakable. He had his father's eyes.

But even greater than Adam's struggle was the storm raging in Kal. The little man was going through the motions of wiping the baby in his arms clean with water-soaked clumps of wool and preparing to wrap it in woolen strips set aside for that purpose, but his mind was tortured.

The sight of Eve's distress during birth—the blood, gore and newborn wails—were bringing forth horrific memories for Kal. The man's protruding eyes stared down at the babe in his arms, but he was living another moment: the beloved Eliana in travail, his own baby in his arms.

Rapha was pulled into Kal's emotional sphere even as he completed the stitches on Eve, cleansed the site one last time and added a light poultice of herbs to strengthen and protect the vulnerable wound.

Now he must tend the babies' cords, cut them short and burn the end to staunch the flow of blood. After heating the sacrificial knife Rapha stepped toward Kal.

Horror and fear flooded Kal's features as he leapt to turn his back to Rapha, his bent body forming a living shield for the newborn in his arms. "No! It is not his fault! You will not harm him!"

Rapha reassured Kal. "No, my friend. I will merely burn the severed cord. No harm will come to him."

Kal's hands remained ready to intervene as the blankets were parted and the glowing knife approached. When the scent of burned flesh assaulted his nose, the stoic warrior succumbed to his darkest nightmare. Rapha tossed the knife back into the fire in the center of their shelter just in time to catch Kal's crumpling form.

Smoke everywhere. Flickering shadows and a sickening scent of burning herbs... the smell made his head heavy while something in his heart fought the sensation. His heart. It was his heart he cradled against his breast. He was handing her over. No! He must snatch her back from them, from the men with their flowing robes and noble faces that flickered in the wafting fumes to become hideous, grasping beasts, licking their lips, eager for a kill.

When Kal came to, he was on his back outside the shelter with a cold rain lashing his face and Rapha's concerned expression above him.

Panic once more flooded in. "Where is the baby? What have you done?"

"Both the babies are with Adam. All is well." Rapha's hand was on Kal's shoulder. "No, do not rise. You… fell over."

Kal leapt to his feet. "Ugh! A great lot of help I am! Get in there and tend Eve. I am fine!"

Rapha, noting the pounding vein in Kal's temple and his trembling hands, knew this statement was far from true. "Of course," Rapha said as he stepped back inside the shelter's heavy animal skin doorway.

But Kal's memories continued to assail Rapha's mind and he peeked out just in time to see Kal sink to his knees, knobby hands covering his face.

With a quick invocation of Adonai's peace, Rapha had to train his thoughts once more on the newborns... and their parents.

So much balanced on the knife's edge of that moment. Eve's life hung by a fragile thread and, as Rapha continued his ministrations to her, he felt the turmoil in Adam's heart.

There the young man stood, cradling the spawn of his enemy in his arms, his face a mask of fear, revulsion and, remarkably, pity.

"I cannot," Adam gasped, "please, Adonai, do not ask it of me."

Rapha did not need to ask what the Almighty required. The words were pounding through his frame as well.

Adam, with dark circles under his eyes and Eve's blood yet staining his garment, spoke Adonai's directive, though each word ripped through his lips as if composed of flaming thorns.

"Teach them My ways. Love them with My love. Nourish, cherish, and instruct them as your own flesh."

Soon, Eve revived enough to reach for the babies and Adam took them to her. With coos of adoration she snuggled them close with an unquestioning maternal instinct. Even the second-born babe responded well, grasping to a fold of her robe and drinking deep with an expression of bliss.

Physically, it appeared, all would thrive. But Rapha needed no divination to know their struggle had just begun.

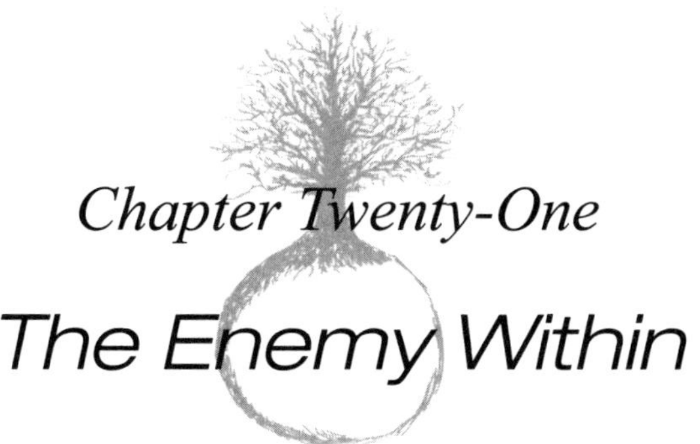

Chapter Twenty-One

The Enemy Within

Rapha surveyed the surrounding land. It was a glorious sunrise with streaks of bright, awakening light kissing the tops of distant mountains with molten pink and gold while a salt-laced breeze teased a flock of waterfowl inland to rush overhead in a frantic, squawking V. He loved this land. Ever since their little band had settled here nine years ago, he felt they had found the closest thing to paradise the world could offer. With hard work and patience they had carved beauty and function and even, he fancied, gratefulness from the rescued terrain that had responded to careful cultivation, rewarding them with a dwelling that flowed with plenty.

For the most part, their borders had been peaceful. Beyond the occasional wandering wild animals and their constant struggle with nature's unpredictability, they had dwelt unmolested, well fed, and content.

Adam and Eve insisted their animal sacrifice was all the protection they needed, while Kal, who had the deepest reverence for their worship, never relaxed his guard.

Rapha's own views fell between the two. Yes, the sacrificial lamb held back Lucifer's claim, *and* evil required constant vigilance. Once again he sensed the brooding tension of those last days in Eden. In their years of apparent peace, reports had continued to reach his ears, mostly from the ravens who knew no borders, of men of immense size who fought and conquered, then destroyed all within their grasp. Thus he knew Lucifer's breeding program flourished.

Rapha longed to forget their enemy, to focus only on their flourishing family and rich harvests. He could hope Lucifer would forget his seed born to Eve but Rapha was too well acquainted with Lucifer's ways to accept complacency. Rapha had no doubt Lucifer knew of Cain and Abel, of their height and strength that proved their angelic lineage. And though Rapha no longer held counsel with the heavenly host, he could read the stars and understand the overriding mood of nature that pointed to the same conclusion: Their little corner of this land was an island in the midst of a fast-rising sea of evil.

He took a deep breath, cleansing his mind of Lucifer's threat as his eyes swept the valley's horizon.

"Never let him steal the 'Now,'" Adonai's words from the garden again resounded in Rapha's heart. For this moment, this sweet breath of fresh day with the rim of sunlight peeking over the edge of their land, Rapha would enjoy the hum of bees, the musky scent of freshly tilled soil, and the warmth of morning's first light on his face.

Soon he expected to hear Cain and Abel's young voices raised in the excitement of continuing rivalry. What would today's challenge be? Throwing the spear for distance? Perhaps target practice with the same? Last week it had been wrestling and footraces. The strapping lads were constantly inventing new ways to compete.

Such had been the way of things since their birth when the two were lifted from Eve's womb seemingly interrupted in a struggle for supremacy, a struggle that almost cost Abel his life. How the three men had cried out to Adonai in that crucial hour and how grateful they had been when both mother and second-born babe had recovered.

Day by day the lads had flourished, consuming more food than Rapha could have imagined. Long and lean, both boys possessed handsome faces, abundant hair, and razor-sharp minds that quickly grasped and mastered any new skill. But they differed in other aspects. Cain's hair was lighter, containing the hues of sand and sun-bleached wheat while Abel's was deep brown with burnished streaks of copper. Both kept their long hair secured in braids for ease and simplicity. Thus far the boys were humble regarding their beautiful faces and perfect bodies since they were only nine and did not concern themselves with such things. Besides, except for Kal, others in their lives were also tall and perfectly proportioned. Cain was broader, thicker of muscle and bone while Abel remained slightly taller and more slender. In this way each was built for a different type of strength. Cain excelled in contests based on brute force and distance while Abel bested his brother in endurance and accuracy.

When they had outgrown wrestling with their mother, they roughhoused with Adam and Kal (who could get the upper hand with dirty tricks). Rapha remained slightly taller and broader in build, but the boys were growing at an alarming rate. If the size of Cain and Abel's feet were any indication, they would soon be at least two heads taller than Rapha. Even now he refused to wrestle with the lads since, if put to the test, *he* possessed the maturity of self-control, but the twins, Cain in particular, threw off all restraint in order to win.

This fact marked one of the overriding differences between the boys. Abel had an uncanny connection to the emotions of others while Cain viewed most emotions as weakness. The thought of being the cause of another's pain was unconscionable to Abel. Rapha felt this was one of the reasons the animals in

Abel's care trusted the boy so implicitly. Cain, on the other hand, had his mother's love of growing things and reserved his empathy for them. He reveled in the backbreaking labor of tilling the stubborn soil and nourishing the crops, trying to improve them year-by-year. He doted on his vines, trees and stalks just as carefully as Abel cared for his flocks, with an instinctive, protective, practically maternal attachment. In fact, one thing sure to puff Cain's chest with pride, almost as much as besting his brother in physical contests, was a compliment at mealtime comparing his handiwork to the unsurpassed fruits of Eden.

If only… Rapha caught himself. Once again he was wishing Cain could be more like his brother. Abel was a happy lad, whistling through his days and bringing cheer while Cain tended to be moody. Abel took worship of Adonai more seriously and begged to hear Adam and Eve's stories of dwelling in the garden over and over, whereas Cain would appear distracted or even bored.

For Abel, it was simple to love and be loved. Not so for Cain who was easily angered and grew sulky when he was not the center of attention, which was often since Abel was a gifted jokester.

Rapha chuckled as he recalled Abel's antics at a recent evening meal as he re-enacted Kal's anger toward a butting ram. "Stupid beast!" The boy had imitated Kal's gravely growl to perfection as he aimed a kick at the imaginary ram's rump. When Abel had raced around the room, exaggerating Kal's bow-legged pursuit of the unfortunate ram, even Kal had laughed until he cried.

Before the laughter had died, Cain had stalked from the room.

But the next morning it had appeared Cain's foul mood had passed when he whooped with joy as his spear outdistanced Abel's.

Thus, though each had their own strengths and areas of expertise, they tended to be evenly matched.

But their greatest rivalry was for their mother's favor.

Eve reigned supreme in their eyes. One touch from her graceful hand or one smile of approval was their greatest reward; therefore, they pursued these tokens with even more determination than they ran their races. And if one ever felt the other had bested him for her regard, civil war was inevitable. Rapha tried to stay abreast of the twins' moods so he could be on hand when tempers flared and fists began to fly, but they had become adept at cloaking their emotions and thoughts from him—a talent Rapha had only encountered in Lucifer—until they could sneak away and beat the fire out of each other without interruption.

Suddenly Rapha felt panic flow over him in a wave. "Cain! Abel!" Adam's voice broke the morning's peace. Rapha leapt to his feet, his mouth set into grim lines, as the familiar feeling of frustration and fear from the thoughts of Adam, Eve, and Kal crashed upon his mind. Those two rascals had run away—again.

As Rapha ran to join the search, he thought back to the first time Cain and Abel had snuck away in the night. For two harrowing days Adam and Rapha had sought Cain and Abel only to come upon them in the foothills of the mountains, hungry and wounded but glowing with pride because they had fought off a mountain cat. They were unrepentant about causing worry until Adam spoke of their mother. When they heard of Eve's tears they had apologized profusely and submitted without a peep to Adam's lashing of their backsides with a thin reed.

On the long journey home with the boys traipsing ahead rubbing their sore hindquarters, Adam had confided to Rapha his pride in Cain and Abel for their bravery but his concern for their curiosity. "I want to tell them the truth of their heritage but what will that do to them? Will they hate me? Will they become fascinated with Lucifer? How can we know the time is right?"

All good questions—for which Rapha had no easy answer.

He should have seen this coming, Rapha chided himself as he went through the motions of checking the boys' favorite haunts—though his heart knew they were headed once more toward "the others" who dwelt beyond the mountains. Just the night before the boys had begged Kal to speak of the cities beyond the mountains where he used to dwell. He had indulged them, spiking the stories with plenty of battle strategy and intrigue to quench their boyish lust for adventure. Usually, after Kal's reminiscence, the boys would press their father to take them on the long journey to Kal's former home, to which their father always replied, "When you are a bit older."

But not so last night. The two had thanked Kal for the stories without bringing up their usual request and had retired early.

Now, from all appearances, Cain and Abel, gone once again, had taken only skins of water, a bit of food, and their spears.

To add to their alarm, Eve had been tormented with dreams of winged beasts swooping from the heavens to snatch Cain and Abel. Adam said she had awoken screaming, convinced Lucifer had finally come for the boys and she would never see them again.

So Adam and Rapha packed a few essentials and set out quickly leaving behind a panicked Eve and the ever-faithful Kal. On they trudged, following the boys' fresh trail out of the valley and up into the mountains, stopping for only a few hours each night for rest and a scant meal.

Even with such a pace, they did not catch up to Cain and Abel until the third day. They came around a bend to find the two boys perched upon a large rock, their eyes red-rimmed with fatigue but their minds clearly set on continuing the journey.

"We are not children anymore!" Cain insisted and, indeed, because they were tall enough to look their father in the eye, Adam could hardly argue the fact.

"We can take care of ourselves!" Abel chimed in. "Besides, how can we prepare to defend our lands if we have no idea of the enemy's strength?"

"That's right," Cain added, building to his most convincing argument. "Is there something you think we're not ready to see? Something you're trying to hide? You have always said we should be honest with each other."

Adam glared at his headstrong boys, then raised questioning eyes to Rapha who watched the proceedings with a wry smile. Adam did not even have to ask. His old friend was amused by how much the boys were acting like him in younger days. With a sigh Adam voiced one last protest.

"But your mother is sick with concern for you. She needs to know…."

"Right. So you go back to let her know we're okay…."

"And we can continue on with Rapha." Cain finished Abel's thought.

Adam tried in vain to mask a smile at their well-rehearsed arguments. "So you want to be rid of me?"

"No, but Rapha has been here before and you haven't." Abel referred to Rapha's tales of wandering these lands long before Adam was even born.

After a private conference, Adam and Rapha agreed to the boys' plan, deciding a guided exploration was preferable to another boyish escape.

With one last admonishment from their father, the three watched Adam begin the solitary journey home. The boys' excitement overflowed. They let out whoops of victory as they once more turned to delve further into the unknown. Rapha was struck with misgivings but their sense of adventure was contagious. He began to enjoy the holiday, revisiting the role of instructional guide to enthusiastic minds.

For their part, Cain and Abel were glad to have a guide who never failed to locate water and food. Exploring was much more fun when their stomachs were full. The boys were excellent marksmen with their spears. They rejoiced to have the challenge of hunting for survival or fending off a ferocious animal, although the latter did not happen often enough for their satisfaction; just a hungry she-wolf who tried to steal their felled duck in a barren mountain pass. (Rapha did not allow them to kill her, explaining she had a hungry litter of pups nearby.) The next day they intentionally left another duck at that spot. Also, when night began to fall in the mountain passes and a cold wind blew, they were immensely grateful for Rapha's finesse in building a snug shelter.

Indeed, those quiet nights tucked into a lean-to of stripped bark or, when it was warm enough, a tent of their animal skin cloaks with a fire and fresh game roasting on long sticks, were the height of adventure for the boys who felt someone was finally treating them like men.

But, ten days into their journey, disaster struck.

They had been descending the mountain passes the day before and spied evidence of humans—the leavings of a campfire, footprints in soft ground. Therefore the boys, overflowing with excitement for their first glimpse of "others," had been eager to press on as soon as the sky was gray. Before long, they were peering down into a wide valley.

For a long moment Cain and Abel were silent as their eyes darted, trying to absorb everything at once. Then Cain gasped and pointed. "There it is, the fortress where Kal told us their warriors stay." At the same moment Abel discovered the huge, pillared arch carved into solid rock that marked the entrance to the place of sacrifice as well as the giant statues representing the gods they worshipped. Although the sun had still not risen, here and there people moved along wide pathways of shaped stone.

Rapha explained that, in an age long past, the large mound in the middle of the plain had been the center of worship and commerce. "The place where the people traded what they had for what they needed," he explained.

"But that is only a flat mountain with grass on top," Abel observed.

"Thus it has been for many lifetimes of men, but there was a day mighty pillars rose into the sky and a carved, ascending pathway flanked by fruit trees and enormous statues led from the floor of the valley." Rapha pointed. "See the large stones at the base on the right? Note the rounded part sticking out. That is a portion of pillar. Unfortunately the path and stairs have long been covered by rock and soil but, ah!" Rapha drew their attention farther down the slope. "There, see the rectangular shape? That stone was part of the foundation."

Cain made a snorting noise, "You would have us believe these men moved that stone, the one as large as our family's dwelling, to the top of that mountain?"

"The people possessed skill in artistry and construction but they also had among them men of great stature to whom these feats were simple."

The boys exchanged dubious glances.

"I will tell you something I told your father many years ago, 'Just because you cannot imagine something does not make it untrue.'"

Again Cain snorted.

"You find this difficult to believe?"

"Our *father*," Cain mumbled.

"How large?" Abel cut in quickly, "The men… how large were they?"

Rapha answered Abel's question even as he studied Cain's sneer out of the corner of his eye. "Various sizes. Some were three and even four times your height but such stature put incredible demands upon their bodies, therefore the length of their lives was greatly diminished. In truth, they were worshipped for what was a weakness. If their breeding had continued without interruption, if their wars and cruelty had not been checked, all men in that ancient time would have ceased to exist."

"But the fire from heaven came," Abel murmured.

"Yes. And much that was good and much that was evil perished." Rapha paused, his eyes once more seeing the carnage and chaos of that day, his ears recalling the shrieks of man and beast as the stench of their scorched flesh rose to the heavens.

A hand was on Rapha's shoulder… a hand that stretched into his soul, entering the painful memory with him. He looked up at Abel whose eyes were shut, a grimace of pain on his young face. Abel's eyes flew open and he jerked his hand away. For a long moment they regarded each other.

Obviously, Abel's ability to read another's emotions went much deeper than Rapha had realized. But this was not the time to discuss that talent because what Abel had absorbed had left him gasping and pale with horror.

"What did you see?" Cain asked.

But Abel ignored his brother, his eyes fixed on the high mound in the middle of the valley. "Why?" he whispered. "Why did Adonai destroy them?"

"The lore of their people teaches that Adonai sent the cataclysm—but this is not true. The fire that fell from the sky was of Lucifer's making."

"How do you know this?" Cain's expression was suspicious.

"Because I was there," Rapha said as he stared toward a tower of stone across the valley.

Someone in that tower was focusing a fixed, intent look their way. "We have been seen," he said as the sound of a ram's horn echoed from the rocks around them.

"Come," Rapha pulled both boys down beside him and moved to propel them uphill but Cain and Abel's bodies were stiff, their mouths gaping, their eyes fixed on movement in the valley.

Rapha followed their gaze.

What he beheld filled his heart with dread.

Men armed for battle were emerging from the rock fortress, their feet stepping in tandem as they filed out, ten abreast, line after line. But for Cain, Abel, and Rapha, it was the one who led this procession who demanded their attention.

The young man was beautiful. Clad only in a short leather garment that covered his loins, and leather wrappings for his feet that extended up to his knees, the perfection of his form could not be denied. His bearing was proud—chin lifted, back and shoulders straight—as he strode before the other soldiers.

Just then the sun's first rays shot through a cleft in the surrounding mountain range and lit a golden circlet on his brow. For a moment the young man stood still, basking in the glow, tossing back long waves of hair that matched his crown.

Then he turned his head toward them and, despite the light shining into his face, he locked eyes with Rapha.

Immediately Rapha's mind was under siege. The infiltration was backed by absolute confidence, the brash assurance of one who has never been denied, one who has never met his equal, one who never expects to apprehend anyone or anything as magnificent as himself. As if the young man grasped his throat in a vice grip, it took all Rapha's strength to simply expand his lungs and breathe.

"I know you," the young man's mind spoke, *"you are the fool who rejected my father's friendship."*

Rapha's mind raced. My *father?*

The reality crashed in. Lucifer had secured Adam's seed. With it the fallen angel had crafted this superior being.

"Yes. You know it is true."

"Who is he?" Cain asked.

"I will explain later. Come," Rapha said as the young man on the plain shouted the order for his men to advance. But the voice was wrong, too high-pitched, too… young.

Of course, this one could be no older than Cain and Abel yet his proportions were manly and body hair covered his limbs and chest.

With an unexpected wave of pity Rapha probed the leader's mind.

A heavy weight bore down on his chest. It was all up to him. He was the chosen one. He must be perfect. He must endure the cruel training and the foul-smelling drinks and the isolation from other children. He was not like them. Their inferiority would taint him. He was called "Ish-el."

He was the only one of his kind. He was lonely.

He was… scared.

A shriek of outrage erupted from the golden-haired leader. Rapha was shoved with such force out of the young man's thoughts he was thrown to the ground. Cain and Abel blinked down at him in surprise.

"I should not have done that. I have angered him," Rapha said as he once more started up the mountain path.

Rapha had taken no more than two steps when another howl of anger, this accompanied by shouted curses and insults, echoed up from the leader. One look at Cain's face gave the reason for the second outburst.

"I did it!" Cain exclaimed. "I've never tried it from a distance…" he looked from Rapha to Abel, elation lighting his features, "ha! It worked!"

But the golden-haired leader was running across the plain in their direction, all semblance of decorum abandoned, while the men behind him followed, trying to maintain their lines.

"You inserted thoughts? From here? I could not throw a rock that far." Abel observed, his expression eager, his hand reaching to give Cain's back a congratulatory slap. "What did you tell him?"

But Cain pulled away. "Oh no. Your secrets first."

"What?" Abel asked.

"Tell me Rapha's memories you saw earlier or I won't…."

"Can you argue as we run please?" Rapha said, grabbing the boys by the forearms and propelling them ahead of him.

"Do we have to run? Do we have to be their enemies?" Abel looked back with longing toward the plain where the leader had reached the rocks at the bottom of the mountain.

"If you had visited his mind," Rapha scrambled up a steep ravine, "you would know he plans to carve us into pieces."

"That is a shame," Cain said. "He would be so fun to tease."

"Please tell what you said to him," Abel begged.

"Well, alright." Cain shot a smug smile toward his brother as he grasped a vine and heaved himself up through thick undergrowth. "I just told him I had not known the women here were so beautiful," he paused to snicker, "with their long, gold hair and bare chests."

As both boys burst into laughter another shriek of rage rang out from behind.

"You are not helping," Rapha began as two long blasts from a horn again split the early-morning chill. Rapha paused to draw in the thoughts of their pursuant once more. "That was a call to outlying guards," he ducked down and pointed toward a hill topped by trees. "Right there. We must hurry before we are surrounded."

"What did you find out from his thoughts?" Cain whispered as he followed Rapha into a cluster of straight trunks and prickly undergrowth that buffered the noise of their passage. "Who is he?"

Rapha took a deep breath and searched their young faces. "He is your brother."

Both boys appeared to stop breathing. They stared at Rapha with matching stunned expressions. Immediately though, Cain's face flushed with anger while Abel turned to look back the way they had come.

A fierce baying broke out behind them followed by answering barks in the direction of the hill Rapha had pointed out. "Come. Quickly."

For several minutes there was nothing but scrambling for hand- and footholds. On one short but sheer cliff they were again able to climb by utilizing strong vines, which Rapha then ripped from the ground and tossed over the edge. "That will at least be difficult for the dogs," he commented before plunging up through a tight gorge of loose rock that gave way as they climbed.

Finally they came to another cliff but this time no convenient vines were in sight. "I will go first," Rapha instructed as he began the inch-by-inch effort. "Follow my hands and feet exactly," he said through gritted teeth as every muscle strained. There were a few complaints as rock and dirt dislodged to fall on those behind but soon Rapha was reaching a hand to assist Abel over the edge. When he reached for Cain, however, the boy ignored his outstretched hand, insisting on gaining the last few feet unassisted even though his muscles quivered as he clung, cheek pressed against the rock, veins standing out on his forehead with the effort. At last, Rapha reached under Cain's shoulders and hauled him out of danger, though the boy shook free as soon as he was on solid ground.

As they rested, puffing and blowing to regain their breath, Rapha took note of Cain's tight jaw and clenched hands. He also noticed when the boys' eyes met. Cain's narrowed and Abel's widened in response to the unspoken communication.

Rapha broke the silence. "We have a moment to talk if you do not mind including me in your discussion."

Cain glared at Rapha. "Why should we? You will just tell us more lies."

"When have I lied to you?"

Cain opened his mouth to speak but Abel placed a hand on his shoulder. Another look was shared between them, then Cain turned away.

"Tell us about the prince," Abel interjected. "Why did you say he is our brother?"

"When Lucifer deceived your father and mother in the garden, he secured Adam's seed. From that seed he has bred this 'Ish-el.'"

"Who is his mother?" Abel asked.

"That I cannot say but Lucifer and his followers have knowledge of how to manipulate the elements of life. Instead of Adonai's simple plan of one man and one woman creating life out of mutual love, Lucifer toys with the seed and the egg, creating new species and undermining the stability of Adonai's plan. It appears, with Ish-el, Lucifer joined Adam's seed with angelic flesh. Though it may be hard to understand, my guess is that Lucifer, in his lust to create a ruler in his image, injected his own essence into Adam's seed. In this way, *he* is Ish-el's mother—even if the babe was implanted in a woman until birth. This boy is able to read others' thoughts, he has grown to full maturity in half the time of other men, and his strength, height, beauty, and intelligence surpass all in his acquaintance."

"So he is the best of angels and men? That doesn't sound so bad." Cain observed.

"But he is lost between those worlds. He will never fully belong to either—so, even though he conquers all, he is alone."

"As we are." Cain stated, "Neither of us has known our true father."

"It matters not from whose loins you came. You have a father who loves you for more than your height and strength, a mother who taught you kindness and compassion, and a brother who understands you—a true family. All are gifts Ish-el has never been given, things he will never understand."

Abel shut his eyes, his head cocked to one side as if listening. "You are right. He has never known a mother."

"Perhaps that is for the best," Cain spat the words, "love is weakness. To trust someone is to allow them to hurt you."

Rapha stiffened as if Cain's words were blows. "Who taught you those words? Is there something you need to tell me?"

Both boys were silent. Abel kept his gaze on the ground while Cain stared back at Rapha, eyes cold, chin lifted in defiance.

Rapha hit the issue head-on. “When did you meet Lucifer?”

“Wha… I don’t—” Cain sputtered.

“Do not lie to me. That is not what your father and mother have taught you.”

“Our father?” Cain’s face flushed with anger. “Our life has been a lie! We have been kept from our true father, the one who would make us stronger… like Ish-el.”

“Cain, lower your voice.”

“What? Are you afraid we’ll draw his attention—our *brother*?” The boy’s angry voice continued to rise in volume.

“Come. We will discuss this when we are out of danger,” he put a hand on Cain’s shoulder and tried to move him from the cliff’s edge but the boy struggled and yanked away. The anger on Cain’s face, however, changed to fright when he slipped on the rocks and toppled backwards. In horror, Rapha and Abel watched Cain hit a small outcropping with a thud and then continue to roll and slide down the steep slope.

“Cain!” Abel shrieked and began to climb down, almost tumbling as well. With Rapha beside him, he raced to the spot where Cain, one arm and leg sprawled at a strange angle, lay among thorny bushes at the bottom of a ravine.

Blood pooled beneath the boy’s head but he was breathing. Rapha set about cleansing the head wound. The boy’s heartbeat was weak and his eyes, when he came to with a moan, were unfocused. With the sounds of pursuit closing in, Rapha instructed the boy to hide.

There were times the abilities of his human body that yet recalled angelic ways was a mystery to him. Usually Rapha felt limited, caged by his inability to fly or shift at will through time and space.

But this moment was an exception.

As Rapha cried out to Adonai and tore strips of cloth from his own garment to bind the boy's wounds, he was aware of three separate realities playing a vital role in this moment. There was, of course, Cain's blood flowing over his fingers but, as if a portion of his consciousness had flown back down the hill, he could see men studying the ground under the trees where he, Cain and Abel had crouched moments before. They shouted and others convened with them then looked up the hill. They were coming.

But, just as clearly, though he was at least seven days' journey from home, Rapha could see Eve rising from her bed to pace the floor. She was outside the house crying, staring toward the mountains. Then she was striding away from the house, increasing to a run, with the dog, Eden, keeping pace with her.

Even as Rapha tightened a strip of cloth to slow Cain's loss of blood, the two other scenes continued; the men, crouched over, following the trail below them; and Eve who was now stopped by Eden, doggy eyes sad but determined as she blocked Eve's path. Into the scene ran Adam and Kal. "Something is wrong!" Eve's lips said though Rapha could not hear the sound. Adam put an arm around Eve's shoulder and tried to pull her toward the house but she would not budge. "They are in danger. I can feel it," she wriggled herself from Adam's grasp.

As Adam held out beseeching hands and Eve continued to shake her head, Kal stepped between them. Rapha did not need to hear Kal to know that his voice would be quiet and gentle as when he soothed a frightened animal. Soon it was obvious Kal had brought calm to the strained situation as the three knelt down in the grass.

Now a fourth realm opened before Rapha's eyes. He was surrounded. The men from the valley were fanning up the mountain and closing in from all sides… but they could not see the shining ones, Rapha's friends and brothers who glowed brighter by the second.

"Abba, Adonai!" Rapha whispered as his fingers probed the wound on the back of Cain's head. The skull was cracked. "Abba, Adonai!" Rapha said again, beseeching Adonai's intervention. Heat flowed through his fingers and heaven's language poured from his lips.

He heard a voice raised in triumph. The men had discovered Abel.

But heaven's speech continued to flow as Rapha's hands pressed against Cain's head and Adonai's power coursed through him. There were whispers on the wind, the familiar voices of Adam, Eve, and Kal mingled with heaven's battle cry. A warm breath rushed past his cheek, then raced with tumbling leaves up into the sky and back to the ground to surge away in all directions, building to a screeching gale that drove branches and rocks before it.

Chapter Twenty-Two

Discord

Rapha inhaled heaven's scent. It revived him, renewing his hope and bringing peace.

A moment later, frightened cries greeted his ears as the heavenly guard drove the pursuers back down the mountain. He breathed his thanks even as his hands continued their ministrations to Cain's torn body. If only he had access to a certain plant that had flourished in Eden….

The sweet fragrance flowed around him once again and his eyes were drawn to a spot of bright light a few paces away. Once again he breathed his gratitude just as Abel reappeared.

"Rapha! It was amazing! The wind blew and there were noises and voices in it and the dogs ran away and the men screamed and—"

"I saw it, too," Rapha said as he pointed toward the light. "Bring me some of that plant. Quickly."

Abel grew quiet at the sight of his brother's broken frame and hurried to obey. Rapha rinsed Cain's wounds with the fermented juice he kept in the small flask attached to his waist, then applied the new plant's sticky, cleansing sap, pressing torn flesh together as if a layer of protective skin had been applied. When Rapha reset the bones in Cain's arm and leg, the boy came to painful awareness, but long draughts from Rapha's flask numbed his pain.

It was the head wound that worried Rapha most. Once again he sought heaven's assistance and focused on the cleansed area that continued to swell until, finally, a new stream of fluid flowed from the wound and the pressure eased. Although this was the least obvious of the day's miracles, he sensed the direct presence of Adonai, knitting what Rapha could not see.

Rapha felt a bit of the tension relax in his shoulders. He took a deep breath and sat back on his heels. "Thank You, Adonai."

"He'll be okay?" Abel whispered.

"He will mend but we must hurry. We have to carry him."

By the time they were pulling Rapha's cloak tight over the frame of branches they would use to move Cain, the sun was high in the sky. Then, as they groaned and lifted Cain's weight up to their shoulders to struggle through a steep cleft, a horn's blast echoed from the cliff walls around them, followed by the excited baying of dogs.

"What will we do?" Abel asked, voice cracking, muscles straining and eyes wide with fright. "They are all around."

"Pray and keep going," Rapha stated. "The rocks are deceiving your ears. They are not as close as it seems and there are none directly ahead."

"But they can move much faster. What will we do if they catch us?"

"Have you forgotten so quickly how Adonai drove them away? Pray and keep going," Rapha said again as he was forced to use one hand to climb and the other to steady the heavy frame.

But as the sun inched toward the west, their path remained rocky and steep while the sounds of pursuit grew nearer.

"What did you do before to make the wind rush at them?" Abel asked as they paused at the top of an especially grueling incline. "Perhaps you should do it again."

"I prayed," Rapha adjusted his grip on Cain's bed, "Adonai and the celestial host moved the wind." A shout of triumph sounded from below. "We have been seen," Rapha stated.

They began moving uphill but their path led over open terrain with another steep, rocky hill at the far end. "Perhaps we can slow them down," Rapha said when he spied a circling hawk far above. With a thought, Rapha summoned the bird.

"You just called him, didn't you," Abel stated.

"I pictured him descending to us."

Abel squinted up at the hawk that began spiraling toward them. Soon it landed a few feet away, one bright eye fixed on Rapha.

"He is impatient and wants to get back to his hunt, right?" Abel whispered.

"Yes," said Rapha, "now I am asking for his aid."

Abel stared hard at the hawk that gave one "Skree!" and flapped into the air.

"He agreed, didn't he," Abel stared, awestruck, after the bird. "That was amazing. It was more feeling than words, but I got it!"

Rapha took a tighter grip on Cain's bed, "Be amazed later. We must hurry or the diversion will be in vain."

As they raced over the level stretch of ground the hawk's cries continued and were joined by the squawks, chirps and caws of other birds. By the time they reached the cliff, the noise was almost deafening as a feathered cloud amassed above them, growing steadily as birds continued to materialize from the surrounding trees and rocky crags.

But their pursuers were closing in. As Rapha and Abel struggled to heave the unconscious Cain up the cliff that barred their way, the dogs reached the base and the golden-haired leader was standing at the edge of the trees, a rallying cry on his lips.

Many things happened at once. Several dogs yapped and struggled to climb, their powerful jaws snapping at Rapha's feet. Cain groaned and Rapha discovered the boy's eyes were open—just as Ish-el burst from the trees, screaming commands and racing ahead of his men onto the grassy expanse. But Ish-el's voice, in turn deep and resonant, then cracking with immaturity, was swallowed up in screeches as the cloud of birds lowered and became a barricade of flapping, clawing cacophony. Dogs yelped, men screamed, and the birds, a darting, undulating mass, fed the frenzy.

But Ish-el raised a hand toward the diving flock and, as if a mighty wind blew them off-course, the birds in that direction were scattered.

Cain and Abel gasped. "Did you see that?" they asked in unison.

"Do not stare! Climb!" Rapha commanded the awestruck Abel. "They will continue to dive until we are away."

"Make the birds stop. The men are stabbing them!"

"Abel, we have to get Cain to safety."

"But the birds are not hurting them."

"Which is what I instructed," Rapha heaved himself up to another foothold.

"It's not right," Cain pleaded weakly.

"Rest, Cain," Rapha said, "there is a place close by. I will tend you there."

But Cain's eyes were riveted to the drama below. "No!" he strained against the straps holding him to the bed as a harsh "Skree!" filled the air. "You!" Cain yelled, "Get him!"

Rapha turned, following Cain's gaze, and the situation was all too clear. Ish-el had skewered a hawk and, with a shout of triumph, was swinging the still-shrieking bird in the air like a banner, unaware that a monstrous eagle, talons extended, bore down toward his golden head.

In an instant the sharp claws were imbedded in Ish-el's bare shoulders and blood poured down his back as the bird pecked and dug. Ish-el flailed his arms and screamed.

"Cain! Tell him to stop!" Abel begged, just as the eagle's beak aimed for Ish-el's eyes.

"No! Peace!" Rapha's shout reverberated around them, echoing and multiplying from rocks, trees, and hills, building until the command became the voice of an army of thousands raised in one accord.

All fell silent.

Men and birds gazed around them in stunned confusion.

It was Ish-el who broke the spell. His gaze locked on Rapha and, with muscles straining and veins bulging as if the very air resisted him, he lifted his spear and aimed it toward the eagle that had broken off its attack at Rapha's command.

But the eagle snapped to sudden attention and dodged the spear, then extended its talons toward Ish-el's eyes.

As Ish-el's panicked cries filled the air, men and birds glimpsed the horror of his bloodied face and resumed their attack, more fierce and deadly than before. Soon the ground was littered with the feathered, maimed bodies of man and beast.

With a mighty effort, Rapha shoved Abel and the cumbersome bed up the remaining portion of the cliff, then commanded the stunned Abel across several hundred paces of rocky terrain and into a maze of caverns.

As soon as they lowered Cain's bed in a narrow alcove with faint light filtering down from an opening in the rock above, Abel turned his face to the wall and his shoulders shook with sobs.

Cain's gaze was still unfocused. "Stop it, Abel," he gasped as he tried to turn his eyes toward his brother. "They would have killed us. This way, it's… over."

"No." Rapha paced back and forth, the carnage of the men and birds replaying over and over in his mind. "No. It has begun… once again. Lucifer's ways are loosed on another age. By using your ability to command the bird to attack your enemies, you continue a horrible inheritance of man slaying man, of war between man and beast, of might triumphing over weakness, of flesh ripping and tearing flesh in self-preservation and fear." Rapha's voice caught on a sob as he relived the endless years of striving, celestial brothers at war, the waste of ruined creation, of distrust and fear being their daily food.

"But he deserved what he got," Cain said. "He was about to kill the bird. He would have killed us."

"It would have been better if he had!" Rapha turned to glare at Cain. "We do not defeat evil by becoming even more evil! Have you learned nothing from your father, Adam? He is a man of peace. He loves and serves you and your mother with selflessness. He does not demand a crown or a kingdom. He only desires what is best for you, just like Adonai. *That* is your inheritance. *That* is the hope you should be passing on to future generations, not the continuation of war and the shedding of blood!"

"But it wasn't right," Cain tried to move but a wide strap secured his head. "You told the birds not to harm them?" He tried to reach toward his head with his good hand but another strap around his chest prevented it. "They needed to protect themselves."

Rapha reached to untie Cain's cords, "How many birds were saved by fighting?"

Cain was silent.

"None," Abel's ragged whisper, spoken to the wall, reverberated around them. "None were flying. All were wounded… or dead."

"And the men," Rapha asked, "were any saved by commanding the birds to attack?"

"Why should I worry about those who want to kill us?"

"Because," Rapha stopped working at the knot securing Cain's arms, "they are part of Adonai's creation and He loves them."

Cain sneered, "So we should *love* them so much we allow them to kill us?"

"If that is Adonai's desire, yes."

The conversation ceased a moment while Rapha checked Cain's splints and bandages.

"Why is Adonai so weak?" Cain accused through gritted teeth as Rapha dressed his abrasions again.

"Are you weak because you feel pain?" Rapha asked.

"No. I am weak only if I cannot endure it," Cain answered.

"Then Adonai is strongest of all because He endures the most. Only in Him can we be strong enough to love even those who hate us."

"Then the ones who hate would win," Cain observed, "because they would kill those who obey Adonai."

"No. God's creation is built upon laws. When you sow seeds, you expect to see more of what was planted, right? Therefore, if you sow violence, you will reap it. And if you sow peace…."

Cain's jaw jutted with stubbornness and he looked away.

"You reap peace," Abel's quiet voice supplied.

In the coming days, their mood was somber as they kept a wary watch and waited for Cain to heal sufficiently to walk. Gone was the easy camaraderie and sense of adventure. Cain was sullen as if he blamed Rapha for his wounds. Abel was quiet, obviously lost in thought. Rapha was grateful to begin the long trip home. But, though he was eager to deliver the boys back to Adam and Eve with every limb accounted for, it seemed their hearts remained behind on a lonely mountain pass.

When Rapha and the boys were still far from the house, Adam and Eve came running to greet them. "I thought we had lost you," Eve sobbed as she clutched her sons.

Adam too was overcome with emotion, "Welcome home," he said as he grasped them in a powerful embrace.

Even as Abel responded with tenderness, Cain was stiff and unsmiling.

Rapha opens his eyes to the ruin Earth has become. Over and over in his thousands of years in this tired body he has had to witness hopeful beginnings, fresh young faces so full of promise, so committed to Adonai, so fervent in their commitment, yet, at their core, flawed. Over and over he abandoned hope, even abandoned faith in his Maker, as his heart broke with each betrayal of Adonai's ways.

The faces parade before him: Esau, Saul, David, Solomon, Samson, Absalom, Judas; so many hopes crushed, so many mistakes, so much pain.

But Abel... Rapha had such hopes for the boy. Abel was gaining understanding. He would have raised his children to know Adonai's heart. But Rapha just didn't see it coming.

Or was it that he did not want to see?

His mind races back to the dawn of Cain and Abel's thirteenth year. Like every other day, Rapha began by communing with Adonai, by gathering news of their borders from the birds and roaming beasts and speaking the ancient words of protection over their domain.

Had he become complacent? Had he watched so carefully for invasion from outside that he had ignored the growing threat under his nose?

Alas, on that day, the scales were ripped from his eyes.

Three full celestial cycles and several moons had passed since that harrowing flight through the mountains and slow journey home. Life had resumed its ebb and flow; sowing and reaping, tending and building; the seasons marked by the regular pilgrimage up the mountain for the sacrifice of blood that secured their covenant with Adonai.

Tomorrow marked the day the boys would bring their own sacrifice, the day when they shouldered responsibility for their relationship with Adonai.

How Rapha's heart went out to Abel who planned to sacrifice his special pet, a yearling calf fed and coddled by the boy's hand from birth. All the family loved the spoiled beast who had a habit of poking his head through the stone window of Abel's room each morning to wake him and request breakfast.

Rapha looked down the hill where the brothers were having a contest with their spears, this time a test of accuracy. Cain went first, his muscles rippling as he grasped the weapon, his eye riveted to the target, a particular knot on a tree. With a grunt of effort he stepped forward and released the spear that flew, unwavering, slicing the morning's quiet with a whiz and thud as the point landed in the direct center of the knot. Cain leapt and gave a shout of victory. Then, laughing, he stepped aside for Abel to have his turn.

Rapha watched Abel take aim. Like Cain, Abel was stunning. Tall and perfectly proportioned, the lad cut a slightly leaner figure than Cain whose muscles were thick from working the land. In wrestling and contests of brute strength, Cain continued to hold the advantage while Abel remained quicker and more agile. Both boys had abundant hair they kept secured at the base of their neck. Although Cain's hair remained lighter, both sported locks that reflected the sun's rays with multi-hued brilliance.

The most remarkable feature for both, however, was their eyes, eyes that fluctuated in color according to whether the day was overcast, misty, or sunny, growing more colorful when the light was bright and dimming to a uniform darkness when it was faint. And when the boys stared into the sun or even watched flames dance in the fire, light would stir in their eyes until they blazed with an answering glow.

Now, Abel had his eyes riveted to the mark where Cain's spear yet quivered in the sun's rose-colored glow. Though the scene around them was tranquil, a just-waking world of mist-shrouded mountains and a lazy breeze, Rapha leaned forward, left hand clenched as if it bore the spear's weight.

When the spear flew, Rapha once more marveled at the perfection of Abel's technique, graceful and effortless, every movement flowing like a dance down to the extension of the fingertips that remained poised in the air as if willing the shaft to his desire.

Rapha gasped. The spear was slicing toward its target, closer and closer on an impossible collision course until, with an audible crack, it splintered the shaft Cain had thrown, knocking it aside and taking its place in the center of the tree's trunk. With a whoop of joy, Abel ran to reclaim his weapon.

But Rapha's amazement turned to shock when he looked at Cain. The young man's eyes were narrowed and his lips were pulled back in a feral expression while every line of his body strained toward Abel, a beast lunging against invisible bonds. However, when Abel turned toward his brother, the tension was gone as if it had been a mirage and Cain was simply a disgruntled brother conceding defeat.

The lightning transformation was alarming… and familiar.

Was this talent to mask feelings ingrained or taught?

The second possibility sent a grim shiver down Rapha's spine. Could it be Lucifer had gained access to the boys—under his very nose?

Rapha continued to study them. This time, Abel was first to throw. As the lad focused on the mark, Cain stood a few paces behind, weighing the heavy shaft in his hand. When Abel raised his spear, Cain matched the movements, his eyes riveted to his brother's back. Time seemed to slow as Rapha felt cold dread grip his being. Cain's arm was back. He was stepping toward the point of release. His shoulder rippled with power as the shaft passed his ear, its point still aimed at Abel.

Cain was extending, mirroring Abel. A cry lodged in Rapha's throat just as Abel released his spear… and Cain completed the movement, spear shaft still gripped in his fingers, its length pointing at Abel.

When Abel's spear embedded in the direct center of his target, Cain smiled, his eyes still on Abel's back.

As the day progressed, so did Rapha's concern. Later, he approached the wall of smooth stones that enclosed the nursing ewes and their lambs in time to hear Cain's teasing voice say, "That is just because she preferred *me*."

"How would she know who she preferred? I never even spoke to her."

"Because you ran away," Cain laughed, "a scared little boy."

There was a "whump" as Rapha rounded the wall in time to see Abel launch himself at his brother and push Cain's face into the dirt. "I'll show you who's scared," Abel declared.

Usually Rapha would have had a vicious struggle before him to end the brothers' fight but as soon as Abel was aware of Rapha's presence he jumped off his brother, face flushed and surprised. Cain leapt to his feet, a calm expression flowing over his features like a mask.

"Rapha," Cain began brushing dirt from his garment. "Did you need us?"

"No. I was coming to retrieve the lamb for tomorrow's sacrifice." Rapha paused, "Who is *she*?"

Abel shot a glance toward Cain whose face remained serene. "Our mother, of course. What other 'she' do we know besides cattle?"

And Cain had looked calmly into Rapha's eyes, without a shred of guilt for the lie.

That night, when Adam gathered the boys to impress once again the importance of the sacrifice, Rapha's apprehension increased.

"Tomorrow, you are responsible before Adonai to provide your own sacrifice," Adam stated. "Your mother and I pass that responsibility on to you. In this way you choose obedience to Adonai and continue the protection from our enemy."

"Yes, father," Cain interrupted. "You have told us the story many times. We know."

"But it is good to hear it again," Abel cut in, "since we need to remember, without the shedding of blood, we are vulnerable." His eyes shot toward Cain who smiled and ruffled his brother's hair.

"Have you decided on your sacrifice, Cain?" Adam asked. "The animal will need to be prepared…."

"All is prepared, *Father*," Cain cut in. "As you have said, it is *my* responsibility," Cain's words were clipped but he added a smile. "It is a surprise."

"How about you?" Adam turned to Abel. "You know, son, another calf would do. There is no reason it has to be—"

"Should I choose what means less to me?" Abel asked. "No. This one has been committed to Adonai before his birth. I will fulfill my vow before the Most High. Only the most precious is worthy to be placed upon the altar. Anything less would dishonor Him."

Adam clapped Abel on the back as Eve choked back a sob and leapt to embrace her son. "We are so proud of you." Unshed tears glistened in her eyes as she kissed Abel's cheek.

Even Kal had turned away, wiping a sleeve across his eyes.

But Adam's gaze had followed Cain's quiet exit, his brow knit with concern.

The next day unfolded in a cacophony of beauty, triumph… and pain.

At midday, they prepared to trudge the path to the family altar, each accompanied by their sacrifice: a milky white lamb for Adam and Eve; a strong ram for Rapha; a gentle goat for Kal, which he carried across his shoulders; and, of course, Abel's calf, who trotted beside the boy without harness, happy to be next to his master.

But no Cain.

"Where is your brother?" Adam asked Abel.

"He refused to come, father," Abel replied. "I tried. I begged. But he wouldn't listen."

To Rapha, it felt as if the sun had just been stolen from the sky. Never had the trek up the mountain seemed so steep or grueling as each step widened the gulf between Cain and his family.

By the time they reached the summit and the stone altar lay before them, each member of their party was stealing glances back down the path. As the animals were fed their final meal, choice grain mixed with plentiful fruit of the vine to calm them, Eve's tears flowed. When the other sacrifices had been offered and Abel led forth his calf, all were weeping.

Just as Adam spoke the sacred words and lifted the knife to slay the calf, his upraised arm froze and the others turned to see what held his gaze.

There was Cain trudging toward them, two large baskets hanging from a pole across his shoulders. They rushed toward him with joy, relieved he would not remove himself from Adonai's protection. Then, one by one, their steps faltered and confusion replaced their relief.

"Son, where is your sacrifice?" Adam voiced the question on all their minds.

"Here." Cain whipped out a dirt-encrusted harvest tool from the sash at his waist and sliced the ropes that held the baskets to the branch across his shoulders. Leafy vegetables, fruit and grain spilled onto the ground at Adam's feet. *"Father."* The defiance in his eyes begged confrontation.

"Why you foolish—" Kal leapt forward but Adam held out a hand to restrain him.

"Cain, I don't think you realize—"

"What? That this is not the way things have always been done? Maybe it's time for change."

"But, the sacrifice—" Eve began, but Cain cut her off as well.

"Is right here." He waved a hand over the spilled produce. "I know what I am doing, Mother." He looked toward his brother. "Do you?"

Abel glanced with regret toward the calf that bawled on the altar.

"If Adonai loves you so much, why would he cause you pain?"

Abel doubled over with a sob.

"That's enough, Cain." Adam strode forward and stood between them, "On this mountain we worship Adonai with our best. You dishonor Him with those words. You dishonor us."

"No, it is a good question. I have wondered the same," Abel admitted. "I don't understand." With slow steps he made his way toward the calf and reached a hand to scratch behind the animal's ears. Immediately the lowing ceased and the liquid eyes fixed on his master. Although Abel was encased in the body of a man more than three hand breadths taller than Adam, in that moment he was just a boy grappling with powerful emotions as large tears coursed down the still-smooth cheeks.

"Adonai asks for obedience, not understanding."

After a long moment, his left hand remained stroking the calf's head, but with the other he reached toward the knife still grasped by Adam, and, meeting his father's eye, gave a slight shake of his head.

Adam struggled to mask his shock. He placed a hand on Abel's shoulder. "You can choose another. Adonai will understand."

Abel wrenched the knife from Adam's hand.

"Then we have truly failed," Eve whispered.

"Think of what you are doing," Kal shouted.

"Yes, brother. It's time to throw off barbaric practices," Cain said.

Abel leaned down and kissed the calf's head. Then, with one hand over the animal's eyes, the sacrificial knife fell.

Silence.

For a moment, all were too stunned to move or speak.

The boy froze, still gripping the knife that was wedged in the calf's heart, a mask of pain on his young face.

When Abel melted over his calf and wept, a white mist that hummed with power descended on the mountain and all fell to their knees as a piercing light from on high settled on the grief-stricken boy.

Then came a voice that shook the ground.

"You are fully Mine. Your stain is cleansed. The favor of The Most High is upon you. From this day forth, the blood of your sacrifice shall resound throughout the earth."

As these words yet rang in the air, Cain began to back away.

"Cain," Adonai spoke again, **"what is this you have brought to my altar?"**

"My… sacrifice," Cain said. For a moment he stood, eyes locked on the ground. Suddenly Cain threw up his hands and turned away, his face tight with anger.

"Why are you angry? You know what is required. You can yet choose to turn from evil."

"I have made my choice," Cain said through clenched teeth.

"Please, son," Adam reached toward him, "it is not too late."

"I am *not* your son!" Cain spun to face Adam. "And I will not be kept from my true father any longer."

"Lucifer will consume you, Cain," Rapha warned.

"Don't be a fool, boy," Kal growled.

"Cain! Please!" Eve sobbed. "You don't know what you're saying."

For a brief instant, regret filled Cain's eyes. "I'm sorry, Mother. I can't… I'm… sorry."

Then Cain turned and ran back down the mountain path.

Cain still had not made an appearance when the sun began to sink behind the mountains. Kal and Adam set off to seek him.

"Watch over Eve," Adam instructed Rapha as he slung an extra skin of water over his shoulder.

"What will you do if you find him—put him in bonds and drag him back?" Rapha asked.

"I see no problem with that plan," Kal mumbled.

"Maybe he will not return but I must do all I can," Adam replied, then marched off into the fading light with Kal. When Eden loped from the dwelling to join them, Adam knelt down and caressed the shaggy head. "Stay here. Comfort her."

Eden whined and licked Adam's hand before the two men walked away, then she turned back and trotted to the dwelling.

Rapha watched her disappear into the entrance and a pall of grief descended on his heart as the late afternoon light cast shadows on what had been a happy home, a haven.

He could hear Eve praying in her room, her grief pouring from her lips in gasps. "Abba, Adonai! Save him from himself. Abba, Adonai! May Your love embrace him when I cannot. May he see through lies. May he long for You. May his heart turn toward home no matter where he goes," she trailed off in a spasm of sobs.

Rapha stumbled as he felt the impact of her broken mother's heart. He would go to her. She needed him.

But Adonai whispered the same directive Rapha had once heard in the Garden.

"Let it drive her to Me."

He peeked into her window and saw Eden pressing close to her weeping mistress' side.

Rapha stepped away from the dwelling.

In the deepening shadows he saw Abel skirting the sheepfold, his sash wrapped around his head and shoulders as if to remain unseen.

"Abel!" Rapha called.

For a moment the boy increased his pace but then he stopped, his shoulders sagging with resignation, and turned toward Rapha's approach.

"Are you looking for Cain?" Rapha asked.

"No," the boy answered. Then he shuddered. "I hear his thoughts. I see what he sees. I know where he is."

"Then we will go to him."

"He would not hear us. His mind is filled with visions of power and… beautiful women."

"Where were you going?"

"Please, I don't know what to do," Abel's voice broke. "My heart is torn, I can hardly breathe. I feel the hold on him."

Indeed, now that Rapha was close enough, he saw that Abel appeared pale and weak. His body was quivering and a thin layer of perspiration beaded on his forehead.

"It is all right, Abel," Rapha soothed, "Adonai's hand is heavy on you to intercede for Cain. Go ahead and do what you must. But I will go with you."

Rapha followed Abel across the stream and into the dense trees onto a steep path. Higher and higher they climbed, chasing the waning sun's light.

Abel led the way into a clearing. At the foot of a rocky precipice he removed the coverings for his feet and Rapha did the same. The need of this became clear as they began to climb, grappling carefully for finger and toeholds.

Rapha followed, gripping at barely sufficient chinks. But, when they finally heaved themselves atop a sharp outcropping and paused to catch their breath, the view of their valley was breathtaking, an artist's palette of dusky rose, gold, and amethyst that stretched as far as the eye could see.

Abel stood and squeezed through an opening comprised of a tall, standing rock and the sheer mountainside that towered on to impassable heights above. After a few moments' passage through the narrow cleft where Rapha's broad shoulders threatened to become wedged, they emerged into the last golden rays of the setting sun.

"He's been coming here often in the past few years, well, since our trip through the mountains when he… was injured."

Abel stepped forward into the sun's glow toward a monstrous stone chair. Its back stretched high into the rock and its seat appeared wide enough for their entire family to sit side by side. "He told me he felt the arms of his true father wrap around him when he sat there. He saw pictures of his future and knew our father was calling him."

"And you," Rapha asked, "did you ever sit there?"

"I did once, when Cain first brought me here, but I became sick and he laughed." Abel gripped at his stomach. "I feel it again now."

"Then let us leave this place," Rapha urged.

"No. Adonai has directed me here. Here I sense Cain's thoughts even stronger. Here I can… feel what torments him."

Abel fell to his knees at the foot of the stone seat.

Something was stirring, a power so intense Rapha desired to escape… but it was not evil. For him, the scene that followed on that mountainside would be forever etched in his memory with holiness too pure for the temporal world.

Sobs wracked Abel's body as he cried, "Adonai, have mercy." The moments passed, Abel's prayers for Cain becoming more passionate until he was reduced to garbled mutters as he rocked on his knees, gripping his shoulders. "His pain," he gasped. "Adonai, ease his pain."

The glory of heaven sparkled and hummed in the air and Rapha could see dim shapes in the mist as ministering angels gathered around the boy. As Abel shook with the violence of his grief, his countenance became brighter, the pain acting as a furnace to cleanse bitterness and sorrow.

Rapha sank to his knees and gripped the rocks under his hands, sensing the need to brace for a powerful storm.

Then he was given a great gift. Suddenly Rapha was not simply an observer, but was flooded by Abel's thoughts and emotions, swept up in the flow from the throne of The Most High. He was no longer aware of the rocks beneath his knees or the sweet scent of mountain air as he was joined to Abel's heart's cry. At the same time, a living line of power also connected him to the tormented soul of Cain who grappled in desolate places with an ancient malevolence that drained all purity.

Thus Rapha was assaulted by empathy that threatened to rend his mind. Yet, since the flow originated from Adonai, Creator of all the living, even as strength was sapped and awareness of his own being faded, he felt more alive—a kinship to the hours he had spent as a celestial when he would go to restore his strength before heaven's throne.

"AHHHHHHH!"

A shriek of venomous anger yanked Rapha to consciousness. Lucifer was there, fuming and striving to gain access to Abel but the presence of heaven was an impenetrable wall. In his fury he turned on Rapha, eyes boring into Rapha's soul, hands like unsheathed knives groping toward the former angel. Rapha braced himself, knowing he had no power to resist but, to his surprise, Lucifer could not touch him. The evil one's rage was deflected like a stone skimming the surface of a frozen mountain lake.

With a jolt of joy Rapha shut his eyes and rejoined Abel's lament, crying and laughing at the same time, one for the depths of their grief, the other in response to Lucifer's ineffective attack. So he aligned himself with Abel and, with a sense of power he had never felt toward Lucifer even when he bore heaven's strength in his body, he asked Adonai to remove the evil one from his sight. Like a mist vanishing before a rising sun, Lucifer faded.

With all noise aside, Rapha could attend to Abel. Eventually, the fervency of the boy's spiritual struggle eased, replaced by sweet comfort and peace.

"Please, Adonai, turn Cain's heart back to Your ways. Help him see where this path will lead. Open his eyes to the evil that tempts him. May he long for the open arms of his family."

On and on the boy's words flowed from a heart made fertile by grief.

But Abel's next words caught Rapha off-guard. "Whatever it takes, Father," he prayed, his voice steady, his features bathed in peace. "I sense Your presence and Your favor. They are more precious to me than life. However," and here the boy's voice broke as he gasped in real pain, "please take my favor through sacrifice so Cain will not die in his sin. Yes." The agonized whispers poured from lips pressed to the ground. "My father's favor rests on me and I am heir to all. Your favor flows and Your blessing is assured for my future generations. But," the young shoulders convulsed again, "Cain suffers. Evil consumes him." His voice became a shout of travail. *"How can I dwell in comfort while he is in torment?"*

For a few moments there was no sound in Rapha's ears but the boy's sobs.

Then Abel spoke these immortal words, "Everything that is mine by right—I reject. I count all gain as nothing if my brother would perish. I bequeath it all to Cain—even my life. Though I perish, even if I be cast from You forever," again the voice broke, "I will trust You, Adonai."

All was silent but Rapha could sense their Heavenly Father sigh with pleasure. The boy's heart had conformed to the will of Adonai. His words carried eternal impact.

Wait. What had just happened? Was Adonai simply pleased with the prayer, or was He accepting its terms?

But Rapha's ponderings were cut short by a flow of power so strong he felt his bones would melt. He gasped as he felt himself expand. His name, his past, his present, even the unending war with evil, meant nothing when compared with this overflow. Emotion was too small a word. All things were contained—love, joy, peace, hope, fulfillment, grief. Thirst and hunger did not exist. There was only that moment of breathing in as the Most High exhaled.

Abel and Rapha remained, forgetful of everything but Adonai's embrace, until the sun looked down on a new day.

Chapter Twenty-Three

Brotherly Blood

They told Adam, Eve, and Kal about their time on the mountain, and the family took hope.

For forty days afterward, the family heard nothing. They mourned as they went about their tasks, each scanning the horizon for Cain's return, each wondering what they could have done to keep his heart rooted in Adonai's ways. Often, Abel would disappear into the hills, and Rapha knew he went to pray.

On the morning of the fortieth day, Abel joined them to break his fast, a wide smile on his face and cheerful greetings for all.

"Who needs the sun to rise with Abel around?" Kal quipped.

"Adonai… is," Abel replied. "How can I remain in sorrow?"

"So you visited the mountain again?" Adam said, "Do you sense a change in Cain?"

"I believe so. His thoughts are turning toward home. And, father," Abel leaned forward, childlike joy filling his eyes, "one message kept coming to me. **'All will be well.'** Over and over Adonai's words filled my heart. I think we may see Cain very soon."

With an affectionate squeeze for his mother, Abel whistled on his way out the door to tend the livestock. For Rapha, it was as if the sun had been allowed to rise when Adam and Eve's long-absent smiles lit their faces.

But later in the day, a growing unease made Rapha seek the solitude of the hill overlooking their land. He sat under the shade of olive trees trying to discern the truth, but it was as if the heavens were cloaked in fog. Even the sight of flourishing fruit trees and the orderly grapevines, laid out with Cain's attention to beauty and function, did not calm him. But when Abel strode into the fields, still whistling as he picked a cluster of grapes, Rapha sighed, encouraged by the sight.

Grape harvest was upon them, a task usually overseen by Cain, but the elder brother had not been home since the day of sacrifice. Ever since, Abel had maintained that Cain would return to do his duty—but the fruit could not wait. They would bring in the rewards of his labor without Cain even though every inch of that fruitful ground was a testament to his hard work and expertise.

"Brother!" Cain's shout echoed across the expanse of fields and up the hill.

"Cain!" Abel's voice was filled with rapture and he broke into a run toward his brother whose head and shoulders also rose above the young fruit trees.

"Get out of my fields!" Cain shouted.

Abel halted, hit by the wall of Cain's fury.

"So it is true," Cain said, "you continue to steal what is mine."

Even from that great distance Rapha could discern Cain's deranged, disjointed movements and wild appearance.

"No," Abel answered, "you were not here…."

"Adonai has decreed all is yours. *Adam* has decreed all is yours. Can you deny it?"

"Adonai loves you. We all do. You will be restored…."

"Lies!"

Rapha could not hear Abel's reply as the boy drew close to Cain with his hands outstretched, but he spied the sharp harvest tool in Cain's hand and he could easily read Cain's posture—a predatory beast ready to pounce.

Cain leapt toward his brother and both boys crashed down, out of Rapha's sight. He ran, shouting their names as he hurdled the rows of vines and dodged tree branches that grasped at his clothing. He paused to listen, his own heart pounding in his ears. Silence, all the more deafening after his determined crash through vines and branches.

Then he smelled it. Blood. And more. A breeze brushed his cheek laced with the scent of fluids… gases… organ tissue….

A strangled moan escaped Rapha's lips.

There was a rustling noise ahead as someone moved away. Rapha ran, the horrible smell leading him forward even as choking dread caused him to stumble.

"Abel!" he shouted. No answer. "Cain!" No reply.

Suddenly he broke through to a small clearing.

Immediately Rapha was on his knees beside the still form of Abel who was face down, one arm behind him. Too horrified to make a sound, Rapha gingerly rolled the huge boy onto his back. His eyes were wide and blood trickled from his nose and mouth. There was the harvest tool, imbedded to the tip of the handle within Abel's chest. But the wound did not start there. Abel's tunic was a red gash from abdomen to throat.

Rapha gasped and looked into Abel's eyes. The boy's lips moved soundlessly. He had no air. His eyes were wide with confusion and tears trickled toward the ground. With shocking strength he gripped Rapha's arm, his mouth moving again.

"Forgive… him," Abel mouthed, attempting another breath, the air hissing uselessly from pierced lungs, blood pulsing over the handle of the tool imbedded in Abel's chest.

All else faded as Rapha's only focus became easing Abel's passage. Blessedly, the boy thrashed for only a few seconds before a slow smile spread over his features.

"That's right," Rapha assured in a soothing voice, "go with them. All you ever hoped for awaits."

Abel's hand relaxed and he was gone, leaving behind the empty shell of his handsome face and muscular body. How Rapha wished in that moment he could follow Abel out of this world to that place of Adonai's perfection. How he wanted to escape the pain to come.

He was vaguely aware of howling. Eden. She knew. Soon the dog crashed through the stalks and bounded to Abel's body where she first sniffed and licked his cheek, nosed his neck and ear as if to rouse him, and when this effort failed, lay beside the boy's body and resumed her howls.

In a fog of unreality, Rapha eased the harvest tool out of Abel and gently pressed bowels and organs back into his chest cavity. As he was wiping the blood and dirt from Abel's face with the sleeve of his garment, Adam and Kal broke into the clearing.

"Abel?" Adam ran and fell to his knees at the boy's side, then looked to Rapha and whispered, "Cain?"

Rapha nodded.

"Is he… will he—" he lifted the torn edge of Abel's tunic that covered the wound. "Aah! No! No!"

Adam placed his hands on Abel's face. "Fix him, Rapha," he sobbed. "Please! Just like you did for Eve. Now! Kal, go get what he needs."

"Adam," Kal said in a low voice, "a wound like that… it's too late."

"What?" Adam's head whipped toward Kal. "You know nothing!" he shouted. "If Adonai lives it is never too late!"

Adam sat back and wiped his face, "Get stones. We will build an altar and…."

Rapha laid a hand on his shoulder, "Abel is gone."

"Get away from me!" Adam shook off Rapha's hand. "Faithless! Godless! Go!"

He turned from them and gathered Abel into his arms, weeping and crying out to Adonai.

"Stay with him," Rapha instructed Kal. "I will go to Eve."

She was already at the edge of the sheepfold and walking toward him when he saw her. Her face was pale and her eyes were wide with shock.

Something in Eve's bearing, in the way she stumbled forward, eyes staring as if she beheld a dream, made Rapha remain silent.

"Abel came to me," her tone was calm, though her movements were jerky, as if her body moved without her consent. "I was patting out the cakes when suddenly he was beside me, smiling. His face was so bright. He said, *'All will be well, Mother. I love you.'* Then he was gone."

She gripped Rapha's arm, "What does it mean? What has happened? Why do I hear Adam shouting?"

When he told her, Eve's knees gave way. Rapha caught her and tried to guide her back to the dwelling. "No," Eve said, her voice quiet and steady. "Take me to him."

Never had putting one foot in front of the other been so painful. Every step brought them closer to the scene of Abel's slaying, closer to the horror he wanted to spare her, closer to Adam's heartrending pleas to the heavens.

Then he was leading her into the clearing where Kal sat weeping while Adam yet clutched Abel to his breast, begging Adonai to come and mend.

Then Eve was sinking to the ground beside Adam and bending over Abel's body. "Oh my son, my son," she cried, stroking the boy's cheek and hair as if to wake him as her tears washed the dirt from his face.

Kal was indispensable on that painful day. He was well-acquainted with death, and so took care of odious details Adam and Eve could not fathom in their grief. It was he who located a suitable cave for Abel's grave and prepared the boy's body for burial. Kal's prayers and tears never ceased as he worked.

Rapha was consumed with those yet living. Where was Cain? His heart broke for the torment the young boy was enduring, a torment that allowed no peace for Rapha since the prayerful link had never been severed. So, as Kal ministered to Adam and Eve, Rapha gave himself over to the devastating empathy, conversing with Adonai as he connected with Cain's soul, stripped of sanity by horror and grief.

The next day Rapha set off into the hills, drawn by a torment carried on the wind, stronger even than the boy's bloody trail. Eden would not be left behind, so Rapha utilized her keen senses to aid his own. Soon the trail was unmistakable. When they were still not far beyond their fields, the blood became, not the hours-old flow from Abel, but fresh. Soon after, they were discovering fabric shredded from Cain's clothing, and clumps of Cain's hair rent from his head.

They heard him before they saw him. In a deep gully, carved like a gaping wound in the earth, his cries, mumbles, and shrieks echoed down the narrow canyon, bouncing against the dry riverbed.

"He fell. That's right, he tripped and fell against the tool in my hand and when I tried to pull it out…." Fresh sobs exploded, "Oh, Abel!"

When Rapha rounded the last bend and caught sight of Cain, he halted in horror. Even Eden froze with a whimper and lay as flat as she could, repelled by the pungent evil pervading that gorge.

"Thank you for coming, *dear* friend," a soft, young voice spoke in Rapha's ear while Eden yelped and backed away, snarling. Startled, Rapha turned to view a young woman clad in clinging garments that draped provocatively on her blossoming body. A slow, knowing smile spread across her features as she relished his surprise. "I was so proud of the guise that hooked him on their way through the mountains, I thought you should see it. Quite fetching, I think." The girl turned slowly to fully display her curves. "They saw me bathe in a mountain stream. Abel hid his eyes and ran—but Cain—" her eyes gleamed, "Cain was *fascinated*."

Rapha shook with rage. "Your perversion knows no bounds—to utilize beauty to lead a boy to murder."

"The desire was there, I simply met it."

In his torment, Cain used sharp rocks to score his forearm again and again, his blood dripping onto the ground as his cries filled the canyon.

"Enough!" Rapha moved to intervene but unseen cords ensnared his feet and he fell accompanied by the girl's tinkling laughter. Soon though, her proud expression hardened and when she spoke again, the voice was Lucifer's. *"This one is mine."*

Rapha turned from the unholy specter. "Cain!" he called the boy who muttered, eyes staring into the gloom, darting with paranoia as he viewed terrifying scenarios racing through his mind.

"He can't hear you," Lucifer gloated. "Even if he did, my grip on his mind would twist your words before they reach his ears."

"Cain!" Rapha strode toward the boy who leapt to his feet, teeth bared, muscles spring-loaded to defend himself. Abruptly, Rapha stopped and opened his hands. "I am here to help you."

But Cain was lost in hallucination. He ducked and swatted at unseen foes, spinning to see all sides at once. With a quick request of the Most High, Rapha opened his spirit to view the scene through Cain's eyes. Suddenly the narrow gorge was filled with gruesome warriors, hatred pouring from their flaming eyes as they advanced.

"Abba Adonai! Abba Adonai! Bring peace!" Rapha shouted, then slipped entirely into the language of the heavens to implore Adonai's presence on Cain's behalf, weeping to view the deranged expression on the beloved face. Fury erupted among the spiritual army but they were forced backwards, their murderous eyes fixed on this former angel who hobbled their powers with his words.

"See, Cain, how Adonai yet loves and protects you," Rapha implored. But Lucifer, still wrapped in his female guise, whispered in the boy's ear. As her words infiltrated his mind, Cain's expression hardened.

"I am to be grateful you called off your dogs?" the boy snarled. "Finally I see you for what you are, a deceiver who turned my family against me!"

Rapha swallowed hard, steeling himself against the accusation. Instead, he spoke again to Adonai, asking that the boy's mind be freed from Lucifer's grip. At his words, the girl writhed in pain and Cain mirrored her movements until she shrieked in his ear, "Kill him!"

Then Cain was running at Rapha, fists flying, mouth hurling obscenities. His hands clutched Rapha's throat, the nails biting into the flesh and shutting off Rapha's air with frightening power. Rapha gripped Cain's hands but they were locked tight.

In that moment, Rapha was overwhelmed by a surprisingly calm thought as he felt Cain's hands, empowered with Lucifer's strength, tighten as his vision grew dim. Perhaps he would die. Perhaps Cain would release his spirit back to Adonai. The thought filled him with joy and Rapha relaxed into the pain. But, through the pounding in his ears, Rapha heard a vicious growl as a furry blur flew through the air and hit Cain in the chest. Surprised, the boy released his hold on Rapha and grabbed the still-snarling Eden, throwing the dog against the canyon wall where she hit with a dull thud and crumpled to the ground, silent and still.

As Rapha fell to his knees, gasping, Cain froze and stared at Eden. The young man moaned and took a step toward the dog.

Suddenly, the voice from the mountain spoke, making the ground beneath their feet tremble.

"Cain, where is your brother? Where is Abel?"

Cain licked his lips, his eyes darting as if seeking escape. "I don't know." His volume rose and he added, "Why should I know where he is? Am I my brother's keeper?"

The ground rumbled and Cain cowered, "You have no right to slay me! No one can prove anything! No one was there!"

"That's right," Lucifer's voice spoke through the girl's seductive lips, "there are no witnesses. You are safe!"

"I am safe…." Cain echoed her words.

"Cain," the voice of Adonai spoke again, **"your brother's innocent blood cries out from the ground. Its stain is yet on your hands. The soil testifies against you. These witnesses to your deed cannot be silenced."**

"He lies! No one knows!" The girl hissed in his ear.

"Only I can cleanse your stain," the Holy One said.

Hope dawned in Cain's eyes, "You can restore me? My parents need never know?"

"Your parents?" the girl hissed, "they have rejected you! Your *true* father is your past, present, and future!"

But the hope in Cain's face died at Adonai's next words. **"True repentance is willing to be humbled. Hiding your sin leads only to further evil."**

"Ha!" The girl gloated, "see! The best *he* offers is assurance of humiliation, while your true father lays the world at your feet. Slavery or a crown... not much of a choice, eh?"

"You would steal my crown!" Cain accused, his expression once more mirroring the girl's hatred. "You would keep me a slave, groveling and sacrificing in a land with no women to carry on my father's lineage—a lineage that threatens your kingdom. A noble bloodline you would snuff out!"

"Cain," Adonai's voice was quiet, **"you have chosen. Since you will follow Lucifer, denying My offer of redemption, you are therefore banished from this place. Never again will you dwell in the blessing of your childhood. Wherever you go, since by your hand Abel's blood was spilled, the land will no longer submit to you. For your labor, you will reap only thorns and hardship."**

In that moment Cain was no more than a frightened child. "My punishment is more than I can bear! How will I survive? Surely others will see I am cursed and slay me!"

Adonai answered, **"Your brother's tears and prayers in your behalf yet ring in my ears. With his own lips he rejected his inheritance and gave you his eternal blessing. I honor that prayer."**

The voice swirled around them and Cain followed its sound with his eyes as if preparing for attack.

"You and your offspring will be mighty rulers of men but, since your flesh remains in sin, your corruption will tear at the fabric of creation."

The voice ceased. The trembling ground grew still.

"Wait!" Cain cried out, "he *gave* me his blessing?" He looked down at his bloody hands and tears filled his eyes.

"What stupidity and weakness!" the female-ensconced Lucifer scoffed in his ear. "Abel was a fool! He has handed you the whole world."

But Cain's ears were filled with news of his brother's selflessness. Tears trickled down his blood- and dirt-crusted cheeks. "Abel," he whispered. Then he fell onto his face and wept, his huge shoulders heaving with gut-wrenching sobs.

Chapter Twenty-Four

Mourning

When Cain left the land of his childhood, Adam and Eve were consumed by despair. For weeks Eve did not rise from her bed and Adam did not speak. While Eve's grief was debilitating, Rapha was most concerned about Adam. The man's faith and confidence had been so crushed everything was bitter to him. He took no joy in the challenge of sowing, reaping and tending. Since he no longer wanted to live, what was the point? His wife's melancholy was a constant reminder of the sons they had lost, and thus her presence pained him.

Even the beauty of nature ripped at his soul until no joy could bypass the scars. Everywhere he looked he saw the same message inscribed like a banner over his life: *Adam. Has. Failed.*

When Rapha tried to speak to Adam of these things, the result was always the same. Rapha would remind Adam of Adonai's promise about his seed redeeming the entire earth—and Adam would walk away.

Once again, Kal was an anchor in the storm. He cared for the flocks, oversaw the fields. and continued to treat Adam and Eve with gentle deference. But finally, when three moons had passed since Adam had joined them for a meal or even tended his own hair and beard, the faithful man suggested a plan.

"He must be jarred a bit out of his grief or it will continue to eat away at his soul."

"What are you suggesting, a large branch to the back of his head?" Rapha asked.

Kal chuckled and a teasing gleam lit his eyes, "Believe me, I have considered it. But no, if we simply put him in a place where he cannot escape, we will say what needs to be said and pray he can hear it."

Thus they planned their ambush, following Adam on one of his meandering walks, and finally cornering him when he ducked into a cave to escape the biting wind.

When he saw them, Adam tried to push his way out of the cave, but they stood their ground and held their hands out as if calming a wounded animal.

"Adam," Rapha said, "we are concerned for you. Those yet living, those who love you, those who have not gone away, need you."

"You still have a wife. You have a home and friends," Kal added. "You have the favor of Adonai and His promises to hold onto."

Adam snarled, "It would be better if I did not. I am a curse to all I touch."

"No, Adam," Rapha reassured, "Adonai's promises cannot be broken. Go home. Love Eve. You will see a new beginning. In Adonai, there is always hope."

"Hope?" Adam exploded with bitter laughter. "Hope is the most painful weapon of all. With it Adonai has carved out my heart. Abel is dead. Cain serves Lucifer. Eve's womb is cursed. There is no hope for me here."

"In Adonai, there is always hope," Kal said. "I too lost a child."

Adam looked up with vague interest.

"A baby girl with dark curls." A spasm of pain rolled across Kal's face and he gulped, unable to speak for a long moment.

"I… gave her… to the gods… she was… burned. My mate, Eliana," again he stopped, swatting with impatience at the tears on his face, "returned to the temple later and threw herself in."

Kal's eyes flamed with rage, "I had nothing. I threw all away to evil! Even so, Adonai brought me out. He forgave me. He gave new life, new purpose." Kal gripped Adam's arm. "Where Adonai is, there is always hope!"

"Then Adonai is not with me!" Adam shouted. "He pitied you, raised without truth. I do not deserve that! I invested my heart, my *life*, in my enemy's offspring—for nothing! One is dead. The other is worse than dead. My wife's *womb* is dead. This is what I have earned. There is no hope for me."

Rapha moved to embrace him, but Adam recoiled and smashed his fist into Rapha's face. Kal, with his warrior instincts, detained Adam with a none-too-gentle twist of the arm that forced Adam to his knees.

When he finally stopped struggling, his face was pressed to the ground, "Look, Adonai," Adam whispered, "the hope of all creation is a madman. Was this Your plan?"

When Kal realized Adam's fit had passed he loosened his grip and helped Adam to his feet. With an apology, Kal knelt before him.

"Do not ever bow to me again," Adam said. "You are the better man."

With that, he pushed past his two friends and exited the cave.

The next morning, Adam was gone.

He had taken little with him; a water skin was missing as well as one of their sharp cutting flints and a spear, so they wanted to assume he had gone to patrol the borders. However, when Eve emerged from her chambers, pale and hollow-eyed, she informed them it was Adam's intention never to return.

"He asks that you do not try to follow him," she stated, her beautiful face shadowed by grief, her abundant hair hanging dull and neglected about thin shoulders.

"But where did he go?"

"I do not know," she replied, staring at a loose thread of the shawl she wrapped and unwrapped around a trembling finger. "He knows there is no future here, no sons to fulfill Adonai's promise. Perhaps he will be blessed with another wife, one who can give him children."

"But you are his mate. You are his flesh and bone," Rapha said.

Eve yanked the shawl from her shoulders, ripped it in two and threw it down. "That bond was torn by Lucifer. Adam *should* go away. Why should he hold to vows that were broken before they were made? Why should he remain chained to a woman whose womb is broken?"

Rapha and Kal finally gave up trying to convince Eve to listen to hope. When she stumbled off, alone, to her chambers, they wrestled in prayer for the man and woman who had been the hope of creation.

In the coming days, Kal and Rapha were all that stood between life and hopeless fading for Eve. They convinced her to eat scant amounts but only due to the fact she was too numb to resist. They dragged her to witness the birth of newborn lambs and goats; however, these events that usually produced joy now could not penetrate her cauterized emotions.

But Eve had been blessed with a firm foundation of Adonai's unending affection. So, even though it took a complete cycle of the constellations, a day dawned that once again witnessed her smile. For the devoted Rapha and Kal, not to mention their attendant menagerie, the sun finally shone a bit brighter.

Nonetheless, she had formed new habits in her grief. She still sang, but her melodies had a melancholy tone. She took her customary long walks through the fields but they ranged farther, her feet leading to steep mountain slopes and her eyes to the distant peaks, ever drawn to scan the horizon for a glimpse of her mate returning home.

So their lives continued. Kal and Rapha patrolled, protected and cared for flocks and fields while Eve wove, tended the fires, and developed her love of beautiful things by weaving pictures into the fabric. In this endeavor Kal was her tutor, having learned this artistry among his people.

Thus Eve busied her hands to salve the emptiness of her heart. But always, her weaving would slow and she would dream of the day loved ones would find their way home through the beautiful landscapes she recreated with her fingers.

In the coming years, others joined their small band, refugees from the surrounding lands where wars and strife never ceased. Whether human or animal, they were drawn by an irresistible desire for paradise, a desire woven into their hearts by the Creator. The canny few slipped through their defenses but most were ensnared, discovered by Rapha or Kal, and granted refuge. Sadly, a good number were women and children, abandoned or bereft by incessant war, desperate to escape the cesspools of humankind where they were easy prey.

Their quiet existence became more complicated but less lonely. For the first time, Eve enjoyed the company of other females and delighted in caring once again for the simple but constant needs of children. Early mornings heard the chatter of women stirring fires, fetching water and tending to the needs of their households along with the squeals and laughter of their young.

In this burgeoning society, Rapha began to withdraw to the solitude of the hills to "keep a more efficient watch on the land," but Eve knew he wished to avoid the constant probing questions of their new inhabitants who insisted, with one glance at the former angel, that he descended from "the gods." Therefore, his visits were sparse and usually conducted under cover of night.

Nevertheless, lively discussions regarding the handsome visitor abounded throughout the camp, fueled by the clandestine nature of his arrivals and also by gossip—some true, most fabricated. The refugees had come from a life of serving might and beauty. Although Eve and Kal continued their worship of the One True God and encouraged the new arrivals to learn Adonai's ways, the newcomers found it easier to focus on this magnificent stranger whose humble clothing and mysterious ways only heightened their fascination.

As a result, Rapha lived the life of a nomad and hermit, committing himself to Adonai, and seeing to the needs of Eve and their land from afar. During a time of drought, a mountain stream would redirect its course overnight and life-giving water would once again flow in their valley. When disease struck their flocks, Eve discovered fresh game hanging in the courtyard, skinned and ready for the morning fire.

Kal journeyed often with Rapha, patrolling beyond the borders to gather news of distant lands and assessing any threat to their valley. In these forays Kal gleaned much regarding the pulse and rhythm of the earth, how to read signs in the trees, stars, wind, and wildlife that advised of things to come and warned of mistakes from the past. "But these signs were created by Adonai and are not intended for worship," Rapha would caution. "His image is etched in them—but we serve Adonai, the Source of all life, not His reflection."

But this wisdom was not heeded by most of the women in their valley who saw in the mysterious Rapha a rich source of fascination and speculation. They sensed his veiled power. Many a girlish daydream was fueled by the thought of this mysterious stranger who came and went like the wind and watched over the welfare of their little community.

Often Rapha entertained thoughts of disappearing entirely from the affairs of men, until rumors of great evil reached his ears. The birds informed him that a new sovereign ruled the lands outside their valley. The fierce tyrant Ish-el, called "Cyclops" by his enemies, was now dead, murdered by his successor who was ruthless in his quest for absolute power. The birds told tales of murders, destruction, perversion, and atrocities the likes of which had not been seen since the past age. Every day evil pressed closer, rising like a cursed tide to swallow what was good. Rapha decided he could not leave those in their valley unprotected.

The opening of Rapha's dwelling faced east, the better to absorb the first warm rays of dawn, that moment when he felt the veil between the realms of heaven and earth stretch thin. He could, for a brief moment, sense the peaceful charge of Adonai's breath, blowing His favor across the land.

Everything else—sleep, food, companionship, even shelter—he could ignore for extended periods, but his daily basking in Adonai's presence through prayer, while not as effortless as when he was a member of the celestial court, was, nonetheless, a non-negotiable of his existence, more precious to him than his next breath. Always he was left gasping for more, as if he took a gulp of air only to plunge back into deep water once again. But it was enough to survive.

On this morning, seventeen years since the day Cain had departed their land, Rapha sat in the mouth of his cave basking in Adonai's presence, tears rolling down his cheeks, his heart breaking with the longing Adonai felt for creation, the desire to gather all into His arms and heal every disease, correct every wrong, fill every being to overflowing with His love.

This time, however, when the rim of molten light peeked over the eastern horizon, the bright fire continued to come, a blinding flare that suddenly took shape before him. Rapha's heart quailed before heaven's presence as he heard a beloved voice.

"Greetings, Rapha, emissary of the Most High."

Though his body shook with frailty he looked up into the face of Gabriel, whose form became solid as the light of his visage dimmed, conforming to the earthly realm.

For a long moment the two simply stared into each other's eyes. To an outsider it might have appeared there was nothing to say but in truth their connection was far deeper than words. In a moment's time they reestablished a camaraderie that stretched back to the dawn of creation.

Finally, the severe demeanor of the heavenly visitor relaxed and a smile lit his eyes. *"It has been too long, my friend."*

Rapha nodded but said nothing, sensing the urgency of Gabriel's mission.

"I bring both commendation and warning," the angel continued. *"Adonai is well-pleased with your faithfulness but would warn of days to come. Creation once again hangs in the balance and the role you play in this crucial time will reverberate throughout eternity. Protect the woman, Eve. The root of the Messiah will issue from her. Fear not. The Most High goes before you. His love never dims even when all around is darkness."*

Gabriel paused, the briefest flicker of pain crossing his stoic features, then he covered the distance between them in two strides to embrace and kiss Rapha—a rare expression of affection among the celestial host, since their inner communion requires no physical manifestation.

Forehead to forehead Gabriel gripped Rapha's shoulders and whispered, *"We are with you, my brother. Though you cannot see us, we fight beside you."* His image melted, once more melding into the morning light.

Rapha stumbled to his knees, his heart racing as if ready to explode as the force of Gabriel's contact reacted upon his flesh like a brush with pure lightning. The embrace both encouraged him and exposed his weakness. Never before had Rapha felt so alone, the fact of his solitude underscored. He was a being caught between the fabric of earth and heaven, not quite suited to either and yet destined to remain, an eternal soul trapped in the prison of an earthly body unable to fade.

But he had made this choice.

His thoughts turned to Kal. The scarred but sprightly man had become stiff since their first meeting. The sparse tufts of the little man's hair were white and he walked with a pronounced limp, wincing as he trotted to match Rapha's stride on their long treks. Even Eve, though still lovely, sported fine lines around those golden eyes. How his heart grieved to contemplate a future without Kal and Eve's companionship.

His gaze was drawn to the first stirrings of life in the human encampment below, to the women rushing to draw water while the few men and some of the older children, answered the demanding low and bleat of their flocks. How these mortals would struggle against the inevitable fading of their bodies when strength and beauty passed. How they strove to discover ancient wisdom to make them "like the gods," beings of eternal beauty and power.

But how Rapha envied them, these finite humans whose brief, painful sojourn so quickly could be traded for the unfading glory of Adonai's presence. He would gladly sacrifice his strong limbs, flawless teeth, and unlined skin for such a promise.

An uncommon sight interrupted his ponderings. One among their number was entering the trees, bent as if beneath a heavy burden. He watched this one's progress, noting feminine grace encumbered by the awkward gait of one close to the time of child-bearing. The female doubled over, then stumbled into the shadows of the trees. His last glimpse of her brought a shocking sight as, from the folds of her robes, he saw the gleam of a long blade, the shape of which could only be the sacrificial knife. What did she intend?

His thoughts reached for those of the lone woman, and her despair filled his mind. She was suffocating in fear and self-loathing. She saw only one escape….

He ran. With an urgency he had not sensed since that horrible last day in Eden, Rapha leapt fallen logs and bounded through undergrowth, sensing this one's pain stronger and stronger with every step until, suddenly, he stumbled over the small bundle of a sobbing woman. With an "Oof!" the sacrificial knife flew from her hand.

She peered at this crumpled, massive being through tears that shimmered on her dusky cheeks. Although her eyes were red-rimmed and filled with grief, the bared, ferocious soul behind them took his breath. For a moment Rapha simply stared, struck dumb by her agony.

For her part, the girl's mouth opened to emit a scream but no sound came. Finally, she surprised him with a burst of mocking laughter. When she spoke, her words dripped with hatred.

"And so the gods would send my greatest fear to torment me. But I am one long since dead. There remains nothing to steal so why should I fear?"

Even as the words left her lips, a spasm of pain swept across her face and, with a gasp, she hugged her bulging womb. To his horror, Rapha saw a bright red stain appear on the ground beneath her.

"What have you done?" he asked, though the despair and determination on her face confirmed his fears.

"There is no other way," she gasped again and stifled a cry of pain. "He will claim his own. It is the only way."

Her strength was fading with the passing blood. Rapha knew there was not much time. He reached to lay a hand on her womb, thankful she was too weak to fight, and felt the babe inside struggling for life. Without another word he scooped up her frail, bleeding form and strode toward his dwelling. In later days he would review his actions over and over again, always coming to the same conclusion; what else could he have done?

Chapter Twenty-Five

Sheatiel

Flames everywhere. A small girl cowers as the fire licks at her feet and burns the edge of her garment. She screams for her mother. A hand is reaching through the tongues of fire. She sees the face of a beautiful woman.

A familiar face.

A trusted face.

The child is yearning, struggling toward the haven of the woman's arms. She touches the outstretched fingers.

Immediately the woman's hand becomes clawed and grasping and the long hair becomes vipers hissing about her head. Her smile becomes rows upon rows of sharp, pointed fangs dripping gore. The fangs open wide and lunge for the child who is screaming, running, but everywhere fire blocks her path.

She is falling, down....

Down into darkness.

Rapha woke, covered in sweat, to stare at the dim fire's glow on the cave wall. Once again, the violence of the girl's dreams had invaded his own. He shut his eyes, wishing for a moment's release from her pain but the images remained. At least these dreams helped him understand why one so young and gifted with such beauty would desire death. This one had experienced horrors beyond human capacity. Though her nighttime terrors were disjointed shadows, he understood those she trusted most had betrayed and abandoned her, leaving her vulnerable to—what?

He sat up and studied the young woman who flinched in her sleep. Her garments, though heavily mended, were of the finest silk with threads of pure gold woven throughout and, though she was well along in pregnancy, her limbs and face could not have been more perfect. With her thick, waist-length braids, dark-lashed eyes and inborn grace, she was the type of woman sure to attract the attention of kings. Rapha sighed as he turned away to stir the fire and the herbed liquid he had left next to the coals overnight. Her beauty had most likely been her curse. Men ruled by Lucifer's ways knew only how to manipulate and destroy, not nurture.

As he inhaled the fragrance of fresh lavender in the steam, he felt her awaken, her eyes a scalding hatred that pounded his skull along with her intense desire for a large rock to smash that skull and escape… or a knife, or a poisoned dart….

"Greetings," he turned, interrupting her murderous thoughts. "No, please do not move." He spoke as soothingly as possible and took a step back to disarm fear. "You will re-open the wounds."

"Did you take the baby?" The genuine concern surprised him.

"No. For the time being, the babe is safe in your womb."

Relief and fear, love and panic raced across her features and beat against his thoughts. But her anguish assured him of one thing: she could never again try to harm the child within.

Rapha could see the band of iron behind her eyes working to dam the flood of emotion. Never, even among stalwart warriors, had he beheld greater self-control. The opposing forces required to forge such strength must have been formidable indeed.

"Are you hungry?"

"No."

The lie hung between them.

"Help me to understand," he filled a bowl with broth and set it within her reach, noticing how she stiffened at his approach. "You try to kill yourself, yet you fear poison." He reached for the cooler, larger bowl containing the solution for bathing her wounds, inhaling the scent of pungent herbs. He inserted a finger to taste. Yes, it was ready.

"Bring that one to me," she commanded.

"But this is—"

"I trust actions, not words. Do as I say." She winced as she propped herself on an elbow and glared, daring him to speak.

Rapha obeyed and backed away. She brought the second bowl to her lips, her eyes watching his every move as she took a wary sip. Immediately she gagged and coughed, gasping at the knifing pain. Rapha rushed to support her, holding the original bowl to her lips. She thrashed at his touch and the braids of her hair lashed him like metal-tipped whips.

"Please. You will harm the child."

She stopped struggling and took a sip, but the feral expression remained.

When he released her they regarded one another. Even without his empathic abilities the message screaming from her eyes would be clear. *You touch me again and I will kill you—or die trying.*

But she needed his skills. With every second the color was draining from her face as the red stain once again spread beneath her. Abruptly he turned to exit the cave. It was time for reinforcements. Rapha whistled and a large raven flew to his outstretched hand. After the message was encoded, the bird rose and began its graceful descent into the valley.

Within the hour Eve was at his door.

"What is it?" she asked, her face flushed by the climb.

Rather than answer, he led Eve by the hand into the cave. When her eyes adjusted to the dimness, she gasped and rushed to the young woman's side. "Sheatiel!" But at the sight of the blood she took over and Rapha assisted, bringing the warmed water and clean strips of cloth.

"Go away," the girl, Sheatiel, commanded Rapha, though the words seemed to take the last of her strength.

Eve gathered Sheatiel's cold hands into her own and spoke calmly. "I need him here, but only I will touch you."

Shealtiel gave the slightest of nods and lay back but her eyes remained watchful.

Rapha faced the cave's entrance as Eve explored the girl's wounds. To her credit, Eve did not allow even a gasp to escape her lips as she pulled aside the blood-soaked wrappings.

"The cuts are deep," Rapha stated. "For now the babe is safe but she must remain still and calm. The wound must be thoroughly cleaned and," he hesitated, "sealed."

"I will go with you to retrieve sufficient water," Eve said with a stiff smile as her fingernails gripped Rapha's arm and propelled him out of the cave and out of the girl's hearing.

"How do you plan on sealing the wound when she will not let you touch her?" Eve hissed, her face growing pale at the thought of what she had glimpsed beneath those wrappings. She crossed her arms and shook her head, "If you were assuming *I* would do it…."

"No. The tear within and without must be mended by a skilled, steady hand, and quickly. Every moment mother and babe are in greater danger."

A hint of color returned to Eve's cheek. "Then how…."

I know where to acquire a certain flower that, when properly prepared, will cause her to sleep but," he sighed, "someone will need to explain."

He waited, watching Eve's eyes narrow as she bit her lip in thought.

Finally she gave a decisive nod and turned toward the cave, her chin jutting at a familiar, stubborn angle. Rapha smiled. Never when he had seen that expression had Eve failed to accomplish her desire.

But in the realm of strong wills, Eve had met her match in Sheatiel.

"No," she was still saying when Rapha returned to the cave, the bright blooms in his arms. Sheatiel was pale and her voice was weak but she was adamant. "Never. Do what you need to do," she looked to Rapha, "but keep your… your… *sorcery* away from me."

"I am simply trying to spare you pain," Rapha replied.

"Better to have pain than to leave my soul unguarded."

"But my hands must be steady. If you were to move suddenly—"

"I. Will. Not!" Sheatiel's dark eyes flashed with panicked determination that told Rapha further argument was useless.

And since the work had to be done before she lost any more blood, Rapha began.

"You truly trust him?" Sheatiel asked, not even bothering to keep her voice low as Eve bathed away the blood once more.

"Yes. With my life."

"How long have you known him?"

"Always. In fact, I was once in your position and he saved my life… and the lives of my children."

Sheatiel lay back, gripping Eve's hand as the procedure began. Throughout the ordeal, no cry escaped her lips, even when tears ran from the corners of her eyes and she had to squeeze Eve's hand so tightly the fingers turned purple.

"I can give you just a bit of the water from the flowers to ease you…."

"No," she gasped before Rapha could finish his offer.

But later when Sheatiel's face was pale and she bit her lip to stifle a scream, Eve put the liquid to her mouth and Sheatiel drank a few sips.

When she finally gave up consciousness—whether from the drink or from pain he could not be sure—Rapha sighed with relief. The obvious torture on her face and the dark memories the pain resurrected in her mind had been distracting to say the least.

"Will she be alright?" Eve asked when Rapha at last finished his ministrations.

"Her body should recover," Rapha replied, "but the heart wounds in this one are much more serious than those I stitched. Only Adonai can heal those."

That night Rapha fell asleep with a hand on Sheatiel's wrist to ensure her heart continued to beat, hardly realizing when his own slowed to match her rhythm.

Rapha pauses in his memories. Sheatiel's image provides a welcome respite to his painful thoughts. Ever after, next to the image of the Holy One who had cleansed his stain, hers was the face in his memory that brought comfort.

Agony was to come, more than he could have imagined, but in the beautiful, tortured soul of Sheatiel, Rapha tasted the sweetest nectar of all his years in exile.

So he savored those days, moving slowly through every recollection of her slightly husky voice and expressive hands, graceful and tapered, gesturing when she spoke. Like her personality, her eyes were multi-layered with flecks of green and gold in the brown. They seemed to grow darker or lighter with her mood but always they reflected deep waters of thought and feeling, ranging from turbulent to tranquil more quickly than leaves tossed before a storm.

Sheatiel—the rose that bloomed among the thorns of that turbulent time.

Two days and two restless nights had passed since Rapha's operation on Sheatiel.

Rapha woke to pressing fear. In the valley he saw bright pinpoints of fire rushing toward the settlement. Invasion! With one swift movement he swung the cloak from his shoulders onto the small campfire at the cave's entrance, extinguishing its telltale light. Then he listened.

He could feel the malice. Closer and closer a hideous intent was slinking toward them. He crept to where Eve slept, placed a hand over her mouth and whispered instructions. While she went to Sheatiel, Rapha crept out of the cave and up the rocky slope.

Yes, desperate measures were in order. He could sense ten distinct entities but one among them wielded sorcerous power. It was this power that drew them like wolves after the scent of blood.

He felt an excited quickening of their pace. Their quarry was near. They were aiming directly for the women… no. It was Sheatiel they wanted. Her image was clear in the sorcerous one's thoughts. Now Rapha's physical ears detected their approach.

Only one thing remained. He slipped back to the cave and located the rope he and Kal had placed behind the rocks by the entrance. After he ensured the women were well back from the opening, Rapha pulled.

As the deep rumble descended he threw his cloak over Eve and Sheatiel and there they remained, hands over their ears, while the cave floor shook under their feet and the world crashed around their heads.

"What have you done? We are trapped," Sheatiel said between coughs that caused her to choke with pain.

"There is another way out," Rapha replied. Then he paused and reached with his senses.

"But—" Eve began.

"Ssssh."

A tense moment followed as they sat in the smothering darkness with no sound but their breathing. "Five yet remain," Rapha whispered. "There is one who can sense us. He knows her face. He is—"

"AAAAAH!" Sheatiel thrashed in the darkness and Rapha felt her cower against him with her hands over her ears, "No, no, no…" she repeated over and over as she shook her head and moaned until another shriek escaped her lips and she slumped against him, deathly still.

"Sheatiel!" Eve screamed.

"Abba, Adonai," Rapha gathered Sheatiel's cold body into his arms and pressed his lips against her hair as intense evil assaulted his mind.

He was barely aware of Evc's whispered prayers as he wrestled for Sheatiel's life, commanding, rebuking, cursing, and pleading as the evil presence pounded down, enraged by their resistance.

Finally, Sheatiel gasped for air and Rapha felt her heart thump against his chest. "Alleluia," he murmured as relief coursed through him.

A thunderous "CRACK!" shook the cave floor and rumbled away into the mountain above their heads.

"Hurry!" Rapha stood with Sheatiel in his arms, "Eve! Take my arm! Do not let go," he ordered, feeling his way blindly to the back of the cave as rocks crashed around them.

They moved as quickly as possible in the suffocating darkness. Finally the crashing ceased behind them and Rapha paused to wrap Sheatiel against his back with the long sash of his garment. Her heart was beating but she had not regained consciousness.

"What happened to her?" Eve asked.

"Sorcery. Someone trained in evil tried to kill her."

"But, why?"

"They want the child."

"Why?"

"They serve the father of the child. He sent them."

"But—" Eve's words were cut off by another rumble and rocks began once more to crash around them. Rapha pulled her forward until he felt an opening on the left. They huddled there until the noise ceased. Rapha reached behind him until he felt the folds of a bundle. "Thanks to Kal we will now have light in the darkness." He pulled out a torch and the sparking stones.

"Do you know, Rapha, I could see you."

"Hmmm?" He struck the stones together.

"When Sheatiel screamed and you were praying, you… got brighter. Then, right before she began breathing again, the light passed into her."

Rapha blew gently on the tiny spark until it ignited the oil-soaked fabric. In the flame's glow his face was thoughtful. "I could feel Adonai's power, but I was unaware it was visible. Perhaps you are gifted to see what others cannot." He brought out a length of rope and tied it around his waist, then attached it to Eve. "The path, if it is still there," Rapha added, "is treacherous ahead." Then he stood and held up the torch revealing a lofty cavern with pointed rocks coming up from the floor and dangling from above.

"I have always wanted to ask," Eve's words echoed around them, "what, exactly, *are* you now?"

Rapha chuckled as he waved the torch, seeking the correct passage on the far side of the cavern. "Ah! We could be buried at any moment but Eve has questions."

"You told us you chose to stay and Adonai changed you but, how? You eat and sleep like me but you are... different. Come now," she said when Rapha hesitated, "distract me from the fact we are trapped inside a crumbling mountain. I may not get another chance to ask."

He sighed, "I will tell you what I can but, in some ways, I too am trying to define what I am."

"You still have power with your words. Is that because you retain the knowledge of angelic language or because that power remains? And you communicate with animals and know the thoughts of others. Again, is this knowledge or remnants of former power?"

"I believe it is both," Rapha turned to assist Eve off of a high ledge. "I saw Adam display power over the earth's elements on our last day in the garden. That authority was placed in him from birth and was lost to Lucifer but Adonai promises it will be restored. As for me, as long as I do not mix my flesh with that of mankind I will remain as I am. I will not… fade."

"Are there others like you?"

"Many joined Lucifer and were banished. But I have not heard of any of them existing in human guise." Rapha paused, his face thoughtful in the flickering torchlight, "However, the one who tried to kill Sheatiel is also able to shake this mountain. Those feats require ancient knowledge and power. Yes, it may well be one of the fallen of my brethren."

"Lucifer?"

"No. But most assuredly one in league with him."

Eve was quiet a moment then she said softly, "So will Lucifer fade… die… since he mixed with mankind?"

Rapha took a deep breath, "No. I am sorry to say, he implanted the seed in you. Even in regards to Adam, Lucifer safeguarded himself and only collected Adam's seed. He has been mastering the art of corruption for many ages."

"We were such young fools," Eve whispered.

"But Lucifer's evil has taken its toll on him nonetheless. Remember the sacrificial blood from the lamb? Every step away from Adonai galls him. By his actions, he tortures himself."

They stopped and Rapha held the torch up to light a narrow path with a sheer drop to unseen depths below.

Rapha checked the rope attaching them, then moved forward. "Can you hear the water? We will follow this path to where it leads down to it." He stopped speaking as images assaulted his mind. "Kal."

"What is it?"

Rapha shut his eyes, pain etched across his features. "The warriors have discovered Kal's hiding place. He is protecting the women and children." Rapha felt fear grip his heart. "They did not acquire what they sought, so they will punish and destroy." He clutched his head. The images were so real. He had not sought these visions. He had not been praying. But they were so vivid.

Fear filled the children's eyes. The acrid smell of charred flesh assaulted his nose along with the agonized screams of the animals with no escape from the flames.

"No! Adonai, no!" Rapha's strength drained away as he watched the carnage. "Please! Brother angels, intervene!" he shouted.

"Rapha," Eve's hand was on his shoulder, "perhaps it is more sorcery. Perhaps these things you see are lies," her voice pleaded for it to be so.

Again the mountain around them rumbled, a huge stone fell two paces behind and they were forced to stumble forward onto the narrow path, the sheer cliff rising above and the water rushing far below. Rapha prayed as he walked, his mind still seeing the torturous scenes, his heart reliving those horrible last hours in

Eden. Why was evil triumphing here? Why was Adonai allowing it? Tears ran down Rapha's cheeks as the path narrowed until he and Eve had to slide forward gripping the cliff.

And all the while they prayed. Over and over Rapha tried to wrest his mind from the visions of destruction but they would not relent. Again the mountain rumbled and in the fight to hold to the cliff the torch fell from his hand, its light flipping end over end until, with a distant splash, its flickering glow was quenched.

Eve screamed, "Rapha, I am slipping!"

"Pray and move forward. We will make it," Rapha instructed even as a new vision played in the darkness.

It was Kal's face, teeth bared, the sharp harvest blade slashing into his enemies as he shouted words that Rapha could not hear. Into the picture leapt Eden, vicious and fearless beside Kal. The dog dove at a man who clutched a small girl, and ripped out the man's throat. The man released his hold on the child and fell, dead, with a startled expression still on his face.

A spear slammed into Eden's side. Rapha could see Kal's face as he saw the dog fall, his eyes wide with horror. In the momentary distraction an arrow struck Kal's shoulder.

Kal twirled and fought as more arrows pierced him and the enemy forces, glowing red from the surrounding flames, closed ranks.

"Rapha!" Eve's panicked voice pierced his grief. "I… can't…." She screamed and suddenly her weight was added to Rapha's crumbling handholds. He inched forward, every movement a strain, convinced at any instant the rock would give way as he clung to scant grooves, sweat pouring down his body, the fact only too clear that three fingers on one hand prevented them from plunging to the rocks below.

"There's nothing!" Eve cried out. "I'm reaching. Nothing is there," she sobbed, her cries amplifying off the cavern walls like the despair of a multitude.

Again, the image of Kal was forced before Rapha's eyes.

Kal's face was bleeding, his eyes swollen shut, the white tufts of hair gone, ripped away. He was pushed, kicked and beaten until he was thrown to the ground, broken and defenseless.

All was dark. Hope was gone. Rapha clung to the rock weeping, his head beating against the rock as if to remove the horror, sticky warmth now running down his face. He could feel nothing. He could hear nothing.

Let go.

He could not stand the pain. He could not care anymore.

Adonai?

Adonai has abandoned you, his tortured mind hissed. *You have failed. Every choice, a mistake. Every hope, destroyed. The Most High turns His face from you, ashamed.*

Give up.

Let go.

End the pain.

Let... go.

The hopeless litany beat against him. He was drowning beneath fierce waves, thrown down out of remembrance, forgotten, destroyed.

Let. Go.

He began to loosen his cramped grip.

Through the haze of searing pain he felt something. A heartbeat thumped against his back, beating when his heart longed to cease. Warm breath was on his neck. As if emerging out of deep water, sound returned to his ears. There was a moan and the weight on his back struggled against the ties that held it there.

"Rapha! Rapha! Please! Move!"

That voice. He remembered it. Eve.

As Eve's weight on the cord kicked and the injured woman on his back struggled, Rapha breathed one word—"Adonai!"

The weight of the women grew tenfold and the blood pounded in his ears, its throb the only sound as repeatedly his anchors on the rock gave way. The voices in his head multiplied.

You fool! You can save nothing, not even yourself. You have led them from danger to certain death!

His strength was gone. He could feel no further chink for hand or foot. The rock to which he clung leaned slightly out over the unknown abyss and the weight of the women pulled him down… down.

"I am sorry," he gasped as his fingers slipped.

"Rapha! Rapha!" He felt a yank on his waist and realized the weight had lessened. "My foot is on a ledge," Eve's breathless voice echoed up, "I see some light ahead."

Rapha could not see light. He slid down, his feet finally reaching solid rock. It was the last thing he remembered.

Chapter Twenty-Six

Death

When he came to, he heard voices and the trickle of water. For a reason he chose not to recall, he kept his eyes shut.

"Here, drink," Eve's voice spoke.

A loud gulp caused Rapha's tongue to flare with thirst. "What about him?" Sheatiel's voice whispered. "Is he alive?"

"Yes. He still breathes."

"How did we come to be here? There is no path."

"He carried us."

"That is impossible!"

"Yes," Eve answered again. "How are you?"

"Better than him, from the look of things," Sheatiel answered with a hint of humor in her voice.

The weight of hopelessness on Rapha's mind lessened.

After a pause, Sheatiel spoke again. "I prefer him this way, weak and sleeping."

"He has saved you time and again. Surely you do not still fear him."

"His kind bring only pain." With those words all was dark once more.

"There is not another of his kind, as far as I know."

"There are many… and they bring pain."

The despair of the girl's past wrapped around his exhausted mind like dense smoke. It was worse than fearing physical death.

This torture chained from within. Rapha struggled against the suffocating darkness. He threw an arm over his eyes as if to shut out her pain.

"Rapha!" Eve was beside him. "Drink."

Like a weak child he obeyed, feeling each cool drop of water flow through his body.

"Give me your hands."

He lifted heavy arms, wincing as wetness set fire to his fingertips. When he tried to open his eyes, they remained shut as if stout thread had sewn his lids.

"Patience, Rapha." She wiped at his face until he was able to open them to the dim light.

He moved to sit up but his body screamed in protest. Instead he turned his head to look around. Yes, the cliff above was sheer. It appeared a large chunk of rock had fallen from the pathway since he had last ventured to this cavern. No wonder they had lost their footing in the dark.

"How did you get to the water?" he asked Eve.

With a smug smile she pointed down. "Look."

As if a giant hand had positioned them, huge rocks lay off the side of their ledge forming an almost perfect staircase down to the stream. In amazed silence he studied the place above where he had clung, realizing Eve's feet must have been dangling a mere hand's breadth from the highest rubble. His greatest, Herculean effort, and they hadn't even been in real danger. He was ridiculous, covered in dirt with most of the skin from his hands and legs left behind on the rocks. How Lucifer would gloat to witness this humiliation!

As if the fallen angel whispered in his ear, Rapha heard what he would say. *"I told you it would come to this, old friend,"* the words hissed, *"you wear their filth well,"* Lucifer's cackling laughter leapt from Rapha's memory with such force he could hear it pounding from the cave walls like a fresh avalanche.

He curled into a ball and covered his bloodied head with his arms.

"Pa-the-tic." That single word pounded over and over.

How could he fight truth? Why should he? He felt pulled into gaping jaws and the wounds on his body awoke as if each had become hungry insects devouring him inch by inch.

"Why cry out to Adonai? Even the Most High mocks you."

Where was Adonai when Rapha had hung from the cave wall in fear? Surely this shame was His will. Again Lucifer's laughter filled his ears. *"Behold! The angel who became a worm!"*

His body was quivering, aching, burning. He was helpless. He was drowning in torment. *Please, Adonai.* His mind screamed though his tongue formed only gasps and groans. *Slay me!*

A splash of cold hit his face and his eyes flew open in surprise. Sheatiel was there, eyes wide and determined. "The voices in your head. Resist them!" she commanded. "They light fires and weave spells. They devour with thoughts."

"The whore knows nothing," the vicious words accompanied a vision of Sheatiel, eyes vacant as from too much wine, body swaying provocatively. The image scraped across his soul, arousing both desire and disgust. Was she simply Lucifer's latest guise?

"Whore," he whispered, barely realizing the word had left his lips.

Whack! Her palm struck his face.

But as he grasped the offending wrist while it was still in motion, he knew this was not his old enemy. Humility and shame filled Sheatiel's eyes—two things of which Lucifer was incapable. Rapha dropped her hand but still he felt its warmth, on his face as well as his fingers.

"Come, Sheatiel," Eve took the trembling girl by the shoulders and shot Rapha a murderous look.

But Sheatiel, pale beneath her burnished skin, resisted Eve and held his gaze. "I am what you say." The dark circles under her eyes deepened as she spoke. "But I know what torments you. They devoured me long ago. Once hope is gone you are their slave. Cling to what is good, no matter how small."

Without pause she addressed Eve. "Please help me to the water."

Then the two women left him and descended into the dimness toward the chattering stream. Alone on his ledge he wrestled with the evil that assaulted his mind. Finally, by thinking of the cool water cleansing Sheatiel's stain, he knew peace.

In the coming days Rapha led Eve and Sheatiel, foraging for their food by cover of night, then retreating to the cave's protective shadows while the sorcerous evil scoured the land, caused the ground to rumble and continued to taunt Rapha, calling him out, pressing images of suffering women and children on his mind.

"You hide because you are weak," the voice echoed over and over in Rapha's mind but Adonai's will held him back. Repeatedly in prayer he was convinced his most important mission was to keep the women safe. No visiting angel appeared to assure him but his heart was certain.

At night, the images almost drove Rapha to madness as the screams of women and children filled his heart. If not for the undeniable mandate from Adonai, he would have stumbled out of the caves for a daring, most likely ineffective, rescue. As it was, darkness would press in, surrounding them with the maddening pursuit until the breath of evil brushed their cheek and whispered death in their ears. But they had learned. Eve and Sheatiel would draw close to Rapha as he painted a picture of Adonai's glory with his words, sometimes whispering heaven's language when the words of men fell short. Therefore, though their bed was cold stone and fear hovered, they learned the art of weaving peace. And when Rapha lay in the darkness, watchful and cramped with the women drawing close to his warmth and their breathing growing deep and steady, he realized he no longer felt alone.

Finally, a day dawned when the brooding presence was gone and they could emerge, grateful for the sun's warmth. But as they drew closer to their former home, dread clutched their hearts.

At the borders of their land, carrion fowl fed on two fallen warriors. Why so few? Why were the majority of their traps undisturbed?

At the grove of olive trees, Rapha finally saw evidence that brought a brief smile. No, their attackers had not been caught off guard at their borders. But they had underestimated Kal. The wily old warrior had lured dozens of the enemy into the open arms of his trip wires and booby traps, where explosions and pits with spears had greeted them.

Every structure was a burned-out shell but, thankfully, no bodies were found among the ashes.

However, as Rapha followed Kal's trail that led toward a large rock, the stench of death was strong. Several enemy soldiers had fallen there along with… Rapha parted the bushes to discover, not Kal, but a mystery. There lay the body of a frail woman, stabbed in the heart, her arms folded over her chest as if prepared for a grand funeral.

Rapha called Eve who moaned and knelt beside the woman's body. "This is Moria. She is finally released from her pain." Eve looked toward the dwellings. "But she could not walk. How did she get here?"

Rapha studied the ground, “She must have been carried. Look. Kal’s steps lead away.”

“Follow them. Perhaps he is still alive. I will see to Moria’s remains.”

So Rapha followed a meandering path of the enemy’s feet. The only evidence that he was also following Kal’s footsteps was the occasional trapped or crushed enemy.

The site of Kal’s last stand was a rock at the end of that valley. Rapha was sure the final volley had been an amazing site. At least twenty of the enemy lay pierced by Kal’s arrows and a circle of warriors had fallen to his sword.

But, it had not been enough.

In the middle of their fields that had been picked clean by the enemy, Rapha found Kal, impaled and burned on a tall wooden stake. Rapha crumpled to his knees. “I am so sorry, my friend,” he whispered as tears ran down his cheeks and he collapsed to the ground.

A loud “Squawk!” interrupted Rapha’s pain and he looked toward the sound to discover his raven friend perched on Kal’s shoulder. “Squawk!” the bird said again, then flew to the ground before Rapha, taking a few waddling, determined steps forward as he flapped and bobbed his head. Obviously, something was on his mind.

Rapha wiped a sleeve across his face and nodded encouragement to the bird who stepped closer. He obeyed the bird’s direction and laid a hand on its sleek feathers.

Once more he was plunged into Kal’s last hours but this time, rather than the sorcerous connection that had revealed only despair, it was related through the bird’s pragmatic eyes.

He was soaring over the hills on the outskirts of their domain. A dark mass of men was approaching from the west.

"The only safe entrance is between those two stones," the man at the front said. "One long line and stay quiet."

The wind whispered through his wings as the bird looked for the short man with white feathers on his head. The man was not in his bed. Bright points of fire were approaching the fields when he located the one called Kal standing among the fruit trees with the dog at his side.

The bird landed a safe distance from the growling dog and croaked the news of men approaching.

"How I wish I could understand you. Are you telling me we're being invaded?"

The bird bobbed his head.

"I knew it! If you can understand, friend, alert Rapha," Kal said before running toward the dwellings. "You old fool," Kal muttered as he ran, the dog at his heels. "Feeling it all day and hesitating."

The bird flew to Rapha's cave in time to see rocks falling to block the entrance.

By the time he descended again to the valley, Kal was leading a group of mostly women and children toward the mountain behind which the sun appeared each day.

"Where are we going?" a small boy asked in a loud whisper.

"You will escape into the hills," Kal whispered back.

"You, too?"

Kal ruffled the child's hair and smiled, "Not yet."

"Elanor," Kal addressed the woman at the boy's side, "straight through the pass and over. You know where the provisions are. Do not look back. Adonai is with you."

The woman nodded and took the boy's hand.

"Eden. Go with them!" Kal pointed toward the group moving off into the darkness. The dog hesitated, whined, but then obeyed.

Kal ran back toward the settlement. In the small dwelling closest to the well he entered the dark doorway and came out a moment later carrying a frail woman, Moria.

"You can stay in the cave until it is safe," he said.

The woman murmured something the bird could not hear.

Kal chuckled, "Yes, I am an old fool but I'm still getting you to that cave."

A flaming "whoosh" sailed over their heads and struck the thatch of the neighboring dwelling. Kal ducked his head and ran faster. Suddenly he stopped as out of the shadows two young boys and a girl appeared with Eden at their heels.

"What are you doing here?"

"We came back to help you," the taller boy replied. "We know where the trip wires are. We can fight."

"Tess!" Kal addressed the girl. "You run into those trees right now or I'll kill you myself!"

The girl took one look at Kal's angry face and ran.

"But she's only seven and she's scared of the dark," the taller boy spoke again.

"Tonight the darkness is her friend. All right, Eli, Jason, you man the rocks. Then get out!"

"No." Eli stood with his fists clenched. "You taught us to fight, now you want us to run?"

There was a scream in the trees followed by harsh voices.

"Tess!" Kal gasped then commanded, "Tess! Nose, eyes, ears, now!"

There was a man's yell, "Ow!" followed by a string of curses and, "Where'd she go?"

"Good girl," Kal breathed. "Eli! Go!" He hissed and the boys shot away into the darkness.

Then more arrows flew through the air and lit the dwellings while Kal ran beneath an arching branch and behind a large rock where he deposited the woman in his arms onto the ground, "I'm sorry, Moria," Kal pulled out the blade from his belt, "I will be back if I can."

But the woman grabbed Kal's hand that held the blade and pulled it to her chest. "Please don't ask this of me," Kal begged.

Moria put her other hand on the blade's handle, "I am old enough to be your mother," she said. "What would you do for her?"

The orange glow of torches lit the place where Kal knelt and a harsh voice said, "There! By the rock!"

Kal kissed the woman's forehead and, with a sob, plunged in his knife."Go with Adonai. I follow soon," he whispered as he pulled out his blade and laid her on the ground.

He hesitated a split second, then his knife came down on a cord beside the rock. There was a whizzing noise as the arched tree beside him shot back. Shouts of pain and thuds of bodies followed along with more curses.

From beneath the rock Kal extracted his bow and a quiver of arrows.

Off he ran, slashing at branches and singing, "Incha, bincha, it's a sincha!" at the top of his lungs. He led the enemy into hidden pits. Some were snatched up and dangled by a cord on their foot. Others followed Kal into a low-lying area and sunk down into clinging mud while he hopped safely across.

Closer to the mountain he led them, "Come lads! Don't give up!" he taunted. The rocks rumbled behind him and more cries of pain filled the darkness.

"Good job, boys," Kal breathed.

But always there were more. Finally, as the sky became tinged with gray, he was surrounded and shot his arrows, bringing down an enemy with each one and several more with his blade as the men closed in. In the midst of his fury Kal swung and dodged, oblivious to his many wounds. But when they dragged Eli and Jason into the light, Eden leapt, snarling, out of the brush and dove for the throat of the man who held them. The man dropped the boys and fell as Eden shook her head back and forth, ripping and tearing with vicious precision until one of the men pierced her with his sword.

Eden yelped and crumpled to the ground.

Kal released a primal yell and slashed his way through the surrounding men. An arrow slammed into his shoulder but he pushed forward and the whole group moved with him, slashing and stabbing while his own sword fell again and again.

Finally, with his back to a large rock he paused, panting as he faced them. "I have a secret," he said in a sing-song voice.

Kal wagged his hindquarters and opened his bulbous eyes wide, "My father is King!" The arm with the arrow hung limp but Kal raised the other in acknowledgement as the men guffawed.

"The king of what? Fools?" One of the men shouted.

"He's mad!" another jeered as they laughed and beat their blades against their wooden shields.

Kal stomped his foot with slow purpose, gradually increasing the pace until the blades joined his rhythm. The stomping became a hop, then a hop with a kick. Gradually the beat increased and Kal's dance became more vigorous until he was cavorting like an agile monkey as the men gradually increased the speed, their whistles and laughter growing louder as he began to spin, his blade clearing a wide circle about him.

Suddenly Kal tripped and sprawled to the ground, gasping. Blood was dripping from his nose and mouth and seeping through his clothing in the many places he had been pierced.

"What? No more dancing, old man?" the leader stepped forward and kicked Kal in the stomach.

A fresh stream of blood gushed from Kal's mouth. He spat then chuckled weakly, "Bow to your king, fool."

Once more the leader kicked and his men joined in, punching, spitting and beating Kal with their fists.

Finally the leader leaned over Kal's blood-covered body and said, "Come, oh king, let us worship you."

He dragged Kal off the ground, and to the tree that some of the warriors had already stripped of its branches and hewn to a point at the top. Two groups of men climbed onto each other's shoulders forming two columns and handed up Kal's limp form as the rest yelled and beat their shields. Then they shoved Kal onto the tree, drowning out his cry of pain with their noise.

Soon, however, their shouts faltered.

"He is smiling," one of the younger warriors observed.

"Mad to the end," another said.

Suddenly the leader looked around, "Where are they? The boys?"

The others jostled and gazed about in confusion.

Eli, Jason, and Eden were gone.

The leader looked back to Kal's smiling face and gave the command, "Push those branches beneath him."

Soon flames licked up the shorn tree. But just as the fire reached Kal's skin and he threw back his head with renewed agony, an arrow thudded into his chest and Kal's head dropped forward.

Rage flooded the leader's face and his head whipped toward the young soldier who had delivered the merciful bowshot. "He had suffered enough." The soldier stated then stood his ground as the leader glared at him with murder in his eyes.

At last the leader's gaze faltered and he backhanded one of the gawking warriors beside him. "Don't just stand there. Tend wounds! Find food! Move!"

As the others turned to obey, the leader glanced over his shoulder toward the young soldier who still stood looking up at Kal's mangled form.

Rapha took his hand off the bird's head and it stepped back with a satisfied "Caw!"

"Thank you, my friend," Rapha said.

The bird bobbed his head then flared his wings to resume his watchful perch on Kal's shoulder.

Rapha looked up toward Kal's blackened body.

With a cry of rage, Rapha shoved the tree with all his might, never pausing to remember that his strength to push trees had waned. But, whether from the power of his grief or due to the burning of the trunk, the tree broke at its base and Rapha was able to remove Kal from it.

For a full day and night Rapha did not move from the body of his friend but wept, begging Adonai to allow him to follow. But the heavens were silent. When he was once again aware of his surroundings, he discovered in the gray pre-dawn that a hollow-eyed Sheatiel had kept watch over him.

Her pain-stricken eyes seemed to read his soul as she reached to cup his cheek with her hand, "He was fortunate to have a friend like you. Kal is with *Him* now. His pain is over."

Rapha nodded, unable to look away though his eyes felt gritty from his long vigil.

"The Holy One has spoken to my heart. He wants you to know it was not your fault. You are fulfilling your appointed role in this dark hour."

The choking sob burst forth, a sudden rush that would not be denied, as Rapha felt the agony of recent days flood his being. Hardly realizing how he came to be in that position, Rapha found himself weeping on Sheatiel's shoulder as Adonai's presence flowed through her slight frame, filling his soul and overwhelming his exhausted body.

Her lips were at his ear and her hot tears mingled with his as Sheatiel whispered, "He is very pleased with you."

Somehow, he felt enfolded in Adonai's being as an unspeakable joy, a sensational overflow he had not thought to experience again until his sojourn on earth was over, wrapped him in quiet, contented, blinding perfection. Rapha was too overwhelmed to wonder why, all he could do was drink in Adonai's breath as if he had been holding his own for a millennia.

The eternal moment stretched on as he felt every hurting nook of his existence flooded by the persistent, sweet, pervading holiness. Slowly, as if emerging from deep fathoms of liquid warmth, Rapha became aware that Sheatiel was slumped against him. A gentle snore told him she was fast asleep. Moving slowly so as not to wake her, Rapha inched Sheatiel onto his lap in order to carry her to where Eve was sleeping.

But when her head rolled against his chest and her small hand grasped a fold of his robe, Rapha stopped to enjoy the warm sense of companionship, the absence of alone-ness, that had become an accepted element of his circumstances. The feeling was so unexpected and sweet, he froze, gazing at Sheatiel's velvety cheek and perfect, full lips, parted in the absolute peace of sleep only an innocent child enjoys.

Rapha felt a wave of rage as he considered Sheatiel at the hands of evil men who would abuse such beauty. He hugged her closer and ran his large hand through the shining hair, letting the rippling curls slide through his fingers. Again the blissful scent of Adonai was in the air. Again tears ran down his cheeks, this time for the horror and cruelty she had endured. How could Adonai *know* and not intervene?

Clearly the answer resounded in his heart, **"I AM intervening now… through you."**

And he was there, looking through Sheatiel's eyes, feeling every violation, the sting of every blow, the despair and shock searing his mind to numbness. In the midst of this torture, the image of the Holy One, holding Sheatiel close in the same way Rapha held her, stroking the hair from her bloodied and bruised face, whispering endearments and weeping as Sheatiel lay, shivering and naked but too frozen inside to cover her body, hating herself too much to care.

Then came peace; Adonai covering her with his mantle of love, and healing, salving every wound, inside and out.

In her sleep, Sheatiel whimpered and buried her face in Rapha's chest. Reflexively, his arms tightened around her and he whispered the language of heaven, his voice and heart slowing until there, on the hard ground at the site of Kal's cruel death, Rapha too slept, breathing in the essence of her grief and freedom.

Chapter Twenty-Seven

Love

The next few days, though filled with watchfulness and grief, became the most treasured of Rapha's existence. Sheatiel, heavy with child and approaching the time to give birth, asked probing questions about Rapha's origins and, because her eyes would come alive with hope, he divulged much more to her than he had to any other, telling her of that place where all enjoy immediate and unlimited access to Adonai's throne.

"You have really been there?" she asked one day as they sat beside a chattering mountain stream braiding the grasses that grew beside the water.

"Yes."

"But how do you survive?

"I eat, I breathe, I sleep—just like you."

"No, no, no," she laid a hand on his arm, her eyes searching his face. "How can you bear to be removed from… *Him*?"

With that question she exposed Rapha's torment.

"I cannot bear it," and his hands trembled as he began threading the rope into a tight spiral. "But I remain. Therefore I continue to breathe."

After a moment's silence Sheatiel said, "When I was alone in the wilderness, I came to a place where my food and water were gone and I had no strength. I lay down under a small bush expecting to die. Then I fell asleep and dreamed, and I heard a voice say, **'Eat! Drink!'** When I looked, bread was on the stones beside me and a stream was bubbling out of the ground. I embraced the blessing of insanity, ate and drank my fill, and slept again.

"Then, a man was there where the bread and water had been. He told me if I would eat the bread and drink the water he offered I would never again be hungry or thirsty. He was not handsome or tall like you, but somehow I knew he was what I had been looking for since the time I was a child, frightened by the images we were forced to worship. When I looked in his eyes, I felt clean, like all my pain had never happened."

Rapha felt as if he were watching the sun appear and transform a dim world when he saw Sheatiel's eyes glow with a childlike joy.

"When I woke," she continued, "I was sad because that moment with him was all I desired." She sighed and brushed away a lock of hair. "There are times I feel I would rather die than breathe again without Him."

Her eyes searched his and Rapha was shocked to discover an understanding between them, she, harlot to evil, and he, misplaced son of heaven.

"Yes," he answered the unspoken question. "It is like that."

They wove in silence, allowing the wind, water and swaying grasses to fill the space between them. To Rapha, those sounds had suddenly become the sweetest music.

"I believe He was real." Her words were so quiet Rapha almost missed them. "When I woke, my thirst was quenched and my stomach was filled so it must have been more than a dream. Every time I sleep I beg Him to come again. It was my hope when I lay dying, before you found me, that He would be there, but…." Sheatiel tied off the braid in her hands with a yank.

"But I came instead," he finished her thought, then laughed when Sheatiel wrinkled her nose as if at an unpleasant smell. "So I am to be despised for saving your life?"

But she was in no mood for jokes. "I had no choice but to end the life of this one in my womb."

"Because you fear the prince of evil who spawned it?"

"You have heard my thoughts," she accused.

"I would not enter your mind uninvited but I see the truth. Evil followed you here because you carry its seed."

Sheatiel took a deep breath. "I have told no one because I could trust no one." Again she paused, lost in memories. "He was the shining ruler of our land. He was perfect, tall, and strong. Other men looked pitiful beside him. They say he descended from the sun and that the blood of the stars ran in his veins. I was bred to please him, chosen for my beauty and intelligence. It was the highest honor to be taken to the palace."

She paused once again and shuddered. "But horrible things happen behind those walls. Soon I realized it was a prison. I saw the evil in his beautiful eyes and it repulsed me. But the more I hated him, the more he desired me. The more my tears flowed when I was forced to witness the horror of his sacrifices the more he chose me, out of his many women, to be by his side. He enjoyed my pain. Once he even confessed it made him feel alive again. He would beat me—and laugh."

As she spoke, Rapha saw a picture developing of this prince, as if her words and even unspoken thoughts were coming to life in his mind. The tall, muscled body, the cunning and cruelty, even the occasional wit and charm could have been a perfect description of Lucifer in human form. In fact....

"What was his name?" Rapha asked.

"He had many. He preferred 'My Lord' but he was also called 'Ra' and 'The Ba'al.' Not exactly a name a mother would bestow." When she spoke again she kept her eyes on the ground.

"Only once did I feel I saw behind the mask he showed the world. He had… hurt me… worse than ever. He probably thought I was not conscious. I wished to be dead. But he spoke of his mother, how she would hate what he had become. Then he began to cry. I knew if I moved he would hurt me again so I lay still as he wept and said, 'Oh my brother!' over and over again."

The image in Rapha's mind was clear. There was no doubt.

"It is Cain. The child in you is his."

"You know him?"

"Know him? I aided in his birth. I shared his home."

"Then, you knew his mother and his father?"

"*You* know his mother."

"Eve?"

"Yes."

"And… his father?" Sheatiel shut her eyes as if bracing for a blow.

"It is a lengthy tale and a complicated one," Rapha said. "But I will tell it if you like."

When Sheatiel nodded, Rapha began. As the sun climbed high into the sky and then began to descend they remained, one unfolding the past while the other drank it in, the bitter as well as the sweet. When she smiled his heart soared. When she cried it eased the burden of his memories. It was only toward the end, when it was nearing the time she became part of the tale, that Sheatiel became silent, arms wrapped around her swollen belly.

When Rapha stopped speaking there was a moment's silence, then Sheatiel was on her knees at his feet.

"You must help me! Give me the strength to end this! This 'Cain' will not rest until…." She wrapped the cord in his hands around her neck. "You are strong. It will be over quickly."

Rapha knelt with her. Sheatiel's eyes were shut tight but a tear escaped to trace a shining path down her cheek. He reached to brush it away and she flinched, her eyes flying open. "Please! Before I become weak."

He removed the cord from her neck, "You are brave but the Holy One you met in the wilderness would ask you to be braver still. He preserved your life. Therefore I can do no less."

"No. He gave me the sacrificial meal to prepare me for death."

Rapha took her clenched fists in his hands. "That is not Adonai's way. Evil demands death to prove devotion. Adonai asks more. He asks you to *live* your devotion. As for the babe in your womb, Adonai's gift of life must never be taken lightly. He knew you before you were born. It is the same with your child."

Touching her was connecting him to so many powerful emotions: fear and courage, love and hatred for the unborn, an artist's sensitivity scarred by cruelty, self-hatred striving with God-breathed destiny, distrust of feelings, and now a deep trust for him.

Ah. Her affection for him had become deeper than her fear. In fact, when her hands touched his, she no longer wanted to die, she longed to live—she longed to… love.

He dropped her hands as if they burned him.

Rapha mumbled something more about Adonai and stood. The words made no sense. "Eve!" he called.

When he found the elder woman he told her of the child of her flesh in Sheatiel's womb. He also instructed her to stay close to the cave at night. He would not be far away.

Why was he leaving? He needed to spy out the land. He would seek a mountain goat for milk. The ravens had news for him.

Lies.

Rapha ran.

He raced like a young Adam to the top of the mountain, running until sweat poured from his body and the heart of flesh pounded in his chest.

What good would it do to protect them from outside invasion if the greatest threat dwelt in him?

The cave at the top of the mountain was the setting of his greatest battle. He never slept, ate, or drank as the sun rose and set three times and his mind stormed with confusion. His flesh was betraying him; therefore he would slay it by neglect. He welcomed the suffering. It proved he could yet master it.

No celestials brought a comforting message. The Holy One who had absolved his guilt so long ago did not appear. Thus Rapha raged and cried out, even beating the rocky floor of the cave with his fists until it was stained with his blood.

Still nothing.

All was quiet except for a lark chirping on an overhanging branch, observing him with a bright eye.

Surely heaven had closed its ears to him, the fool who loved a human. For no other word could describe the feeling he had for Sheatiel. But this love was far different from what he felt for his angelic brothers or the fatherly affection he had for Adam and Eve. His passion for Sheatiel contained all those feelings and more. It was need and desire and tenderness for her presence as if she both completed and weakened him.

He had not been aware this emotion was possible since in his former life angels, at least those who remained faithful to Adonai, had no need of physical coupling. This issue had been Lucifer's effective strategy in his war with heaven. He corrupted both earthly and celestial flesh by joining them—in direct rebellion of Adonai's command. That perversion had been the demise of creation and Adonai's heartbreak for time immemorial.

Rapha had no idea how long he wandered in his memories of grief, back to memories of Adonai's perfection and peace on Earth; to the joyful manchild, Adam, with hopes as high as the heavens; beyond mortal understanding to a teasing, deadly ambitious angel, Lucifer, desiring to ascend to the very throne of Adonai; back even farther to the time before Earth's remembrance, when celestial voices sang in perfect harmony, aiding The Most High in creating the wonders of the universe.

He was neither asleep nor awake, his mind and body losing their grasp on life, his soul hoping to leave behind the husk of flesh, when Adonai whispered to his heart, **"Rapha, arise. Your battle is not complete. Trust My everlasting love. Your weakness is strength in My hands."**

How Rapha longed to drown in that voice. But no, he was more aware, second by second, of his aching body and his swollen tongue until, with a cry of disappointment, he opened his eyes to bloodstained cave walls. But a cleft in the rock before him held clear water. He drank it. When he sat up, he discovered he was not alone.

Lucifer stood at the cave entrance.

"Let me look at you, old friend," he circled around Rapha tsk, tsking mournfully, *"ooh! The years have not been kind!"*

He stopped before Rapha's glazed eyes and grimaced as he sniffed and put a hand to his nose. *"My magnanimity amazes even me. I am prepared, for the sake of our long association, to forget our past differences and lift you out of this deplorable pit. I cannot bear that one of my noble brothers should be so,"* he waved a hand toward Rapha as if words failed him, *"disgraced."*

When Rapha remained silent, Lucifer squatted to eye level, an intoxicating perfume flowing from him. *"Say the word.* One word *and I have the power to restore you. There is no need to be debased any longer. What good can you possibly accomplish devoid of power, devoid of dignity?"* There was a sob in his voice.

But if there was one thing Rapha's self-denial had accomplished it was a slaying of pride. The thought of beautiful raiment and power would be nothing but farce to one who felt less worthy of life than the bright-eyed bird who looked on from its customary branch.

"Go away," Rapha rasped. "Those things mean nothing."

"At least let me feed you!" With a wave of his hand, Lucifer produced a banquet between them. Rapha was assaulted by the scent of roasted meat and fruits bursting with sweetness. His mouth watered but he turned away.

"Oh come!" Lucifer exclaimed, grasping a chunk of meat and tearing into the moist, steaming flesh.

Rapha watched some of the pink juice run down Lucifer's chin. "I thought you preferred it raw."

Lucifer's voicc was so cold it chilled the air. *"You despise my kindness when I could so easily destroy you."*

"Please. Do."

Lucifer's eyes narrowed. *"Yes, it would be kindness to end this pathetic existence. But then you would remain... un-in-struc-ted."* He pronounced the word as if relishing its flavor as he continued to study Rapha, from his lank hair to the soles of his dirty feet.

"Something is different about you," Lucifer finally stated.

Rapha felt the penetration. His thoughts were being invaded. Sheatiel's face pushed to the fore but he forced himself to focus on the memory of Kal, pierced and rotting in the midday sun.

But he could not resist for long. Soon he heard Lucifer's satisfied chuckle as the memory of Sheatiel, eyes shut in peaceful repose, a curl of dark hair draping across full lips, was wrested from his mind.

"Ah! You have excellent taste, old friend." Lucifer's hand was beneath Rapha's chin. *"Believe me. Cain has relished her... fruits. He is most eager to retrieve this bird who has flown."*

Lucifer sat back and sighed. *"Ah, Rapha. My war is not with you. For the sake of our old friendship, I will give you the best of advice. You love this woman. It is all too simple. Join with her, take her as your wife, live a life of peace far from all this strife of war."*

Lucifer leaned in and whispered, his words sweet as honey in Rapha's ears. *"What did it do for the humans to mix with our flesh? It brought death.* Death, *Rapha! Imagine, you grow old, you die, you are* freed*! It is your way out. Become one with her. Reach out and take the joy before you."*

The images in Rapha's mind made him weak with longing.

> *He was falling asleep with Sheatiel in his arms.*
>
> *They were living a life of contentment and simplicity far from intrigues and violence.*
>
> *Sheatiel was glancing up at him, joy in her eyes as she nursed his child.*
>
> *His child.*

"And what of my offspring?" Rapha whispered. "They would be part of your corruption, the way you have destroyed from the beginning. Adonai created perfection and harmony but you continue to corrupt. Why, after all this time, do you think I would be grafted into that vine? The war would continue in their flesh; earthly and celestial, incompatible from the beginning, burdening Adonai's heart, hastening earth's destruction yet again. They would further the tyranny, envy and strife you have unleashed."

Again Lucifer sighed. *"You take yourself too seriously, Rapha. You always have. The seed is sown. It* will *grow and spread. It cannot be stopped. The actions of one outcast from the heavens will be of no consequence. Besides, you have already been altered. What if you are compatible now?"*

Rapha's heart beat faster at those words.

"Who knows but that Adonai has opened this avenue to happiness—if you will reach out and take it."

A wild hope flared in Rapha's heart.

"Have you even asked? You've always had a special connection to the Most High. No reason for fear, eh?"

At that moment the raven landed at the mouth of Rapha's cave. He flapped his wings and backed away when he saw Lucifer.

"Ah! News from below," the fallen angel's eyes glittered and a malicious smile spread on his face.

The bird fixed his gaze on Rapha. The message encoded there caused Rapha to jump to his feet.

"Alas! Adonai gives," Lucifer chuckled, as Rapha raced from the cave, *"and he takes away!"*

"SHEATIEL!"

This time Rapha ran toward her. Lucifer's delighted laughter echoed around him. It didn't matter. Reason called. Rapha shoved it aside. Adonai's one rule since the beginning of all things, to maintain purity—separate and distinct worlds between men and celestials—was tossed to the wind.

He loved. He felt passion beyond himself, beyond law. He would be by her side. He would fight. If he was destroyed, all the better.

As he raced down the mountain, oblivious to rocks against his bare feet, heart torn by this new madness, he sensed a surprising companion.

Adonai was in the madness. His presence was unmistakable.

"Now you begin to understand," Adonai whispered to Rapha's heart. **"My love is beyond law, beyond barriers. What I have declared is established. What I have made pure is redeemed."**

It was a strange moment for clarity. What he felt toward Sheatiel was just a taste of the passion Adonai felt toward all creation. That passion consumed and defined and—Rapha gasped—*forged a way through impossibilities*.

Was Adonai endorsing his love for this woman? Would He somehow bring joy from what was forbidden?

For the second time in his existence, Rapha felt reformed. For the first time… ever… he felt the true human joy of discovery heightened by a sense of limitation, by a sense of—mortality.

Then he heard her cry. He raced toward the sound expecting at any moment to meet Lucifer's murderous hordes—but no enemy confronted him.

Her voice came again on the wind, a terrified shriek. Surely only torture would cause such pain.

Nothing would stop him. If Adonai was with him what could stand against him?

So he stumbled upon his greatest fear—Eve's tragic eyes, Shealtiel's tortured cries—with the peace of heaven overflowing his being. The babe was emerging but it was destroying Sheatiel like an abandoned chrysalis. So Rapha set to work doing what he did best, to bring comfort and mend bodies. How he prayed as her blood flowed over his hands. How forcefully he spoke heavenly commands to ministering angels. How he worshiped Adonai and sang praises to the creator of all things even as he discovered her ruptured womb and the infant foot that protruded, blue in color.

He took the babe quickly, that abnormally large child who was, nevertheless, not ready to thrive outside the womb. And as his hands continued to press down, trying to stop the relentless draining of Sheatiel's life, his tears blended with her blood.

He was failing.

There was no time to wonder why. There was no opportunity to scream at the heavens demanding intervention. He had only moments to love.

Sheatiel grasped his bloodied hand and placed it beneath her chin. For one eternal moment her eyes held his. What he saw there stilled his soul as she smiled with the radiant glow of perfect peace.

Finally she spoke. "Please, if you love me, do not try to keep me here."

Rapha's eyes widened in surprise.

"He told me of your love," she said. "I would not have believed the words from anyone else." Sheatiel smiled and squeezed Rapha's hand. "He was with me through the night, through the pain. He promised you would join me one day—when your task is finished."

Circumstances were unchanged but everything was transformed.

"He says the child is a gift to you. Through you this one, though intended for evil, will be grafted into holiness." She choked with emotion and her tears flowed. "My life is redeemed," she whispered and kissed the tips of Rapha's fingers. "Eve?"

Eve stepped forward, the child in her arms, and Sheatiel said, "My son will be a comfort to you, filling your empty arms. I leave him in your keeping." With that she reached for the baby with feeble arms and Eve laid it on her chest where the child turned its face, eager to suckle. Though quickly fading, Sheatiel said, "Take my strength, dear one. I no longer need it."

The baby swallowed, its sounds of life filling the silence with hope as its eyes fixed on hers.

"Please name him Rapha," Sheatiel whispered, "Teach him to be just like you."

"Today I am his father," Rapha sensed the affirmation of heaven in those words even as he felt himself attaching to her soul, sucking hungrily at its strength, needing that sustenance for survival as surely as the babe in her arms.

He placed a kiss on Sheatiel's forehead and rested his head on her shoulder, breathing in the perfume of her skin and the pulsing life rising from the newborn's still-wet head. He felt his heart tear loose as a lifetime of emotion broke over him.

Like rain on a desert, his tears opened her mind and invited him into that secret place, laying her naked soul before him without reserve, exposing every shame and wound without fear. He gasped at the depth of its treasures and pains, marveling at the palaces of riches and whole worlds of virgin lands, an entire universe of Adonai's likeness embossed on each cell of her essence. And there, in a childlike nook of her heart, he discovered a need, an unspoken but desperate yearning. Rapha lifted his head to look in her eyes.

"I claim you as my life mate, my wife," he whispered, and then paused to drink in her sigh of pleasure. "My heart and body are yours forever. We are one."

"We are one," she echoed and smiled.

Rapha prayed, speaking Adonai's will in heavenly words until he could finally accept it.

A look of rapture dawned on Sheatiel's face and she gasped with childish delight, "I have a family, a husband, a sister, a child. I am loved. It is all I ever wanted." Then she laughed and the air sparkled with the beauty of her soul taking flight, and even the baby stopped suckling to gaze at her.

It was a moment of dazzling beauty Rapha tucked away in his soul. He felt Adonai's kiss bestowed with the gift of her joy.

Sheatiel died as the babe suckled the last drops of life from her breast, his large, innocent eyes closing in contented slumber, one small fist tucked beneath his chin, mirroring his mother who still clutched Rapha's blood-crusted hand.

Then, one more gift dripped from Adonai's throne. A vision of what was, that very moment, taking place.

He saw Sheatiel, running with a shriek of delight to the Holy One who swung her into the air and spun until they both fell into a field of wildflowers, dizzy with joy, laughing in their delirium. Finally, with bits of vibrant petals in her hair, she looked toward Rapha. "You're here!" and she ran to him, leaping into his arms and kissing him on the lips with an abandon reserved for children unacquainted with pain.

But Rapha was not there to stay. He knew if he remained longer he would be unable to return to his new son. Indeed the thought of leaving that place was already destroying him.

"I love you, Sheatiel," he cupped a hand to her perfect cheek and kissed her lips, then walked with her toward the Holy One where he placed her hand in His.

Immediately he was dropped back into the dim world of blood and death where her cold hand yet clutched his and the babe slept at her breast, its steady breathing accompanied by the sound of Eve's quiet weeping.

There Rapha remained, drinking deep of the peace and pain.

Adonai inhabited both.

Chapter Twenty-Eight

Rafe

It was a strange new frontier for Rapha. As soon as he thought he understood the parenting process, the rules would change. The baby would be wakeful all night or he would cry for no obvious reason or he would have a day when he only desired Eve followed by a time of screaming unless attached to Rapha's broad back. He was a needy child, much more challenging than Abel and Cain had been, even considering the fact that since they were twins, the workload had been double.

Thankfully, the baby's challenges were not physical. The mothering instinct had brought the miracle of Eve's milk so he was well fed from the start. But Rapha knew exactly how the baby felt. He too missed Sheatiel. There were days he wished he could join the child in wailing at the top of his lungs but there was no time for this indulgence. Mere survival was too demanding. Their patchwork family lived a nomadic life, following the flocks and milder weather and Rapha's limitless knowledge enabled them to thrive even though they longed for the stability of their former life. But they agreed the child's heritage must be hidden. Thus their home was a portable shelter of animal skins, and the sum of their wealth was the few items they could carry on their backs. Luckily, Rapha could carry as much as the strongest beast of burden, so they knew no lack. Occasionally they could milk a wild goat or discover eggs, but the addition of stock animals for a constant supply was impossible. Even with the ability to move at a moment's notice, danger loomed.

When the baby was only three weeks old that fact was made all too clear. After a restless night of enduring the child's crying (none of Rapha's salves or prayers soothed him) he took the child outside their shelter where fresh air, night noises and the sight of bright stars finally lulled the babe to sleep. There, wrapped in his warm cloak and listening to the lullaby of the baby's peaceful breathing, Rapha too slumbered. The sun was already in its second hour when he was shocked to wakefulness by the plodding lope of an approaching camel.

Berating himself for his lapse in judgment, Rapha remained seated as the rider approached. Every detail of the man's clothing and appearance was cataloged as Rapha assessed this possible threat, from the fine weave of the man's brilliantly dyed cloak to the well-fed state of his camel. The stranger was unaccompanied and his emotions exuded intense agitation and fear, not a recipe for disaster, even so…. "Eve!"

She came, bleary-eyed and startled, to retrieve the still-slumbering baby and then reentered the shelter just as the man brought his camel to a halt. Though his eyes glanced her way, the man's attention centered on Rapha.

"Greetings!" Rapha's smile did nothing to decrease the stranger's unease.

"Good morrow!" The man answered without dismounting. "My son said he heard a baby's cry during the night as he kept the flocks and he reported where you lodged. I hope you are refreshed," the words were cordial but the true reason for the man's visit was screaming in Rapha's mind.

The man got right to the point. "Fierce men are approaching. My sons who roam our borders saw them." He wiped a trembling hand across his brow. "I come to extend protection."

"What are the enemy's numbers?" Rapha asked.

"More than one hundred, well-armed." The man hesitated. "It is reported some stand as tall as trees."

"What are your defenses?"

"High earthen walls and the strength of my sons."

Rapha continued questioning, though already convinced the man's cause was hopeless.

"You must flee to the hills. Your family will not survive if you remain."

The man's expression became shrewd. "You have enjoyed the hospitality of this land. You are obligated to assist against our enemies."

"My assistance is this advice. Flee while you can."

"Why do they come to my lands? Are you what they seek?" Rapha's hesitation confirmed the man's suspicions. "Either assist us or I will lead them to you." The dark eyes were hard as flint. "I know what you are. The only reason a descendant of the gods would travel thus, with only one wife and no possessions, is because you have stolen something of great value."

Rapha stood and the man's eyes widened as he beheld Rapha's height and girth. The man was smart and would not hesitate to be cruel if it would ensure the safety of his family and possessions, especially the latter. "I have a daughter, lovely and tender in years. She is yours, along with seven camels, if you assist us." When Rapha seemed to be considering the offer the man continued, "or my youngest son, if you prefer," the shrewd eyes glinted as he assessed Rapha's reaction.

Rapha shrugged and took a step forward but his eyes were fixed on the camel. He reached for the bridle and lifted the animal's head as if for inspection.

"Yes!" The man adjusted his proposition, "You drive a hard bargain. The boy, the girl *and* the camels—" But his words were cut short as the animal turned tail and streaked away as fast as his long, loping legs would carry him while the man flung himself forward and held on for dear life.

Rapha felt remorse for the terror he had injected into the beast's mind. He knew the camel would not pause until he collapsed, trembling, at his customary shelter, but it could not be helped.

He turned to find Eve already prepared, the sleeping baby wrapped securely to her chest, her few possessions on her back. Moments later they were on the move and nightfall found them miles away in a mountain cave.

The next day dark smoke rose from the valley floor and the scent of death was carried on the wind.

Horror ran rampant in the land. Daily the ravens brought news of death and destruction. Even Rapha found the reports unbelievable—of men as tall as trees who possessed an insatiable appetite for conquest. But when their party of three came upon the remains of these conquests the truth was confirmed. Protective ramparts were ripped from their foundations, men were impaled and burned and any remainders of livestock were simply skin and bones, as if the marauders had devoured them alive. There were some traces of women and children among the ruins, usually victims of unmentionable horrors, but most had vanished. And all around these scenes of destruction were prints from feet twice as large as Rapha's. It appeared Lucifer's new breeding program flourished.

Rapha was of the firm opinion those already dead were the more fortunate.

These events made it more imperative than ever to avoid human association since even normal-sized men viewed Rapha with murder in their eyes, assuming with one look that he was in league with the aggressors. So their lives became even more isolated. Rapha taught Eve and the child the art of blending with their surroundings, an art he owed in great part to Kal. Their cloaks were woven of nature's hues—mottled gray, muted green, and shades of brown—which enabled them to pass under the sun like drifting shadows, and the coverings for their feet left almost indiscernible tracks. In fact, when the young one stepped through soft earth, he learned to leap lightly on his toes as Rapha had taught him, so his imprint more closely resembled a small hoof.

They even developed their own method of communicating with their hands. It was useful not only when they did not want to frighten a wary animal but it also came in handy when they needed to evade humans.

Their primary dwelling was a well-hidden cavern where sunlight shone through a high cleft and plentiful water flowed. When the weather was too hot or too cold the cavern provided protection from the elements and a fairly temperate clime. In this sanctuary, Eve and Rapha coaxed many species of food-bearing plants to thrive but they also tended small gardens not far from the entrance to their dwelling, making sure their fruit trees, vegetables, or plots of grain were intermingled and thus would appear as random growths to anyone who stumbled into their domain.

Once in a while Rapha and Eve would bemoan the child's lack of society but Rafe, as they dubbed him, knew no other company but theirs, and therefore he was content. If the child desired other company, that need was met by the animals that often gathered around him with ready trust and affection.

Even at a tender age, Rafe was a marvel within the animal kingdom. He was gentle, and, through careful observation and Rapha's expert guidance, he had learned to gauge the creatures' moods and mimic their methods of communication. Rapha and Eve soon stopped worrying about these interactions since Rafe had demonstrated the ability to disarm the most distrustful of animals—from the venomous vipers to the hungry mountain cats. Also, due to his size (by the age of seven he was as tall as most human men) none dared to consider him prey. Thus their main directive for the boy when he went out to explore was, "Do not be seen."

Usually this was a simple accomplishment since their dwellings were so remote, but Rafe insisted that when humans were near, "everything tells me it is so. I can smell them on the wind, the animals are quiet and their ears point toward the danger." Although large in size, Rafe possessed amazing agility and stealth. Sometimes even Rapha's keen eyes blinked in wonder when the boy seemed to melt from sight, blending in with the tall trunks of trees and the swaying shadows.

Once when Rapha went out of doors to retrieve the boy for the night, he searched in all Rafe's usual haunts but found no trace. When he finally returned to their cavern entrance, wondering how he would inform Eve that the child was lost, his attention was drawn to a bush that quivered although no wind stirred—a bush, tall and wide, where no bush usually grew. Even then, the guise was convincing, but Rapha reached out with his thoughts, probing the mysterious phenomenon.

Ah! Rafe had learned to shroud his mind as well as his body. Later, Rapha would rave to Eve, "He is truly gifted! Not even eight full cycles of the seasons from birth yet even Adam did not possess such unity with creation!"

But for the moment, Rapha had to correct the misuse of this ability. "Rafe!" he commanded, "Your talents must never be used selfishly. Come out!"

Slowly, the overhanging branches of the tree snapped back into place and Rafe unwrapped the dark cloak from his legs. The boy's expression was meek, but mischievous sparks lit his dark eyes, eyes that reminded Rapha of Sheatiel. Despite himself, Rapha felt a proud smile tug at the corners of his mouth. Rafe, always intuitive, read the forgiveness in his father's eyes, "I'm sorry, father, but," he strode forward brushing a hand through his thick mop of curly dark hair, another trait inherited from his mother, "I did it! I finally fooled you! Nothing ever fools you! I watched the trees and I thought like the trees, and I felt the breeze like the trees…."

On and on the man-sized child enthused as love warmed Rapha's heart. The boy treasured creation. It was a part of his soul. He loved the simple delights of beauty and peace. These gifts would enrich him throughout his lifetime and, someday… would he have children to teach those same values?

So they enjoyed a contrived peace. Rapha and Eve invested the best of themselves in the offspring of Cain, and their own friendship flourished, never replacing the loves they had known, but forging a formidable team nonetheless.

But in a world slipping into madness, this momentary respite could not last. When Rafe was only nine years old, chaos severed their patched home.

Perhaps Rapha had become lax in his vigilance; trusting in their hidden stronghold and his family's ability to melt into nature. But, looking back, Rapha was assured that Adonai had directed even the horror of that fateful day.

It was the cries of a child that drew them. In the late afternoon of a day heavy with oppressive heat, a child's terrified screams reached their ears.

Rapha could sooner have held back the ocean's waves than prevent Eve and Rafe from responding to that cry. It was one thing to ignore evil running rampant far away but quite another matter when suffering was on one's doorstep. Even as the words, "We must be cautious," were on his lips, the others were rushing toward the cries, keeping to the shadows but determined to reach the child without delay. As they drew closer to the source of the sound Rapha smelled Lucifer's calling cards—fear and human blood. Marauders were close, their cruel thoughts filling Rapha's mind. They were searching for the child. Their heavy footsteps and harsh voices echoed as they sought a way down to where the child had fallen. Fallen?!

Rapha sensed another with thoughts centered on the child, her mother, but the woman's frantic desire was that the child *not* be found. *"I hear you, love. You're alive. Run! Please run!"* The mother's heart begged.

Then they saw her in the fading light, a small girl, not far from the age of suckling, with bloodied hands and gashed legs that peeked from beneath a torn, muddy garment. The cause of her screams was obvious. She had apparently tumbled into a patch of mountain nettles. With a gasp of maternal sympathy, Eve rushed forward murmuring endearments and assurances, and soon returned to the shadows with the crying child nestled in her arms. However, when the girl beheld Rapha and Rafe, terror filled her eyes and she screamed as visions of horror filled her young mind and pummeled Rapha's.

Big men. Auda screaming. Da drug away. Heat. Stink. Scared.

As Eve tried to calm her, Rapha found the antidote that grew nearby. He spread the sticky sap on a strip of cloth, then applied the cloth to the nettles in her knees and hands. When he pulled the material away, the child's cries ceased and she looked at Rapha, then down at her knee, in astonishment.

"That's right," he spoke soothingly, "let us take you where it's safe and we can doctor your wounds."

Like an abused animal responding to kindness, the child reached toward Rapha. He took her in his arms and she clung to him as they moved through the shadows, an ever-growing threat pushing him to move as quickly as possible even as the girl hid her small face in his shoulder and her heart pounded against his chest.

Once more he felt it, that sorcerous push against his mind that had haunted them in the caves. That same intent now followed their trail. Rapha's thoughts became confused and his breath came in gasps as he wrestled, attempting to shroud those who ran with him from this piercing hunter.

"Rapha?" Eve gasped. "It's hard to breathe."

"Yes, I feel it."

"It… knows me," she added.

"I can hide us," Rafe suggested.

"Quiet," Rapha admonished. Their predator's thoughts had fixed on them with renewed intensity when they spoke. Rapha moved faster but soon the crash of pursuit could be heard.

Suddenly Eve gasped and her footsteps faltered.

"What?"

"Cain. I saw Cain."

"It is a lie. They are coming," Rapha hissed.

"I must go to him. It is Adonai's plan."

"No! I am commanded to protect you!"

But Eve looked at Rapha with that stubborn, immovable expression, "I am certain. They would catch us soon. You know it. This way the rest of you will have a chance. Go!"

The crashes and harsh voices were upon them and the child buried her face in Rapha's neck, whimpering, her tiny body shivering with fright.

"Take the children to safety. Please!"

As he looked into Eve's eyes, Rapha discovered the pure peace of Adonai.

"I will preserve her. Trust her to My hand."

"Come!" Rapha grasped Rafe's arm and propelled the bewildered boy ahead.

"No! We can't!" Rafe protested.

"Hurry. It is Adonai's command."

"No!"

"Be still deep inside. Hear Him for yourself."

Rafe's face flushed with anger and he pushed toward Eve.

"Rafe," Eve's quiet voice addressed him, "I am in Adonai's hands. You must help Rapha protect her."

The little girl reached toward Rafe and he lifted her from Rapha's arms. With solemn eyes she reached to wipe the moisture from Rafe's face.

"Now go!" Eve urged.

So they stumbled ahead, their feet heavy with grief. It was only a moment until triumphant shouts resounded on the path behind them.

Rapha kept track of the marauding party that had settled a few miles away like locusts to devour whatever was good in that land. Daily he sent birds to gather news from their camp since he did not trust his attempts to hear Eve's thoughts, now warped somehow, as if by a net of confusion. Little could be gleaned of Eve's fate other than brief sightings by the ravens—who reported she appeared unharmed, and was usually surrounded by women and children who, like her, were captives.

On the seventh morning since Eve's capture a raven's caw woke Rapha from sleep. He moved with care so as not to disturb the child they called Auda (the only word she would say) who insisted on pressing her small back against his and wrapping herself in layers of bedclothes even when she slept in a puddle of sweat.

Eve's message through the bird was short and direct, "I am safe. Stay away. Cain is here. He sought Sheatiel. She is dead. His search is over."

He probed the bird for more information, gleaning the fact that Eve was well fed and unwounded. Also, the raven, bold when food could be obtained, had entered Cain's tent to pick at the leavings of a feast and had spied Cain drinking heavily of the fruit of the vine with his head in his hands.

"So," Rapha mused aloud, "lordship is not all Cain had anticipated."

For his part, the raven could not understand the concept of low spirits when one had plentiful food. Speaking of food, having delivered his message, the raven was eager to seek his breakfast, so he cocked his glossy, black head and gave another insistent caw.

Rapha pointed toward a patch of ripe melons. "Help yourself, brother raven. And thank you."

He stepped away from the cavern entrance to savor his relief free from the noise of the bird's meal.

The eastern sky began to burn with the fast-approaching day. Rapha smiled as the weight on his shoulders lifted. When the children woke he would greet them with a lighter heart and perhaps take them to fish at his favorite stream. With Adonai's help he would delight in those who remained.

In the coming days, Rafe's gentleness was further enhanced by the tenderness he showed Auda. Other than that one word, she never spoke of her former life. But Rapha perceived the slaughter of her family, all but her mother, who was a recurring player in Auda's violent dreams of a beautiful, blonde woman surrounded by leering men.

Caring for Auda required all the finesse of handling a poisonous viper. Even if they woke in the night to the sound of her cries, they quickly learned to avoid her clawing fingers and biting teeth. But in spite of her fiery temperament, a keen intelligence flashed in the depths of her blue eyes, eyes Rafe said reminded him of the color of peacock feathers.

How they missed Eve. Though Rafe and Rapha were able to supply bountiful food, something more than sustenance was needed. They tried to duplicate her homey touches—fresh flowers and sweet-smelling herbs—but now those things were only ghosts of Eve's presence.

Rafe insisted they should rescue Eve. For the first time the boy became belligerent and disrespectful toward Rapha, even accusing him of cowardice since he had not fought the men who took her.

"She wanted to go," Rapha said yet again.

"Of course she did! She didn't want us hurt, but we could have trapped them when they passed through the canyon."

"And what would have become of her, if we had been captured or slain?" Rapha indicated the small figure with yellow curls who slept wrapped in Eve's heavy cloak. This brought a momentary end to the argument.

In truth, Rapha second-guessed his own actions. How he desired his secluded mountain cave where he could seek Adonai without distraction, but his responsibilities demanded he stay close to Auda, who became terrified when he was out of her sight, and to Rafe, who entertained thoughts of daring rescue even in his dreams.

In quiet moments Rapha would reach toward Eve with his thoughts but these attempts were still unsuccessful as if she had entered a realm blocked from his perception. So he had to continue relying on his winged friends for news.

On the tenth morning since Eve's capture, their raven messenger woke Rapha with news. Eve was close by and requesting a meeting.

"Is she alone?" Rapha asked.

The bird gave no indication of danger.

"When is the meeting?" Rafe, stealthy as always, was at his side and had intercepted the communication.

"Now."

"But Auda still sleeps."

"Good. I will try to return before she wakes."

"But…." Rafe started to protest.

"Ssssh. If all is well, I will send for you," Rapha assured the boy.

As he was exiting the cave, Rafe stopped him. "In case I don't get to see her, please give her this for me." Rafe laid a hand on his shoulder and a scene played out in Rapha's mind.

Eve and a much younger Rafe, perhaps four years old, chased each other through a forest carpeted with falling leaves. Over and over they fell onto the golden piles and she would tickle Rafe as he shrieked with delight.

When Rafe pulled his hand away they were both crying. "It was the best way I could think of to send her my love."

When Rapha reached for him, the boy's shoulders shook with quiet sobs.

Eve was waiting for him in a glade at the foot of the mountain. When he saw the dark circles under her eyes and the sadness in her face, Rapha wanted nothing more than to toss her over his shoulder and escape.

"Have they hurt you?"

"Oh no. It is known whose mother I am. They wouldn't dare."

"Have you seen Cain?"

"Yes."

"How is he?"

"Miserable. But he is powerful, feared, honored… everything he desired," she wrinkled her nose in disgust. "Listen," she hurried on, "I have news and I have only a short time." Her face crumpled with grief and she struggled to continue. "The child's mother, Lael, is… has… she took her own life."

"Were you able to tell her her daughter is safe?"

"Yes," Eve answered, "it was the only time she smiled. But the fear for her child was all she lived for. Once that fear was gone, she stopped living." Eve shut her eyes tight. "I couldn't blame her. The things the men did… oh, Rapha, the way they used her." Eve's face flushed and she jumped to her feet, tears shedding unheeded as she paced.

"I am glad she killed the last one to use her! Adonai help me, I am! She rose as he slept, found his blade, slew him, and then… turned it on herself." Eve fell to her knees, "Oh Adonai! How has Your creation come to this?" The rage and sadness warred across Eve's face but after a moment's despair she leapt to her feet to pace again.

"I took her body to Cain. I screamed at him, of what I thought of his kingdom, of his… these savages he calls warriors.

"'You should die for speaking to me this way,' he said, and I dared him to do it. I called him a coward and a murderer and begged him to kill me since I could not bear what he has become." Her tirade of words stopped and she wilted to the ground.

"That's when I saw it, Rapha. For one short moment, the Cain I love was looking out of those eyes. He is lost. He is tortured. I want to hate him but… he is my son," she wiped her sleeve across her face. "He agreed that I could come see you but I made him promise to release the other women and children when I return. He knows I cannot abandon them. I pray there is enough honor in him to keep his word on this."

"Is it safe to send for Rafe and Auda?"

"Is that what you call her? Good. That is what she called her mother. No. I do not trust Cain enough to endanger them." Again tears flowed down Eve's cheeks. "Hug Rafe for me. Tell him he filled the longing of my heart. Tell him I will always love him, and I lift his name before Adonai."

When Rapha presented Eve with the memory Rafe had sent, she sobbed. "Please don't tell him it made me cry. I will treasure it. I will treasure every memory spent with both of you."

With one last embrace, she ran in the direction of the warrior's camp.

Chapter Twenty-Nine

Auda

The cycles of the seasons melted away and, to Rapha's ancient eyes, the children grew at an astonishing pace. Yes, he had experienced childhood before but never as the primary caregiver, where he was so busy with the demands of daily life they seemed to sprout up when he blinked.

At fifteen, Rafe towered over Rapha who had to look up to see the boy's chin. Auda, whom they guessed to be eight, was tall by human standards but only reached Rafe's mid-thigh. However, this did not prevent her following the lad like a faithful puppy, climbing, cultivating, and spending hours observing in companionable silence. For his part, Rafe could have gone much farther afield on his excursions if the determined imp with flaxen curls had not bounded up each morning and rushed through her duties to be certain she would not be left behind. Rafe made the mistake of departing before she woke only once, but the red-rimmed eyes coupled with the cold shoulder sufficiently chastised him. He never did it again—at least not without a good explanation.

Rapha's heart warmed when he would watch the two traipse off together, Auda trotting and Rafe matching his pace to hers, lending a hand to help her leap their creek, a hand stubbornly refused by Auda whose motto in life was, "I can *do* it."

But on the morning of Rafe's seventeenth year, as Rapha noticed that the traveling cloak Auda used to trip over no longer reached her knees, he felt a chill of foreboding. Rafe was a man in so many ways and his devotion to the girl was evident. Rapha's shoulders slumped as he realized his duty, a duty he could delay no longer.

That night when Auda slept, Rapha motioned to Rafe, who followed him out of the cave's entrance. A cool breeze swept down from the mountain, stirring the pungent fragrance of their herb garden. As they sat to study the nighttime sky, another of Rafe's favorite pastimes, the boy reached for a mint leaf, crushing it in his fingers before placing it on his tongue. Rapha's stomach was unsettled as well. Their meal that evening had not been his best, for he had been distracted, rehearsing the words he would share with his son. With a sigh he reached for the mint.

"We need to talk about Auda," Rapha began, pausing to recall the exact wording he had rehearsed. But Rafe was way ahead of him.

"I think I'll go away awhile," Rafe said. "I see the birds and the foxes, how their young leave the nest and make their own way. Adonai has made it clear it is time for me to do the same."

"How will you tell her?"

The stark grief in Rafe's eyes tore Rapha's heart. "I don't know. She spoke today of how many children she wants to have—only two babies at a time so they can be carried on our backs when we walk." The boy's head sank lower. "Don't worry. I… I know I am a combination Adonai never intended. At times I feel wickedness in me and wonder, if I had lived with my true father…."

"*I* am your father, Rafe."

"But the blood in my veins is not yours. Those who share my blood roam the land to destroy. Will I become one of them? Will I hurt Auda when the beast inside grows stronger?" The boy's eyes, so dark and intelligent like Sheatiel's, begged him to disagree.

Rapha sighed. The rehearsed speech was useless. Rapha reached to Adonai for wisdom while Rafe drowned in despair.

Rafe answered his own question, "The tiger is a killer at heart. The gazelle feasts on the grass. When they grow they cannot deny their nature any more than an apple tree can produce figs," the bitter edge in Rafe's voice cut through Rapha's stupor.

"No, son. I have also witnessed a tree of the best seed, raised with the purest of sunshine and water, produce only thorns." Rapha said, recalling Lucifer's origin.

"How much harder is it for a bad seed, then, to produce good?"

"I cannot explain Adonai's ways but what *we* think is impossible, *He can do.*"

Rafe leapt to his feet as if the ground burned him. "I want to believe that! If you only knew…" He glanced toward the cavern entrance, his face contorting with grief. "I must do what creation has taught me. I will not wait until the evil in me rises up to hurt those I love."

"Please, Rafe, I have seen both—goodness can spring from evil—evil corrupts what is good. Lucifer was raised in purity while my old friend, Kal, grew immersed in poison. There comes a time *each seed chooses* what will feed and mold it. With Adonai as your source you *will* produce good."

A flicker of hope shone in Rafe's eyes but it dimmed quickly like a quenched spark. "But there is more," he whispered. "If Auda remains with us, with me, she is cut off from others of her kind."

Rapha could not argue the truth of that statement.

"How will she bear the children she desires? Will she remain content hiding in caves?"

Again Rapha was silent.

"I have enjoyed playing that we are a family but it is best for all if I dwell alone." A spasm of rage caused the strong jaw to clench. "That is what you were going to tell me, right— that we, those like me, should never reproduce, that the offspring get larger and more evil with each generation?"

Rapha bowed his head. How could he lie? So far, that had been the trend, as if Lucifer had known from the start his mighty hybrid would eventually consume all creation. That was like him. Win, even if no prize remained when the war was over.

"Adonai is cruel," Rafe said. "He allows me to love when I should not have lived."

"No," Rapha protested, "He led my steps to your mother. I loved her with all the passion a life mate could ever feel. You were a gift to me."

"But you did not mate with her. Did Adonai kill her to prevent it?"

"No—I… cannot say what might have been." That question opened uncomfortable possibilities, so Rapha hastened on, "There was something wrong, the birthing process was difficult, perhaps if I had not run away because I feared to love her, I would have been there... soon enough."

"I was too large for her womb?"

He wanted to spare the boy but what else could he say? "You were large."

Rafe winced as if that word sliced his heart. His head fell into his hands. "I have no choice. I will leave tonight."

"Where are you going?"

They turned to see Auda's bright curls shining in the moonlight. "How did we not hear you?" Rapha asked.

"Easy. You were not listening."

She was right. Rapha must have been deaf and blind not to see the depth of Rafe's attachment to the girl. Though the light was dim, Rafe's face appeared pale as if a knife had plunged into his heart.

"Tell me," she demanded.

"It is time I learned to care for myself," Rafe said.

"You do that already." Auda stated.

"Maybe when you are older, I will explain," Rapha said. "For now, you need to get back to sleep." He rose to usher her inside.

But Auda would not budge. Her eyes were still on Rafe. "I will wake in the morning and you will be gone."

"It is not forever…."

"Yes it is! Your body says so."

Rafe's eyes pleaded for help but Rapha only shrugged, palms held out in defeat. They had taught her too well. Now, instead of reading wildlife, she was reading them.

"Why were you sneaking away without telling me?"

The pain in Rafe's eyes disappeared when he turned to look at her. "I must go alone to seek Adonai's path—without short legs to slow me."

It was a direct hit. Auda's eyes opened wide as if her lungs would never expand again.

Rapha placed an arm about her thin shoulders, "It is like the birds when the young leave their—"

"Good!" Auda yelled and shook off Rapha's arm, her eyes brimming, "I am tired of trying to keep up with your stupid, long legs, and, and you make snort noises when you sleep, and," she wiped a hand across her cheek, "j-just go live with those stupid, big, giant people and, I hope you never get to sleep, because you all *snort!"*

With a loud hiccup, Auda turned and ran into the cavern.

For a moment, even the insects were silent. Finally a nearby cricket gave a tentative chirp as Rafe let out a long breath. "It is better for her to hate me."

"That was fear and panic," Rapha sought to soothe the lad, "a long way from hatred."

"But as the years go by, that is what it will become."

Rapha took a deep breath of his own. "Remember what happened before she came to us? Her family was slaughtered, all but her and her mother, who were salvaged for the men's…

entertainment. Her mother pushed Auda down into a ravine to save her. She still has a hard time believing she was shoved for the sake of love."

"And now I have done the same thing," Rafe whispered. "Will she ever know it was for love?"

"Do you want her to?"

Rafe's answer was almost too quiet to hear.

"No."

The next morning Rafe was gone and the light was gone from Auda's eyes. When Rapha asked her to walk with him she cried. When he asked her to fish with him she cried. When it was time to eat her favorite meal of tender fish with herbs she would not touch it.

In the coming days, Auda stopped laughing and talking. In fact, though she was taller than when she came to them, she reverted to the sad child Rapha first met. On rare occasions she would smile when they came upon a kit of fox pups or a baby goat, but the smile would soon turn to sadness.

Once in a while Rafe sent a raven to gather news but he never gave a report of himself. However, as time went by rumors circulated of a large man who would warn villagers of an approaching raiding party and then melt back into the trees to ambush the marauders, often using trained birds to peck at the eyes of the enemy. Thus Rafe, son of Sheatiel, adopted son of Rapha, became both a legend and an outlaw.

Chapter Thirty

Finding Family

Four years later…

"How can they bear to live like that?" Auda whispered as she stared toward a small group of earthen shelters nestled at one end of a wide valley.

As fragrant morning woke and spread its light, Rapha and Auda observed the scene displayed before them. For years Rapha had scoured the land for just such a settlement.

"Their way of life is comfortable," Rapha said, "food growing in the field, animals giving milk and even their meat when necessary, and a snug home to keep out the cold wind."

"But look at that woman," Auda indicated the eldest female bent under the weight of heavy water skins balanced on a long pole across her shoulders. "Why do they not just go to the water instead of dragging it back? And the way they push everything away to plant row after row of what they choose? Much of what they destroy would feed them."

"That is what they know," Rapha answered, suppressing a sigh of frustration. "I am sure they would find our way of life difficult to understand as well."

"But how can they spend day after day dwelling within a small, brown cave—hardly large enough for rabbits—while so much remains undiscovered?" Auda's nose wrinkled, "They are to be pitied."

This was not going the way Rapha had planned. Finally he had discovered a thriving group of humans dwelling in a sheltered valley far from slaughter and oppression… a difficult scenario to achieve in troubled times when most had given up resisting the stronger species, opting rather to appease their conquerors. These humans, therefore, must be of a hardy, independent spirit. Plus, the stone structure erected on the mountain overlooking the valley had the appearance of an altar. According to Rapha's winged friends, this family offered sacrifices to the One True God. Rapha longed to hear how they had come to that knowledge.

And there was one other crucial element.

At the sound of laughter, Auda paused in her critique and looked toward a group of three males emerging from the trees. One was short and moved with the eager, energetic motions of childhood as the taller men ambled beside him, both bearing half a large stag on their backs. The leader of the party sported a full, dark beard and a shaggy thatch of wiry hair while the other….

Ah! She had noticed. The third was as tall as the bearded one but his cheek was smooth and his physique, while muscular, had the coltish, narrow build of one suspended in that fleeting moment between boy and man.

Rapha glanced at Auda from the corner of his eye, noting with satisfaction that her mouth was agape and her thick-lashed eyes were narrowed as she studied the lad. But when she turned a suspicious gaze Rapha's way, he feigned intense interest in the stag. "Eight prongs! That was no easy kill. They are skilled hunters."

"They are disgusting! They are like boar who have groveled in filth!"

Even without the influence of a mother in her life, Auda had perfected that look of feminine disdain. In the four years since Rafe had left them she had developed into a formidable, beautiful young woman who moved with the feline grace and watchfulness of the mountain cats she admired, and had, on rare occasions, even coaxed into wary affection—when they were well-fed and not protecting their young. But, like her feline companions, she had an especially heightened sense of cleanliness, though she had an affinity for the water they could not abide. During the heat of the day she was often occupied with grooming, her flaxen curls combed to smoothness and her skin kept supple by Rapha's shared knowledge of nature's apothecary.

"This is foolishness to skulk in the shadows. Let us greet them." Rapha rose.

"No!" Auda's hand gripped the sleeve of his leather cloak.

"What do you fear?"

"I do not fear!" Her hands smoothed the thick hair secured at the nape of her neck with a narrow strip of leather, "I just have no desire to…."

"Come. They will think us unfriendly if their beast discovers us before we announce ourselves."

At that moment a large dog with thick gray and black fur and the loping gait of a wolf emerged from the trees behind the men and paused, his nose detecting a new scent in the morning breeze.

"They are downwind. You did this on purpose," Auda hissed.

But Rapha was already on his feet, his hand raised and a shout of greeting on his lips. Soon there was no recourse but to move forward and meet the strangers.

That day was thereafter filed among Rapha's memories as "notably unbearable." When introductions were made, Auda would not allow the people to grasp her forearm, their method of greeting, choosing instead to clasp her hands behind her back and ignore their outstretched hands. This strategy backfired, however, when the father mumbled his approval to Rapha for raising his daughter, "with the meekness becoming a young woman."

Immediately, Auda's hand had shot out to grasp the forearm of each as she forcefully introduced herself, this being the first of many ways she sought to offend their hosts. When the women, a mother and three daughters, came to greet her and subsequently referred to Rapha as her father, Auda made it clear this was not the case but made no effort to clarify the matter. Thus Rapha became the target of dark looks and when the wife found the proper opportunity to whisper in her husband's ear, the situation became dangerous.

"Why are you here?" the man's long knife was in his hand, and the older son, after shooing the women into the shelter, stood behind Rapha, his knife's blade aimed at Rapha's back.

"This is a lonely land. We seek the society and mutual protection of friendship."

But the man was unconvinced. Blood might have been spilled if Rapha had not said with a steady voice, "You are wise to be cautious, since so few bow the knee to the One True God."

The man's jaw dropped in astonishment, "Few indeed! We know of only one!"

After a few piercing questions, he embraced Rapha as a newfound brother.

"I am Ochim and this is my son, Elden. You are very welcome here."

Soon the entire family gathered to marvel at the story of Auda's rescue while she sat just outside the shelter, refusing to enter. But when Rapha explained, "Poor child. Enclosed spaces remind her of captivity," the group, clucking and murmuring their sympathy, rearranged the party in the open air.

Auda, looking as if she sat on a hill of ants, was forced either to be civil or to endure their pity when Rapha credited her lack of social skills to "an understandable distrust of strangers."

In truth, if Rapha had not been so disappointed his plan was failing, he would have greatly enjoyed goading his stubborn daughter. When she refused their food, pulled away from the youngest child who fingered her hair with shining eyes, or refused to be seated next to Elden (who could not hide his admiration) Rapha would flash a look of pity and pat her hand with humiliating condescension.

But later in the evening, Ochim told stories of the homeland they left behind. The oldest daughter sang a song of their peoples' defeat by a violent race, and the mother stepped forward in the firelight to dance, a small drum under her arm keeping rhythm as they paid tribute to the slain. The woman's graceful movements combined like magic with the young girl's pure voice forming the perfect key to unlock Auda's heart.

When the dance ended, Rapha asked, "How did you learn to worship the God above all gods?"

The man's face was thoughtful, "It was several years ago, another time such as this when a stranger came to our door. Oh! He was a sight! He was dressed in ragged animal skins, hair and beard covering most of his face. He was large so we assumed he was one of *them* and commanded the dog to attack—but when he got close, the beast sniffed the man's hand and licked him. I can usually trust that animal's instincts so I asked the man what he wanted. 'Just some food and company,' he said. 'In return I will tell stories.' And that is what he did. He spoke of a beautiful garden where the God over all gods walked and talked with him, where there was no war and even the animals dwelt in peace. *'The lion would lie down with the lamb,'* he said.

"The more he talked, the more I wanted to believe his story was real. But then," Ochim stared in the fire, "the story became sad. The man and his mate in the garden listened to a serpent who tricked them into betraying the God of all gods, and they had to leave that place. The man told us the only way they were protected from the evil one outside the garden was to sacrifice. 'The blood of the animals covers us until the day the One True God restores creation through the,' what was that word?" the man turned to his wife.

"Messiah," she supplied.

The man looked up at Rapha, his eyes reflecting the flames of their fire, "Ever since, we have sacrificed several times a year to the One True God."

The group was silent a moment while the fire crackled.

Finally Rapha asked, "Who was this man? What did he call himself?"

"He said he had no name," Ochim replied, "that he was simply a wanderer with a story to tell."

When the moon was high, Rapha and Auda took their leave. It was a silent walk, a surprise to Rapha who had expected to endure her venom at the first opportunity.

"Do you want to be rid of me?" she asked as they reached their encampment nestled beneath close-knit pines that sighed in the wind.

"Yes, if that will bring your happiness."

"I miss Rafe."

It was the first time she had mentioned his name in three years. Surely this was a good sign. "He would want you to be happy," Rapha said, "to have children, to dwell surrounded by love."

Auda was silent a moment, her eyes scanning the stars. "Is this Adonai's plan?" She turned that piercing gaze toward him.

"I admit, I do not know for sure, but it is good for you to spend time with… those like you."

"I don't like them," Auda stated, "and I am *not* like them. But if it makes you happy I will try to be… nice."

Her face bore such snobbish revulsion Rapha had to laugh. "Do you consider them beneath you, my queen?"

"No!" she retorted, then hesitated. "Well, they *are* rather dirty and they are messy when they eat…."

"And have you been raised in marble halls?"

A faint smile lit her features, "No. Usually we had no walls to keep out the night wind and no roof to hide the stars."

Rapha sensed her brokenness as she walked away into the shadows of the trees, but he allowed her solitude. This was a rite of passage she must make on her own.

He also noticed the large raven that rose on whispering wings, the same that had watched them the entire day.

One thing he knew for sure. That night, Auda's would not be the only grieving heart.

It should have been a happy time for Auda, a time for discovering young love, for dreaming of the future, for reveling in the fact that a family was eager to open its arms and make her a part of them.

Rapha had to admit she tried. She made a valiant effort to smile at the young man, Elden, to enjoy the chatty intimacy of female friendships she had never known before. But when she would walk away looking as if a heavy burden was pulling her into the earth, Rapha would encourage her eager suitor, Elden, to honor her privacy. “She has lived free as a bird on the wind. Give her time.”

But as her smiles grew more rare and her appetite all but vanished, Rapha had misgivings. Was the most logical path truly the one to make her happy? Was this Adonai’s will or was Rapha merely encouraging what was safe?

The morning Rapha woke and Auda was gone from her bed, he feared she had fled rather than face further pressure to play the role of a love-struck young woman. His worry was short-lived, however, for soon she walked into camp, face streaked with dirt, eyes swollen and red, but lit with a fierce determination.

“I had a dream,” she announced. “A shining man told me to find Rafe. He said you could help me.”

Before Rapha could answer she continued, “He also said I would be the mother of a mighty people, redeemed and dedicated to Adonai.”

“What was his name?”

She wrinkled her brow at the question. “What?”

“The man in your dream. Did he tell you?”

“He called himself ‘Gabriel.’”

“Gabriel!” Rapha’s heart raced as memories of his former life—eons of battles, joys, and sorrows—flooded his mind.

“Why is it important to know his name?” Auda asked.

Rapha wrestled his mind back to the present, “Beauty and might are not gifted only to those whose motives are pure,” Rapha said, “but be assured, Gabriel is a faithful servant of The Most High.”

Auda burst into tears, sobbing with an intensity of emotion she had never expressed, not even as a small child who missed her mother. When the flood of hurts dammed for a lifetime had soaked Rapha’s tunic, she wiped her face and said, “I was so afraid. Afraid to believe him, afraid to hope, afraid of losing hope again, afraid you would say it was my own wishes taking form as I slept, just the dream of a foolish girl who wants what she cannot have."

"As a rule," Rapha felt obliged to warn as he wiped her face with his sleeve, "heavenly messengers are sent when the road ahead is especially difficult."

"I had believed Adonai hated me. What road could be more difficult than that?"

"Did he say anything else?"

"Um, yes," Auda wrinkled her brow and put a hand to her head, "his words were, 'Say to my brother, Rapha, all is well with Eve. Great joy will come of her sojourn in a wicked land.'"

A wave of gratitude flooded over Rapha. His latest messengers sent to inquire about Eve had never returned.

"He called you 'brother.' You really *were* one of them once," her eyes were wide with wonder. "I always loved your stories about life in the heavens. I would fall asleep and dream of angels and that perfect garden and all the animals and… it's all *true*. There really was a garden and you were there with Adam and Eve."

Her expression grew thoughtful, "Then the rest is true as well. Lucifer corrupted creation, Cain killed his brother and Rafe is…."

"Yes, his son. But remember, Rafe chooses his allegiance."

As Auda fought back tears, she shook her head, amazed. "Yet Adonai says He will bless our union. 'A mighty people redeemed and dedicated to Adonai.'"

"Yes. His will is clear."

After a moment of silence that buzzed with her racing thoughts, Auda said, "I cannot consider joining with another, even if Rafe will not have me."

"Unless I am mistaken, we can have his answer before sunset." He turned to address a large raven who watched from a high branch. "Correct?"

The glossy bird rose into the air on silent wings.

"I should have known," Auda watched the bird climb higher until he disappeared into the sun. "He has appeared every day for weeks now. He goes to Rafe?"

When Rapha nodded in answer, Auda laughed, a delightful sound that seemed to sparkle in the air around them.

Soon, however, she groaned, "What do I tell Elden and his family? They have been so kind." Her expression brightened, "I could make him glad to release me. His patience is stretched already…." Then she clapped a hand to her mouth as understanding dawned. "That was what Rafe did the night he left. He was trying to make it easier for me."

"How well did it work?" Rapha inquired with a smile.

She wrinkled her nose, "Not well at all."

But Elden was pushed quickly from her mind as Auda realized Rafe was summoned, and here she was, bedraggled from her night of weeping.

Later, when darkness had once again settled over the land, a tall man with broad shoulders, a full beard and dark, curly hair, stepped into the light of their fire.

At first, Auda was wary. Rafe the boy had turned into a formidable man, even taller than she remembered.

"Auda?"

The caressing tone with which he said her name carried a myriad of questions, all of which she chose to answer by walking to stand before him and look up into his eyes. After a moment, she smiled.

"There you are," she reached a hand toward his face. He went down on one knee and she touched the unfamiliar beard and traced the lines of care around his eyes before taking a long lock of thick hair in her fingers and tugging—hard. "What took so long?"

Then he grabbed her up in his arms and spun her around the way he used to when she was a child. But when the fit of laughter had passed, and he looked into her eyes with a much different expression than he had when she was a tormenting imp with messy, blonde curls, Rapha saw fit to intervene.

"Alright, that's enough," he said as he pulled Auda from Rafe's grasp. "Unhand my daughter!"

Even then Rafe tried to convince Auda to stay with the family in the valley. He told her of his life running from those he defied, that they would not have time to sow and reap or maintain flocks, that he could not abandon those whom evil would destroy. But his eyes could not lie. He had been tortured by thoughts of her belonging to another; so when he gazed at the breathtaking young woman who vowed her devotion with the stubborn persistence of the little girl who would not be left behind, his eyes shone with the gratitude of a starving man set before a feast.

Dawn was about to break when the exhausted Auda retired, and Rafe remained, staring into the fire. "I do not dare remain in this valley. My enemies seem to find me wherever I go. In fact, the birds report that a raiding party fast approaches."

So while Auda slept, Rafe and Rapha descended into the valley to warn the family of their danger.

Elden and Ochim looked with narrowed eyes from Rapha to the tall, handsome stranger at his side. "Where is proof of this enemy?" The boy's hand rested on the knife at his waist. "How do we know you will not take this valley as your own?"

"Come now, Rapha is our friend, soon to be family," the father said though he shooed the younger children behind him. "Surely we can trust his words."

"Where is Auda?" The youngest daughter asked.

Confound the child. Rapha had hoped to delay their other news.

The father read much in Rapha's hesitation. "If we go, Auda is with us, eh Rapha?"

"Auda goes with me," Rafe stated.

Rapha could only shake his head as that conversation deteriorated. "Take the children inside," Ochim ordered his wife, even as she begged him not to fight, while Elden leapt to draw the hunting knife from a strap at his side, and the dog advanced, teeth bared.

"Where is she? What have you done to her?" Elden shouted as Rapha placed himself between the young men who faced each other like bulls ready to charge.

"Please!" Rapha shouted. "Allow me to explain!" But his words were drowned by their yells and the dog's excited barking.

When the younger boy tossed a spear to his brother saying, "Kill the giant, Elden!" Rapha intervened, his ancient abilities disarming the boy in one blurred, instinctive movement. As the dog leapt for his throat, Rapha triggered a nerve in its neck, causing the beast to crumple to the ground, stunned.

The family looked on in shocked silence and, though Rapha's actions had averted catastrophe, their expressions were more fearful and murderous than before.

"You are one of them!" the father roared. "Get off my land and take your giant with you!"

"Rafe can help you. He has resisted this enemy for years. At least allow us to show you the way to safety."

"I have seen what his kind do," the father growled. "The only giant I will trust is a dead one."

"And I have seen the gratitude of your kind," Rafe countered. "I fight at your side, save your women and children, and then am rewarded with your knives pointing at my back."

As Rapha grasped Rafe's arm and pulled him away he attempted to salvage a shred of civility. "My thanks to your family for the kindness you have shown—"

But Ochim cut him off. "Enemies descend upon us and my son has lost his mate. Be gone!"

"Rafe! You said that? No wonder he was ready to kill you," Auda tried to appear angry at the turn of events but the report of Rafe claiming her as his own made her blush with pleasure.

Later, as they lounged beneath spreading limbs of the towering trees and watched the first stars appear, Rapha tried to speak of the fast-approaching enemy. But Rafe was deaf and blind to all but Auda. Rapha walked a few paces away to give the couple a measure of privacy. It warmed his soul to hear their murmured endearments and shared laughter. He breathed deep, grateful for the magic of young love.

However, now that there was some distance between him and the couple's overwhelming emotions, Rapha could detect more on the cool night breeze than the musty spice of pine and shuffle of nocturnal creatures. A fearful, angry, wounded ego was creeping closer.

Rapha rose noiselessly and crept toward the source of this disturbance, guided by the panting breath of a dog and the pounding of a young heart bent on revenge.

Threading his way through the undergrowth, Rapha paused behind a tree trunk to watch the cloaked figure and accompanying canine creep closer to where Auda and Rafe lounged against a rock, her slender body tucked close to his side, her small hand entwined with his as they continued the quiet conversation and laughter.

For a moment the intruder observed them, but when Rapha saw the hand reach back, spear poised for flight, he leapt to wrench away the weapon and pin the would-be attacker to the ground.

In the ensuing scuffle, the cloaked figure struggled while the dog crouched and snarled. But the creature maintained a safe distance from Rapha, obviously remembering their earlier encounter.

"Stop fighting and you will not be harmed," Rapha instructed as the hood fell back to reveal Elden, face flushed, eyes wild with fright and fury.

"If that thing has harmed her…."

"Quiet, Elden!" Auda commanded as she entered the clearing and strode to face him. "Call him 'that thing' again and I will kill you myself."

"You will join with it by choice?" Elden said with a look of disgust. "It is an abomination!"

Her fist moved with the speed of a striking snake to connect with Elden's nose. "He is more of a man than you will ever be!"

"You whore of giants!" Elden cried as he cupped his bleeding nose. He was given no chance to continue the insults since he suddenly found himself looking at the sky, held aloft by Rafe's hands.

"This abomination can tear you in two," Rafe's voice shook with fury as he tossed Elden into a thorn bush. "I will try to understand your anger at losing her, but call her that again and those words will be your last."

Rapha rushed to lend a hand to the bleeding Elden. “Your family needs you. The true enemy will be upon you in two days!”

“There is no proof of that!”

“When you have proof it will be too late.”

“For too long have we run from his kind,” Elden nodded toward Rafe. “We will not abandon our home and fields.”

“Then your fields will burn and your family will be slaughtered, or tortured in ways you cannot imagine,” Rafe said.

But Elden would not listen to reason. “Giants lie! Giants charm, and then destroy. You are no different from all the others! And you,” he turned to Auda, “are worse. A traitor to your own kind!”

Rafe’s hand went to the knife at his belt, but Rapha forced himself between them, “Enough! We will overlook your words because you are angry and young—but do not deprive your family of an able protector with your foolishness. Now go to them. Get them out of that valley or they will die!”

In the end, Rapha, Rafe, and Auda rushed to help Elden’s family when stormcrows were on the horizon, forcing the stunned group to abandon their fields and flocks.

“Leave it. You must not be seen,” Rapha ordered.

“You think us cowards?” Elden accused.

“No. Just a fool if you do not take your women to safety now!” Rafe lifted the youngest child and handed her to Auda even as the child cried to bring the baby goat. “No! Nothing must slow you. Go!”

As the family followed Auda to safety, Rapha and Rafe were left with the unpleasant task of destroying what would have fueled the marauders for weeks. They built fires, and then directed the blaze toward the ripened fields that flared and spread with a wind that flowed from the mountain. It was heartbreaking to witness the panic of the stock animals set free from their pens and maddened by the flames. At least they would not remain to feed the enemy.

But Rafe could not help himself. As he and Rapha ran toward the shelter of the trees, he scooped up the bleating baby goat and placed it on his shoulders.

As they watched from a high hidden cleft, the enemy swept into that valley with all the fury of hell itself, led by a huge being who swung a spiked club the size of a tree.

"Oh no," Rafe breathed.

"You have seen this one before?"

"I killed his brother—and, uh, set… fire… to his hair," he glanced at Rapha's surprised expression. "The flaming arrow was meant to kill him. He must have called reinforcements."

Rapha was grim as he took note of the well-armed troops and their leader, the crazed giant with a head that resembled a scorched hillock. The fire drove the giant to such fury he swung the club at his own troops, skewering a dozen with each sweep of his arm.

"Today is not our day of victory," Rapha said, "unless victory is measured by survival. Come."

Luckily, the sound of the goat was drowned by destruction as Rapha and Rafe made their way to meet the others, little realizing how many seasons would pass before they once again walked freely under the sun.

Chapter Thirty-One

Full Circle

Seventy years later…

Rapha watched the caravan coming closer like an ever-lengthening snake in the desert sand. How this land had changed since he had explored these hills with the young Cain and Abel. It was where their home had stood and where their flocks had grazed, but then the valleys had flowed with streams and the trees had been home to innumerable species. Today the scars of ceaseless war had rendered the land barren and desolate. However, since ruined, at least no one fought over this valley, thus there was a momentary peace. Perhaps it was the peace of death—but any reprieve was welcome. Not to worry. Rapha knew where water was available, enough to make this land flourish once again.

A glimmer of bright orange, like a miniature tongue of flame, caught his eye and Rapha watched as a desert flower opened its petals to the warmth of the rising sun, a vibrant defiance to its bleak surroundings. Hope brushed Rapha's heart as he pondered the miracle of that seed. Through destruction and drought it had waited, a germ of life unquenched. This tiny flower was the first of spring's blooms that lay just below the surface, sleepy but growing, thriving. Soon these hills would be ablaze with their short-lived triumph.

He glanced up again, shading his eyes against the sun's rays. He had distracted himself with an hour's concentration on the blossom but grew impatient. He had been so for weeks, ever since the raven had carried her message over the mountains.

His reply had been brief. "Come home."

Ah! Good. The caravan was making steady progress though the trek through deep sand was slow, and camels, as a rule, did not like to be rushed. Anticipation of this meeting made his heart race. A feeling of youthfulness flushed his ancient veins. He hardly dared to name the emotion. He did not even trust the wind to know that Rapha, demoted angel, had reason to hope.

He studied the procession until he detected a diminutive figure swathed in white with a canopy suspended above. That must be her. Not able to contain himself any longer, Rapha directed a command to the camel that bore her, chuckling as the beast broke into a run and the white-swathed figure shook a fist toward Rapha. He began to stride across the sand toward her. He had waited almost eighty years for this meeting. That was long enough.

Finally.

The camels were unloaded, servants were deposited in their tents, everyone had received their fill of water and, when the coolness of evening descended, the old friends could speak freely.

"Not quite the same land you left behind, eh?"

"Nothing stays the same for long. It is the one thing on which I can rely."

"Except for Adonai."

"Yes. Adonai never changes. He has been my sanity and my strength," the still lovely face smiled, bringing a glow to the golden eyes. But a hint of great sadness hung about her like a cloak.

Rapha leaned into the cushions and studied the woman before him. She glanced up and met his gaze. "Counting the new lines in my face since last we met?"

"No. Still I see the tree-climbing girl in you. Would your servants be surprised to know how unrefined you once were?"

"Every day I would climb, but it was the stairs to my roof where I would go to look in your direction and dream of escape."

"I was happy to assist in that regard."

"Yes," she laughed, "the crows, ravens, and vultures that blanketed the city were very convincing. The darkest symbols of their superstitious fears come to life! They were willing to speed me on my way with Cain's body. By the time the new king had changed his mind, deciding I would be a fitting sacrifice to appease the gods, I was already far away with Rafe.

"Tell me of Rafe."

Joy flooded her features as she spoke, bringing to mind the teasing girl who had mesmerized the young Adam. "Rafe's land is fruitful, his family flourishes and, best of all, they are hidden. Even my eyes were covered as we passed through the deep caverns leading to his kingdom.

"His kingdom," Eve mused. "Rumors had reached my ears even in the palace, impossible tales of the might and riches of a people hidden in the depths of the earth." Again she grinned. "Rafe was pleased to hear how he sports venom-filled fangs and prefers human flesh to that of his friends, the vicious beasts he controls with his mind who stalk any who are cruel to animals. It was a tale I told to palace children I caught throwing rocks at a sickly dog—the pampered, mean-spirited brats—and now it is repeated as fact."

"And Auda?"

"She is the daughter I always wanted." Eve paused to wipe her eyes. "The virtue of Rafe's land, its healthful water and rich soil, prolong her life, Auda's children adore her, and she reigns supreme in Rafe's eyes. Never have I seen two people more in love, except for…." Eve's voice trailed away and the shroud of grief again settled over her.

After a moment's silence Rapha asked, "You brought Cain with you?"

She nodded, "It was his final request, to be returned to the land of his youth."

"It is the answer to countless prayers."

"Yes. I learned to praise Adonai for my captivity, for it put Cain in my sight. I could pray and love daily. And, when he was ready, I was there to lead him back to the arms of Adonai."

"What of his wives and children?"

"They were poison to him, for that is what he made them. The son who murdered Cain was murdered by the next in line for the throne, and so the legacy continues. A mold of his body was made many years ago so they yet have his image of gold to worship, to remind all of them of their own importance—whose blood runs in their veins—of their right to continue his oppression."

She sighed and took a sip of wine from her trembling hand before continuing. "Oh, Rapha. How I wanted so many times to flee that place. Innocence is consumed so quickly there. It seems babes come from the womb ready to devour everything within their grasp. Cain's children, my own family, were corrupted, and continued the tradition before my eyes. It became impossible to watch them and keep my food down. Such hopelessness. Such foolish waste."

The tears ran down Eve's cheeks as she unburdened herself of the years of residence in Cain's kingdom, of the horrors visited upon the helpless, and the delight taken in cruelty toward man or beast—in the name of spectacle, sport, or even worship. "My protests were met with scorn, just the ramblings of the king's eccentric mother. Very few were saved by my efforts. Even the slave girls assigned to me would heed my teachings only until they were taken to the pleasure palaces, where any purity was burned from them. I felt almost cruel to offer hope since I knew what was in store."

She paused, the bleakness of those years haunting her eyes. "There was one, Leda, she reminded me a bit of Sheatiel, who listened to my ramblings about the garden and Adonai's plan for redemption. How her eyes lit from within and how she grasped my hands and asked me to whisper tales of the One True God's love, for we did not dare speak of these things aloud. But we were found out. She was taken, and, when she claimed allegiance to the 'God above all gods,' she was included in the next public sacrifice—burned to the 'glory of the gods.' After that, I was given only deaf and mute serving girls."

She glanced up with a hint of joy. "Now the truth of Adonai thrives among those who cannot hear—who in turn pass on that truth to the outcasts: the blind, the crippled, those with wasting disease. They are shunned and despised, even feared—not useful for profit or breeding—therefore they enjoy freedom in their poverty. I consider them my true offspring in that country. They suffer horribly, their lives are often short, but their faith is pure."

When Rapha questioned whether she was included in the breeding program, Eve laughed. "Oh no. Cain would not allow it. He alone could claim to have issued from my loins. I was placed in a seat of honor at all the public functions, revered as a wife of the gods—but was absolutely off-limits since it was well known any man who touched me would be burned with fire from heaven." She notched her chin higher as if she would have ensured the burning with or without heaven's assistance. "But enough talk of that hateful place."

The old friends spoke deep into the night, enjoying a depth of communion they had been denied for decades. At last, when a dim gray light shone through the flap of their shelter, Eve found the courage to ask what was foremost in her mind.

"Have you heard aught of Adam?"

Rapha related the tale told to him and Auda by Ochim and his family. He sighed before continuing, "Since then, only rumors from the ravens of a tall specter who hides from God and man alike and resembles a great, walking tree with bushy hair sprouting from his head and face. Even heaven is silent about him, as if he exists somewhere between heaven and earth."

Eve's eyes swept the dim horizon, visible through the open tent flap, "Cain had hoped to see him once more. In fact, I bear a message from Cain for him. He said, 'Tell Adam he was the best of fathers.'"

The talk of Adam appeared to have drained the last of Eve's strength so, with a hug for her old mentor, she slipped away to rest saying, "I think I shall sleep tonight."

And she did.

Rapha did not see her again until the sun rose on the third day.

Chapter Thirty-Two

Second Chance

Once Cain's bones were buried next to his brother's, Eve aged before Rapha's eyes day by day. She explained that after so many years in a hostile environment she just wanted rest, but Rapha knew better. The fight was gone from her eyes like a soldier who languishes when the war is over.

She ate and drank only the least required to sustain life. One faithful servant remained from Eve's years in Cain's land; without that kind woman's stubborn, mute insistence, Eve might not have eaten at all. The woman had been called Ilda, meaning ill-favored—resembling an old, knotted tree, her body bent and knobby at every joint—but Rapha changed her name to Isla, explaining through the signs of his hands that she had now become an island of refuge to her mistress.

Daily Eve fought the kind woman's ministrations, but Isla was nothing if not persistent, ignoring Eve's hands that waved away food, anointing her mistress with fragrant oils, and maintaining the gloss of Eve's still-lustrous hair. And when the day came that Eve would not rise from her bed, Isla concocted healthful drinks from the plants that thrived in their mountain oasis.

But still Eve declined as if she had chosen to end her days on Earth. Try as he might, Rapha could not rally her spirits, and even his own talent with herbs and tonics was wasted.

One night, Isla moved Eve's bed to the opening of her tent for the cool breeze and view of the stars. Rapha joined her.

"Look at the heavens," Rapha said. "The celestial hosts speak of new hope and comfort."

"Not for me, old friend," Eve said. "I have remained too long. I have seen too much. Evil thrives and mankind worships those who devour them. My comfort lies in leaving the pain of living to those young enough to hope."

Rapha spoke of Adonai's goodness and power, of His love for all creation. "Remember how He made all things new, how He held you and Adam close to His breast and promised redemption through your seed."

"We chose evil," her voice was flat, dead. "We are corrupt. I am old. Adam must hate me, or he has produced children with another and has forgotten me. What good can come from us now?"

Rapha leaned forward and grasped Eve's cold hand. "Adonai does not change. Therefore we have hope."

"Stop!" she snatched her hand away. "It hurts too much. I have failed Adam. I have failed Adonai. I have accepted that."

Rapha walked away from her tent with the despairing words still ringing in his ears. She was right. Hope was gone. Eve was far beyond the age of childbearing and, with her mate wandering the earth shrouded in madness, it would appear Adam's line was ended, while Lucifer's offspring enjoyed no opposition. Rapha could only imagine, with their hopes so vanquished, and his kingdom thriving, that Lucifer no longer even considered them a threat.

But, for one fleeting instant, Rapha had seen a flicker of agony in Eve's eyes. Good. A live coal yet burned beneath the ashes.

A strange peace settled over Rapha as he gazed upon the bright star in the east. Adonai's best work was always accomplished when all was lost.

He came on a day when smokes of war hung in the wind and the sun's heat had not allowed a whisper of cooling breeze for days. He was battered, had taken the long journey through despair and madness, but his heart had led him home.

From his seat among the tall poplars that forever point heavenward, Rapha watched this shadow of a man stumble up the stony path toward him. Throughout the night he had waited and prayed while Adonai whispered joy and renewal. Now, the miracle stood before him.

Adam had come home.

The reunion of Adam and Eve was a quiet affair, no shrieks of joy or weeklong feasts. Eve rose from her bed, smoothing a shaky hand through her hair while Adam, still covered with the dirt of countless hills, and sporting long, mud-encrusted braids on his head and face, knelt before her. Down she fell to join him, heedless of the hard ground, and there they stayed, melting, leaning into one another's tired bodies, and taking deep, contented breaths.

When Rapha stepped unnoticed from Eve's tent, he stumbled back to the poplars and fell on his face to weep—his heart so full, so amazed by the Holy One's quiet wisdom, so stunned by heaven's beauty radiating through brokenness, that he remained there, floating outside of time, nestled in Earth's bosom and basking before the celestial throne, until a thick mist rose around him, the physical presence of heaven's glory flowing from a grateful heart.

Ten years later…

Rapha stepped into the small, stone home, out of the frigid night, and into peace.

"Come see, old friend." Adam rose from his stool by the crackling hearth with a snuffling bundle held tightly in his arms and crossed the room with an agility Rapha had not seen in him for a century.

"He will never look at me again, Rapha," Eve's tired, contented voice quipped from her pallet in the corner where Isla hovered, discreetly bathing her mistress and whisking away blood-soaked linens. "I am forgotten. Booted from the throne of his idolatry by that tiny foot."

"You are a miracle, my love," Adam laughed and rushed to her side. "You may vex me every day as long as I live, and only make me more your devoted servant." He leaned down and, with the bulky bundle pressed between them, kissed her with a noisy smack on the lips, and then remained to gaze at her smiling face—his eyes devouring every plane of her flushed cheeks, sweat-beaded brow, and eyelids that fluttered, losing the battle against slumber.

"So, my beauty," Adam whispered, "shall I send the discarded angel and meddling woman away so I can ravish you in peace?"

A hand leapt from the covers for a slap to his shoulder. "Hush, you old goat," she admonished, but her fingers lingered to caress his face. "You will teach our son bad habits."

As if on cue, a wail like the bleat of a tiny lamb rose from the folds of the blankets. "Come Rapha," Adam beckoned. "See if you still possess your old magic."

Rapha approached and held out his arms to receive the bundle with one tiny fist flailing from the warm folds. As the squalling weight settled into the crook of his arm, he pulled a corner of the swaddling back to look into the wrinkled, red face. When he saw Rapha, the babe grew quiet and blinked, its over-large, clear eyes proclaiming a wordless, "It's you!"

Rapha pulled the babe closer, his hair forming a curtain around their communion, and placed a kiss on the velvet skin of the babe's brow as he drank in the most glorious scent in all creation, Adonai's breath of new life.

He reached to stroke the tiny fist that opened to grasp his finger, and felt every fiber of his being bow in awe.

"Adonai is good," Rapha managed to choke the words past the lump in his throat. The favor of the Most High filled the air and Rapha heard words well up from his innermost being. He opened his mouth and Adonai's promise leapt from his tongue.

"Behold, when all is darkness, My light shines forth. Through this seed will I bring my Holy One, the hope and redemption of all creation. Remember, My promise cannot fail. I make a way where there is no way."

Then Rapha took the babe to Adam and clasped his old friend's broad shoulder. "He looks just like you."

Adam gazed down at the baby boy, wonder etched in the wrinkles of his handsome face. "We will call him Seth."

A fresh, cold wind whisked a cloud from the moon's face as Rapha stepped into the night and held his face toward the silver glow. Surely the stars had drawn closer since he had met the babe.

He shut his eyes and listened, a slow smile spreading across his features. Yes. The sound was getting louder, swirling in his heart and rushing throughout the depths of the earth before galloping back to the heights of creation.

Thousands of celestial voices shouted with joy as hands of light applauded, the chorus building until earth's weight dropped from Rapha's shoulders and his soul shot up to the clouds, taking flight to join the dance.

The End... of the beginning

The Story Behind Rapha Chronicles:

The Fall

The journey of The Rapha Chronicles caught me completely by surprise and, to this day, I'm a bit stunned by the ride.

It began in a quiet, pre-dawn summer prayer time in 2007. There, face down on the beige carpet of our walk-in closet that doubles as my private sanctuary, after a few minutes of praise and stretching (good tip for staying awake) the moment developed laser-like clarity. There are few moments like this in life—the birth of a child, a rainbow that stops you in your tracks, or even staggering catastrophe such as those first images of the Twin Towers on 9/11—the moments when there's no past, no future, just the right now. This was one.

Understand, I believe God is always right now, and right there, but I rarely unplug from distraction long enough to soak in that fact. That's the power of entering His presence through praise. It helps us to focus. Anyhow, in this moment, I was fully aware He was there, humming with power in my humble closet. That thought blew my mind. Everything ground to a decisive halt and I melted—realizing my own insignificance as I grappled with the fact that, "He. Knows. My. Name."

For a long moment all I could do was weep. My heart and mind were so filled they were literally bursting as I just drowned in… do I call it love… purity… holiness? At any rate, it was the most blissful pain I could endure. For once things were in proper priority—God IS. Everything else is nothing in comparison.

Every now and then the vague thought would flit through that my hubby was going to come in and promptly call the men in white jackets to report I'd lost my mind. But the moment stretched on, feeling for all the world like I was breathing in as God exhaled and I might, at any moment, just step on through to heaven.

Finally, it was absolute peace and my satiated brain was in a stupor. No audible voice. No vision. Just felt God ask, **"What do you want?"**

A strange question for such a moment. For once, I couldn't want anything. For once I was completely free of self-absorption, stress and hurry. I didn't even want to remember my lengthy prayer list. But you don't take such an offer lightly.

My first reply was something along the lines of an overawed, "You tell me," since God obviously has a much better view of what I need. Finally though, I began to realize this overwhelming, fulfilling, scorching love from the Creator of All just didn't fit. There were things I had been taught, things I had assumed, characteristics I had attached to my image of God, that were blown away by basking in just one pure drop of the presence of I AM.

So I asked a question. I thought it was a simple one, something about the angels, but it was like reaching out and grasping a rocket during countdown. The answer blew my mind and I yelped, "Oh my God!" to the silence of our still sleeping household.

It was just one bit of information, one missing piece of the puzzle that, when slipped into place, lit up the switchboard of Bible stories and Scripture I'd been exposed to all my life. It was shocking, giving instant stretch marks to my brain, but it made perfect sense, especially regarding those nagging questions about God's true character.

So began a discussion that had me waking before the sun for the next three months as this new factor wedged its broad shoulders into my narrow spiritual worldview. This was both an exciting and painful process as many "truths" fell apart like poor construction during an earthquake, revealed in the glaring light of God's love for what they were: assumptions and prejudice.

Each day, I grappled with new insights like a blind man suddenly seeing what he's imagined all his life. I typed the journey into my computer, trying to wrap my brain around concepts that fried its circuits. At the end of those months, I knew the 200 plus pages contained vital information, but I really didn't know what to do with it. I called it "Fruitbasket Turnover" and showed it to my husband who graciously did not label me a heretic. His assessment: "This needs to be a novel."

Hmmm. Sounded like a LOT of work and this little pilgrimage had already absorbed three months of my "normal" writing time. Couldn't I just publish it "as is" or stick it online alongside other off-beat ideas? Besides, who the heck was I to assume I could pass on spiritual revelations? No theological degrees. No political aspirations. Nothing famous or infamous enough for people to care what I had to say.

For a second opinion, I sent the manuscript to Adam, a writer friend, who came to the same conclusion: "This needs to be a novel."

The next morning, a story began to take shape during my prayer time as if I was getting glimpses of a movie. So, I went to my customary coffee shop table and worked my way through the first scene, keeping my eyes on the simple step I could accomplish that day rather than the huge mountain ahead.

When I got home and checked e-mails, there was one from Adam titled "Some inspiration for you." I opened the attachment to discover a full-screen image of warring angels with the words "FALLEN—a novel by Chana Keefer," inscribed on it.

About a month later I had a complete summary, scene by scene, of the entire novel—twenty-five pages worth that told me loud and clear this was just the beginning of a huge undertaking. But my husband's feedback after reading it was the spark I needed to take a huge gulp and plunge ahead. "I knew you could write but… damn!"

Adam's assessment was both humbling and daunting: "This has the potential to be the Screwtape Letters of this generation."

Whoa! Now I knew it was beyond me. But the task drove me to my knees every day. Not a bad working environment.

Even now, after three and a half years, several drafts and rewrites-I-thought-would-never-end as well as countless moments of facing an impenetrable, unscaleable wall of writer's constipation, the task still amazes and humbles me. It was much more than writing a novel. It was a pilgrimage that crushed, shaped and changed me; the way I think, the way I pray, the way I love, even the way I view current events.

And the real beauty of it? There is no end in sight.

The Fall is a novel that demands response. Perhaps your response will be anger and offense. I wouldn't blame you a bit. But my prayer is that, like me, this story will take you on a journey of deeper fascination with your Maker and spark a lifetime of questions and answers of your own.

Sincerely,

Chana

Study Guide

1. A worldview is a particular set of beliefs we hold regarding the foundations of life and our universe. Whether we realize it or not, our worldview is like a lens through which we perceive what we regard as truth. How has your worldview been affected by reading *The Fall*? Positively? Negatively? Expanded?

2. God is a major character not only in this book but also in the course of human history. What are your thoughts on God? Does He/She exist? Do you believe God is accurately depicted in the Bible? In this book?

3. If God knows everything, even the future, why would he create Lucifer? How did Rapha answer this question? What do you think?

4. Do you believe Adam and Eve's relationship with and faith in God grew or lessened after Eden? Discuss.

5. What character qualities seemed to predispose Cain toward Lucifer's temptation? What character qualities drew Abel to choose God over Lucifer? Do you believe even Cain could have received God's forgiveness?

6. Throughout the Bible, stories are told of rivalry, even enmity, between brothers—Cain and Abel; Isaac and Ishmael; Esau and Jacob; Joseph and his elder brothers, etc. Do you think this might underscore the rivalry Lucifer felt toward Adam, and mankind in general?

7. In the story, God's plan tends to follow directly on the heels of a monstrous defeat. Put another way, God can make beauty from ashes. Have you experienced this phenomenon in your life? Discuss.

8. It's very easy to look at the evil in the world around us and wonder how God—if He even exists—could allow it to happen. What are your thoughts??

9. The Bible says in 1 Corinthians 13:8 (New International Version) that "Love never fails." Do you truly believe love is stronger than evil? Discuss.

10. How do you think Adam and Eve were different when they had Seth than they had been when Cain and Abel were born? How do you think this difference might have affected Seth's upbringing?

11. It's hard for us to grasp the depth of God's holiness, grace, and love. Where do you unwittingly draw the line between forgivable vs. unforgivable? Terrorists? Pedophiles? Abortionists? Murderers? Rapists? Fallen Televangelists? Fallen Angels? Lucifer? Yourself?

12. Read Isaiah 53 aloud emphasizing verse 5.

    "But he was pierced for our transgressions,
    he was crushed for our iniquities;
    the punishment that brought us peace was on him,
    and by his wounds we are healed."

    How do you believe Jesus fits into history and world religions?

Do you need a speaker?

Whether you want to purchase bulk copies of *The Fall* or buy another book for a friend, get it now at: www.imprbooks.com.

Do you want Chana Keefer to speak to your group or event? Then contact Larry Davis at: (623) 337-8710 or email: ldavis@intermediapr.com or use the contact form at: www.intermediapr.com.

For your publishing needs, contact Terry Whalin, Publisher, at Intermedia Publishing Group, (623) 337-8710 or email: twhalin@intermediapub.com or use the contact form at: www.intermediapub.com.